Praise for Talia H̶̶̶̶̶̶̶̶̶̶̶

"Talia Hibbert is a rock star! Her writing is smart, funny, and sexy. . . . She'll make you fall in love with her sweetly imperfect characters, who are so real you'll wish you could give them all a hug."

—Meg Cabot, #1 *New York Times* bestselling author of the Little Bridge Island and the Princess Diaries series

"Hibbert joins important voices in contemporary romance who write steamy page-turners where the characters look nothing like they did a generation ago—and that's a wonderful thing."

—*Washington Post*

"*Get a Life, Chloe Brown* is . . . a warm, laugh-filled, life-affirming tribute to the hard work and rewards of healing, honoring the courage it requires to love oneself."

—*Entertainment Weekly* (Best Romances of 2019)

"Hibbert shows how standard romance tropes—misunderstandings, meddling sisters, a steamy camping trip—can be elevated to sublime pleasure in the hands of a brilliant writer. . . . An extraordinary book, full of love, generosity, kindness, and sharp humor."

—*New York Times Book Review* on *Get a Life, Chloe Brown*

"A rom-com with depth, one that explores living with illness, the benefits of therapy, and how two people can better communicate when they slough off their own rough exteriors."

—Shondaland on *Get a Life, Chloe Brown*

TAKE A
HINT,
DANI
BROWN

Also by Talia Hibbert

Get a Life, Chloe Brown

TAKE A
HINT,
DANI
BROWN

A Novel

TALIA HIBBERT

AVON
An Imprint of HarperCollinsPublishers

TAKE A HINT, DANI BROWN. Copyright © 2020 by Talia Hibbert. Excerpt © 2021 by Talia Hibbert. All rights reserved. Printed in the United States of America. No part of this book may be used or reproduced in any manner whatsoever without written permission except in the case of brief quotations embodied in critical articles and reviews. For information, address HarperCollins Publishers, 195 Broadway, New York, NY 10007.

HarperCollins books may be purchased for educational, business, or sales promotional use. For information, please email the Special Markets Department at SPsales@harpercollins.com.

FIRST EDITION

Designed by Diahann Sturge

Emojis © Popicon / Shutterstock, Inc.
Twitter icons © MAKSIM ANKUDA / Shutterstock, Inc.

Library of Congress Cataloging-in-Publication Data has been applied for.

ISBN 978-0-06-294123-7

22 23 24 LSC 11

For the Hopeless Romantics, and for myself

ACKNOWLEDGMENTS

This book had teeth and it sucked me dry. I flatter myself that it's a fairly funny read, but imagine me crying and bleeding for every line of witty sarcasm and you'll get the picture. I couldn't have produced this bad boy without all the support I received from the lovely people in my life.

Thanks first and foremost to my family for keeping me alive while Dani and Zaf spent months trying to kill me. Mum, Sam, Tru, I don't know how you lived with me, but you did. Props. I owe you each a Coke.

Thank you, of course, to my lovely agent, Courtney Miller-Callihan, and my editor, Nicole Fischer, who talked me off of many authorial ledges and gave me exactly what I needed, when I needed it. If it weren't for the both of you, I probably would've rewritten this book ten times instead of three.

Thank you to the incredible team at HarperCollins for all of your support, and to Georgina Kamsika and Aimal Farooq for helping me represent a culture not my own. I hope I did the Ansaris justice.

Finally, thank you to Kenya Goree-Bell, Layla Abdullah-Poulos, Mina Waheed, Therese Beharrie, Ali Williams, Yusra, Yasmin, Chiara, Umber, and Laila for your invaluable advice and encouragement.

Also, thank you to Bree Runway for "2ON," the motivational bop of the century.

AUTHOR'S NOTE

Please be aware that this story involves sensitive topics, such as dealing with the death of close family members and handling general anxiety disorder. I hope I have treated these issues with the care they deserve.

PROLOGUE

The moon was high and full, the night was ripe for witchy business, and Danika Brown had honey on her tit. The left one, specifically.

"For fuck's sake," she muttered, and swiped it off.

"Daydreaming at worship, now? Tut, tut." Dani's best friend, Sorcha, sat across the tiny table that served as their altar, all bright, brown eyes, thick, dark hair, and crooked smile.

"I wasn't daydreaming," Dani said, though she absolutely had been. "My chest just sticks its nose into everything."

"Here we bloody go." Sorcha rolled her eyes and imitated Dani's crisp accent with unnerving accuracy. *"Oh, pity me and my incredible rack, even though I selfishly refuse to share any of it—"*

"I don't think we can share breast tissue, Sorch."

Sorcha glared. "Well, if we could, would you give me some?"

"No. As you say, my rack is incredible. Now shut up and focus."

"Selfish, fiendish woman. Vain, daffodil-brained . . ." Sorcha could always be relied upon when it came to creative insults.

Her gleeful mutterings faded into the background as Dani set aside her pot of honey, placing the dish she'd filled near the center of the table. Behind that dish, standing back-to-back with Sorcha's Black Madonna, was a small golden statue of the goddess Oshun.

Like any self-respecting deity of love, beauty, and abundance, Oshun was covered in jewelry and not much else—unless one counted the bees and the enormous hair. Dani had little hair, zero bees, and no established habit of public nudity; nor did she devote any attention to romantic love, empirical evidence having proven it was a drain of energy that would distract from her professional goals. But the fact that Dani and the orisha didn't see eye to eye on that particular topic wasn't hugely important. The golden statue was an heirloom passed on from Dani's dear, departed Nana—the same woman who'd once told her, "There's power in knowledge passed between generations, whether it's by those books of yours or by an elder's mouth."

Danika agreed. Plus, following in her Nana's witchy footsteps was fun and came quite naturally. Must be something about the elaborate nighttime rituals and the history of dogged womanist defiance.

"Come on, then," Sorcha nudged, apparently done listing Dani's character flaws. And so, at a table shared by two different idols, in a room where candlelight and the full moon's glow twined lazily together, Danika took her friend's hands and closed the circle.

"You first," Sorcha whispered.

"Oh, darling, are you certain?"

"Don't start. I know you're gagging to invoke something or other."

Well, yes. In the month since Dani's last situationship had ended, her vagina had developed cobwebs (the vagina was, unfortunately, prone to dramatics), and this invocation would hopefully end that awful state of affairs.

She took a breath and began. "Hello, Oshun. Hope the twins are well. This month, I have an intention I think you'll support: I require another fuck buddy."

Sorcha's eyes popped open. "Hang on. Is this a good idea?"

"Shut up," Dani said sternly. "I'm busy."

Sorcha, being Sorcha, plowed on regardless. "I thought you were still upset about Jo?"

Dani produced a withering glare. "I was never upset about Jo. Getting *upset* is the sort of pointless, time-consuming emotion I work very hard to avoid."

"Really." The word dripped skepticism like the candles around them dripped wax. "Because I could've sworn that when she dumped you—"

"She didn't dump me. We weren't together, a fact that she wanted to change, while I did not."

"When she dumped you," Sorcha continued, because Sorcha was a twat, "you bought a box of cake mix and added an egg and ate the whole thing raw in a big old mixing bowl—"

"I have a sweet tooth," Dani said coldly, which was absolutely true.

Sorcha sighed. "You do realize it's not good for a witch to be so out of touch with her own feelings, don't you?"

"Rubbish. I am entirely in touch with my feelings, thank you very much."

"Except for the times when you don't know how to handle someone you slept with falling in love with you, so you go on a Betty Crocker binge."

"*That wasn't about Josephine,*" Dani repeated. "I must've been pre-menstrual or something." Because Danika Brown didn't mope—or at least, she didn't mope over interpersonal relationships. Hadn't since the day she'd walked in on her first love merrily boinking someone else, and never would. Jo wanted romance, and Dani couldn't think of anything less suited to her skill set, so they'd ended their friendship with benefits and gone their separate ways, and everything was fine.

Except for the fact that they didn't talk anymore.

Except for that.

"Stop trying to throw me off," Dani said firmly—because, clearly, the only way to end this god-awful conversation was to be firm. "I know what I'm doing and I know what I want. I am a grown woman of reasonable intellect, on track for tenure within the next fifteen years, with a deep desire for frequent oral sex and absolutely nothing else. So shut up and let me ask for it."

"Oh, whatever," Sorcha tutted. "Fine, then. Ask." And a miracle occurred: she rolled her eyes, heaved a disapproving sigh, but ultimately shut her mouth.

Well. One must always take swift advantage of divine happenings.

Dani closed her eyes and began again. "Oshun, I need a regular source of orgasms." She thought of Jo and added, "Someone who won't expect more from me than I can give. Preferably a sensible sort with a nice arse who's focused on their own goals. I haven't had much luck, myself, so if you know anyone who meets the criteria . . . just . . . point me in their direction. Give me a hint." When Dani finished, a warm and rare peace washed over her like the waters of a sun-touched river, as if the goddess had heard and promised to do her best. She let a tentative smile curve her lips and basked in the glowing silence.

A silence that was promptly ruined by Sorcha. "Christ, you're such a Sagittarius."

"Murder. I am going to commit a murder." Dani opened her eyes and rose up on her knees, studying the table calmly. Should she smack her best friend over the head with a religious icon—potentially disrespectful—or a hefty wax candle? The candle was aflame, so it'd have to be the statue. Only, when she reached for it, something fell out of her dress's many hidden pockets to land smack-bang on the altar.

In fact, it landed at Oshun's feet, balancing perfectly on top of the honey dish.

Dani supposed that was some sort of sign. Likely one that said, *Please don't kill Sorcha, you will eventually regret it and I doubt you'd enjoy prison.*

Sorcha squinted in the candlelight, clearly unconcerned by

her near brush with death. "Hang on, is that a cereal bar? I'm ravenous."

"It's a protein bar," Dani corrected, picking it up and handing it over.

"Since when do you eat protein bars?" Crumbs flew as Sorcha broke off pieces with her fingers like the mannerless heathen she was.

"I don't. Someone gave it to me. God, Sorch, you're making an awful mess and we haven't even finished our invocations. Didn't you want to do something for that creative writing competition you entered?"

"Doubt it'd help." Sorcha snickered. "We are *shitty* witches."

Dani sniffed. "Speak for yourself. *I* am focused on the present and attuned to the magic of my reality."

"Since when?"

"Since I made a request and now I'm waiting for a sign!"

Sorcha tossed the protein bar's empty wrapper onto the table. "Knowing us, you'll probably bloody miss it."

CHAPTER ONE

Five Months Later

The student union's coffee shop was like a bad pop song: painfully repetitive and unnaturally upbeat. Milk was steamed, names were chirped, and baristas beamed as if there were any call for such abominably perky behavior. (There most assuredly wasn't.) Dani was late for work, and the churn of coffee beans acted as background music to her fantasies about murdering everyone around her.

Come to think of it, she'd been considering murder quite a lot, lately. Perhaps she should see someone about that, or perhaps it was simply a natural consequence of living on planet Earth.

"Christ," Sorcha muttered, stirring half a kilo of sugar into her latte. "Are people always this loud?"

"It's March. The end of the semester is in sight. They're"—Dani let her gaze drift over the far-too-perky students filling the shop—"*hopeful*."

"Someone should cure them of that. It's disrespectful on a Monday morning."

Before Dani could wholeheartedly agree, a barista slapped two takeout cups on the counter. "Green tea and a black coffee for Danika?"

"Thanks." Dani grabbed the drinks and made good her escape.

"Black coffee," Sorcha murmured as they wound through the mass of bodies. "That'll be for your gorgeous security *friend*, am I right?"

"He has a name."

"And I'd like to scream it."

Dani almost choked on her own laughter. "Sorcha, you're *gay*."

"Thanks for noticing. Really, Dan, this is just coffee-shop banter. Girls being girls! Speaking of, this is the part where you admit all the filthy things you'd like to do to your so-called friend Zafir."

Dani scowled at the name—mostly because if she didn't, she might smile, which Sorcha would willfully misinterpret. "I'd never do filthy things to Zafir. He's a nice boy."

"*Nice?*" Sorcha squawked the word, incredulous. "Zaf? Zafir Ansari? That big, grumpy fucker who terrifies half your building?"

Dani sipped her green tea. "He's very sweet once you get to know him."

"*Sweet?*" Sorcha was approaching glass-shattering pitch.

Perhaps she was right; *sweet* might be overstating the matter. But Zaf was kind, and Dani had always had a soft spot for kind men; they were fabulously rare. Unfortunately, Zaf also avoided staring at Dani's chest with the kind of Herculean focus that suggested either disinterest or an excess of chivalry—and Dani couldn't stand chivalry in a man. It frequently led them to make ill-advised decisions, like inviting her to have dinner before sex, or hanging around and talking *after* sex.

"Zaf, gorgeous as he may be, is not an option. I'm waiting for a sign," she reminded Sorcha. "I'll just wank to thoughts of his beard until my perfect fuck buddy materializes."

Sorcha considered that for a moment before shrugging. "Fair enough. Speaking of yummy unsuitables, want to have lunch with me later at that pizza place with the hot, straight waitress?"

"Can't. Working."

"You're always fucking—"

Before Sorcha could finish that doubtless true statement, a man popped into their path like a mole from the earth. Dani blinked, coming to an abrupt stop. "Oh. Excuse me."

The man didn't seem to hear. He was tall, blond, and in possession of an easy, handsome smile that said he'd never met a boundary he couldn't bulldoze. Case in point: "Good morning," he purred, his eyes landing on Dani's chest like tit-seeking missiles. "I don't mean to bother you—"

"And yet, here we are," Sorcha sighed.

Tall, Blond, and Witless valiantly ignored her. "—but when I see a woman wearing red lipstick before nine A.M."—he winked—"well. I simply have to reward her."

Dani stared. "Reward me? With what? Because I only accept books or food."

The flicker of irritation on his face suggested that Danika

actually *speaking* was not part of his brilliant script. But he recovered smoothly enough. "There's food." He smiled. "Or there will be, if you let me take you to dinner."

Dani shook her head sadly and turned to Sorcha. "Do you think this ever works? It must, mustn't it, for them to continue?"

Sorcha managed to inject a bucketload of disgust into a single sigh, which was a skill Dani had always envied. "Maybe. Or maybe they're just not clever enough to make the connection between interrupting women and never, ever being voluntarily touched by one."

The man jolted, a scowl twisting his flawless brow. "Hang on," he snapped, "are you talking about *me*?"

"It's quite obvious that we are," Dani told him gently.

The blond spluttered in outrage for a few moments before deploying a dazzling "Fat fucking slut," and storming away.

"Oh dear," Dani sighed. "He thinks I'm a fat slut. I might die of a broken heart."

Sorcha rolled her eyes.

The voice in Zafir Ansari's ear murmured, "What are you thinking about?"

"How much I want you."

"Then have m—"

Zaf paused the audiobook, the sound from his single earbud cutting out. Sometimes, it was possible to read while he was working. This scene was not one of those times.

He unplugged the earbuds and wrapped them around his

phone, shoving both into his pocket. All the while, he kept a sharp eye on the door of the Echo building, scowling when one reed-thin boy, wearing what looked like pajamas under his hoodie, tried to skulk past without holding up his ID card like everyone else.

"Oi. You." Like most things Zaf said, the words came out as an irritable rumble. "Get over here."

The kid stopped walking and held up his hands, which were currently filled by a phone and . . . a bagel. "I can't reach my ID," he said apologetically, and made to keep walking, as if that would be o-fucking-kay.

"Get. Over. Here," Zaf repeated. Then he stood up, which tended to make people listen to him, since he was a former rugby union flanker.

Eyes widening, the kid swallowed and approached like a scolded puppy.

"Now," Zaf said patiently, "put your crap on the desk."

Both phone and bagel were glumly dropped.

"Well, would you look at that? Hands free." One eye still on the door, where the morning rush had slowed to a trickle, Zaf ordered, "I.D."

Huffing and puffing, the kid checked a thousand pockets before producing the student I.D. that said he probably wasn't here to nick a dead body or steal explosive gas. "I'm going to be late," he muttered as he handed it over.

"Not my problem." Zaf took the card and flashed it against the automated checker on his desk. "You know what I *could* do? I could make every last one of you line up while I ran you all through the system. But I'm a nice guy." Not strictly true, but he also wasn't a complete prick. "So I use my eyeballs instead. Easy for you, easy for me. Unless you don't put the card *in front* of my eyeballs. Then it's not so easy, since I don't have X-ray vision. Let me show you something." Card verified, Zaf held it up by its blue lanyard, stamped with the university logo. "You know where this goes? Right around your neck. Then you don't have to choose between holding your bagel and pissing me off. Sound good?"

"I can't put it around my neck," the kid spluttered. "I'll look like a dick."

"You're wearing *Adventure Time* pajamas to a lab, mate. You already look like a dick, and in five minutes' time your professor will tell you so."

"I—what?" He looked down. "Oh, for fuck's sake."

"Come here." Zaf slung the lanyard over the boy's messy hair. "Now piss off."

With a few glares and muttered comments, off he pissed.

Then a slow, sarcastic clap started to Zaf's right, which was all it took for him to realize that his niece had entered the building. He turned to face her, his standard bad mood evaporating. "Fluffy! What are you doing here?"

She widened her kohl-rimmed eyes in warning, jerking her head pointedly at the group of girls behind her.

Zaf cleared his throat and fought the twitch of his lips. "Sorry. Fatima, I mean." He gave the girls a little wave. "Hello, Fatima's friends."

"Will you relax?" she whispered. "You're so embarrassing."

"I was aiming for mortifying. I'll have to try harder."

She growled at him like a little lion and turned to wave off the girls. "I'll meet you upstairs, okay?" When they nodded and melted away, she turned back to him. "I see now why you chose this job. You get to bitch at people on a professional basis."

"Dream come true," Zaf said dryly, and sat down. Tucked behind the tall security desk was the table he actually used for work. He tapped his computer to bring up the time . . .

Not that he was watching the clock for anyone in particular. He had absolutely no reason to do that.

"You look tired," Fluff was saying. "Mum reckons you run yourself ragged and you'll regret it in your old age."

"Add it to the list. And I don't look tired, I look mysterious."

"Mysterious like a zombie," Fatima said.

"You're such a rude girl. Respect your elders."

She narrowed her eyes at him, tilted her head mockingly, and simpered, "Please, dearest Chacha, sleep eight hours a night instead of writing charity letters or whatever it is you do, and maybe you will not be at work looking like a dead thing, inshallah."

She was just like her father. The thought was bittersweet. "I'll think about it. Why are you here? There's nothing wrong, is there?" In the months since Fatima had enrolled, Zaf had only caught glimpses of her on campus from afar. He usually pantomimed his best Embarrassing Uncle routine, and she usually skulked away while shooting daggers in his direction—but now here she was, in his building. A kernel of anxiety skittered within his chest, always ready and waiting to blow. His Protective Uncle routine was even more intense than the Embarrassing Uncle one.

But Fatima rolled her eyes—she had a minor eye-rolling addiction—and sighed, "No, Chacha. Nothing is wrong. I just moved a class around to fit in Level 1 Punjabi."

Zaf raised his eyebrows. "Your Punjabi is fine."

"Exactly. I look forward to my distinction. Of course, I didn't know my rescheduled lit seminar would be"—she wrinkled her nose, looking around the foyer with blatant disgust—"*here*." Echo was a squat, gray relic of a building halfway down University Road where medical-science students did weird things to dead bodies and animal organs.

"Ah, it's not so bad," he told her cheerfully. "At least you'll get to see your favorite uncle more often now."

"I see you almost every day, and you are my *only* uncle," she tutted, shifting her handbag from her left arm to her right. He'd told her countless times to wear a rucksack for even weight distribution, but she was a little fashion plate like her mother.

"Grouch as much as you want, Fluff. I know you love me. Now hurry up to your lesson, or you'll be late."

"Nag, nag, nag. This is what I get for checking on your welfare, ah?" With another epic eye roll, she turned to leave.

"Niece," he called after her, "be good and bring me breakfast next time."

She ignored him, increasing her pace as she walked away.

"A snack, even. Fluffball! Are you listening to me?"

The flick of her headscarf over her shoulder was an unspoken *Fuck you.*

And then Fatima was gone, and Zaf was alone—a realization that made him tap his computer again. If he was the type to obsess over women, he might notice that a certain someone was late, but he wasn't, so he didn't. Instead, he rubbed at his short beard, clicked his tongue against his teeth, and checked his emails. There was a reminder from the team leader about the evacuation drill planned today, because Echo housed a ton of dangerous gases as well as weird organs. There was another email from the university's staff rugby team, inviting him to play—but, as much as he'd like to, that might be asking for trouble. Zaf was rarely recognized these days, what with the beard, and it was almost a decade since he'd last played pro. But getting on a pitch with local rugby fans could jog someone's memory, and if anyone said to him, "Hey, aren't you the guy whose family died in that car crash?" he might accidentally punch them in the face.

While he trashed the email with a sigh, Echo's automatic door heaved itself slowly open. In his peripheral vision, Zaf registered a familiar figure, and something inside him grew quiet. Watchful. Hungry.

He turned, and there was Danika Brown.

She walked like she'd never stumbled, studying the empty foyer with feline eyes he had a bad habit of falling into. Her dark skin glowed prettily under the same fluorescent lights that made everyone else look ghostly, jaundiced, or gray. And even though he'd told himself a thousand times that panting after a friend—a *work* friend, a work friend who might also be *gay*—was tacky at best and creepy at worst, lust slammed into Zaf like an illegal tackle.

"I'm late," Danika declared, because she rarely said hello or good-bye. Her long, black dress swirled as she approached him, the loose fabric occasionally clinging to her hip or her waist or her thigh. Not that he was looking, because that would be inappropriate. "Here you are," she said, sliding a cup over the desk that separated them. "One extra-hot, extra-black, extra-bitter coffee for our resident prince of darkness."

"Cheers, Princess," he shot back, and his reward was a million-dollar smile from that soft, scarlet mouth. The sight crackled through his veins like electricity. He kept going. "Out-gothed any teenagers, lately?"

"Scared any old ladies shitless?" she replied sweetly.

"Old ladies love me."

"Wow, hot stuff."

He flushed, but hopefully his skin tone and his beard would hide it. "Erm . . . because I mow their lawns and that. Is what I meant."

She grinned. "This just gets better and better."

"Fuck off."

Usually, she'd smirk at him and do as instructed, always in a rush to get to work. But today, she huffed out a laugh and ran a hand over her short, pink hair, from the razored edges to the longer curls on top. That hair had been black on Friday. Blue last month. Red the first day he ever saw her.

Aaand he should probably spend less energy cataloging this woman's hair colors, and more on . . . you know, important shit. It wasn't like he didn't have other things to think about—workshops to write and goals to chase and nonprofits to get off the ground.

But then Dani sighed, and he was distracted from common sense again.

"That was a hell of a sigh," he murmured, because it had been.

"Of course it was," she replied absently. "I'm a hell of a woman."

True enough, and a typical Danika comment, but her gaze was distant and her heart clearly wasn't in it. With her narrowed eyes and her pursed lips, she seemed unusually . . . *agitated*, and that gnawed at Zaf harder than it should.

See, if she was pissed about "culturally biased research" or "two-dimensional claims to feminism," he would have heard about it the minute she entered the building. Which meant something else must be bothering her, maybe something serious—but she hadn't *mentioned* that something, so it clearly wasn't his business.

He wouldn't ask. He wouldn't pry. He wouldn't—

"Everything all right?" blurted his big fucking mouth.

Dani startled as if he'd pulled her out of deep thought. "Well—it's just—" She hesitated. "I should probably go up. You know I try to be early to class in order to give the impression of omnipotence."

She was ridiculous, as always. Unselfconscious, as always. Made him want to grin, as always.

Zaf resisted, as always.

"Fair enough," he said. "I'll see you—"

She produced another sigh fit for the stage and announced, "Fine, fine, you *dragged* it out of me."

"Did I," he deadpanned.

"I'd tell you not to be sarcastic, but I don't think you can help it. No, be quiet, you awful man, and listen to me moan. You did ask."

"That I did." Fuck, but he enjoyed this woman.

"You wouldn't *believe* what happened to me outside the coffee shop."

He sipped his coffee like he wasn't desperate to know. "Feel free to tell me anytime now. It's only been a century since this conversation started, after all."

That earned him a quicksilver smile before she confessed. "Some arsehole asked me to dinner."

His next sip seemed to burn. "Hope you told them to get fucked."

"Well, yes." She must have approved of his response, because her gaze went all warm and sweet like treacle. "Yes, I did."

"Good."

Good, as in, women deserved to go about their business without being drooled on at the arse-crack of dawn; not *good* because he didn't want any fucker taking Danika out to dinner. That would be weird and possessive and pointless, because she was categorically none of his business. Sometimes he got this burning urge to *make* her his business, but he was pretty good at squashing that before it got out of control.

See, what Zaf really wanted was to be happy, and he'd read enough romance novels to know how to make that happen. First, you reached your goals and shit. (He was working on that part.) Second, you found a good woman who made you think bad thoughts and you lived happily ever after with her.

Dani was a good woman who made him think *filthy* thoughts, but he'd known her long enough to realize there'd be no happily ever after. They wouldn't even get to "once upon a time." First, because she talked about banging Janelle Monáe kind of a lot, and when he'd asked what she thought of Idris Elba (everyone who was into guys liked Idris Elba, right?), all she'd said was "He's great. I really enjoyed *Luther*." And then there was the fact that, according to staff gossip (not that Zaf approved of staff gossip—he really didn't, he absolutely didn't), Danika Brown was the queen of one-time things. Zaf wouldn't know what to do with a one-time thing if it showed up with a fifty-page instruction manual and slapped him on the dick.

So she wasn't for him and he wasn't for her, and they were friends, so he shouldn't even think about it. Which was why he swallowed his ridiculous jealousy and joked, "Hope that guy falls down a manhole or something."

"From your lips to the universe's ears," she purred, and twinkled at him. That was the only way to describe it. She looked at him, and she just—she fucking *twinkled*. All of a sudden, he felt a little bit warm and slightly dizzy and way too horny for a Monday morning at work.

Zaf cleared his throat and pulled himself together. Clearly, that was more than enough Danika for one day. "Anyway. You're late, remember?"

Her eyes widened in degrees as if she was a sleepy kitten. "Oh. Oh, shit! Yes, I am."

"Hang on." He reached into his pocket for Dani's morning protein bar, a habit he'd fallen into since she'd started working at Echo months ago. It was only fair, since she always brought him coffee. And since she never had time for breakfast, a fact he'd learned after seeing her chomp down a bag of Skittles at 9 A.M. And since she was a bleeding-heart vegetarian who might die of malnutrition without him.

"Thanks, Dad," she said, and snickered, holding out her hand because she knew the drill.

Zaf snorted. But what he found in his pocket was hard and cold and definitely not protein-rich: his phone. Wrong pocket. As he let go and withdrew his hand, sound filled the air.

"Then have me. I'm dying for you, and you know it."

Oh, shit.

Shit, shit, shit.

Of course he'd managed to press Play on his latest audio-book. Zaf grabbed his phone and fumbled with the earbuds wrapped around it—the same earbuds that hadn't stopped him from hitting Play but now acted as some kind of impenetrable fucking shield protecting the Pause button. This must be one of his teenage nightmares, because his hands were way slower and clumsier than usual. The audiobook narrator warned, *"If I touch you tonight, I'll make you mine,"* and across the desk, Danika made a choked noise of—horror? Yep, probably horror—and put a hand over her mouth.

"Zaf," she half-shrieked, "is that *porn*?"

"No!" The word came out a bit too loud to seem honest. "No," he repeated through gritted teeth, trying to sound like a calm, sensible man instead of a raging pervert. He finally managed to pause the app, then opened a desk drawer, shoved his traitorous phone inside (technology, like most apparently good things in life, clearly couldn't be trusted), and slammed it shut.

"That was definitely porn," Dani said, and Zaf was so busy wanting to jump off a bridge, it took him a long while to realize she was laughing. One hand still covered her mouth, but little chuckles escaped between her words, and her eyes creased at the corners in an unmistakable smile. The relief that hit him was so fucking intense, he almost passed out. With every good-natured giggle, a bit of his instinct to think the worst faded away.

"It wasn't porn," he repeated, and this time he didn't have to shout over the frantic pounding of his heart, or the urgent moaning of his phone. "It's an audiobook."

"What the bloody hell *kind* of audiobook?" But she asked with a grin on her face.

"Doesn't matter," he muttered, not because he was embarrassed about reading romance novels, but because now didn't seem like the best time to explain it. "Listen, I really didn't mean for that to—"

"I know," she said, no hesitation, which was good. Because if she'd taken that fiasco as some kind of creepy, quote-unquote *accident*, Zaf would've had to run away to Guatemala to herd goats for a living. And he'd never been great with animals.

His cheeks still burning—thank fuck for thick beards and brown skin—Zaf stabbed a hand into his other pocket, found the protein bar, and handed it over. "There. Now piss off."

"Rude," she said, but she was smiling as she walked away.

"You'd better eat that!" he groused.

"Enjoy your sex book!" she called back. Then she swung open the door to the stairwell and disappeared.

Zaf exhaled and dropped his head into his hands. "Kill me," he murmured to no one in particular. "Just kill me now."

CHAPTER TWO

It was absolutely typical that Dani's first year as junior teaching staff—*good*—had coincided with her unfortunate transfer to the hideous building that was Echo—*bad*. She should be teaching next door to one of her Ph.D. supervisors right now, in the tiny, cozy building on campus dedicated to literature and women's studies. But back in October, there'd been an unfortunate incident involving a group of first years, clown suits, a piñata, and a surprising amount of asbestos. In the chaos of relocation, Dani had helpfully and foolishly volunteered to take the classroom no one else wanted to touch. After all, Jo worked in Echo, so how bad could it be?

Now that Jo was no longer her good friend and regular lay, the answer was: quite bad. Even the best thing about Echo—one rather entertaining security guard—had a habit of making her late. Or later than usual.

"All right!" Dani clapped her hands as she strode into her temporary classroom. "I'm here, shut up, hope you did the reading, because if you didn't, you're buggered." She carefully removed her laptop from her rucksack, put it on the desk, then dumped the bag unceremoniously on the cold, hard floor. Uncapping a whiteboard pen, she pointed at the table of students waiting for her, all of whom looked slightly unnerved—which was just how she liked them. "Christina Rossetti, 'Goblin Market,' let's discuss. Emily, start us off."

The sleepy-eyed teenager wrapped a strand of long, blue hair around her finger and said promptly, "Totally about banging."

Dani approached the board and wrote *Goblin Market* in a bubble. Traditionalists might find writing on the board unnecessary, but not all learners were aural, no matter their stage of education. So she scrawled a little arrow coming out of her bubble and wrote: *Banging*.

Then she turned back to Emily and said brightly, "Please elaborate."

"Well," Emily hedged, "I mean, it's either banging or Christianity. One of those. Maybe both."

"I think it's both," added the boy beside her, Will.

Dani nodded, drew another arrow, and wrote *Tits out for Christ?* Then she asked, "Anything more specific?"

"Tits *in* for Christ," Will corrected.

"Tits wherever you want for Christ," Emily said firmly, "because he'll totally forgive you. It's an allegory. Lizzie suffers, right, for Laura's sin?"

"Now we're getting somewhere." Dani grinned, grabbed a board cloth, and replaced *Tits out for Christ* with *Allegory: original sin, savior's suffering.* "Okay, someone else . . ." Her eyes landed on an unfamiliar face—the new girl. She'd received an email from scheduling about that. "Fatima, yes?"

The girl nodded, small and serious and alarmingly well dressed. "That's right."

"Did you have time to read?"

"I did."

"Hit me, then."

Fatima cleared her throat. "I got the Christ thing, too. And I think the goblins are anti-Semitic."

The girl next to her, Pelumi, clicked her fingers. "Like in Harry Potter."

"Hey," someone piped up from across the table. "Don't shit-talk Harry Potter."

"It's not shit-talking if it's true."

Dani clapped her hands. "Robust discussion is precisely what I want from you, but unless you can connect Harry Potter to Rossetti's themes more solidly, I'm going to ask that it's taken off the table."

There was a pause before Pelumi said, "Excess sensuality and the private cost. Hogwarts has magically refilling tables as a result of underground slave labor; the girl in the poem dies of too many orgasms or something because she tasted some dick. I mean, fruit."

Dani nodded gravely. "For sheer ingenuity, I will allow it."

The debate burst to life.

Dani spent the rest of the class listening to a mix of razor-sharp insight and meme regurgitation, directing the conversation when it seemed necessary, shutting up when it didn't. Time skipped ahead of her until the seminar was over, notebooks were being stuffed into bags, and the cupcakes at the union stall started calling her name.

As the students filed out with waves and good-byes, Dani paused to open her laptop and take a quick look at her emails. One had to stay on top of these things. Someone might need her to—

Ah.

There was a new email at the top of the screen with a bolded subject line that made her gut squeeze. Whether that squeeze was excitement or a warning sign of nervous diarrhea, it was hard to say. All things considered, it might even be both.

DAUGHTERS OF DECADENCE, THEN & NOW: A PUBLIC RESEARCH SYMPOSIUM.

Hi, Dani . . . the preview read, and was doubtless followed by something like: *Just need final confirmation re: topics for discussion panel with Inez and co.!*

The discussion panel was a public speaking event Dani had foolishly agreed to take part in when she was presumably high on (then undiscovered) asbestos fumes the previous year.

Well, the decision hadn't been *entirely* foolish—or even mostly foolish. It would give her more academic exposure, increase her experience and her profile, and help cement her as a trusted voice in her topic of interest. Taking part would be an honor, and certainly fit with her careful plans to gain a professorship by forty-two. (Forty-five, if she couldn't squeeze everything in within the next fifteen years.)

Really, the only reason she was close to shitting herself was that she'd be speaking on the panel alongside *Inez fucking Holly.* You know: one of fewer than thirty black female professors in the United Kingdom, the woman who made feminist literary theory her bitch, Dani's eternal Beyoncé-level idol, et cetera, et cetera. The one woman she would rather die— literally, she would rather *actually* die—than embarrass herself in front of.

Not that Dani tended to embarrass herself at work. Her profession was straightforward and easily controlled and required qualities she naturally possessed, such as laser-like focus and an enthusiasm for close reading and analysis, instead of qualities she didn't, such as the ability to process and express irrelevant rubbish like her own emotions. So, no, embarrassment at work wasn't likely. But still. Stranger things had happened.

She pressed a hand to her chest and touched the moonstone hanging beneath her dress, letting calm sweep through her in waves. Then she exhaled, typed out a painstaking reply, and snapped the laptop shut.

"Everything is under control," she told herself. "This is your work. This is your *thing.* This is the kind of pressure you can handle."

She was still repeating that mantra a few minutes later, when she sailed out of the lab and came face-to-face with her ex–friend with benefits.

Well, shit.

"Dani," Jo blurted, stopping just short of what would have been a mortifying collision.

"Jo," Dani managed, inclining her head, hoping she looked incredibly cool and generally unaffected by this awkward situation. A quick inventory of her own body revealed she had a death grip on the trio of crystal pendants hanging beneath her dress, which rather suggested the opposite. She let go.

She still felt them, though, skin-warm against her chest: moonstone for destiny, garnet for success, rose quartz for determination.

Rose quartz was supposed to help with romance, too, but Dani had decided a long time ago that hers was broken.

"How are you?" Jo asked stiffly, patting her dark, silky bob with one hand.

Dani blinked, caught by surprise. "How *am* I? Are you really asking me that?"

Jo's tight smile disappeared. "It's called being polite."

"Polite? The last time we spoke you told me I was emotionally stunted and ruled by fear." Both of which were patently ridiculous accusations and, more to the point, quite rude. "Honestly, it's indecent of you to expect conversation after bruising my heart." Well, that might be overstating the matter. "After exacerbating my spleen," Dani corrected.

Jo stared. "Your spleen?"

"Yes. It's a lesser emotional center."

"No, it's not. It's an immuno— Oh, for heaven's sake, never mind." Jo's bob looked a bit less smooth now, her cheeks flushed, her scowl ferocious. "Stop acting all wounded and brooding," she whispered sharply, as if they might be overheard by the bloody walls. "According to you, we weren't even in a relationship."

"According to *both* of us," Dani snapped. "We agreed from the start. You're the one who changed your mind." Who started demanding dates and affection and commitment, things Dani had learned not to bother with because she always got them wrong. Not that she cared. Her system was more efficient, anyway.

If she'd tried to give Jo what she'd asked for, Dani's efficiency would've been the first complaint. *Are you seriously scheduling me in? What, am I just another job to you?*

She knew the drill. And avoided said drill like the plague, or the dentist, or both.

"Look," Dani began, meeting Jo's steel-gray eyes and trying to find the easy friendship that used to warm them. The friendship that never should've disappeared. "You know I don't do that sort of thing—and trust me, you don't want me to try. It'd be a waste of everyone's time."

Jo's frustrated expression flickered, then faded, replaced by something that looked disturbingly like pity. "You really believe that, don't you?"

Dani swallowed. "Can't we just be all right again? I . . ." *I miss being your friend,* she wanted to say. Except that would be mortifying.

But Jo waited until Dani's pause grew into a chasm. And then she shook her head slowly. "No. I don't think we can."

Well. *Well.* "Fine." And that was that.

Dani gathered her dignity and swept down the hallway with as much dramatic disdain as she could muster. Which, she fancied, was rather a lot. Since Jo had been headed toward the stairs, escaping her presence took Dani to the lifts, where she frantically pressed the button and refused to look back. She pinned her eyes to the slightly dented chrome doors as she waited, Jo's words circling in her mind like a children's merry-go-round. Perhaps the motion was why they made Dani feel slightly nauseous.

The battered old lift arrived with a groan, and she slipped gratefully inside, releasing a heavy exhalation as the doors closed. What a bloody mess. At this rate, she might have to top off her cupcake with some Skittles, just to soothe her nerves.

"Actually," she muttered, flicking a wry glance up at the ceiling, "you know what would really soothe my nerves? Sex. So, you know. Not to rush you, darling, but chop-chop. Still waiting on that hint."

The fluorescent lights cut out and an ear-rending shriek filled the lift.

"Oh, bloody *hell*," Dani shouted, slapping her hands over her ears. "Fine! I don't see how any reasonable higher power could expect me to go this long without oral sex, but if it means so much to you, I'll be patient."

Apparently, those weren't the magic words, because darkness still reigned, the siren continued to scream, and Dani remained eager for a snack without any obvious path toward a nice packet of sweets. All in all, a terrible state of affairs.

"All right," she murmured to herself. "No lights, completely obnoxious and unnecessarily shrill alarm, the lift has stopped working, and . . ." She pulled out her phone, which had no signal, used the flashlight to find the lift's buttons, and pressed the one marked EMERGENCY. Nothing happened. "The lift has stopped working," she repeated calmly, "and so has the emergency call. I suppose I'm in a bit of trouble." What did an alarm mean in Echo, again? Could be fire, could be gas. Neither sounded particularly positive.

Dani stood for a moment, biting her lip, trying not to think about tragic deaths, because Nana had always taught her that one's thoughts influenced fate. And Dani was far too fabulous for her fate to involve dying from toxic inhalation in a bloody elevator.

So, after a few minutes spent weighing her options, she initiated a highly sophisticated two-step plan. Step one involved sliding her fingertips into the slight gap between the closed lift doors and attempting to pull, hard. Step two involved engaging her diaphragm, taking a deep breath, and bellowing at the top of her lungs: *"Help!"*

The scream of the gas alarm was shrill enough to shatter the glass on Zafir's emergency-only adrenaline store. Once upon a time, he'd felt this urgent, explosive focus before every game, the roar of the crowd battling the rush of blood in his ears. But he was an old has-been now, so he took his thrills where he could get them, and if that meant handling a routine, semiannual drill like he was Jason bloody Bourne, so be it.

George, the secondary officer responsible for Echo, appeared from a nearby corridor, took one look at Zaf, and snorted. "You do know this is a drill, yeah? Why are you giving me Terminator vibes right now?"

Zaf rose to his feet, let the vibes intensify, and said grimly, "Shut up, George."

George shut up.

"All right. As discussed, I'm your point, timer's set, go." They split apart and got down to business. While George took the primary sweep, Zaf opened all exits before going to hunt down anyone who might have unregistered mobility issues. He had a database of staff and students who'd need emergency assistance in situations like this, but none of them were in the building right now. Still, there might be someone who'd broken their leg last week, or someone whose knee stopped working when it rained, or some shit like that. It was Zaf's job to keep an eye out for those people, because, as his line manager had said, "I reckon you could lift anyone, if you had to."

Bit presumptuous, but not exactly wrong; Zaf could do anything if he *had* to. Like wearing a uniform jacket that didn't come in a size big enough to cover his wrists.

After a sweep of the building showed staff and students evacuating without issue, Zaf went back downstairs to coordinate with the professors checking their class registers. He found the pavement outside Echo a mess of pure chaos, because, routine drill or not, people loved a fuss—and, he was discovering, they rarely checked their bloody emails. Students in particular were shouting useless questions at each other, shoving like trapped animals, and generally fanning the ever-glowing coal of his anxiety.

Well, maybe it wasn't the students doing that last part. Maybe it was the fact that he still hadn't seen Danika evacuate, even though he knew full well she hadn't left with her class half an hour ago.

By the time George returned, Zaf was outside scanning the crowd for cropped, pink hair while using a bellow honed on the rugby pitch to make sure everyone knew, "This is just a drill! You're safe, and there's no need to panic. There is no threat to you inside, but we can't let you back in until the building is secure."

"But you just said there's no threat inside!" A nearby student scowled.

Obviously, one of the email ignorers. *Give me bloody strength.* Zaf sighed. "I know. This is part of the drill."

"Well, if it's all just fake, I don't see why you can't—"

He speared the man with his flattest look, the one that made his mother smack him on the head and call him a shark. "Do you know what the word *drill* means, mate?"

The guy swallowed, shrugged, and turned away.

George appeared at Zaf's shoulder to mutter, "Anyone ever tell you that you have strong supervillain energy?"

"Be quiet. Final sweep?"

"All clear."

Zaf studied the crowd again. "Did you see Danika? Because I haven't."

"Er, no." George scratched his ear, brow furrowing. "Probably took one of the emergency exits."

Probably should be good enough, in a situation like this,

right? Clearly it was for George, because the man looked annoyingly unconcerned. For all they knew, Dani could be trapped in a supply closet by some evil academic rival whose theories she'd called "woefully uninformed." Or maybe a cult obsessed with worshipping her had seen their chance in the chaos and swept in to steal her away. Or something.

"All right," George was saying, "I think that went well. Let's shut it down."

"No."

A slow blink. "Erm . . . pardon?"

"No," Zaf repeated. "I'm going back in." Yes, he was paranoid about safety, and no, he didn't give a fuck. Maybe if *everyone* was paranoid about safety, his dad and big brother wouldn't have died in a car accident seven years ago. And if that was a messed-up thought process, oh fucking well. He was a work in progress.

"Back in? Why?"

Zaf pushed through the crowd, ignoring George's obvious confusion. "Danika Brown," he called, his voice rising over the chatter and the sound of passing traffic. "Who's seen her? Pink hair, teaches English lit, about this tall—"

"I know Dani!" chirped a blue-haired girl a few feet away, turning toward him. "I had a seminar with her, last period."

Relief rolled through his body. "Did she leave with you?"

"Uh, no," the kid said, twisting the end of her ponytail around her finger. "She stayed behind on her laptop, I think. But I'm sure she's fine—it's just a drill, right?"

"Yes." Zaf nodded calmly. "This is just a drill. What floor?"

"Third. Hey, are you okay? You look—"

"I'm fine," Zafir said over his shoulder, already running. "Remain calm," he shouted as he raced back toward the building. He yanked open the power-assisted door so hard it actually smacked into the wall. Fuck. Had he just broken the motor? Never mind. He turned back to the crowd and reminded them, "This is just a drill!"

Then he sprinted in and took the stairs three at a time.

CHAPTER THREE

After what felt like an hour of yanking at the lift doors and making as much noise as possible, Dani was starting to worry just the teeniest, tiniest bit. It had occurred to her, approximately three minutes ago, that if the building had indeed been evacuated due to the presence of dangerous gas, she probably shouldn't be breathing so deeply to power her yells for assistance. So she'd switched to slamming her hands against the doors while trying not to breathe at all, which seemed less effective but also less likely to speed up her imminent carbon monoxide poisoning. Now she was trying to figure out if she felt light-headed because the poisoning had begun, or because she wasn't fucking breathing.

It could possibly be both.

When she heard a voice shouting her name on the other side of the doors, she wondered for a moment if she was hallucinating as her body suffocated on ricin. Then she pulled herself together, patted the trio of gemstones hanging beneath her dress, and shouted back, "Hello?" *Bang, bang, bang* went her hands against the door, her left wrist aching and swollen because she'd wrenched it a little, back when she'd tried to open the lift. "HELLO?"

"Danika!" The voice was closer now, much closer, and almost familiar over the scream of the alarm.

She hesitated. "Zaf?"

No answer. But there was an odd, metallic wail, as if an iron elephant had been struck down, and then a high screech. She leapt back instinctively from the doors, and a second later, a tiny slice of light appeared right down the center. She caught sight of one dark eye and almost collapsed with relief.

"Hang on," Zaf called through the gap, and then there was another wail and the door opened a little more. She saw his blunt fingertips at the edge of the chrome and realized he was actually succeeding in the endeavor at which she'd so tragically failed.

"You can't just pull the thing open! You'll hurt—"

The alarm cut out abruptly, plunging them into silence. Dani clapped her hands over her ringing ears, as if the quiet was attacking them, before blushing at her own silliness and lowering her hands. Zaf, meanwhile, continued the superhuman and technically impossible—shouldn't it be impossible?—feat of forcing open the lift. Unfortunately for him, these doors were the least of their issues. Dani had been trapped long enough that her death by poisonous gas was assured, and Zaf had likely doomed himself to the same fate by rescuing her. For some reason, she was intensely upset by that, and also felt a little bit like swooning.

Must be the formaldehyde inhalation.

Zaf gave one final heave, and the doors opened. She had an

instant to register the sight of him: tall and broad and heavily built, his usual resting bitch face veering into *furious* territory, his warm, brown eyes gentle enough to negate the effect. For some reason, the contrast—the hard precision of his features versus that soft, liquid gaze—made her shiver. The light shone behind him like a halo, and he looked even larger than usual, and it hit Dani like a giant, cosmic fist that this whole nobly-rescuing-her-from-death situation was almost certainly a sign. As in, a *sign*. The timing and the drama were too significant to ignore. The universe might as well have pointed flashing neon arrows in the direction of Zaf's delicious shoulders and screamed, *This one, then, since you're so impatient.*

Dani stared. *Really? Him? Are you certain?* After all, sleeping with a friend hadn't ended well for her last time. Plus, Zaf could be a teeny bit uptight, and then there was that excess of chivalry and the habit some men had of reading commitment into copulation . . . She opened her mouth to ask Zaf if he might, against all her previous instincts and assumptions, be up for no-strings shenanigans. Then she remembered that they were dying, which made the whole thing immaterial, and anyway, he looked to be in a foul mood. His jaw, beneath its short, black beard, was tight, his lush mouth was a hard line, and his thick hair was an outrageous mess, perhaps because he'd just forced an elevator open with his bare hands.

Before she could comment on that strange, if impressive, behavior, he reached into the lift, dragged her out by the front of her dress, and plastered her against his massive chest. An almost silent "Alhamdulillah" rushed out of him on a sigh. Dani was just thinking, rather ungratefully, that he better not have creased her bodice, when he wrapped his arms so tightly around her that she could barely breathe.

Or maybe that was the mercury vapor.

"Why the fuck were you in the lift?" he demanded, his words hard, the rest of him . . . not. She was quite certain he was nuzzling her head like a cat. "You don't use the lift in emergency situations!"

"I know that," she griped, her voice muffled against his chest. And what a lovely chest it was, like a big, meaty pillow. His belly was nice, too, both soft and solid. She wondered if she could get away with grabbing his arse, since her brains were probably melting out of her nose as they spoke. "I was already in the lift when the alarm started. It just sort of . . . shut down."

He growled. He actually *growled*—she felt the sound rumble through him. "This shitty old *fucking* building. The outer doors weren't even closed."

"The emergency button didn't work," she said, enjoying the tension in his body as he wrapped himself around her. "I was trapped in there for hours."

"Er . . . I don't think it was hours."

"One hour, then," she corrected.

"Danika, it's been twelve minutes since the alarm started."

"Oh." Well, it had *felt* rather long. "Perhaps my grip on time wobbled a bit because of the strain."

His growl came back. "I'm going to kill someone."

"I think *we're* going to be killed."

"What?" Zaf pulled back a little, looking down at her, and

she tried not to whine at the loss of contact. At least his hands were gripping her upper arms now, his thumbs sliding back and forth over her skin in a shower of sparkles. He'd never touched her before.

He really should touch her again, if possible. Soon.

"We're being poisoned," she told him sadly. "By gas. But at least my last sight on this earth will be your wonderful beard."

His response was slow, as if he doubted her cognitive function. "Dani, this is a drill. There is no gas."

It took her a moment to process those words, but once it happened, she blushed hard enough to combust. "Right. Erm. Sorry about the beard thing. My mind's all over the place. It's the gas."

His gorgeous mouth kicked up at one corner. "The . . . nonexistent gas?"

"Placebo effect," she told him firmly, and stepped back, breaking the contact between them. If there really was no gas, then it must be touching Zaf that was making her dizzy. And silly. And mushy. That needed to stop. She had nothing to feel mushy *about*, since he hadn't actually risked death by cyanide to come to her rescue, and anyway, mushiness was strictly prohibited.

"What's wrong with your hand?" he frowned, thankfully oblivious to Dani's mental ramblings. He caught her right wrist and studied what she hadn't noticed: her nails, torn and slightly bloodied from the force she'd used trying to open the doors.

"Oh, I attempted your method of escape," she told him airily. "Apparently, I don't have the biceps for it."

He didn't laugh. His frown deepening, he grabbed her other

hand for inspection, then dropped it like a hot potato when she let out a hiss of pain. "What—?"

"Sorry. I, er, pulled too hard, I suppose. That wrist aches a little bit. Perhaps I wrenched it."

"Right," Zaf said, his eyes burning something awful. He looked mutinous, but evidently not with her, because he stepped forward and slid her rucksack gently off her shoulders. "I'll take this," he murmured.

"Oh, no, it's okay, I—"

"Danika," he said, iron in his tone. "I. Will take. This."

"I knew you were bossy, but I had no idea you were *this* bossy."

"Yeah, well," he muttered, "now you know. Just like I know you have a dodgy grasp on time. We're even."

She shot him a glare. "Why do I put up with you?"

"I think it has something to do with my wonderful beard."

"Shut up, you awful man."

He sighed. "No gratitude. That's the problem with posh girls." Before she could formulate a response to that outrageous comment—which she absolutely was *not* tempted to laugh at—he said, "Come here." Her rucksack now safely on his back, he scooped her up in his arms like a bride.

Her stomach swooped, and she let out a mortifying little shriek—but really, it couldn't be helped. Because Zaf's grip on her waist and her thigh sparked electricity, and her mouth was just inches from his bare, brown throat, and who could blame her for making undignified noises under circumstances like that? It was all very irregular and unreasonably *good*. Perhaps she should stop doubting the universe and accept this man as her goddess-chosen fuck buddy, after all. He looked down at her with a tiny smirk, a quirk of the lips that seemed to say, *Bet you didn't know I could do that*, and she almost melted into a puddle pussy-first.

Of course, she couldn't let him *know* she was melting, since he was a handsome man, and handsome men must never be allowed to know the full extent of their sexual appeal. They couldn't be trusted with the knowledge. So she tried her best to look outraged and demanded, "What on earth are you doing?"

"You hurt yourself," he said calmly as he carried her toward the stairs.

"I hurt my *hands!*"

He grunted. "You were trapped in here during a gas leak. Probably aren't steady on your feet."

"I thought it was a drill?"

"Emotional trauma," he said without missing a beat. "You should really check your emails, by the way. Everyone got one. About the drill, I mean."

"I had other concerns," she said ominously.

"You always do. Someone should keep an eye on you."

"I *beg* your pardon?"

He fought back a smile as they crossed the foyer. "What? Is that not allowed?"

"It's not *necessary*. Smirk at me all you like, but I doubt you'd let anyone keep an eye on you."

"Depends on the eye," he said dryly, and kicked open the building's front door, which swung far more easily than usual. The students milling around in front of Echo seemed thrilled by Dani and Zaf's sudden appearance, pointing and whispering among themselves like she was someone exciting rather than an ordinary and extremely tired Ph.D. student with a throbbing wrist. Perhaps they thought she'd been poisoned by amatoxin and were eagerly awaiting her gruesome death. That would certainly explain why they started aiming their camera phones at her.

She gave them a sunny smile—as her bonkers grandmother Gigi would say, *Always put your best foot forward*—and Zaf looked down at her with obvious bafflement. "What are you doing, Danika?"

"Being beautiful for my people."

He let out a burst of laughter. "I wish I could carry you around all the time. You do wonders for my mood."

Silly, to glow at such an obvious joke, and yet Dani did. There was something in the warmth of his eyes as he studied her through lowered lashes, in the tender curve of his smile, all fond exasperation. Like lemonade and vodka, the sweetness contrasted so sharply with the way he held her—tight—and the way he'd dragged her from the lift upstairs, with that feral note in his voice that said . . .

She didn't know what it said. But she did know they were now staring at each other like mooning teenagers, which was the sort of ridiculous behavior she should put a stop to.

As if he'd read her mind, Zaf looked away and cleared his throat. "I should . . . I really need to talk to someone about that lift. And—"

"And I have things to do," Dani said firmly. "Cupcakes to eat, research to continue."

"First aiders to visit," he added, "about that wrist."

"Yes," she lied through her teeth. Professors didn't knock off work after twinging a wrist, so Dani certainly wouldn't. She didn't have the time to waste, anyway. Symposiums to prepare for, and all that. Inez Holly waited for no sprain!

Zaf stared at her, dark eyes narrowed.

"*Yes*," she repeated, attempting to look trustworthy. "Absolutely. First aid. Medical professionals. Et cetera." As Gigi always said, *Men are much less time-consuming when you lie.*

Except, apparently, for this man. "If I find out you haven't had that looked at, you'll be in deep shit."

"Duly noted," she said dryly, which was impressive, considering she was in fact extremely wet.

Zaf sighed and took her over to the little wall surrounding the building's flowerbed, setting her gently down as if she really was injured. "I mean it, Danika," he said, propping her rucksack by her feet. "I'm watching you."

But when he turned to find his supervisor, she was the one watching him. Specifically, his arse.

She had to take some pleasures, after such a stressful day.

Dani did as she'd been told. Sort of.

Her wrist was aching quite a bit, and if it got any worse it might slow down her typing speed. So she popped some painkillers and went to her older sister Chloe's house at the end of the day.

Their youngest sister, Eve, answered the door, a smile on her face and a single AirPod in her ear. "Dan! I didn't know you were coming over."

"Yes, well, here I am."

"You changed your hair again. We match!" Eve flicked one of her own pastel-pink braids and shut the door behind them.

"Wonderful," Dani murmured, slightly distracted. Memories of being held tight against Zaf's chest had haunted her all day, and after failing for hours to escape the bastards, she'd decided to let them simply wash over her.

Now she was all hot and shuddering inside like her battered old laptop, so distracted she almost missed Redford, Chloe's boyfriend, calling, "Hey, Dani," as they passed the room where he painted.

"Hi, Red," she called weakly, and walked on into the living room.

"Dani!" Chloe, the eldest Brown sister, perched on a throne of cushions and blankets formerly known as the sofa. Chloe would tell Dani to buy a new laptop, because she didn't understand that old technology could hold character and luck. "Thank goodness you're here," she said now. "Eve's been boring me to death—"

"Hey!"

"With Pinterest boards and Instagram hashtags and all sorts of rubbish."

"You are both jealous," Eve sniffed as she sat down, "because I am the youngest, but neither of you have ever been wedding planner of honor before."

Dani briefly considered investigating that baffling statement, then decided it was better left ignored. Holding up her wrist and attempting to look forlorn, she said, "I hurt myself."

"Darling! What happened?"

"I got trapped in a lift."

"*What?*" Chloe stood so abruptly that her cat, Smudge, almost fell off his seat on the arm of the sofa. "Do we need to sue someone? Mum's been quite bored lately, I'm sure she'd enjoy it." She bustled off to the kitchen without waiting for an answer and returned with a mammoth first-aid kit.

Chloe had seen so many doctors over the course of her life, she was practically one herself. Sort of. Years of rigorous study and training aside. So, five minutes later, Dani's wrist was wrapped up in some sort of gauze, her bag was filled with borrowed ibuprofen, and she was sharing her thrilling tale of lift extraction.

"My," Chloe murmured, her eyes wide behind the blue frames of her glasses. "Well. This Zaf fellow sounds wonderful."

"And handsome," Eve piped up, although her focus was on her phone.

"He is," Dani agreed, settling down on the sofa. "I think—"

"And strong," Eve went on.

"Well, yes. He's very—"

"He looks a lot like that hockey player, don't you think? The Canadian one everyone was thirsting over last month."

Dani, who knew nothing about Canadian hockey players or sportsball-type people in general, glared at her little sister. "And how would you know what Zaf looks like?"

Eve held up her phone. "I'm watching the video of him rescuing you from the building on Twitter."

Dani opened her mouth, then closed it. Took a breath to speak, then expelled it. Ran through a thousand different interpretations of that relatively simple sentence, then rejected them all. "I'm sorry," she said, quite calmly, under the circumstances. "You're watching the what?"

"I," Eve said slowly, "am watching the viral video that just popped up on my Trending page, which is tagged #DrRugbae, and features a very huge and handsome security guard identified as ex–Titans star Zafir Ansari, carrying a pink-haired woman who looks rather like you, Danika, out of that ugly building where you work." Eve looked up and batted her lashes, the mischievous little cow. "Haven't you seen it?"

"Give me that!" Dani snapped, and lunged for the phone.

"It's *my* phone!" Eve grunted, trying to hold it out of reach. "Get your own!"

"You know I don't have Pinterest or Instagram or whatever the hell you're—*oof.*" They both toppled off the sofa, and Eve's AirPod fell out. While she looked around for it in the mess of pink braids and tangled limbs, Dani snatched the phone and crawled across the rug.

"I'm so glad," Chloe said, "that we have all grown into such mature adults."

Dani didn't bother to answer. She was too busy scrolling up and down Eve's phone, trying to find the trending topic she'd caught a glimpse of before— Ah. Here it was.

Shit. Here it was. An honest-to-God video of Dani cradled in

Zaf's arms, staring at him like she wanted to eat him for lunch. Which was certainly accurate, but not exactly something she'd expected to find splashed across the internet.

"Oh my God," she breathed. "I thought you were joking."

"Nope!" Eve said cheerfully.

"This has over thirty thousand views!"

"Yep!" Eve sounded delighted.

Dani checked the comments, feeling as if she'd stumbled into some sort of alternate dimension.

YOUVEBEENZIZESED: This vid is cute af regardless, but apparently he's an ex-rugby player???

1h   47 likes   Reply

BASICJELLYBABY: IDK, but she teaches at my uni . . .

1h   38 likes   Reply

TITANSFOREVERNTC: That's Zaf Ansari 100% he played 6 for the Titans until 2012

1h   57 likes   Reply

ITSELLIEEEE: 😊 #DrRugbae #couplegoals

23m   64 likes   Reply

Dani stared. "*Dr. Rugbae?* I have never heard anything so inane or inaccurate in my life."

"You have a hashtag!" Eve crowed.

"I'm not even a doctor."

"Let me see!" Chloe demanded.

"*Rugbae?* Zaf is going to die."

Eve snatched the phone and took it to Chloe while Dani sprawled out on the floor and filed through a sudden influx of new thoughts. Zaf was a famous sports-type person? Famous enough that people recognized him in viral videos? He *did* talk about rugby a lot, but she tended to zone out during those conversations, so she'd never given it much thought. And, speaking of viral videos—was this ludicrous happening another sign that she should abandon her doubts and introduce Zaf to the wonders of her bedroom, her boobs, and her three-speed vibrator? Perhaps, but she was struggling to move past the disturbing fact that people seemed to think he and Dani were *dating*.

Of course, that assumption didn't mean anything. It was just heteronormative bullshit, a societal compulsion to thrust independent and perfectly happy individuals together in a socially accepted way, so they could become vulnerable before ultimately growing too familiar with each other's flaws and engaging in destructive behavior that would result in the heart of at least one party being crushed. Behavior such as, for example, shagging their neighbor and blaming it on their girlfriend's supposed inattentiveness.

Or something.

"This is incredibly impressive," Chloe murmured, her eyes glued to the video. "Please tell me you're sleeping with this man."

Dani sighed, pressing her cheek against the carpet. "Not yet, but the universe seems to think I should be." She considered something awful. "If he wants to, that is. Which I suppose he might not."

"Oh, he definitely wants to." Chloe was clearly thrilled.

"He looks like Superman flying Lewis Lane to safety," Eve piped up. "Only, you know, he's not flying."

"Lois Lane," Dani corrected.

"No," Eve said serenely. "I'm quite sure it's Lewis."

"I still can't believe he rescued you from a lift," Chloe was saying, one hand pressed to her cardigan-covered chest, her lashes fluttering rapidly. "Gosh, look at his face. Look at your face! You two are *electric*."

"Chemistry," Eve said wisely. "Or is it physics?"

"No, you were right the first time. Oh, Danika, look at this. No, don't be awkward, look. His *hand* is on your *thigh*."

"I'm not looking." Dani didn't need to; she remembered the feeling perfectly well. If she watched and remembered at the same time, she'd probably come over all . . . silly. And then she, like her sisters, might lose the ability to speak in anything other than italics.

"He's very *sturdy*, isn't he?" Eve asked.

"He's *massive*," Chloe agreed. "And *strong*."

Chloe's boyfriend, Red, appeared in the doorway with an indignant frown on his handsome face. "Hey. I feel like you're forgetting that time I rescued you from a tree."

"You didn't carry me out of the tree in your *arms*," Chloe said, her eyes still pinned to the phone in her hand, that damned video on a loop.

"And how the hell was I meant to do that? You were up a tree."

"Don't be jealous, darling."

"Now, why would I be jealous?" Red walked behind the

sofa and slid his hands over Chloe's shoulders. Dani watched with no little awe as her hyperfocused older sister dropped the phone and giggled—giggled!—while Red whispered in her ear.

What an absolutely sickening display. Romance clearly melted the brains of sensible women. Dani was horribly glad she had nothing to do with it.

"All right," Red announced. "I'm going to Vik's. I filled Smudge's bowl. See you later." He grinned at Dani and Eve, then looked at his girlfriend again. His voice took on a low, steady warmth that made even Dani feel slightly wobbly inside. "Behave yourself, Button."

Lord.

When he was gone, Eve gave a little shriek. "That man is *so*—"

"Never mind Redford," Chloe said briskly. "Danika has a lot to tell us about her soon-to-be-husband."

Dani's stomach lurched. "Ugh. No. Relax. I just want to sleep with him." The word *husband* gave her hives. As if romantic relationships weren't impossible enough without the extra pressure of a bloody legal contract.

"Well, make sure he wraps it up, because people are already naming your children. And their suggestions are atrocious." Chloe gave a delicate shudder. "*Blitz*, indeed."

Dani gaped. "You can't be serious."

"I'm not surprised they're getting overexcited," Eve said. "It's the way he looks at you."

Though she predicted she would regret it, Dani bit. "And how does he look at me?"

"Like he wouldn't mind sleeping in a pile of your dirty laundry." Eve arched her eyebrows, running her tongue over her purple upper lip. The lipstick clashed with her pink braids and scarlet T-shirt, which read, IN MY DEFENSE, I WAS LEFT UNSUPERVISED.

Dani stared. "I beg your pardon?"

"You know that feeling," Eve said, "when you truly adore someone and also want to sniff their underwear?"

Dani stared some more. "No. No, I do not."

"Chloe, you must know that feeling."

"No comment," Chloe said.

"Okay, let me rephrase: when you truly adore someone and also want to bury your face between their legs for eternity."

"Oh," Chloe said brightly, "*that* feeling."

"If his eyes were penises," Eve went on wisely, "you would be pregnant. With twins."

Dani wrinkled her nose. "Evie, that's disgusting."

"Or is it?"

As one, Chloe and Dani replied, "Yes."

CHAPTER FOUR

That evening, Zaf watched thirty-odd breathless lads drop like flies at the end of their training session. Mondays were for conditioning, and conditioning meant sweat.

Fighting a grin, he grabbed one boy's inhaler from his pocket and held it up. "Usman. You good?"

Uzzy nodded and waved the inhaler away, his breaths deep and deliberate. "Yeah. Fine."

Once upon a time, Zaf might not have believed that. But he'd spent the last six months guiding these lads through practical, sports-based workshops designed to show them that vulnerability wasn't a crime, no matter what society tried to teach them. So today . . . yeah. If Uzzy said he was fine, Zaf trusted that.

"Lucas." Zaf turned to a wing who'd just recovered from minor muscle strain. "How are you feeling?"

"Fucked," the fifteen-year-old breathed, and flopped back onto the grass. The other boys snorted and laughed.

"Language," Jamal interjected mildly. But then, he did everything mildly. Had ever since the day they'd met as teenagers at an

Eid al-Fitr prayer. Zaf's best friend was unshakable, unshockable, quietly immovable, and the king of patience—which made him damned good at running the Meadows Foundation, a charity that supported local kids through music, sports, and tech lessons.

So when Jamal had asked Zaf, a few years back, to coach the foundation's youth league team, Zaf couldn't refuse. It was supposed to be temporary—but, somehow, Zaf was still here. In fact, he enjoyed this shit so much that he'd started Tackle It, his own nonprofit. The Meadows Foundation boys still played rugby, but under Zaf's program they also stayed in touch with their emotions and learned that dealing with mental health didn't make them "weak." Judging by the change in them, Tackle It worked.

Trouble was, the schools and other institutions Zaf had offered his services to weren't biting. And he was low on funding, too. Right now, Jamal's boys were all Zaf had.

His brother's voice floated through his head, as clear as if Zain Bhai were standing beside him. *Hey, Eeyore. Why don't you take a second to be proud of yourself? You can poke holes in it later.*

Okay, yeah. Imaginary Zain was right.

"Another great session," Jamal said quietly. "You know, a few of the lads talked to me before you got here. Apparently they've been stalking your social media—"

"And it's sad as f—as hell," Usman called from the grass.

Jamal rolled his whiskey eyes. "Tactful as ever."

"All right," Zaf barked at the kids. "Off your arses. Cool down."

There were groans and moans, but everyone got up and started stretching.

Jamal caught Zaf by the shoulder and pulled him farther

down the field. "They've been stalking your social media, your website, whatever, and they think you could be doing more."

Zaf sighed and bent an arm over his head, stretching out his triceps. "What, are you feeding them lines?"

"No." Jamal grinned. "I just happen to be right, and the kids are, too. They wanted you to know that if you need pictures of them, videos or whatever, they'd be happy to do it."

Zaf switched arms, and looked over at the boys, who'd gone from stretching to shoving each other onto the grass. Warmth flooded his chest. "That would be great, actually."

"They suggested something else, too," Jamal continued carefully.

In the hollow of Zaf's chest, just below his nervous heart, a bead of anxiety bounced around like a pinball. "I know what you're going to say."

"They think it's weird that your website doesn't mention who you are."

Zaf bent his head to the left, which stretched out his traps *and* helped him avoid Jamal's eyes. Two birds, one stone. "It does mention who I am. Qualified coach, four years' experience in the charitable sector—cheers for that, by the way."

"Yeah, okay. But what about Zafir Ansari, retired pro—"

"*Retired.*" Zaf snorted, straightening up.

"Retired," Jamal repeated firmly. "You decided to stop, so you stopped."

More like Zaf's own brain chemistry had conspired to stop him getting out of bed, but sure.

"And," Jamal went on, "the things you went through, during

that time in your life, are part of why you're doing something like Tackle It. You know it, I know it, potential supporters should, too."

"Sure," Zaf said flatly. "I'll write an essay all about how I was a D-list rugby player who became a tragic story for bored gossip rags after my dad and brother died. Sounds like exactly the kind of attention I want."

Jamal's expression softened. "That was seven years ago, Zafir. The press aren't going to notice an old pro's new charity. But it'd impress head teachers and whoever else, trust me."

"Give them inspiration porn, you mean."

"There's nothing wrong with being inspiring," Jamal insisted, his voice low. He put a hand on Zaf's shoulder and squeezed, looked him in the eyes. "Listen to me. I remember how things were. I remember when your anxiety got so bad you were scared to get out of bed or let Fatima out of your sight. And I remember how hard you worked to get that under control so you could live again. You don't think that's relevant to what you're doing here?"

Zaf knew what his friend was trying to do, but that didn't mean he had to like it. His jaw tight, he said firmly, "When you've moved past something, you don't focus on the rearview mirror. I'm good now. I don't need to go back there."

"Mate, you know there's a middle ground between—"

"Later," Zaf muttered, and turned back to the kids. "You lot, stop tripping Allen up. If you break his ankle, his dad'll burn your house down." While the boys grumbled, Zaf picked up the phone he'd left by a bag of practice balls, mostly to avoid talking to Jamal. Unusually, as soon as he touched it, the screen buzzed to life with a notification from Tackle It's Instagram page.

Speaking of, he should really get better at posting on there.

The phone buzzed again. Twice.

Jamal frowned in his direction. "Who's texting you? No one texts you except me, and I'm here."

"Charming." And true. *Buzz. Buzz.*

"It's not Kiran, is it?" Jamal asked casually. "I mean—home. Everything okay?"

Zaf shot him a strange look. "Why would it be Kiran?" *And why is the first worry on your mind my brother's widow?*

Jamal shrugged, his gaze sliding away. But Zaf would bet his car that the man's dark skin hid a blush.

"Seriously," he pushed, "you and my sister have been acting—"

He was interrupted by yet another buzz, only this one . . . this one didn't end. *Buzz-buzz-buzz-buzz-buzz,* just like Zaf's heart when his anxiety really kicked off. He stared at the screen as notifications flared out of nowhere, moving so fast his eyes couldn't follow.

After a moment of stunned silence, he said slowly, "I think my phone is having a panic attack."

Jamal cracked up, which wasn't helpful.

"Lucas!" Zaf snapped. "Get over here."

The teenager scowled as he dropped his bike and peeled away from his friends. "What?"

"My phone broke."

"It's not broken, Zaf," Jamal snorted. "People are . . . following you, or commenting, or—" He broke off with a shrug. "Something."

"Why?"

"Oh my *days*." Lucas sighed and snatched the phone. "Put your finger on the button."

"What? Oh, yeah." Zaf unlocked the phone and watched Lucas tap rapidly at the screen. He wondered if the younger generation had the strongest thumbs known to mankind. Maybe from now on, kids would be born that way, like evolution.

A few more taps, and the angry buzzing cut out.

Zaf exhaled. "What did you do?"

"Turned off push notifications."

Zaf caught Jamal's eye and mouthed, *What?*

Jamal wrinkled his nose. *Dunno.*

"Now let's see what's going off," Lucas muttered. More taps, and then a moment of frozen surprise on the kid's face. After a second, the surprise melted into a shit-eating grin that made Zaf, who understood teenagers much better than he'd like, feel nervous.

Very nervous.

"What?" he demanded. "What is it?"

Lucas looked up, his blue eyes dancing in a way that didn't help Zaf's nerves one fucking bit. "@FatimaAnsari's tagged you in something."

"Fatima's always tagging me in things." Zaf frowned, holding out his hand for the phone. "What is it?"

But Lucas skipped out of reach and said loudly, "Zaf. You didn't tell us you had a girl!"

The handful of boys who hadn't left yet dropped their bikes, their heads snapping up like predators smelling blood on the breeze. A second later, they swarmed Lucas like piranhas.

"What are you on about?" Zaf demanded.

The boys were jostling to see the phone now, muttering shit like "Give it here" and "Whoa. Who is *that*?"

"Look, look, look." Lucas pointed a gleeful finger at the screen and said, *"Dr. Rugbae!"*

Everyone fell about laughing.

Zaf surged forward, but the kids swerved him like some kind of athletic hivemind. It was Jamal who finally managed to grab the phone. But once he saw the screen, he started laughing, too.

"What?" Zaf growled. "Give it to me before I knock your block off."

"Go steady," Lucas tutted. "Don't think your missus would approve. Since she's a doctor and all."

"What the hell are you talking about?"

"Mate." Jamal shook his head, his laughter fading as he held out the phone. "Just—don't lose it, okay? And don't kill Fatima."

Zaf accepted the phone with a frown . . . and stared down at a video of himself carrying Danika Brown out of Echo like she was a fairy-tale princess and he was a devoted knight. Holy shit. Holy *shit*. Embarrassment flared to life like a forest fire, burning hotter with every second the video played. Dani smiled at the camera like a vixen, and Zaf stared dreamily down at her like she was the source of all sunshine. *Fuck*. Fuck, fuck, fuck. Who the hell looked at their friends like that? If she saw this video—

If she saw this video, she'd probably think he was obsessed with her, or in love with her, or one of those douchebag "nice guys" who only befriended women because he secretly wanted to sleep with them. They'd have to have a painfully awkward conversation where she explained that she wasn't interested, that the coffee and the occasionally flirtatious jokes were just friendship and light-hearted banter, and shit, she'd thought he knew. And it would be especially galling because he *did* fucking know. Of course he did.

So why are you looking at her like that?

"Correct me if I'm wrong," Jamal said, sounding unusually cheerful—practically fucking gleeful, actually. "But I'm assuming that's the woman you're always mooning over, the one who brings you coffee. Yeah?"

"*Coffee!*" the lads crowed, as if Jamal had said, *The one who blows you every morning.* Zaf would have told them all to fuck off, but they were just excited kids, and also, he was too busy trying not to die of embarrassment.

"I don't *moon* over her," he muttered darkly. What the hell did that even mean? And how did you delete a video someone else had posted to Instagram? While he tried to figure that out, his gaze drifted to the number of views and comments—and his heart plummeted through his body like a lead weight. Which didn't feel too healthy.

How many views? And there was a hashtag—a bloody ridiculous one—and his *name*. What rugby-obsessed weirdo had recognized him, bearded and seven years older, on some random internet video? He didn't know, but the fact it had happened at all made his heart pound. And, since his heart was currently rolling around in his stomach, the sensation was even more uncomfortable than usual.

Claws of ancient anxiety sank into his skin, but he closed his eyes for a second and pulled them out, one by one. *It's just*

Instagram. Yes, that's a lot of views, but Instagram isn't real life, and it definitely isn't the press, and even if it was, you can handle it. You have the tools to handle it.

Right. Yeah. He did. By the time Zaf opened his eyes, he was already feeling better. Then something occurred to him. "Wait—Fatima tagged me in this?"

Jamal held up both hands as if calming a bull. "I'm sure she had a good reason. She's a smart girl."

But Zaf's only Instagram account was actually *Tackle It's* account. And according to his notification page, Tackle It now had more likes and comments than the app could keep track of. Setting his jaw, he went back to the video and found Fatima within seconds.

FATIMAANSARI: Look, Uncle Zaf @TackleIt. You're famous!
    1h   98 likes   Reply

"Zaf," Jamal said. "Don't—"

"Can't stay. Have to go and flush my niece's phone down the toilet."

"Did you have a good day at work, puttar?"

"No," Zaf snapped, kicking off his shoes and striding into the living room. "Where's Fatima?"

His mum and sister-in-law were perched on the old, squishy sofa they'd had since Zaf was a kid, Mum's tiny, round frame swallowed up by the swathes of fabric she was working on. Her focus was split between stitching a hem by muscle memory alone and watching an episode of *Come Dine with Me*, so she didn't seem to notice Zaf's tone. "Fatima?" she murmured. "Around, I think. There are samosas in the kitchen."

"I don't want samosas." Zaf frowned, then got ahold of himself. "In a second. I want samosas in a second. Thanks, Ami. But—"

Mum's laughter interrupted him. She nodded gleefully at the TV, where a white woman with feathers in her hair stirred a pot of vomit-colored dopiaza. "Dear me, that looks awful. The other guests will cause such a fuss."

"Is Fatima here or not?"

"All they do is fuss," muttered Zaf's sister-in-law, Kiran, who was frowning down at her own stitches and ignoring Zaf quite happily. Kiran was taller than Mum, paler and thinner than she used to be, her face lined before her time. But Zaf knew exactly what his brother would say if he saw his wife now.

There she is, the one who puts the moon to shame.

Was it weird to think sentimental thoughts about Zain and Kiran while plotting the murder of their only child? Maybe. Just to get everything out in the open, Zaf said, "I'm going to kill your daughter."

Kiran barely glanced up. "Why? Has she been stealing your romance novels, too?"

"Romance novels?" Mum was finally paying attention, scowling at them both from behind her huge, cream-colored glasses. They were Gok Wan, apparently. Height of fashion, apparently. Zaf stayed out of it. "You are both a horrible influence. Romance novels, indeed."

"It's healthy for her, Ami," Kiran said. "She needs to see—"

"This is *not* what I came to talk about," Zaf growled. Then he raised his voice to bellow, "Fluff! Get your arse down here."

Mum tutted disapprovingly and turned back to the TV, where a balding man with a grim expression was complaining about the dopiaza. "Absolutely awful. To be frank, I wouldn't feed that to a dog. I'm sure she tried her hardest, but it's a two out of ten from me."

A few minutes later, the living-room door burst open and Fatima rushed in, a beaming smile on her face. "Chacha! Did you see it?"

Her happiness disarmed Zaf a little. Fatima was a smart kid—a *really* smart kid, just like her dad had been. So why didn't she seem to realize that she had done a Very Bad Thing and was in serious trouble?

"The video? Yes, I saw it. What on earth were you thinking?"

"I was *thinking*," Fatima said patiently, "that views are money, and Tackle It needs money. Is this your regular grumpy face or your angry face? I can't tell."

"Angry face," Kiran offered from the sofa. "When he looks extra constipated—"

"What the *hell*?" Zaf burst out.

"Language!" Mum snapped.

"—that means he's angry. Zaf, sweetie, what's crawled up your behind now?"

"I'll tell you what. *Your* daughter," Zaf said, because he officially washed his hands of Fatima as his niece, "used an embarrassing Instagram video to publicly identify me as the founder of Tackle It."

"Good." Kiran smiled sweetly, because she was an unnatural woman who enjoyed the suffering of others. "Now people will pay attention and you'll finally get it off the ground. Only a child of mine could be so clever."

Zaf's jaw dropped. His righteous anger deflated. *Why* was no one furious on his behalf? What the fuck was wrong with these people? "This—she shouldn't—you sound like Jamal!"

Was it Zaf's imagination, or did his sister-in-law's cheeks flush slightly pink? Before he could decide, she argued, "Fatima's right: views are money and publicity is opportunity. You are, allegedly, a young man. You should know this." Kiran herself was some kind of Instagram model, except she made all her own clothes. She even embroidered her own hijab. Her account brought a lot of business to the clothing store she ran with Mum, so Zaf supposed she knew what she was on about. And he'd been planning to add his name to Tackle It's website anyway. Eventually. Once he'd turned the idea over in his mind long enough to wear away the film of anxiety.

But this video . . . "It's too much," he said, and his voice came out rough and croaky. "Too many people. Attention isn't always a good thing, Kiran, you *know* that." Back when Dad and Zain had died, there'd been . . . a news drought, or something. Zaf had already stood out more than he should, being one of few Muslim pros, non-practicing or otherwise. Journalists had been all over his "tragic" story like flies on shit, and his world had shattered under someone else's microscope. So, no, attention wasn't always a good thing. He'd learned that when the press had turned his family's unhappy ending into a sports section headline.

Kiran looked up, a flash of sympathy in her eyes. The teasing satisfaction left her voice in an instant. "Things are different now, Zafir."

Yeah, they were. Didn't mean he wanted complete strangers asking him about those differences. His gaze drifted to the family photo wall, dominated by old pictures that included Dad and Zain Bhai, frozen in time forever. The poltergeist of his grief curled itself up tight inside him. Pain was private. Some things weren't for public consumption. There were lines.

In life, there were always lines. Good or bad. You just had to figure them out and stick to the winning play. *Stay on track.*

"I did this to help you," Fatima said, "because you're social media illiterate. This is big, Chacha. The hashtag's on Twitter and everything. I knew *you* wouldn't take advantage of your viral moment."

Zaf was perfectly fine with being "social media illiterate" if it meant he didn't say shit like *viral moment.*

"And this particular video has nothing to do with Dad and Dadaji," Fatima went on, her gaze unnervingly sharp. "People aren't talking about that at all. They're talking about your super-romantic opposites-attract love story."

That statement pricked the balloon of Zaf's worry, because as far as he could tell—and he *may* have obsessively scrolled through the comments on his way here—it was true. Hmm.

"This associates your name with something *positive*. The more people think about #DrRugbae, the less they'll remember about . . . before," Fatima insisted.

"Doctor what?" Mum interjected. "What is this love-story nonsense? Zafir?"

"It's not a love story," Zaf gritted out. "My friend got stuck in a lift."

"And you just *had* to carry her out in your big, strong arms," Fatima snorted.

"I think," Kiran said with a slow, dangerous smile, "that I'd like to see this famous video."

Zaf glared at his niece. "I am regretting every time I ever fed you as a child. I should have let you starve."

"You shouldn't be embarrassed about your new girlfriend. If your follower count is anything to go by, she's getting Tackle It a ton of publicity."

That was . . . an interesting way to look at it, but for one crucial detail. "Great, except *she's not my girlfriend.*"

"Well, maybe she should be. I like Dani. She's smart and funny and a good teacher."

Mum made a sound that suggested she was moments from a pride-and-excitement-induced heart attack. "Zafir is marrying a *teacher*? From a *university*?"

Kiran, meanwhile, narrowed her eyes suspiciously. "Wait. Is this the woman you're always telling me about, with the hair and the books and whatever?"

Aaand that was his cue to leave. He pointed at Fatima and said ominously, "I'm not done with you."

She snorted. Kids these days had no healthy fear of their elders.

"Zaf," Kiran said, "you can't ignore me forever. Or even for an hour, usually."

"Fatima!" Mum was practically shrieking now. "Show me that video!"

"All right," Zaf said loudly, "love you guys, gotta go."

"Wait! Zafir! Where are you going?"

He was already at the front door. He *may* have sprinted. "Bye!"

Only when he was partway to his flat did Zaf realize he'd failed in his mission to kill his niece, or even properly shout at her. But every time he thought about it, he saw Fluff's happy little face and heard her calmly explaining how she'd actually done him a favor, and he felt bad about telling her off.

Which didn't mean she was right. Obviously.

Zaf wandered out of the neighborhood he'd grown up in, a working-class one that his family had always refused to leave, occupied by Pakistanis like them, other South Asians, West Africans, Jamaicans. His own city apartment was less diverse and way less familiar, but on the plus side, he didn't have any neighbors to make nice with. Or make eye contact with. These things swung in roundabouts.

As he moved through the city streets, passing the glowing signs and lit-up windows of chicken shops and dive bars, he muttered under his breath, "This is not a good thing. This is *not* a good thing. And what the hell is Dani going to say?" He had no idea, but he didn't think women generally appreciated becoming social media sensations without their consent. This could affect her work or something. And Zaf knew her well enough to realize that if that happened, she'd sneak into his flat and slit his throat as he slept.

But when he got home and checked his phone again, he was . . . thoughtful. Fatima *had* been right about the boom in his follower count. There were more comments and likes under his pictures than ever, most people actually interacting with the content or asking questions about the nonprofit. Other people were commenting #DrRugbae and IS THIS REALLY ZAFIR ANSARI?, which kind of ruined the effect—but no one, he noticed, had posted anything about his "tragic past." People used to call him that all the time. *Tragic.*

He pushed that thought away, along with the flare of old, aching anger it caused, and switched over to Twitter. Typed in that ridiculous hashtag. Took a breath, propped his legs up on the sofa, and started reading.

> **@BEYONCESBANGS:** #DrRugbae 💕 if you know, you know.
> 🗨 694   ↺ 4k   ♡ 63   ⬆

> **@SLYTHERINBIH:** Uhhh everyone at NGU knew about #DrRugbae lol they basically shag on the desk every morning in Echo
> 🗨 86   ↺ 683   ♡ 2k   ⬆

> **@HOLLY_COOKE:** Does this mean nerdy girls get pro sports players now? #DrRugbae
> 🗨 24   ↺ 1k   ♡ 430   ⬆

> **@POPPYANNACOOKE:** Ha, maybe if they look like THAT nerdy girl.
> 🗨 509   ↺ 287   ♡ 1k   ⬆

He scrolled until his eyes blurred and saw not one mention of his brother or his dad, not one mention of death and pain. Fatima's earlier words came back to him, and something hopeful and daring and a little bit ridiculous stirred in his chest. Then he switched over to his DMs, scowled at the influx of messages from strangers—and saw, buried in the chaos, one from the *Nottingham Post*.

Zaf stared. Blinked, hard. Stared some more. He tapped the account, noticed the verified check mark, and fought a spike of anxiety before hopping off the sofa and starting to pace.

"Open it," he told himself. "Just open it. If it's some bullshit question, you can delete it and block them. It's social media. You have control over social media."

Well—you did unless someone filmed you salivating over a work friend and posted it online and it went viral. But still. He had control over *this*. So he sat down and opened the message, and his old, habitual nerves were replaced by a fizzy, sunshine sort of shock. No invasive questions about dark times or personal struggles here—just invasive questions about his nonexistent relationship.

> Hi Zafir,
>
> Hope you're well. Our team is planning to cover the adorable #DrRugbae video, and we were hoping you and your girlfriend might have something to add before we publish. Is there anything you'd like to say about the video? We'd love to mention all the good you're doing with Tackle It, too.

Holy shit. They'd love to mention Tackle It? Maybe Fatima was right. Zaf tapped out the first few words of a response, then deleted it all at once.

You and your girlfriend. That's what the message said: they thought Dani was his girlfriend. If he replied, he'd need to correct them. But if he corrected them, why the fuck would they write about this hashtag bullshit? Why would they write about Tackle It? And how would he do just what Fluffy had said and . . . and change people's associations?

He didn't know. But the hopeful stirring in his chest was a roar now, and the half-formed, impossible idea in his mind was so wrong it made him feel kind of dizzy, and he couldn't make himself type out the words *She's not my girlfriend.* He couldn't. Through the tangle of fevered, guilty thoughts, one thing stood out nice and clear: he needed to talk to Dani.

But first, he better figure out what the fuck he wanted to say.

CHAPTER FIVE

"No umbrella?" Sorcha tutted as she popped hers open. "You trollop."

"It was sunny this morning," Dani sniffed. "I'm sure you can't blame me for the indecision of the weather, darling." Not to mention she'd been somewhat distracted since, erm, "going viral" on Monday. It was Wednesday now, and Dani remained in a befuddled sort of fugue state, which did not lend itself well to remembering umbrellas.

Of course, she'd made sure to apply mascara. Apparently, one never knew when one might be recorded and posted online without permission.

"It's March, babe. What did you think was going to happen?" Sorcha rolled her eyes and held the umbrella between them, though she favored her own head a little more. The bitch. "If this blowout curls up, I'll kill somebody. Possibly you."

"That threat would work better if you ever attempted to follow through," Dani murmured, but her focus had already drifted away from the icy drizzle and toward the mammoth building ahead. Sorcha was a writer, and she tended to get . . . *edgy* every time she submitted a manuscript, so today Dani had paused her symposium preparation to drag Sorcha off for an emergency cupcake in town. Now they were returning to campus, which meant walking past Echo.

Echo, of course, meant Zaf.

Yesterday morning, while she'd waited in line for his coffee and her green tea, Dani had devised a cunning plan: first, she would ask Zaf when on earth he'd been planning to mention the whole "pro rugby player" situation. Second, they would laugh together over silly social media frenzies and the vagaries of human nature. And third, she would somehow segue smoothly from that sparkly bonding moment into the fact that they were apparently destined to bone.

But he'd ruined everything by barely talking to her at all. She'd entered the building to discover that Zaf had lost his marbles and was demanding students line up to scan their cards at his desk, rather than the more casual policy adopted by, oh, *every campus security guard ever.* When Dani had tried to hover (in order to chat about ridiculous videos and lonely vaginas and so on), he'd grabbed his coffee, practically thrown a protein bar at her, and proceeded to look pointedly busy. When she'd come down from her class hours later, George had been at the desk in his place. Apparently, Zaf had *just nipped to the loo.*

The bastard was avoiding her, and heaven only knew why.

Dani didn't teach on Wednesdays, so she probably could've popped in today and caught him by surprise, but that seemed undignified. It wouldn't do for Zaf to see that she was bothered by his sudden distance. Or rather, for him to *think* she was bothered. Which she wasn't.

Sorcha must've followed Dani's gaze toward the building, because she purred, "Planning to visit your boyfriend, hmm?"

"Stop," Dani muttered. The word *boyfriend* made her stomach seize up like a gazelle in the face of danger. "Maybe I'm paranoid, but I swear students keep pointing their phones at me."

"Oh, they are," Sorcha said, sounding disgracefully unconcerned. "Who knew Zaf was famous?"

"He's not *famous* famous." The words were automatic, but Dani wasn't sure if they were true. He certainly wasn't A-list, or even C-list, but judging by the comments Eve had read out last night, Zaf had once been reasonably well known. Which didn't concern Dani—after all, her grandmother Gigi had been something of a musical legend in the sixties and remained a classic sex symbol. But Dani had always known that about Gigi, while she was beginning to wonder if she'd ever known anything about Zaf.

Which was a ridiculously dramatic thought, one she shook out of her head immediately. He was a friend from work, not her lifelong confidante. He didn't owe her bloody confessionals across the security desk. He didn't owe her anything.

Still . . . "Did you know," Dani said out loud, apparently unable to help herself, "that he runs some sort of charity?"

"Does he?"

"Eve showed me his account last night. It's supposedly his account, anyway. He uses rugby to teach boys to embrace their emotions. The website was all, *something-something-something, toxic masculinity.* You know."

"Hmmm," Sorcha said slyly. "Interesting. And speak of the devil."

Dani knew exactly who she'd see even before she turned her head.

Huddled just inside the entrance to Echo's underground car park stood an unmistakable, imposing figure in a security uniform. Zaf was eating what looked like a sub from the union restaurant, his hair spilling over his eyes like black ocean. But it was obviously him. No one else had those thighs, which were thick and muscular and looked in danger of splitting his uniform trousers, or that torso, which seemed, beneath his navy-blue jacket, like the kind of solid core an Olympic shot-putter or possibly the Hulk might possess. And no one else, Dani might as well admit, made the constant thoughts and ideas whirring in her mind stutter, momentarily, to a stop.

Being as effortlessly sexy as Zafir Ansari should really be illegal, or at least regulated. He must represent some sort of danger to the public.

"I should probably go and talk to him," Dani said absently, because it was true. They had things to discuss, such as their sudden viral fame and why the fuck he was acting so strangely. Again, not that she cared.

"Talk to him? About your feelings? In the *rain*? How romantic."

"No one mentioned feelings," Dani muttered. "I'll meet you in the library."

Sorcha batted her lashes. "Unless you get lost in Zaf's eyes on the way there."

"Oh, *gag.*" Dani wrapped her cardigan around herself—why hadn't she brought a jacket this morning?—and left the umbrella's protection behind.

Everything was muted and cool in the concrete entryway of the car park, the sound of rain fading a little and the air growing sharp. The closer she got to Zaf, the more she noticed the shadows beneath his eyes and the tense line of his jaw. He'd looked like that yesterday, too, slightly haunted as he avoided her gaze and grumped at poor, innocent undergrads. It occurred to Dani all at once that, if he never mentioned his background, maybe he didn't want people to *know.* But now it seemed as if everyone knew.

She was busy frowning at the pang that thought caused in her chest when Zaf finally noticed her. He pulled out one of his earbuds and said with a defeated air, "Danika."

"Sorry. Did I ruin your plan to avoid me?"

He screwed up his face and scrubbed at his beard, and the whole world seemed to hold its breath. Which was both ridiculous and impossible, and yet, that's how it felt. Then he sighed, "Yeah, actually. But I wasn't enjoying it much, anyway, so I'm glad you're here."

Everyone and everything exhaled.

"Of course you're glad," she said. "The real question is why you'd avoid me in the first place."

"And the short answer," he replied, "is that I was, er, thinking about some things."

"That sounds like heavy-duty thinking."

"Well, we don't all have as much practice as you." Before she could formulate a response to that, he changed the subject, a little furrow forming between his eyebrows. "Why aren't you wearing a coat?"

Oh, not this again. "It was sunny this morning," Dani said for the second time in ten minutes, sounding defensive even to her own ears.

Zaf shook his head, unzipping his jacket and shifting his sandwich from hand to hand as he slid out of the sleeves. "You need someone to keep an eye on you."

"Keep saying that and I might decide you're a misogynist."

"Is that what you think?" He wrapped his jacket around her shoulders, then squeezed her upper arm. His eyes met hers, not with a challenge, but with quiet, open care—as if he was actually waiting for a response.

"Well, no. I was joking."

"Oh. Good." He smiled slightly, and they stood like that for long moments, close and connected in the shadows. Dani thought she felt a gentle tug within her chest, as if there was a ribbon tied around her breastbone, connected to the curve of Zaf's solemn mouth.

Then he let go, and stepped back, and took a bite of his sandwich, and the moment dissolved. Which was fortunate, as she had no idea what the bloody hell had just happened and would prefer to forget about it completely.

To that end, she cleared her throat and gave her borrowed jacket an assessing stare. "Hmm. Not bad. And it's almost black."

"Yep. One hundred percent nylon, too. Nothing but luxury."

She laughed, but the sound was slightly breathless. His fault: she could see more of him now he'd stripped off for her. The way his shirt stretched tight over his chest, the corded muscle on his exposed forearms—it was all deliriously visible. The hair on his arms was dense and black and silky. He had ridiculously thick wrists. His hands were big and long-fingered and he was currently using them to unplug his earbuds from his phone.

"Listening to porn again?" she asked, pushing all horny thoughts firmly aside. Small talk, *then* sexual propositions, that was the rule. Although, she supposed discussing porn might be blurring boundaries. Oh, well.

Zaf's cheeks flushed darker. "I was never listening to porn. I listen to romance novels."

Erm . . . what?

"I beg your pardon," she sputtered after a moment. "Did you just say you listen to romance novels?"

He grunted. "Well. I listen in the car, mostly. Read at home."

Dani, in a shocking display of intelligence, repeated, "Romance novels. Actual romance novels. The novels. With the romance."

He gave her a flat, sharklike stare that sent another thrill of arousal down her spine, because apparently, she found him gorgeous even when he was annoyed. Possibly more so, in fact. "And?" His tone dared her to elaborate.

"Oh, behave," she said, her surprise blooming into curiosity. "What do you think I'm going to do, question your masculinity and tell you kissing is for girls?"

After a moment, he admitted grudgingly, "Nah."

"Then what's the murder glare for?"

With complete seriousness, he told her, "This is just my face. I have a murder face."

But when she laughed out loud, his scowl faded, replaced by one of his little smiles. Usually, Zaf was handsome in a distant, angsty, man-on-TV sort of way. But when he smiled, even the tiniest bit? Then his kind eyes glowed like spilled ink by candlelight, and she found herself wanting to kiss the broad curve of his nose. In a purely abstract manner, of course. In reality, Dani would never do something so pointless. Faces were for sitting on, not for kissing.

At least, that was her opinion. She wondered now, more than ever, what Zaf's was. "Why do you read romance?" she asked, sounding a little like a drill sergeant or a police investigator. Oops.

Zaf looked at her as if she'd asked if milk came from fish. "For the romance."

"The . . . romance."

"Yeah. People liking each other and talking about their feelings and living happily ever after."

Now she'd officially entered the realm of *what the fuck*. "*You* voluntarily read about people discussing their feelings?"

"Yep."

"Let me rephrase that," she said. "*Why* do you read about people discussing their feelings?"

"If I was standing here with a thriller, would you ask me why I read about people murdering each other?"

"Of course I wouldn't. You have a murder face, not a feelings face."

It was his turn to laugh, the sound low and rich and unreasonably sexy. "Good point."

"It's just, I would never have guessed you were a romantic." This is what Dani said, but what she really meant was *Oh, hell. You're a romantic.* She hated to question Oshun's verdict, especially after asking for help in the first place—it seemed a tad ungrateful, slightly rude, et cetera—but *really*. A romance novel–reading undercover sweetheart who gave his jacket to umbrella forgetters without a second thought? This was her supposedly perfect fuck buddy? She usually preferred the unsentimental and disinterested type. "Fond of happily ever afters, are you?" she asked brightly.

Zaf rubbed a hand over his beard, looking oddly pensive all of a sudden. "I've seen the alternative. That's not the story I want for the rest of my life."

The words caught Dani unawares, heavy as stone, solemn as still water. A strange ache started beneath her rib cage. "Oh?"

"Mmm." He brushed the moment off with a barely there smile. "I mean, who doesn't want to live happily ever after?"

She studied him for a second, searching for another hint of that serious, hidden sadness. But she couldn't find it, which meant he didn't intend to share it again—and Dani wasn't one to push. She certainly found it rather irritating when people pushed *her*.

So she made herself smile back and say, "I'm more into happy endings, actually." When Zaf stared at her in silence, she added, "That was a joke. You know. About orgasms."

"I know," he said, a smile playing at the corners of his mouth. "I just thought you needed a minute to see how corny it was."

"Oh, wow. *Wow*. Someone's feeling sassy today."

"Maybe you bring it out in me," he said dryly, and took another bite of his sandwich. "So . . ."

"So?"

"Are we, er . . . going to talk about the elephant in the room?"

For a moment, Dani was convinced he meant her raging theoretical hard-on for him. Perhaps he'd noticed her nipples stabbing the shit out of her bra, or maybe her unsubtle questions about his stance on romance had tipped him off. Eve read romance novels, so Dani had learned that the genre created positive romantic expectations in its reader. Maybe Zaf was about to gently inform her that he had higher hopes for his interpersonal connections than frequent snark sessions and casual access to Dani's magnificent breasts. Which wouldn't be the first time she'd heard such a thing.

Then he raised his eyebrows and said, "The video?" And she realized she'd somehow veered down the entirely wrong track.

"Yes. *Yes*." She nodded like a bobblehead, shoving those strangely nervous thoughts under her mental bed. "The video—and your semi-secret identity, let's not forget."

Zaf snorted. "*Semi-secret identity*? Really? That's what we're going with?"

Dani chose to ignore him. "You know, I might've listened to you drone on about rugby more often if I'd known you had a professional interest."

"Would you, though?"

She thought for a moment. "No, actually. Never mind."

His laughter faded far too quickly for her liking. "Listen—about the video. I just wanted to say, I'm really sorry. I probably didn't need to carry you like that."

He was *apologizing*? Really? "Zaf, you do realize it's not your fault that a few students had nothing better to do than film and theorize about two random strangers they saw exiting a building, don't you?"

"Well, yeah. But I don't know if this kind of attention could get you into trouble, or—"

"No. I already spoke to my supervisor, and she's not remotely bothered by what she called 'internet gossip.' Apparently, the whole thing is irrelevant to her life and to the department in general. So please don't worry about that."

"Good," he said. "Good." But he didn't relax. If anything, she could almost see an edgy tension building around him, inflating like a balloon.

"You don't like this, do you?" she asked, because suddenly she couldn't hold the question in.

Zaf faltered. "What?"

"People talking about you."

His gaze met hers, a hint of surprise flashing in the dark. "No. No, not really. Some things are fine, but others are off limits, and people never know where to draw the line. Doesn't help that I—" He broke off, pressing his lips tightly together as if to trap the rest of that sentence.

"That you what?" She wanted to know because she'd always been horribly curious by nature, not because the exhaustion in his voice dug talons of worry into her heart or anything. God, no. Unless that was an ordinary feeling for work friends to have toward each other, in which case, yes, talons ahoy.

"That I have anxiety," he finished, his jaw tense. "I like to think I have some control over my life. Makes things easier. But you can't always control what people say."

"No," she said softly. "You can't. The only thing you can control is what you do, and the things *you* do are frequently . . ." *Lovely.* But that was a disgusting thing to say. "Good," she finished, rather pathetically. "The things you do are good. So. At least there's that. I'm sure it doesn't help much, when you're . . . thinking . . . anxious things . . . but—at least there's that."

He watched her with a slow, quiet smile, his eyes crinkling at the corners, the warmth of his expression spilling over her like sunlight. "Good, am I?"

Oh, God. Oh, Christ. Couldn't some passing, kindhearted citizen just bludgeon her to death?

But then Zaf's gaze softened, and he said, "Thanks," and Dani's passionate wish for oblivion lessened, just a bit.

Still, it was time to move on before she said anything else ridiculous. "Since we're on the subject—"

"I can't wait to hear what completely unrelated subject we're supposedly on," Zaf murmured, because he was a bastard.

"Why don't you tell me about this charity you run?"

Which is how she discovered that there was one topic grumpy, guarded Zafir was perfectly willing to discuss at length and without sarcasm. He lit up when he spoke about Tackle It, as if there were a tiny fire burning inside him, and making kids face their feelings on the rugby pitch fanned those flames. He described his week-by-week program, and she realized she'd never seen him so passionate before. He admitted he'd gone back to college to get qualifications in sports and psychology, and she realized she'd never seen him so focused. He muttered, "It's not exactly successful, though. Yet," and she realized she might actually kill to protect all of Zaf's hope and tentative ambition and quiet, careful drive.

"Yet," she repeated. "But soon. Aside from which, I'm sure your past must help."

He looked up at her sharply. "What?"

"All your, er, rugby contacts and what have you. That sort of thing's got to be a leg up."

He looked strained. "I don't like to rely on that. There are things in my past I'd rather not bring into the present. So I drew a line under it all."

Snooping into the topics that made people turn quiet and rigid was not one of Dani's favorite pastimes; all too often, it ended with someone who'd previously seemed quite sensible blubbering all over you. So she had absolutely no idea why some rogue, instinctive part of her demanded she pepper Zaf with questions until he explained exactly what he meant, and why there were shadows in his eyes all of a sudden.

Fortunately, he moved on before the urge could get the better of her. "Things are looking up since that video, though."

Dani's eyebrows flew up. "Really?"

"Yeah. Tackle It's getting all kinds of attention. The thing is . . ." He shot her a look, one she couldn't quite decipher, and shoved his hands into his pockets. But the flex of his muscular forearms told her those hands had curled into fists, out of sight. And the hard line of his jaw only confirmed that he was nervous.

Why was he nervous?

"The thing is," he repeated, "it's all because people think you and me are together. That hashtag, the couple goals thing . . ." He sounded so uncomfortable saying *couple goals*, Dani had to hold back her laughter.

"It's silly," she agreed, "but if it's helping, that's a good thing. Isn't it?"

He looked up. "So you don't mind? It doesn't bother you?"

"I don't know," Dani said slowly, exploring her own thoughts as she spoke. She knew she should be horrified, or at least uncomfortable—especially given her feelings on relationships. But she and Zaf weren't *actually* together, so the usual, suffocating pressure that accompanied anything to do with attachment was absent. "No," she said finally. "No, it doesn't bother me."

He took a step closer, then another, until his coffee-and-citrus scent flooded her space and she couldn't meet his eyes without tipping her head back. She was used to talking with him at the security desk, while he sat down. This was . . . not the same. Or maybe it was the way he looked at her, the urgent burn of his gaze, that made everything different.

Either way, it was hot. Dani still had a few logical worries about romance novels and sweetness and expectations and *blah blah blah*, but right now, her vagina was pitching an intriguing idea: *How about we trust the universe, stop second-guessing this, and take the fucking hint?*

"The thing is," Zaf was saying in that low, smoke-and-whiskey voice, "I had this idea. It's a ridiculous idea, but it's still an idea, and it—it would help me a lot. Help Tackle It a lot."

She hovered closer to him as if hypnotized. An idea that would help his *charity*? His charity for *children*? Yes. Wonderful. Fascinating. Almost as fascinating as watching his lovely mouth move. "Tell me."

"What if . . ." He hesitated, then pushed on, fast and firm. "What if we let people think we're together?"

As soon as the words left his mouth, Zaf regretted asking. It was as if letting them out of his head and into the light showed him, in painful detail, how ridiculous he was being. Or maybe it was Danika's reaction that made him wince, the way she stared at him in silence for long, long moments.

Shit.

"Never mind," he said gruffly. "I have no idea why I said that. Obviously you wouldn't—I mean, we aren't—so that would be— it's just," he went on desperately, because he should probably explain himself, "the *Post* sent me this message about some kind of feel-good local feature, and they asked about Tackle It, but I don't think they'd want to do the piece if they knew we weren't a couple, so . . ." So he'd lost his grip on good sense, apparently.

Dani continued to stare, sinking her teeth into her lower lip. She was so close, closer than they ever got. He could see the texture of her lips, soft and plump and creased, could trace the smooth dip of her cupid's bow with his gaze. Could drink in the velvet of her skin and the slight indent of a little scar on the bridge of her nose. He could *smell* her: she was warm skin and fresh fruit and the sweet smoke of blown-out birthday candles, delicious and a little confusing all at once.

But now really wasn't the time to lose his head over Danika's hotness. He was supposed to be concentrating on taking back the fucked-up suggestion he'd just made.

"It was a bad idea," he said. "I know that. I've been reading too many romance novels. No one fakes relationships in real life."

"Faking a relationship," she said slowly, as if she were turning the words over on her tongue, examining them as she spoke. "I thought that's what you meant."

He searched her tone for amusement or annoyance or *something*, and came up completely blank. Studied her expression and saw nothing but that familiar thoughtfulness. He'd always liked the way she considered things, the way she learned them inside and out before expressing her thoughts, but right now it was fucking killing him. "Bad idea," he repeated, trying to ignore the thud of his heart against his ribs. "Even if you wanted to, you probably couldn't. You might be with someone. Or gay. Or both. Probably both. I never asked. I know you were dating that professor—"

"You know about Jo?" For the first time, Dani sounded kind of . . . off. Upset, maybe.

"I don't know nothing about nothing." *Clearly.* Zaf shoved the final bite of his sandwich in his mouth to shut himself up. In hindsight, he probably should've done that a good ten minutes ago.

Her lips quirked, and the tension faded from her mouth, her shoulders. "Okay. Well, I'm not gay."

He swallowed. "Right."

"I'm bisexual."

"Got it." He crushed his sandwich wrapper into a ball and reminded himself that just because Danika was into guys didn't necessarily mean she was into security guards with the social skills of a fucking brick wall.

"And, no, I don't have a partner," she went on. "I don't do the commitment thing. Ever."

Well, shit. Zaf wasn't exactly in a *hurry* to find a relationship— he had his own crap to deal with, and sometimes that crap seemed never ending. But he still valued commitment. He still envied old married couples. He still remembered the love his parents had had, the love his brother and Kiran had had, and wanted it despite the danger of loss. If commitment wasn't for Dani, then she and Zaf weren't for each other.

So stop thinking about her like that.

Yeah, yeah. Easier said than done. "Ever?" he repeated, trying not to sound too invested in her response. "Like . . . you don't want to find some nice young, erm, person, and settle down and—?"

"No," she said, looking unusually severe all of a sudden, shadows obscuring the light in her eyes.

"Are you, erm . . ." Right on time, he forgot the technical term he'd been looking for. "You don't . . . get those . . . feelings?" he asked, then wondered why the fuck he was delving even deeper into what was clearly personal shit. Like he hadn't talked himself into enough holes today.

But Dani didn't seem irritated by the question—more by the topic itself. "Am I aromantic? Sadly, no. Coupledom simply doesn't suit my constitution. Aside from which, I am entirely too busy for dating and ego-stroking and sharing my feelings and meeting people's parents." Her expression grew more and more disgusted with each item she listed. Zaf might have laughed, if something about her carefully disinterested tone wasn't setting off alarm bells in his head.

"Okay," he said slowly. "But—you know that sharing your feelings is always important, right? Whether you do the romance thing or not."

She arched an eyebrow at him. "Is this part of your workshop? Are you going to make me throw a ball, too?"

He sighed. "I'm going to pretend you didn't just describe rugby as *throwing a ball*." He was also going to pretend that the cold weight of disappointment in his belly had nothing to do with his personal feelings for Danika Brown. He was only bothered by all this because, if she had no time for a relationship, she wouldn't have time to fake one. It had nothing to do with her smile, or how smart she was, or the fact that she brought him coffee no matter how busy she got, or anything else like that, because if it *did*, he might have to admit that his crush was a little bit more than a crush.

It wasn't, though. More, that is. Definitely just a crush.

"Okay," he said finally. "Okay. No relationships for you. You know what? Can we just forget about—?"

"No relationships for me," she interrupted, "which means that I'm perfectly free to fake date you."

It was a good thing Zaf had already swallowed the last of his sandwich, because if he hadn't, he might be choking right now. "Erm," he wheezed. "What? Wait, seriously? Danika. Are you fucking with me? Because—"

"*Yes.*" She rolled her eyes.

"Yes, you're fucking with me?"

"Yes, I'm serious. It's a smart plan. My grandmother used fake relationships for publicity all the time."

Was he hearing things now? "Your grandmother did *what*?"

Dani waved a hand. "Doesn't matter. If this will help you shine a spotlight on your, erm . . . Tackle It situation, well"—she shot him a wry smile—"I'll consider it my good deed of the season." She turned slightly, her gaze focusing on something to their right. "We have company, by the way."

It took Zaf a minute to process that, since his thoughts were still scattered by disbelief. "What?" He looked up, saw the trio of girls hovering a few meters away with their phones out, and scowled. "For fuck's sake. I came out here to eat because everyone kept staring at my desk like I was a giraffe."

"Do you want publicity or not?" Dani asked sternly.

No was his instinctive response. But the right kind of publicity, he reminded himself, could help in countless ways, so he'd better buck up. "Yeah. Yeah, I do."

"Then fix your face," she told him.

"What?" Zaf was saying that quite a lot at the moment. Understandably, he thought.

"I'm the catch of the century on paper, if not in reality," Dani said. "No one's going to believe you've been blessed with my affection if you stand there glaring at everything like the world pissed on your pillow."

"What does that even—?"

Before he could finish the question, she closed the space between them, her hands sliding over his shoulders and her tits—*holy fuck*—her tits pressing firmly against his chest, so soft and ripe and full he felt like he might pass out. The blood rushed to his cock so fucking fast it left him dizzy. Actual dark spots blinked in front of his eyes for a second. Apparently, Dani's chest was as dangerous as a spear tackle.

Made sense.

In that moment, everything inside Zaf—including the cold marble of worry that lived in his gut—got really still and really silent, really fucking quick.

An instant later, his body boomed back to life, every part of him hotter and harder than before. Raw, animal want ignited in his belly, spreading fiery tendrils through him until he vibrated with the need to touch her, grab her, *something*. His muscles tensed, his body tightened, the pulse of his blood ached beneath his skin. Then her hand cupped his face, and he was decimated. She looked at him with those eyes, those fucking eyes, and it felt . . . it felt like that moment in an apocalyptic film when the nuclear bomb drops. When an invisible force sweeps across a landscape—*whoosh*—and wipes out everything in its path.

What the fuck was this? He'd known she was beautiful, and charming, and hypnotic. He'd known he was kind of—okay, *completely*—into her. But what. The. Fuck. Was. This?

Something entirely new, that's what. An alien species of lust.

Did he kill it before it killed him, or watch and wait and see what happened?

"Try to look enamored," she murmured, a laugh in her voice. Maybe she didn't know he was dying. Yeah, that had to be it. She tipped her head back and looked up at him through her lashes, a dare in her eyes. "You could even kiss me, if you like."

If he *liked*?

Zaf had spent more time than was healthy, over the six months since he'd met Dani, wondering if she might be attracted to him. Now she was looking at him like he was dessert, her tongue gliding over her plush lower lip, asking if he'd like to kiss her. Hell yes, he'd fucking *like*. But . . .

But she'd only suggested it because they were being watched, and knowing that cooled the burn of his desire, just a little.

Not enough to stop, though. She bit her lip again and shifted, every lush curve pressing tight against him, and in that moment, Zaf knew the only thing that could stop him was her. Good-bye, self-control. We barely knew ye.

"Unless you don't want to," she murmured after a moment, "which is also—"

"I want to," he said, because fuck that noise. Fuck even letting her finish that bullshit sentence. And then, before he could change his mind, Zaf made the only sensible choice he could and kissed the life out of Danika Brown.

CHAPTER SIX

Every month, Dani and her sisters received money from the family trust, and every month, Dani donated 90 percent of it to various causes. Considering that charitable history, her agreeing to this fake relationship scheme was *entirely* in character: she was doing it, clearly, for the sake of the children.

Technically, that implied she was going to kiss Zafir in front of a group of spying undergrads for the children, too, but Dani had other reasons. This physical contact seemed a sensible way to determine whether Zaf might be seduced away from his romantic ideals and into her bed—temporarily, of course. Until she got bored of him. Or until he met someone else, someone serious, someone who didn't accidentally work through their partner's birthday parties or, when asked what day it was, respond with "The date of Sylvia Plath's death" instead of "Our anniversary, of course, darling."

Ahem. For example.

So, yes: kissing Zaf was entirely practical. Until it wasn't.

One minute he was staring down at her with a slightly astonished expression; the next his endless eyes were hooded and one of his big hands was cupping her nape, the other grabbing her hip. It was around that point when Dani forgot the definition of the word *practical*, and also how to spell it, and also whether it was English or French or possibly Latin. One slight, restrained squeeze from Zaf, and her thoughts were thrust toward bare, sweat-slicked skin and gasping breaths, moans intermingling and thrusts timed with the pounding of her heart.

Then his lips brushed hers, and everything changed completely.

So soft, so sweet, that butterfly graze. A cautious, barely there kiss that made something in her belly seem to sparkle and fizz, that made her hands shake as she slid her fingers through the rough silk of his hair. Zaf tasted like rich, warm comfort and straightforward sweetness, sherbet-sharp and almost, impossibly, familiar. She could feel the tip of his nose against her cheek, could feel his eyelashes brushing her own. Time suspended, like he'd cupped the sands of an hourglass safely in his palms, and the sensation was so breathtakingly *strange* that she might do something awful, like crack into a thousand tiny pieces, or ask him for more.

He angled his head, increased the pressure, and parted her stunned lips easily, his tongue a dart that sampled her in little, teasing sips. The way he touched her, the way his big body curved around her, all that said *possession*. But the way he kissed her, slow and gentle, tiny gifts of pleasure rippling the surface of her still lake—the way he kissed her said *care*.

And it worked. Dear fucking Lord, did it work. Dani was helpless and hopeless and mindless in seconds, tilting her head and opening for him, rubbing her aching breasts against his chest because she knew without a doubt he was the source of all relief, pressing her thighs together as liquid heat ruined her knickers, clinging to him as the race of her heart and the thick honey of her pulse joined forces to make her breaths faint and her knees weak.

Then everything stopped.

Zaf pulled back, and awareness came to her in slow waves. First was the sound of him panting as if he'd run a mile, and that was satisfying enough to make Dani almost forget that he'd just wiped her mind clean with his mouth. Almost.

Second came the realization that her feet weren't on the floor anymore. Apparently, he'd gotten tired of bending down for her and had simply wrapped an arm around her waist and . . . picked her up. Only a little bit, until their mouths were level. Now he put her down just as easily, her body sliding over his as he lowered her to the floor. There was a close, dark world between them, made up of shadows and those goddamn, dizzying pants. Of the hitch in Dani's breath and the rigid line of Zaf's erection, jabbing her stomach.

As far as seduction went, that was a wonderful start. Now, if only she was more certain of who had just been seduced.

"That was fun," Dani managed after a moment, hoping she sounded more in control than she felt.

Zaf blinked rapidly, each flick of those long, dark lashes almost hypnotic. "Yeah," he said, his voice rough at the edges, crumbling like brick. "Okay. Yeah. That. Fun. You—think so?"

"Yes," she repeated slowly, because he'd clearly gone a bit dizzy. At least she wasn't the only one who'd temporarily lost control of her faculties. Dani leaned into his erection, and felt a wave of reassurance when he sucked in a breath and screwed his eyes shut. This was how things were supposed to go; people touched, bodies reacted, promises of pleasure were fulfilled. She gave what she was capable of, and he accepted.

Yes. All was absolutely in order. And if she'd felt some odd, additional, heart-pounding, hand-shaking need that was flavored distinctly like Zaf, as if he, specifically, mattered—well. Clearly, that was another sign. The universe's final kick, just to make sure she took the hint.

"Are our watchers still here?" Dani asked, because someone had to say something, and she didn't want to scare him off by suggesting they find an unoccupied bathroom somewhere.

"No," Zaf said. "No, they're gone." Then he stepped back, putting some space between them, and said awkwardly, "I need to . . . get rid of this." A nod southward.

A delighted grin spread over her face. "Zafir!" Maybe he'd be up for the bathroom after all.

"Not like that," he snorted. "I meant I need you to leave."

"Oh." She tried not to pout. "Fair enough."

"Sorry, by the way. About, er . . ."

"Stabbing me in the stomach with your massive cock? That's okay."

Zaf coughed, spluttered, managed to choke on fresh air, then bent double as he wheezed. Dani watched him in mild alarm. Clearly, it would take a while to open his starry, romantic eyes to his destiny of being casually screwed by one Danika Brown on a semiregular basis. Aaand Zaf was still coughing. Should she administer the Heimlich? Maybe, but she wasn't entirely confident she could get her arms around him . . .

Before she could further consider the logistics, Zaf caught his breath and straightened up, his cheeks flushed dark. "Bloody *hell*, Danika. And here I was worried about freaking you out."

"What? Am I supposed to be offended that kissing me gets you going? It's just a bodily function, Zaf."

"Oh, never mind," he muttered, throwing up his hands and looking as if he generally despaired of her. "You try to be a gentleman—"

"Attempting to be gentlemanly after fucking my mouth was never going to work."

"I did *not* fuck your mouth," he said, apparently quite outraged. "I just—actually, you know what? This conversation is not helping my dick. Go away. My lunch break ends in"—he checked his watch and swore—"five minutes. Seriously, disappear."

"Fine," she snickered, "but we need to swap numbers so we can coordinate shenanigans."

"Shenanigans," he repeated dryly.

"Well, I'm not going to say 'so we can coordinate our fake relationship,' am I?"

"But you just said it."

She narrowed her eyes and muttered, "Shut up and give me your phone."

Zaf was used to sleepless nights. No matter how hard he tried, nine times out of ten, his brain wouldn't turn off without the help of medication. But, since that same medication made his early mornings at work a fucking nightmare, he tended to save it for the weekends. So, spending Wednesday night staring at his bedroom ceiling? Pretty routine.

But the kaleidoscope of need coloring his mind was nothing he'd ever dealt with before.

Danika, Danika, Danika. Hours had passed since he'd seen her, but she still dominated his thoughts. He'd been trying so hard to stop wanting her so badly—but then she'd agreed to be his fake girlfriend and kissed the sense out of him. So what the hell was he supposed to do now?

Be grateful for the help and wank over the kiss, apparently.

He'd already jerked off twice—once as soon as he got home, once in the shower after a Tackle It session—but he was ready to go again. Which, for a thirty-one-year-old man, could not be healthy. Then again, like she'd said: *It's just a bodily function.*

Right. Except he'd kissed other women and managed to walk away without developing the libido of a fucking rabbit. Of course, he couldn't remember the last time a kiss had sparked in his chest like this, had left him on the edge of combustion in a thousand ways. He'd wanted to grab her the second she'd let go, and his hands still ached to hold her now.

Meanwhile, she'd probably forgotten all about it.

It was depressing, how that possibility—no, that *probability*—got him down.

"I'm too fucking old for this," he muttered—the horniness and the crush. But he was still thinking of her, because he couldn't stop, and his cock was hard and in his hand beneath the covers, because of course it was. The tiny, breathless noises Dani had made as he kissed her filled Zaf's ears like surround sound. His free hand flexed around the ghost of her lush hip. Her taste, cool mint and honeyed brilliance, flooded his mouth like water after a drought. He was remembering the rhythm of her desperate, hitching breaths, squeezing his dick as his balls tightened, when the sound of his phone's text tone startled him out of his skin.

For fuck's sake.

Zaf groaned, teetering on the edge of ignoring that bloody thing for once. Then he sighed, gave up on his dick, and picked up the phone. He never could ignore a text or a call. It wasn't as if everyone in the world had his number, only the people who needed it—the people who might need *him*.

Squinting at the harsh light of the display, he saw Danika's name and felt his heart kick happily in response. Shit. That couldn't be good.

He liked her way too much, and he knew it. In the books Zaf read, making out with a friend usually lead to a happy ending, as did faking a relationship with one. But in reality, she wasn't interested, and if he didn't get these feelings under control, he'd only end up hurting himself.

Not safe, his nervous heart whispered. *Not safe at all.*

DANIKA: Can I tell my sisters we're faking it?

She texted like she talked: no hellos or good-byes, no context. There was no reason for that to make Zaf smile, so he rubbed a hand over his beard and forced himself to frown instead. Yeah. Much better.

ZAF: If you think you need to.
DANIKA: Oh, good, because I already did.

His laughter bounced around the walls of his dark, empty bedroom.

DANIKA: How long is this whole arrangement supposed to last, anyway?

For some reason, his gut response was *forever*. Ha. Not fucking likely.

ZAF: My niece reckons we should milk it, but I think interest
   will die down quickly. People have better shit to do.
   Let's say . . . a month, to be safe?
DANIKA: Oh, so now your niece is on in this? Corrupting
   innocents, hmm?
ZAF: Hard to corrupt a mastermind.
DANIKA: Well, damn. Fair enough. And a month sounds
   doable. By the way, shouldn't you be asleep right now?
ZAF: Probably. Shouldn't you?

DANIKA: Working. This is my breaktime entertainment. So
    try to be more entertaining.

He snorted, shaking his head. Working at this time? Of
course she was.

ZAF: Anyone ever tell you you're really up yourself?
DANIKA: Of course they have. You told me about a month
    after we met.

That one left him staring at the screen for a while. She remembered random things he'd said a month after they met? Maybe
he'd upset her, and it had stuck in her head. Or maybe not, because the phone beeped, and another text appeared.

DANIKA: You've never seemed to mind it, though, so don't
    start now.

It must be exhaustion—or perhaps it was the possibility that
the wrong answer might hurt her feelings. Whatever the reason,
Zaf found himself typing recklessly and sending without thought.

ZAF: I don't. I like it.
DANIKA: My sisters saw the video and they think you like ME.

He swallowed. His eyes felt heavy all of a sudden. Maybe it
was eye strain, maybe it was surprise sleepiness, or maybe his

body was trying to send him into hibernation so he wouldn't have to deal with this embarrassment. Was the fact he had a thing for her *that* obvious?

ZAF: I do like you. You're my fake girlfriend.

A pathetic half lie, but what was he supposed to do? Admit her smile gave him butterflies, and force her to let him down gently? She'd told him loud and clear she didn't do that kind of thing. Friendship and faking it, that was all he should want from Danika—all he *did* want from Danika, because he knew what was good for him.

But then the memory of her mouth smacked him over the head, and he thought about her dazed, hot-treacle eyes the moment after they'd kissed, and . . . She'd said she enjoyed it. Did that mean she wanted more? Would he *give* her more, if she asked? No, he shouldn't. Zaf might not practice his religion, but he'd grown up believing sex meant something. He still believed that. Some people could do casual, but it would probably melt his brain.

Then again, you don't know until you try.

Ah, shit.

DANIKA: I thought as much. Breaktime's over now. I give
　　your entertainment value 6/10.
ZAF: I'm offended.
DANIKA: Keep that fire burning. Hopefully it will motivate
　　you to do better next time.

Next time came three hours later. He was still awake, turn-ing her—all of her—over in his mind, when the phone chirped again.

DANIKA: If you answer this, I'll be deeply worried for your
    sleep cycle.

He was already grinning as he picked up the phone.

ZAF: Be worried, then. I'm worried about how long you work
    between breaks.
DANIKA: Be worried, then.

He was laughing when the phone rang, her name lighting up the screen.

Dani was propped up at her desk, staring sightlessly at her panel notes, listening to the phone's soothing dial tone and trying not to stumble into sleep.

Tiredness wasn't great for mental processing: she knew this. But she also wanted—*needed*—to kill the upcoming feminist lit panel, and since it was a discussion rather than an essay or pre-sentation, there was no knowing what kind of research it might require. So she would complete *all* the research, just to be sure. If there was one thing Dani could excel at, it was this. Inez Holly would *not* catch her stuttering, no, sir.

But even now, self-conscious awareness hummed at the back

of her mind like the low murmur of students before a lecture began. That awareness reminded her, completely unprovoked, that if she had someone waiting for her in the bedroom down the hall, they'd feel annoyed or neglected right now. They'd lose their patience and their temper. They'd try to persuade Dani away from her tried and tested process, as if they knew what was best for her, and if she refused, they'd ask snide questions about whether her degrees would marry her and love her in her old age.

Unless they were sweet like Zaf. If they were sweet like Zaf, they'd probably talk her into bed with gentle, teasing comments. And if they were heavy like Zaf, they'd pin her down in a big soft hug, and she wouldn't even be able to sneak off once they fell asleep, and then she'd *have* to rest . . .

Which sounded awful and was one of the many reasons she preferred to keep potential fuck buddies on the other end of the phone, instead of nestling them into her life. Speaking of, she must conscript Zaf to the cause soon. Preparing for the symposium was proving extremely stressful, and as she'd learned today, his mouth was a magical tool of distraction.

When he picked up, his voice was deep and sleep-roughened, and it shot straight to her clit. Of course, everything about him shot straight to Dani's clit, just like champagne shot to her head.

"Hey," he said, all raspy and gorgeous and *ugh*. "Let me guess. You're working." There was a smile in his voice—no scolding exasperation or heavy disappointment to be found. Almost as if he was amused, rather than annoyed, by her unsociable hours.

"Yep," she confirmed. "Working." But now that she had Zaf

on the phone, work didn't seem half as interesting as getting on his nerves. Hmm. Unfulfilled lust was a funny thing.

"Studying in the middle of the night," he groused, fondness lacing each word. "I don't know how you look so pretty all the time. I come to work every morning looking like I've got two black eyes."

The word *pretty* sent a childish thrill of pleasure through her, which was mortifying, because Dani wasn't in the habit of caring about who called her pretty. If she did, she might also have to care about who called her ugly, and when you were a woman—especially a black woman on the chubbier side—that was never a good idea. The only opinions she valued on that score were her own.

But there seemed no harm in murmuring, "Pretty, am I?"

"Don't start. You know you're a knockout." He paused, clearly considering. "Unless you don't, and you'd like me to tell you. As a friend."

"No, no," she said quickly—because he *would* tell her if she asked. He would tell her in that quiet, rumbling voice, calm and steady and unembarrassed, just to make her feel good about herself. And this weird melting feeling in her middle, as if her insides were spilling out and leaking everywhere, might get even worse. God forbid. As an extra layer of protection, she added, "For future reference, there's never any need to emphasize my attractiveness. As you say, it's already an established fact."

He laughed, the sound sinking into her skin, spilling over tight, tense muscles.

"As for my lack of dark shadows," she went on, trying to sound casual, "it's concealer. Google it."

"Hmm. Maybe my niece will lend me some."

She exhaled, smiled. It was kind of adorable how often he mentioned his niece. "Good luck. But you know, there is an alternative to makeup."

"Yeah?"

"Indeed. It's called sleep, and at this time of night, most people are doing it. Why are you up so late?" Maybe he was busy, too. Maybe he valued his work in the same way Dani did, and maybe, because of that, he'd understand certain things and—

He grunted. "No reason. I don't always sleep that great."

Ah. She dragged her teeth over her lower lip, that softly delivered news making her chest ache. "Something on your mind?"

"Something on yours," he asked, "since you called?"

If Dani bothered to observe things about people, she might note that Zaf had a singular talent for steering subject changes. "I try to take a five-minute rest break every thirty minutes," she told him. "Although time occasionally gets away from me. I thought, since you're up, and we have things to talk about—"

"You're bestowing your five minutes on little old me? I've never been so flattered."

She laughed. "That's not the reaction I usually get." Most people wanted more from her, hungry for bites she didn't have to spare. Dani wasn't good at this sort of thing—at making people feel like they mattered. But according to the universe, Zaf was her perfect fuck buddy—so of course he wouldn't mind. He probably didn't *care* enough to mind.

He sounded like he cared, though. "Is that right?" he murmured, the smile in his voice replaced by something cautious and concerned. "What reaction do you usually get, Danika?"

Dani decided that changing the subject had just become a matter of urgency. "Oh, you know," she managed, and wiped the question away with an airy laugh. "Never mind all that. How goes the publicity thing? What does a fake relationship involve, anyway?"

There was a slight pause. She bit her lip and hoped for the best. Zaf gave it to her. "Er . . . I sent a few lines to the *Nottingham Post*, since you're okay with it. And I guess those kids took a picture of us—*talking* in the car park," he said, because he was adorable, "which got the hashtag trending again. One-time donations are through the roof, so all the attention really is working." She detected a faint note of wonder in his voice that made her want to squish his cheeks and kiss his forehead. Fortunately, he wasn't in the room, so she was saved from the horror of actually following that impulse. "I got an email from BuzzFeed Sports, too," he said, sounding pleased. "They sent me some questions to answer. Everything's amazing, Dan. And it's because of you, obviously."

She made a gagging sound. "Don't start getting emotional."

"Piss off. Let me say thank you."

"Zaf, don't, I'll be sick. You don't want me to be sick."

"Fuck you, then," he said, but there was laughter in his voice. "As for the fake relationship—we don't have to kiss in any more car parks."

She was going to say, *What if we want to?*, but that sort of thing should probably be saved for face-to-face communication. Wouldn't want him to misunderstand her intentions.

"I was thinking we should just have lunch together," he went on, "and try to . . . you know. Flirt."

"Try to flirt? Because we're so out of practice."

She could almost hear his blush through the phone. "We don't flirt."

"If that's what you think, I really need to brush up on my skills."

Judging by the strangled sound he made, Zaf appeared to be having some sort of mental crisis. "You mean . . . we . . . *do* flirt?"

"Well, I try my best. You can be difficult, sometimes." Dani stood up as he spluttered through a response, wandering around her flat's living room to stretch her legs.

"I thought—I thought you were joking," he said finally.

She wouldn't want his head to explode, so she said, "Yes, of course I was joking."

He exhaled.

I was jokingly *expressing the fact that you're mind-blowingly hot.* "So, lunch. Flirting. Anything else? Adorable selfies, et cetera?"

"Fuck, no. You sound like my niece. Fatima told me social media crazes are a flash in the pan, and if we want to make the most of it we should consider starting a YouTube channel." His disgust practically dripped from the words.

"And you said?"

"Absolutely fucking not."

Dani's lips had been twitching as she asked the question; now she laughed outright. "Of course you did." If the words sounded a little too fond and familiar, oh, well. It was the middle of the night and he was being unforgivably cute. "Your niece is clearly a smart girl." And the eucalyptus by Dani's window, for freedom and prosperity, was looking a little parched. She headed to the kitchenette to get it some water, her feet padding against the floorboards.

"Yeah, Fatima's smart. You teach her, you know."

"I do?" Dani frowned as she filled her little watering can, then remembered a new student with huge, dark eyes. "*Oh.* Fatima Ansari. Of course you're related. She looks just like you."

A slight silence as Dani went to water the plant. Then, a moment before it got awkward, Zaf said quietly, "Nah. She looks like her dad."

"Your brother, is he?"

"Mm-hmm." Zaf's tone went from distant and distracted to light and teasing so fast Dani felt slightly whiplashed. "She thinks you're sophisticated. That's what she said to me. *Everything Dani does is so sophisticated.*"

"Poor, deluded girl."

"Ain't she just." Sweet exasperation crept into his tone, a gleaming thread that said, *I know what a chaos demon you are, and I think it's great.*

Dani tried not to beam in response. That would be ridiculous. She watered her eucalyptus, put down her can, heard the beep of her five-minute timer, and realized with a jolt that her break had vanished like smoke.

"Oh," she said, "I have to—it's—"

"Five minutes. I know." But there was no irritation in Zaf's voice, no resentment. He was probably relieved to know she'd get off the phone now and let him sleep.

She, surprisingly, wasn't relieved at all. In fact, the thought of putting down the phone made her feel slightly sad and deflated. For a moment, something in her leaned toward him like a cooped-up plant growing desperately toward the sun, and—

And good Lord, she must be exhausted. Dani shook her head, frowned, and considered going to bed earlier than planned.

"My lunch break starts at twelve thirty tomorrow," Zaf said, oblivious to her spiraling thoughts. "That work for you?"

"I think so. I'll text you if anything changes. Otherwise . . . meet you at the food court?"

"All right," he said. "Goodnight, Danika."

"Go to sleep!"

He grunted and hung up.

Only when he was gone did Dani realize she'd barely tried to seduce him at all.

CHAPTER SEVEN

Somehow, in the whirlwind of setting up this fake relationship, Zaf had managed to forget that he was a shitty actor and a truly abysmal liar. That fact came back to him like a concrete boomerang on Thursday afternoon, when he saw Danika walking toward him in the food court and realized he had absolutely no idea how to greet her.

After a second of mental flailing, Zaf cleared his throat, waved awkwardly, and said, "Hi, er, babe."

Babe? *Babe?* He was 99 percent sure his lips had never formed that fucking word in his entire fucking life. And was it just him, or was every pair of eyes in this food court suddenly pinned to his blushing face?

Before he could weigh the odds of extreme social media

stalkerism versus paranoia, Dani reached him with a laughing smile and dancing eyes. "Hello, handsome."

He short-circuited, just a little bit.

Then she rose up on her toes, pressed her hands against his chest, and kissed his cheek. Holy fuck, she smelled like honey. He wanted to bite her.

In his ear, she whispered, "Am I wrong, or is everyone watching us?"

"I *knew* it."

"Shh. Noodles, conversation, a little light hand-holding. Let's not make this too difficult."

"Okay," he managed, but her hands were still on his chest and he was concentrating on not getting hard, because that would be extremely embarrassing on several thousand levels.

"Zaf?"

"Yeah?"

"Try to look more like yourself and less like seven guilty toddlers standing on each other's shoulders in a security uniform."

A few slow blinks, and his brain started processing normally again. "That . . . does not make a lick of sense."

"Well done for noticing," she said, and patted him soothingly. "Come on, then. I'm starved." Apparently, she'd decided to take charge of this whole thing, which he was absolutely okay with. If you had to stumble your way through a fake relationship with a woman you were *actually* crushing on, that woman being inhumanly calm and scarily smart and a little bit bossy made things a thousand times easier.

But Zaf wasn't supposed to be listing all of Danika's excellent qualities. In fact, he was supposed to be ignoring them, and also her smile, and also her arse, which looked excellent in today's floaty, star-printed dress-robe thingy. Not that he was looking. *Behave.*

They headed straight toward a Thai food truck, where Dani told the old guy behind the counter, "Good afternoon! Hot tofu box, double veg, please."

"Size?"

"Large." To Zaf, she added, "Is there any other size?"

He bit the inside of his cheek to fight a smile. "Not if you're smart. You like tofu?" Was unnecessary interest in someone's food preferences a friend thing, or a sneaky crush thing? The lines were already blurring like smudged paint. Zaf was mentally compiling a list of curries he knew how to cook that might work with tofu—not that he'd ever cook for Danika. That would definitely be a crush thing.

"It's good," she said. "Try it." So he ordered the same, because of course he did. Then Dani added, "And some chips, please. Wait, Zaf, do you want chips?"

He shrugged. "I can share yours if you—"

"Nope. Two lots of chips. Thank you." She smiled up at the man in the van, all white teeth and glossy lips, her doe eyes bright.

"Uh . . . you're welcome," the man said faintly, then stared for a second before turning abruptly away.

Zaf sympathized.

They got their food a few minutes later and sat in the middle of the courtyard. Zaf spent a solid ten seconds dithering about where to sit—was opposite her more datelike, or next to her?—before getting a grip and choosing a seat at random. Danika, meanwhile, ignored him completely in favor of devouring her noodles. So, really, she wasn't that great at this fake-date thing, either. Or maybe she was just super hungry. Whatever the case, the fact that he wouldn't be the only one letting the side down took the pressure off a bit. Zaf swallowed, picked up a fork, and dug in.

Dani had been right about the tofu: it was good—really good, in fact. The chips, obviously, were chips. He finished all his food before she was even halfway done with hers, then asked, "You need some help?" just to get on her nerves.

She froze and gave him a deadly look. "You need my plastic fork up your arse?"

"Might be worth it for more of those noodles."

"Zafir, if cutlery-based orgasms are what gets you going, just say." Out of nowhere, she grinned. The effect was so overwhelming, he actually had to remind his cock that this was all a joke. *Relax, mate. We're not even into anal.*

Then she leaned forward and murmured, "If you're that hard up, I'll shove a fork in there for free."

Zaf's dick looked at him suspiciously and said, *We're not into it? Are you sure?*

He cleared his throat.

She smirked and went back to her food. But she also picked

up her phone and, somehow, typed out a text as she ate. When his phone beeped a second later, he realized the text was to him.

DANIKA: Hey. Strategy meeting.

ZAF: . . . Are you really texting me right now? I'm sitting next to you.

The food court was alarmingly bright and filled with a surprising number of avid eyes—Dani would never get over the baffling popularity of this #DrRugbae phenomenon—so, yes, she was indeed texting Zaf from the same table. And he was clearly unimpressed, because his reply was accompanied by a raised eyebrow and a disapproving look. God, he was such a dad. An adorable dad. An adorable, *sexy*—actually, never mind.

DANIKA: I know, but spies are everywhere. Case in point, that boy to your left is filming us under the table.

And now he looked vaguely horrified.

ZAF: Please tell me you're joking.

DANIKA: Look for yourself, if you dare.

ZAF: You know I'm too obvious for that.

DANIKA: True. Anyway, since we're on camera, we should probably look less text-obsessed and more deeply in love. Idea: feed me some noodles.

ZAF: Feed you? Seriously?

DANIKA: Just do it.

Couples fed each other, right? Yes, they most certainly did. Dani had seen it in *Lady and the Tramp*, plus her parents had done it with cake for their wedding photos. And since she wasn't confident in her ability to seem happily committed and blissfully in love—hungrily in lust, more like—every little helped.

Zaf shot her a dubious look, put down his phone, and reached for her noodles. "All right. Open up."

"Just be careful," she muttered under her breath. "I have an overdeveloped gag reflex."

"Erm . . . okay," he said, looking as if he expected to wake up and find this entire situation had been some sort of weird, cheese-fueled dream. When the waking up failed to occur, he shrugged his massive shoulders and held out a forkful of noodles. They both hesitated for an awkward moment before Dani, in a bid to look comfortable and couple-y, opened her mouth and leaned in toward the fork.

At the exact same time, Zaf moved, too. Because of course he did.

He jabbed, she jerked. Their mutual enthusiasm did not, unfortunately, make for a calm, controlled, social-media-friendly feeding experience.

Actually, Dani ended up with a wad of bean sprouts at the back of her throat, all of which she promptly spat out onto his lap.

@FOZZY99: Did I really just see Zaf Ansari's girlfriend coughing stir-fry all over him in the campus food court? LOLOLOL

♡ 250 ⟲ 7k ♡ 6k ⬆

@SLYTHERINBIH: Oh my god, gross

♡ 68 ⟲ 386 ♡ 1k ⬆

@BASICJELLYBABY: She was cute even semi-throwing up on him

♡ 42 ⟲ 4.3k ♡ 509 ⬆

@HOLLY_COOKE: This is why I love them. They really seem real AF

♡ 615 ⟲ 6.8k ♡ 2.7k ⬆

Friday 12:36 P.M.

ZAF: Noodles again?

DANIKA: All the yes, but don't feed me this time. I'm not ready to die.

ZAF: I told you it was a bad idea!

DANIKA: And I told you about my gag reflex, so it looks like we're both terrible listeners.

ZAF: George asked me yesterday why my crotch smelled like hot sauce. I think he thinks I have some kind of food fetish now.

DANIKA: Does he think you have a Teflon dick, too? Because a hot-sauce fetish sounds extremely painful and also a high UTI risk.

ZAF: Should've thought of that before you threw up on me.

DANIKA: IT WASN'T VOMIT. IT WAS JUST FOOD. IT WAS
UNDIGESTED FOOD. IT WAS UNSWALLOWED
FOOD. HOW MANY TIMES?

Saturday 8:48 P.M.

DANIKA: Are you free for late-night phone calls, or do you
have weekend-type plans?

ZAF: Weekend-type plans?

DANIKA: You know what I mean.

ZAF: Yeah. I just enjoy your nerd phrasing. Have to let it
marinate.

DANIKA: I am strongly considering blocking your number.

ZAF: But if you did, who would be your five-minute
entertainment tonight?

DANIKA: There's a sex joke in there somewhere but I've
been staring at this book for three hours now, so my
brain is too blurry to find it

ZAF: If you've been working for three hours that means you
owe me six phone calls already. So close the book and
ring me now.

Over the weekend, Tackle It hit a milestone: £3,000 in one-off
donations had been made since the Dr. Rugbae video went viral.

Zaf had posted about it online, received an unholy number of likes and comments, and the total donations had bumped up even higher. He'd made Fatima a bowl of rasgulla roughly the same size as her head, because she was a genius mastermind who deserved to be recognized as his niece again, and he'd gone out with Jamal to a milkshake bar in town that offered a ton of old arcade games. Basically, he'd had a great fucking time. But for some reason, when he remembered the highlights, the first thing that came to mind was Danika sending him an emoji wearing a party hat. Probably because she never used emojis.

And the fact he'd noticed that, and was now ascribing significance to it, made Zaf want to smother himself.

It turned out that was physically impossible, though, so he compromised by rereading one of his favorite books on Sunday. A romance, obviously. Happy ending, obviously. That was what he wanted: a happy ending. And yes, he'd learned the hard way that those didn't always last, but he wasn't going to shoot himself in the foot by getting attached to a woman who didn't want one at all.

The reminder worked.

During their Sunday-night phone call, he barely mooned over Danika at all. During his post–phone call wank (unavoidable— she had a sexy voice, okay?) he kept things fast and thoughtless. On Monday, when she turned up at his desk to fake flirt before and after class, Zaf remembered through every smile and lingering look that this was all for show. It. Was. All. For. Show.

And when she texted him later that morning, her messages like little rays of sunshine no one else would ever see?

That was friendship, obviously. Friendship, full stop.

DANIKA: I can't wait for lunch.

DANIKA: Not the fawning all over you and feeding you grapes part. The food part.

Huh. Zaf hadn't realized grape-feeding was on the fake-lunch-date cards at all, but suddenly he couldn't wait, either.

DANIKA: My stomach is eating itself. RIP me.

ZAF: Didn't you eat your protein bar?

DANIKA: Yes, I ate my protein bar, you absolute parent. It's a shame I don't have a daddy kink, or I might get off on those things.

Zaf set his jaw and shifted in his seat. She kept . . . saying things like that, these past few days, and it was getting harder and harder not to bite.

ZAF: Come and get another one.

DANIKA: You want me to choke down two in one day?!

He should probably be offended, but he found himself laughing into his hand, disguising the sound with a cough and a glower when a passing group of students stared at him. Once they were gone, he set his tiny smile free and typed out a response.

ZAF: That's not very polite.

DANIKA: I can't leave my strategic library position to come and get a protein bar. My seat by the window will be stolen. The risk isn't worth the tasteless but protein-rich reward.

ZAF: Are you telling me you don't like my protein bars?

DANIKA: They taste like cardboard.

DANIKA: Keep giving them to me, though.

As if he had any intention of stopping.

ZAF: For food emergencies?

DANIKA: You ask so many questions. I'm working now, I have to go.

And she really did go. There were no more texts during her breaks—not a single one—and she didn't show up to lunch, either. Zaf leaned against a lamppost by the food court, staring longingly at the noodle van and the library in turn, like a man with a desperate craving for chili bean sprouts and books. Or chili bean sprouts and a bookish woman. Whatever. Clearly, he was delirious with hunger, since he'd finished his store of snacks around 10 A.M. as always. *Hours* ago now.

He checked his phone again, but there was no response from Dani to his latest nudge. Since his brain was his brain, his first thought was that she'd died. She'd taken the stairs and fallen, or she'd been crushed between those fancy moving bookshelves— the ones with signs on them saying to shout before you pulled the levers, only no one ever did.

Lucky for Zaf, he was used to shoving unreasonable worries away, so he drop-kicked those ideas into the sun and moved on.

In reality, he'd probably been stood up by his fake girlfriend. Ouch. Of course, knowing Dani, it was equally likely that she'd just gotten distracted—that she was lost in a book or a journal, her phone at the bottom of her bag, time a distant concept she preferred not to play with. Which would be fine, if it weren't for the fact that they had social media stalkers to manipulate into free publicity.

And, *wow*, it all sounded incredibly mercenary when he phrased it like that. But still.

Zaf needed to be seen with Dani before this flash in the pan . . . un-flashed. He wasn't about to let a single fake-lunch-date opportunity slip through his hands. So, for the good of Tackle It—obviously—he had no choice but to hunt down his girlfriend.

His *fake* girlfriend.

Obviously.

The low murmur was a familiar fixture in her dreams. "Hey. Danika."

Danika, said with those soft, round consonants. Dani smiled, squeezing her eyes tight against the light. If she could fall asleep properly and sink fully into this dream, she might see Zaf as well as hear him. And seeing him was always a thrill.

Unfortunately, her inner eye remained stubbornly blank. She might have sulked over that, if it weren't for the feel of a large, warm hand stroking her hair.

"Dani." The whisper was quieter and closer, now. She felt the warmth of a body beside hers, caught the scent of coffee beans and spiced citrus—a scent she usually tried not to enjoy, because sniffing people was . . . just . . . odd. But it was okay to sniff people in dreams. Or to fantasize about taking the whole of them, making them yours, popping them into your mouth like a glossy, round grape, seeds and all, and trusting they wouldn't choke you. For example.

"Sweetheart. Wake up."

She'd really rather not. Even though her position was a little uncomfortable and her pendants were digging into her chest, this dream or half dream or whatever was too heartbreakingly lovely to abandon.

"You're drooling on a book."

"Shit," Dani blurted, and jolted upright in her seat. At which point, a few things became immediately obvious: first, that she had fallen asleep in the library. Second, that she had not drooled on a book, but if the ache in her cheekbone was anything to go by, she *had* used a book as a pillow. And third, that Zaf was here.

Why was Zaf here?

Not that she minded, exactly. He was quite nice to have around, she supposed.

He was sitting beside her at one of the long library desks, and he appeared to have forgotten the meaning of personal space—again, not that she minded. Zaf was close enough that she could count his sinfully long eyelashes, and if she wasn't mistaken, the delicious weight at the back of her neck was his *hand*. A wave of pleasure thrummed through her stomach.

He was holding her neck. He was *holding* her *neck*. His palm cradled the line of her spine and his thumb stroked the side of her throat, and her clit ached in time with every slow sweep. Apparently, she had a thing for being grabbed by large men. Funny how she'd never noticed that until this moment. Of course, she didn't usually let anyone grab her in public, since it had always seemed disturbingly proprietary, and Dani was not property. So why, exactly, was she allowing Zaf the privilege?

As if that thought had deactivated some sort of mental firewall, the last of her faculties returned. All at once, she remembered why Zaf was there, why he was holding her as if they'd been married for sixteen years, and why he was staring at her with a slight, sweet smile tugging at the corner of his mouth.

Fake relationship. For . . . reasons. Lunch. To be . . . seen. And . . .

"Oh, crap," she said. "I'm late, aren't I?"

His smile widened into a grin, which was an absolutely shocking turn of events for a man with such epic resting bitch face. "Maybe."

"I'm sorry," Dani blurted, then wondered why she was apologizing. She was a terminally disappointing date, and *I'm sorry* had never changed that. The phrase was usually just an opportunity for whomever she was with to wrench her flaws wide open and list them all in excruciating detail. Not that Zaf had a right to do that, because they weren't really in a relationship—she was doing him a favor, for heaven's sake—and anyway, she hadn't *meant* to fall asleep, so really, what was to be done?

Except . . . well, she supposed *something* could've been done. Something other than accidentally standing him up. She didn't like the idea of standing him up, not even for a library power nap.

"It's okay," Zaf said, and the ease of his response snapped Dani out of her thoughts like an unexpected static shock. "I brought lunch," he went on, "since I thought you might be busy in here."

For a moment, all she could do was stare. He'd thought she'd forgotten him because she was busy with work, and instead of throwing a righteous fit, he'd . . .

He'd brought lunch to *her*.

A sunrise threatened in Dani's chest, but she shoved it down, barely wincing when the heat stung her palms. They were co-conspirators, after all. They were in the midst of a plot. A plot that *required* Zaf to be around her, and do nice things for her, and look at her with eyes like fire gleaming off midnight water.

"You're very laid back about this," she whispered, arranging her books into a neat pile. "But I suppose allowances must be made for fake girlfriends, as opposed to real ones."

"Yep," he said cheerfully, and there was no reason for that confirmation to pinch at something behind her breastbone. She already knew she wasn't quite up to scratch; every relationship since her first, since Mateo, had taught her that, and it didn't matter. A sensible woman played to her strengths and left immaterial weaknesses behind.

Which didn't explain why she kept asking pointless questions, like picking at a scab. "So if this was real, and your girlfriend missed lunch . . ."

Zaf looked up, his eyes slightly narrowed as he leaned in close and lowered his voice. "You didn't miss lunch, Dani. You fell asleep because you work too hard, and if you were really mine, I'd be less worried about lunch dates and more worried about ways to trick you into slowing down." His thumb swept over her neck again, a slow, soothing stroke that tugged at something sweet and lazy in her. *If you were really mine,* he'd said, and the words seemed to beat a tattoo against her skull, as fast and firm as the pulse pounding scandalously between her thighs.

"Oh," she said, so quiet she barely heard herself.

But Zaf heard and came closer, his scent filling her lungs. "When you ask me things like that, Danika, it makes me think someone hasn't treated you right."

Those words were a wake-up call, swooping in to save her from herself. "Sorry," she said brightly. "No soap-opera sob story here, mostly because I'm humanly incapable of sobbing. Superior tear ducts, you understand."

"Mm-hmm." Zaf nodded. "Obviously. Mechanical heart, too."

"Got it in one. I was just curious about how relationships work when you're a hopeless romantic." She waited for him to deny that judgment, wondering if he'd respond with sarcasm or maybe some masculine bluster. There was a first time for everything, after all.

Instead, he watched her steadily. "Right," he murmured, his dark eyes piercing, and suddenly she felt as if he'd stripped off all her clothes in the middle of the library. And not in a sexy way.

She pushed the feeling away, replacing it with a flirtatious confidence that was as easy as breathing. "If you ever want to know how *I* do things," she purred, "just ask."

He didn't flush, didn't stutter or change the subject. He didn't bite, either, didn't smirk or sway closer. No, Zaf just shook his head, squeezed the back of her neck, and said, "Behave yourself, trouble."

Dani blinked. She had the oddest feeling something about their sexual balance had irreversibly changed, and not necessarily in her favor.

Well. Good for Zaf.

"Let's eat," he said, as if nothing had happened. His hand left the back of her neck, and he turned to riffle through a bag she hadn't noticed before. "No protein bars. Promise."

She bit her lip. "I like your protein bars."

"Thought they tasted like cardboard?"

"I like them," she repeated stubbornly, because it was true, and because she was gripped by the unnerving worry that he might stop giving them to her. Although, why that thought should make her worry, she had no earthly idea. All her feelings were wonky and sideways at the minute. Maybe it had something to do with her nerves about the panel, or her poor, neglected vagina, or both.

"Glad to hear it," he said cheerfully, "because I'll blend them into mush and spike your green tea if necessary. Now," he muttered, almost to himself, "let's see." Out of his mysterious plastic bag came a bottle of water, which she grabbed so greedily, she almost missed the rest: wrapped bagels from the union, little pots of fruit and yogurt, crisps and Maltesers.

"Zaf," she whispered, "you do know we're not allowed to eat in here?"

"So we'll do it until someone throws us out. You're hungry, my break's almost over, and"—he gave her a significant look, his voice dropping to a whisper—"we have to eat together because we're madly in love and all that shit."

"Oh, right. Of course." Dani shuffled her chair closer to his, just so any photos that wound up online would accurately convey how thrillingly intimate they were. Couple goals, and so on and so forth. Milking it, et cetera, et cetera. "How was your day, er, baby?"

He arched an eyebrow. "*Baby?* Can't decide if that's better or worse than me calling you *babe* that one time."

"Oh, shut up. This is the sort of thing couples say."

"I bet it is, doll tits."

Her cheeks heated. "Except that. No one says that."

"Are you sure?" he asked mildly.

"Yes, I'm sure, sugar cock."

Zaf spluttered, then burst into a coughing fit. Dani was searching for another name that might cause a similarly adorable reaction when a gaggle of ruddy-faced, thick-necked boys—undergrads, if she had to guess—appeared out of nowhere. They chose a desk opposite Dani's, dragging spare seats from neighboring tables, ignoring the glares of other occupants as chair legs scraped over the floor. After sitting down in a muttering, giggling group, they proceeded to stare, starry-eyed, at Zaf and tap away on their phones with obvious intent. One boy turned to shove another's shoulder after a particularly loud guffaw, and Dani caught sight of the lettering on the back of his blue jacket: NGU RUGBY.

"Oh, good," she whispered. "I do believe your acolytes have found us."

Zaf rolled his eyes. "I doubt any of them had even heard of me before last week."

"Honestly, Zafir, you're so grumpy you could create your own storm clouds. Entire countries would pay good money to use your services, I'm sure."

"What can I say? It's a natural talent."

"Or maybe it's lack of sleep," she pointed out, then wanted to kick herself. It was none of Dani's business if he stayed up until all hours of the night. She was nobody's mother, thank you very much.

"You're telling me to sleep? Woman, you just passed out in a library."

She blushed. "It's a very restful environment!"

"I've heard beds are even better."

"I don't want to talk about beds with you, Zaf." Not right now, anyway, because it wouldn't do to spontaneously combust in public.

But then it occurred to her that *in public* was the perfect time to push things, just a little. Because if everything went horribly wrong, and he wasn't interested in what she had to offer, Dani could claim she'd been faking it. *Genius.* Suddenly the boys at college who'd once texted her messages like Be my gf? Haha, JK. Unless . . . ? seemed like bold pioneers instead of irritating gnats.

So she murmured the tragic truth with a teasing smile. "Too much bed discussion could tip me over the edge. Next thing you know, I'll be ravishing you on this undoubtedly unsanitary carpet."

Apparently, he hadn't expected that, because for a moment, his face was blank as a new Word document. Dani bit her lip, wondering how he'd respond, and barely noticed the increase in whispers from their excitable observers at the next desk.

Then Zaf's surprise melted into an expression she could only call *hunger*. Without warning, he grabbed the leg of her chair and jerked it—jerked *Dani*—closer. The breath left her lungs, and by the time she remembered how to inhale again, her seat was trapped, sideways, between his spread thighs. His arm rested over the back of the chair, and she felt its heat against her shoulders. His mouth was perilously close to her cheek, and when he finally spoke, his voice was low and rough and *changed*, and it rasped over her skin the way his hands would. "Tell me what it is you want from me, Danika. Explain it to me. Slow."

For someone so repelled by relationships, Dani sure had a lot of questions about them. But then, for someone who wasn't interested in casual sex, Zaf sure struggled with telling her to knock this innuendo bullshit off.

He didn't want her to knock it off.

Maybe he was imagining the way she looked at him sometimes, like he was a surprise, scary but special all at once. And maybe he was imagining the vulnerability in her, too, glittering beneath her surface like fragments of gold underwater. The problem was—call him reckless, call him led by his dick, call him a hopeless romantic, but he *wanted* to believe in it. He wanted it so badly that he dragged her closer and asked her straight.

"Tell me what it is you want from me, Danika. Explain it to me. Slow."

Her teeth grazed the soft, plump flesh of her lower lip, and he felt the action in his fucking balls. Her gaze flicked over to the boys watching them, then back to Zaf. She spoke so quietly he barely heard her. "I want to sleep with you, Zafir. Don't take it personally, though." Her smile was painfully sexy and as sharp as an arrow. It certainly burst his bubble.

No. You've always known how she operates. Don't be disappointed with the sun for setting.

Zaf took a breath as his hopes rearranged themselves into common sense. So Dani had nothing more than sex on the brain—he'd have been foolish to expect anything different, and Zaf refused to be a fool. Here was the bottom line: she wanted him back, at least in one way, and that was hot enough to singe his doubts. Everything in life didn't have to be black-and-white, did it? There was something between searching for happily ever after and outright celibacy, wasn't there? He certainly fucking hoped so, because it had been a year since his last relationship and right now his dick was so hard, he felt like it might break. Which definitely couldn't be healthy.

He leaned closer to Dani, mostly to make sure his hard-on was hidden by the shadows between them. But the arm he'd rested on the back of her chair brushed her shoulders, and she sucked in a breath at the contact.

His focus on her sharpened, and he saw a lust in her eyes that felt as animal as his. She was beautiful, her chest moving with each heavy exhalation, her plump lips parted, the tip of her tongue wet and pink between her teeth. Honey-brown irises swallowed up by hungry, black pupils, her nostrils flaring, her hands gripping the desk. Coming apart at the seams right in front of him, each of her unraveled threads wrapping around him like silk.

Fuck it. Fuck overthinking, fuck playing it safe, fuck saying no when the yes on the tip of his tongue had never tasted so good. He was going to fuck her, and they were both going to enjoy it, and that would be enough. It would have to be enough. He would *make* it enough, because the roar of lust in him right now was louder than his usual feelings about sex. Wasn't it?

You can't do this, Zafir, said a voice in the back of his head. He pretended that voice was anxiety instead of reason, and shoved it out a window.

Then he ran a fingertip over her jaw, savoring the way her lashes fluttered and her gaze grew heavy. For him. She wanted him, bad enough that the ghost of a whimper fell from her lips, and holy fuck, it'd be a miracle if he left this library without coming all over himself.

Don't do that. Seriously, don't do that. The administration might be disinterested in #DrRugbae so far, but they'd definitely pay attention if he jizzed in his pants on university property.

Zaf let go of her and turned away to catch his breath, focusing on the food they'd abandoned on the table. "Later," he told her quietly. His own voice sounded alien to him, rough as sandpaper and thick with suffocating need. He stole a glance at the group of boys a table away, just to remind himself they were there. That did the trick. The reckless fist of desire squeezing his brain eased its grip, and he could think clearly again.

"Later," Dani echoed, her voice high and faint. He couldn't look at her. He couldn't. But that voice tightened the coil of need in his stomach.

"Tonight, after work," he decided, then picked up his bagel. Bread was boring. Bread would help.

"I can't," she said.

Fuck.

"I told my sisters we'd have dinner together, and I—I don't cancel on my sisters."

Warm, sweet fondness flooded his blood, softening the bite of disappointment. Danika, he'd noticed, loved her sisters. A lot. Enough to remind Zaf of his brother, of the way they'd been, thick as thieves despite a seven-year age gap, together forever until the day they weren't.

"Tomorrow, then," he said softly. "Have dinner with your sisters. And give me tomorrow."

He wouldn't waste it.

CHAPTER EIGHT

SUBJECT: Titans Coach 2011

Hi Zaf,

Not sure if you'll remember me, but I coached you for a
while back when you played for the Titans. Always thought
it was a shame how you left. Hope the family's doing better.

Anyway, my kid showed me your hashtag (a doctor, huh?
Nice) and we found your charity's website. Looks good. I
coach the under-sixteens now and I was wondering if you
offer the emotional workshop stuff without the coaching,
since we've already got that covered. Let me know and
maybe we can talk.

Best,

Mac Stevens

Before this whole viral video thing, Zaf had spent his evenings
after work coaching the kids at Jamal's foundation, planning

new workshop sessions, and stumbling through requests for funding from various trusts. Ever since he'd become one-half of a viral hashtag, he'd also started reading articles on social media marketing and checking his emails every half hour for journalists who wanted a quote.

Mac's message blew that routine out of the water, though.

Zaf read it for the third time, or maybe the fourth, or maybe the twenty-fifth. His first urge was to pick up the phone and call Danika, but that was fucking ridiculous. For one thing, she was busy with her sisters tonight. For another, he was trying not to think about her too much in case he accidentally talked himself out of sleeping with her, which was exactly the kind of travesty his anxious mind was capable of if he didn't watch himself. And then there was the most important part: Dani would have no idea why an email from the coach of his old pro team had Zaf so conflicted. Because there was a lot she didn't know.

Like how messed up Zaf had been after Dad and Zain Bhai had died—or the fact they'd died at all. How he'd closed himself off from everything and everyone, letting his dream slip through his fingers because he'd been too numb to want it anymore. How hard he'd worked to get past the grief, to get a handle on his anxiety, to let go of his anger and his regrets. That wasn't the kind of thing you shared with a woman when you were trying to, er, maintain emotional distance or whatever. That was the exact fucking opposite of what you shared.

So Zaf put his phone on the coffee table, firmly out of reach, and studied the email again. Maybe he should think back to his old therapy sessions—hell, to the techniques he taught in his own workshops—and try to untangle his knotted feelings.

Or maybe he should stick to his usual coping mechanism, tried and tested, of shutting down this blast from the past before it could do any damage. After all, Zaf had survived by drawing lines. His old life had been thrown off a cliff when his family shattered, but they were better now. Someone from the section of his life labeled *Before* reaching out to him in the *Now* wasn't a bad thing, but it was—it could be—complicated. No need to blur the edges between the old and the new when he'd done so well at leaving the past behind.

In the end, he clicked away from the email. He didn't delete it, though. He'd . . . think. He needed to think.

But not right now. Right now he answered more emails from press and cautiously interested schools, focusing on the progress he'd made, his overheated laptop burning his knees and a slow smile curving his lips. This publicity thing was working. It was really, actually working. And tomorrow he was going to touch Danika Brown, which he probably shouldn't include on his mental list of accomplishments, except it definitely *felt* like an accomplishment, so—

A knock reverberated through the flat, jerking Zaf out of his thoughts. He closed his laptop, abandoning emails and Twitter notifications, and headed to the door, already knowing who it was.

"Evening, mate." Jamal was like a river: calm, steady, and powerful enough to wear away mountains. As soon as the door opened, he wormed his way into the flat, went directly to the living room, plonked himself down on the sofa, and opened Zaf's laptop.

"Yeah, make yourself comfortable," Zaf muttered.

"Cheers. Put the kettle on."

"Go fuck yourself. What are you doing here?" He sat down, then realized Jamal had already logged into the computer. "And since when do you know my password?"

"Bonkers, right?" Jamal deadpanned. "Who could've guessed your password would be Fatima2001?"

"Shut up."

"And I'm here to take over your social media for a bit, since all your replies sound like they came from a waiter at the end of an eight-hour shift."

"Oh, piss off," Zaf said, but there was no heat in his voice. Jamal was right, and he was grateful for the assist. "Er . . . thanks."

Jamal rolled his eyes and didn't bother to respond. "By the way, Zafir—"

"*Zafir?* What, did I stack your cones up wrong or something?"

"—when were you going to tell me," Jamal went on, "that you and Doctor What's-Her-Face are pretending to date?"

"Never," Zaf lied cheerfully. "But, since you mentioned it—who *did* tell you?"

Jamal looked shifty.

Zaf grinned. "Was it Kiran?"

"No!" The word was twice as loud as Jamal's usual soft-spoken tone. He cleared his throat and said more quietly, "Why would it be Kiran?"

"Because you two have known each other for decades, but over the past few months you've been acting like you've never met."

"What does that—"

"And every time I mention you in front of K, she blushes."

"No, she doesn't," Jamal said immediately. Then he paused. "Does she? No, it doesn't matter. Who cares? I don't care. You're being . . . you're just . . . Don't try to distract me. What's with the fake-relationship bullshit?"

Zaf shrugged, trying to look casual. Unconcerned. The opposite of a man who was planning to sleep with his fake girlfriend. "It's just a publicity thing. Fluffy gave me the idea. And it's working, right?" He nodded at his emails.

"It is," Jamal agreed slowly. "But . . . are you sure you know what you're doing?"

"Well, not usually, but I get by okay." So far as Zaf could tell, life was all about keeping an end goal in mind and sticking to—

Jamal blinked, slow and deliberate, which was code for *Give me strength.* "I meant with her. The woman."

Oh. Zaf set his jaw and looked away. "Her name is Danika."

"I know what her name is." A flash of that familiar grin. "I just like making you say it so I can hear the adoration in every syllable."

"Tonight I'm going to let myself into your house and smother you in your sleep."

"Uh-huh. All I'm saying is, you've been half in love with her for, like, six months, so just be careful."

"I'm not in love with her," Zaf gritted out. Because he wasn't. He couldn't be. There were lines and boxes and sensible paths, and Dani was over the line and out of the box and in the middle of the woods, so no, he was not in love with her.

He just really wanted to sleep with her, and hold her hand, and keep her fed and watered while she worked late into the night, and sometimes he wondered what shampoo she used and how he could make all his pillows smell just like it, and he'd better not say any of this out loud because he didn't think it would help his case.

"Liar," Jamal said succinctly, clicking through Zaf's emails.

Zaf stared. "What?"

"That's your lying voice. It's all tight and scratchy."

"Who are you?" Zaf spluttered. "The bloody . . . voice police?"

"I hope next time you're in the shower, you think of seventy things you could've said just then that would've been way better than 'voice police.'"

"I hope next time you're in the shower, you drown." Although Zaf agreed that, at thirty-one years old, he should probably have developed better comebacks by now.

"Look," Jamal sighed, meeting Zaf's eyes with a seriousness that did not bode well. "You read a lot of books, so you probably don't realize that in the real world, faking a relationship is actually an incredibly weird thing to do—"

"Er, no, I definitely realize that."

"—and if she's agreed to it, that says something." Jamal gave him a significant look. "You know, *something*. So if you like this woman, you should probably let her know."

Zaf swallowed hard and rubbed a hand over his beard, avoiding Jamal's gaze. "I can't."

"Why? This better not have anything to do with your stick-up-the-arse happily-ever-after thing. I don't know how you can be so flexible when you teach the lads about mental health and so uptight with your—"

"I don't have a stick up my arse," Zaf snapped. Really, was dating with purpose so bad? No, it was not. Goals were important in life, thank you very much. "She's not interested, okay? In any kind of relationship." Except a fake one. And a sexual one. If Jamal knew about that, he wouldn't call Zaf uptight, now, would he?

Although, he might say some other shit. Shit Zaf didn't want to hear, like *You're making a mistake,* or *You take sex too seriously.* None of which was true, obviously, because Zaf had this all figured out. He'd sleep with Danika, and then this mind-numbing hunger he felt for her would naturally fade, and he'd be able to concentrate long enough around her to remember she wasn't for him. Or rather, she didn't *want* to be for him. Different angle, same view.

"She's not interested," Jamal repeated flatly, his raised eyebrows screaming disbelief. "And you know this because . . . ?"

"Because she told me. Seriously. She was very clear."

Jamal paused. "Oh. Hmm. That's rough, man."

"It's fine."

"Not really. You gonna be okay with all this?"

Zaf didn't know and didn't want to investigate, so he shot back, "Are you in love with my sister?"

Jamal snapped his mouth shut, then made a sound like a cat hacking up a hair ball. "No," he spluttered, his eyes fixed determinedly on the laptop screen. "Why would you—? *No.*"

Zaf snorted. "Because *that* wasn't suspicious at all. You two are so—"

Jamal's expression changed. "Zaf."

"—fucking weird. If there's something—"

"*Zaf.*"

"*What?*"

"Are you busy tomorrow night?"

"Yes," Zaf said immediately, his mind going back to the library. *Tomorrow. After work.* "Very busy. Hugely, enormously busy. Don't come here, because I won't be here. And if I am here, I won't answer the door."

"I have a key," Jamal said dryly. "But whatever you're doing, cancel it—"

"No."

"—because you just got offered a local radio interview, and they want to talk about Tackle It."

"Oh," Zaf said. "Shit." And then all the possibilities, all the opportunities hit him, and he repeated, slightly breathless, "*Shit.*"

Dani woke up the next morning with electric excitement thrumming through her veins and an enormous, loopy, *I'm getting laid* grin on her face. It was, to be frank, sickening.

Even Sorcha muttered, when they met at the cafe that morning, "You're way too cheerful. This have anything to do with
your"—she coughed dramatically—"*boyfriend*?"

"Shut up," Dani said, and tried to glare. But the loopy smile
was stuck to her face like glue. "If you must know, I'm cheerful
because Oshun's hint was, of course, correct. Zaf is well on his
way to spring-cleaning my vagina, hopefully with his mouth,
exactly as the goddess intended."

"Right. Thing is, Dan, I've known you for ten years, and you
haven't been this cheerful about a bog-standard shag since . . ."
Sorcha frowned, as if thinking back. "I don't know, Mateo? So
basically," she snorted, "the dawn of time."

Dani tried to laugh along. She really, really did. But something about the name of her first boyfriend made her laughter
congeal in her throat.

And by *something* she meant *literally everything about it*.

"Are you sure this whole arrangement is fake?" Sorcha prodded, still laughing. "Because either you have a crush on your
friend, or he's packing some kind of glow-in-the-dark, vibrating
equipment you're not telling me about."

"Shut *up*," Dani hissed, looking around furtively. She wouldn't
even address that nonsense joke about a crush, but using the
word *fake* in public might undo Zaf's professional progress. The
Social Media Forces That Be could be lurking anywhere. The tat-
ted and pierced teenager gloomily gnawing at a croissant in the
corner might whip a badge out of nowhere and arrest them in
the name of publicity stunts. "Don't make me regret telling you."

Sorcha rolled her eyes. "As if I couldn't have guessed. All jokes aside, even Zaf isn't hot enough to cure you of your relationship phobia."

"Another word about this in public and I'll shove you through a window."

"I might believe that if you didn't look as blissed out as a dead saint."

Considering the turn this conversation had taken, that couldn't possibly be true anymore. Yet Dani caught a glimpse of her distorted reflection in the metallic side of the coffee grinder and realized that Sorcha was, somehow, correct.

Well. It had been six months without sex, and for Dani, that was rather a while. A little excitement was to be expected. Which explained why, by the time she sailed into Echo and slapped down Zaf's morning coffee, she was ready to vault over the desk and rip his bodice like a true romance hero.

Until she saw his face.

"Morning," he said gently, the low gravel of his voice standing out above the familiar whining of passing staff and students. His hair was messier than usual, falling over his forehead like glossy ink, which meant he'd been running his hands through it. His heavy-lidded eyes were cradled by shadows like indigo thumbprints, which meant he'd slept even less than usual, and his golden skin looked pale against the black of his beard.

"Oh no," Dani blurted.

He blinked, then arched an eyebrow.

Since she couldn't let the rest of that rogue thought spill out—it ended with mortifying concern, as in, *Oh no, are you okay?*—she searched for something else to say. After a moment of roiling nerves and surprisingly intense worry, she settled on, "You're confiscating the dick, aren't you?"

Because he probably was. He'd been fine, if a little quiet, during their five-minute phone calls last night, but that didn't mean a thing. People hid their feelings all the time, wrapped them up tight until the pressure turned explosive, and then *boom*: your self-image was in tatters and you were throwing someone's clothes out the window in a rubbish bag like Keyshia Cole.

Zaf had probably put the phone down and spent the rest of the night balancing Dani's many faults with his various romantic ideals, and had decided even the majestic power of her tits (bountiful, obviously) and tongue (long and very flexible, in case anyone was wondering) just wasn't enough to lead him into joyous sin. He certainly wouldn't be the first to make a negative worth calculation when it came to Danika Brown. Although, keeping things purely physical was supposed to prevent the outcome of those calculations from actually hurting.

So the hole his dark gaze punched through her chest must have something to do with divine nudges and destiny. Yes, that was it: the fact that her universe-mandated sex buddy didn't *want* to be her sex buddy was what had Dani's mood falling like bird shit—*splat*—onto the pavement. Oshun really must stop messing her around. Or perhaps this was supposed to be character building? Like fasting was for monks.

"No," Zaf said, standing up to lean against the security desk. "I'm not—" His lips twitched, and his voice lowered to a pitch

that rubbed against her legs like a purring cat. "I'm not confiscating the dick."

"*Oh*. Well. Lovely," Dani babbled, trying not to be too alarmed
by the sudden upswing of her spirits. But really, this morning was
becoming almost violent in its ups and downs. She felt slightly
nauseous and somewhat unsteady on her feet. Which probably
had something to do with relief, her clitoris, and abrupt changes
to blood flow.

"I do have bad news, though," Zaf said. Then he took a nice,
slow sip of his coffee, because he was, apparently, a professional
torturer as well as an ex–rugby player. He really had to stop hiding all these past lives. Friends didn't keep friends in the dark
about their wide and varied special skills.

Which was why Dani would soon be teaching him all about
her bedroom expertise.

She was distracted by the rhythmic bob of his Adam's apple
for a few seconds before impatience won out. "What? What's
the bad news?"

Zaf put down his coffee. "Didn't want to tell you over the
phone yesterday, in case you thought I was avoiding you again.
But I need a rain check on tonight." The words were pushed out
on a wave of disappointment, as if whatever had caused him
to request a delay of their frantic bonking was so unwelcome,
he'd barely prevented himself from kicking that thing into the
sun. Which went some way toward soothing Dani's pang of
unhappiness.

Although she didn't know what she could possibly be unhappy about. She'd survived on vibrator-given orgasms this

long, and it wasn't as if she'd been looking forward to spending the evening with Zaf. That would be silly. Especially when she could just call him.

With that fact in mind, she asked calmly, "Everything okay?"

"Yeah." A tentative smile teased his mouth. "Things are pretty great, actually. Aside from us not—well. Yeah. Radio Trent want to interview me."

"*What?*" Dani felt as if a bulb had been lit inside her and now she was glowing gentle pleasure right through her skin. "That's wonderful, right? That's huge!"

"Yep." Zaf nodded, looking away as if he was embarrassed. His smile was cautious, hopeful, sweet. Something about it punched her in the heart, which was highly uncomfortable and made her ribs ache.

"They want to talk about Tackle It," Zaf was saying, "and about us, obviously. I really can't . . ." He paused, his tongue gliding over his tempting lower lip before he reached across the desk and caught her hand. It occurred to her that, for the first time since they'd met, Zaf was completely ignoring his security duties. Usually, when they spoke, his gaze flicked everywhere and he burst out with scowls and orders at random, reminding people to flash their ID. But right now? His eyes were pinned to Dani as his fingers laced through hers, and all that dark, velvet focus sent a thrill racing through her blood, and she felt singularly . . . wanted. Really, really wanted. Her breath rushed out like the tide, and she couldn't bring it back again.

"Thank you," Zaf finished softly. "For all of this. It's ridiculous, I know it is, but it's doing so much."

He was so disgustingly sincere. Dani must be allergic, since every time he thanked her with those big, puppy dog eyes, it made her feel hot and flushed and jittery inside. "Never mind all that," she said briskly. "Do you need me to come?"

Zaf rolled his lips inward. "They asked if you would, obviously. But I told them you're busy, so . . ."

She *was* busy, horribly busy preparing for the symposium—last night she'd woken from a fever dream in which Inez Holly had asked her a question about an obscure Afro-Swedish theory on intersectionality in late nineteenth-century literature, and Dani *hadn't been able to respond.* She should be glad that Zaf didn't need her company. And yet, she found herself asking lightly, as if it were a joke: "What, you don't want me there? I'm wounded."

He laughed a little, because, of course, she wasn't serious. Of course she wasn't. "You're already doing a lot for me, Dan. I'm not about to start dragging you to interviews." His voice lowered as he leaned in. "Or asking you to lie any more than we already are."

All entirely noble points, but none of that was a *no.* And Zaf was the kind of man who knew how to say no when he wanted to.

Dani knew she should let this go. She was mere weeks away from the symposium and the accompanying terrifying panel discussion with Inez fucking Holly, for heaven's sake! She didn't have time to go gallivanting off on last-minute radio interviews with her fake boyfriend, even if it was for the good of the children and so on and so forth, and even if that fake boyfriend was her very real future fuck buddy. So, he was right. She shouldn't come.

Except . . . Zaf clearly didn't like being the center of attention. And when he was nervous, he became particularly, adorably intimidating, only no one else seemed to notice the *adorable* part. And, for fuck's sake, he had anxiety. So, no, Dani wasn't going to let him do this alone. That thought was so urgent, so vehement and intense, that it almost alarmed her—but this caring came from friendship, and friendship was just fine. Friendship was perfectly safe. It might hurt sometimes, but it had never crushed her heart and ruined her from the inside out.

For a moment, the slight hollow in her chest where laughing with Jo had once lived felt unbearably dark and shadowed. But Dani pushed that ache away.

"I'll come," she said.

Zaf looked startled, probably because she'd been silent for a good few minutes. Long, thoughtful pauses were a socially unacceptable habit Dani struggled to break, one she knew from past experience and blunt feedback made her seem strange and/or boring. Zaf never seemed to mind, though. He simply waited for her, and when she spoke again, he always spoke back as if the silence had never happened.

Like right now. "You'll come?" he echoed. "But—"

"But nothing. Let's do this properly."

"You're sure?" His expression was unreadable.

"I'm sure," she said, despite the tiny voice in her ear that was screeching, *What is* happening *here? What are all these warm, glowing sparks and why are* none *of them centered around my genital area?*

The slight tension in Zaf's shoulders melted away, and he gave her a huge, heart-stopping smile—the pesky kind that always made Dani want to kiss his nose (against her conscious will, that is). Then he made things a thousand times worse by sliding a hand around the back of her neck, pulling her close until the desk between them was less innocent plank of wood and more evil cock-blocking barrier, and pressing a kiss to her lips.

It wasn't a hot, hard, passionate sort of kiss. It was a slow, soft, tender kiss, a not-quite-but-almost-chaste kiss, his lips parted but his tongue behaving itself. Sweet, warm pressure, a faint, comforting nuzzle, and then he pulled back just enough to look her in the eyes. His were warm like caramel on the stove and cradled by smile lines.

"How many people," he asked quietly, "know how kind you are?"

"I . . . um . . ." Dani swallowed befuddlement and willed away her blush. "I'm not."

"Right," he said dryly, and then he bumped their noses together, and her entire middle folded in half before melting everywhere like butter. *We're in public*, she reminded herself harshly, *which means this is all pretend*.

Except, most days, Zaf couldn't fake basic good cheer well enough to stop swearing while in uniform. He couldn't even fake a *smile*. Which begged the question—

Don't. Don't ever beg that fucking question, or you might have to give up your first lay in months before you even get a ride. Security walls slammed up in a section of Dani's mind, concrete thicker than Zaf's thighs and higher than her heart rate every time he put his hands on her. Because feelings had wings, but

Dani didn't, and she wasn't about to let herself chase a tiny bird clean off a cliff.

She didn't even feel the urge. Not ever.

So she forced her focus back where it belonged and said, "Maybe after the interview we could . . ."

"I'll come home with you," Zaf said. No hesitation. Just hot, liquid lust.

CHAPTER NINE

That afternoon, Dani watered her plants, salt-watered her goddess, and hunted down a few online articles about Swedish literary criticism, just to be sure. She added a few pink sticky notes to her Wall of Doom, the mind map she'd created beside her desk that contained all her symposium research. Then she found a fascinating essay on race, gender, and the nineteenth-century new woman that she could include in her panel preparation, fell down a rabbit hole, and promptly forgot all her plans for the evening.

She was still playing with pink sticky notes when her grandmother Gigi called to complain about misbehaving grandchildren and difficult yoga poses. Time ticked firmly on but was, unfortunately, ignored by them both.

"Eve has been impossible since that little friend of hers became affianced," Gigi drawled, having moved on from the treacherousness of the wounded peacock pose. "The bride is a nightmare by all accounts, and Eve, bless her heart, is bowing to every whim. I'm beginning to doubt the integrity of my granddaughter's spine."

"Eve's spine is fine," Dani murmured as she scrawled across a new sticky note *A room of* <u>whose</u> *own?* and slapped it onto the wall. "She simply places too much value on being nice."

"I cannot fathom why." Gigi sounded genuinely bamboozled. "Niceness is incredibly dull."

"Mmm." Zaf wasn't nice. He was kind. It was a notable distinction. Rather like the distinction between misogyny and misogynoir. Dani snagged another sticky note.

"She came storming into my yoga studio just the other day—an interruption which *quite* distressed Shivani"—Shivani being Gigi's live-in yoga instructor and girlfriend—"asking me to consider performing at the wedding reception! She told me, 'I would be your eternal household savant and greatest fan,' as though she isn't already! That is, supposing she meant to say *servant.*"

"Probably," Dani replied.

"Well, I said, 'I hope you are referring to *your* wedding reception, darling, because the marriages of you girls are the *only* events that might *ever* inspire me to so exert myself.'"

"Quite right," Dani muttered, switching her Zora Neale Hurston and Zadie Smith sticky notes around.

"Speaking of which, when is that gorgeous white man going to marry Chloe?"

"Promptly, I'm sure," Dani replied soothingly. Gigi, having been abandoned as a pregnant teenager by her first love, and then kicked out in disgrace by her horrified family, had revealed a firm stance on marriage ever since Dani's older sister had moved in with her starving-artist beau.

"And when are *you* going to find yourself a nice girl or boy or otherwise categorized individual to shower you with life-long affection?" Gigi demanded, warming to her topic, which reminded Dani quite abruptly that—

"Oh, shit. I think I'm late."

Gigi gasped in delight. "Late for *what* on a Tuesday evening, Danika Brown? Something other than working yourself into a husk, I hope?"

"*Husk* is a strong term, Gigi." Dani felt mildly affronted. She touched an absent hand to her cheek to see if it was husklike, but it felt moisturized as ever by her Super Facialist hyaluronic day cream.

"Don't tell me you have a *date*?" Gigi went on.

All right, I won't. Since Chloe and Eve had apparently managed to keep their mouths shut on the topic of Zaf—clear evidence that magic really did move through the world—Dani certainly wouldn't be the one to spill the beans. And anyway, this *wasn't* a date; it was a favor. Or a professional engagement, if faking relationships with charity founders for publicity could be counted as a second profession. She'd better hope it wasn't, or Her Majesty's tax office would be all over her.

Not that Dani could see herself ever providing such a service for anyone other than Zaf.

"Danika," Gigi nudged, "don't think so loudly. *Speak.*"

Dani was saved from stammering more excuses by a sudden knock at the door. Of course, *saved* was a relative term, since that knock was almost certainly Zaf, and she'd already let him down by being in her pajamas and on the phone with Gigi when she should be ready to face the music-slash-radio-microphone.

Which, Dani supposed, was no surprise: there was a reason none of her past relationships had worked out, after all. They hadn't all been like Mateo, but she'd always been herself.

"I don't have a date," Dani lied brightly to Gigi. "It's just Sorcha. Must dash, love you, tell Eve to get ahold of herself."

She put the phone down, abandoned her Wall of Doom, and went to the door. Before actually letting Zaf in, Dani took a moment to glance down at herself, just in case her outfit had magically transformed.

Sadly, it had not. She was still wearing enormous, ratty Minion slippers (one purple and one yellow), reindeer-print sleep shorts (*Really, Danika, in March?*), and an oversized T-shirt she'd originally worn to a final Chaucer exam, on which she'd scored a 98. Since Dani despised Chaucer and had no knack for Middle English, that grade had been an obvious miracle. Ever since, she'd worn her lucky T-shirt while working on especially difficult projects.

Unfortunately, said T-shirt was now a faded grayish white

and mildly see-through. Wonderful. She kicked off the slippers and wondered if she should do something to hold up her tits—when left unattended, they sagged dramatically like twin grande dames. Then she reminded herself that if all went to plan, Zaf would eventually see the girls flopping around like drunk puppies anyway, so there was really no point.

Having dealt with that strangely nervous moment, she finally opened the door.

Zaf stood there with his hands in his pockets and his thick, dark hair falling over his brow. Seeing him in street clothes after months of nothing but that navy-blue security uniform was . . . something of a revelation. Dani bit her lip and reminded herself that sensible women didn't swoon at the sight of a man in a Henley, even if that Henley was forest green and clung to every inch of him, from thick forearms to meaty biceps to that solid chest and torso.

Then he produced one of his small, cautious smiles, and Dani was forced to admit that she wasn't a sensible woman after all, because she was definitely swooning. On the inside, anyway. Looking at Zaf was like walking out of an air-conditioned room into a wall of midsummer heat: lust slammed into her, surrounded her, and she proceeded to gently suffocate.

"About an hour ago," he said, "I realized I don't have a clue what you wear to a radio interview."

Her heart melted, *drip-drip-drip*, like an ice pop on a scorching summer's day. Oh dear. "I suppose it doesn't matter," she told him, because if she said, *You look so delicious I'm seriously fighting the urge to sink my teeth into your scandalously plump pectoral,* he might be alarmed. "Come in! I'm afraid I'm not quite ready—"

"Really?" He followed her into the living room, looking around in open curiosity. "I thought the reindeer shorts were a statement."

"Hilarious," she said. "Make yourself at home. I'll be as quick as I can."

"It's okay. I'm twenty minutes early."

Her eyebrows flew up as his words sank in. Dani finally looked at the clock hanging on her kitchen wall and realized he was right. "Oh. You . . . erm . . . so . . . ?"

"I had a feeling," he said wryly, "that you might need a nudge."

Dani supposed she should be outraged by the presumption, or at least mildly annoyed, but frankly, she was just pleased to have one less irrelevant thing to think about. And yes, she was aware most people considered time to be the opposite of irrelevant. But pretending to agree with them had always been exhausting.

Still, she couldn't let Zaf know he'd done something helpful, or he might start thinking they had some sort of *doing helpful things for each other* arrangement, and that was a dangerous dynamic to get into. People tended to take it personally when the other party defaulted. So she scowled and said, "What, are you trying to manage me now?"

His smile was slight, lopsided, and . . . fond. That was the word. *Fond.* "I know you have a lot on your mind, and you don't do well with time when you're busy, so I thought coming early might help. That's all."

He made it sound as if she struggled to remember his

existence—which she certainly did not, thank you very much. But perhaps she behaved that way, sometimes? Dani found that idea infinitely bothersome. Zaf took up a lot of space and spread a lot of warmth and did a lot of good, and someone like that should not be treated as an afterthought. It was the principle of the matter. It was bad for the balance of the universe. So maybe, next time she was supposed to meet him, she'd set an alarm to make sure she wasn't distracted or forgetful.

"I understand, but you don't need to worry. I won't be late again," she said decisively. And then she had to turn away, because something about his expression changed. His eyes seemed even darker and more dizzyingly lovely than usual, and she couldn't bear to hold his gaze. "I'll just . . . get ready, then," she blurted, heading toward the bedroom. "There are glasses in the cupboard over the sink, if you want some water. Or mugs, if you want tea, do help yourself to tea." When he didn't answer, she glanced back to make sure he hadn't fallen through an interdimensional gap or been kidnapped—*giant-napped*—by a team of skilled and silent individuals.

No, he was simply staring, his mouth hanging slightly open, at her arse. Ah. Yes. She'd forgotten about the cut of these sleep shorts, and also about the tattoo on her bottom. Cheeks burning—which was *ridiculous*, since she planned to show him far more skin after they dealt with this interview—Dani slapped a hand over her backside. Zaf responded by bursting into laughter, possibly because her hand wasn't big enough to cover even a fraction of that particular body part.

"Well, I never," she muttered, and hurried off.

"Sorry," he called after her, not sounding remotely apologetic.

"Pervert!" She hoped he was, anyway.

"No, no," he said, utterly deadpan. "I just really like tattoos."

Danika Brown was fucking impossible.

Zaf stood by the living room window, watching her walk away in the dark mirror created by its glass. She was all strong calves and heavy, dimpled thighs, half her arse exposed by those fucking shorts, her palm covering a tattoo that read BITE ME. She disappeared through a door he assumed led to her bedroom, slamming it shut. Zaf released a long sigh of relief and leaned forward until his brow touched the cold glass. He needed to calm down. His pulse was a rhythmic punch against his throat, so violent it must be dangerous. He'd be in the news tomorrow: MAN KILLED BY OWN AROUSAL. ARTERY BURST BY THE FORCE OF HIS BLOOD.

No messing around with Danika, he told himself firmly. Not before they'd gotten this fucking interview out of the way. His nerves about the whole thing mixed with the hot, electric anticipation of what they'd do after, and it was making him shake as if he'd downed three espressos in a row. Or maybe he was shaking because he *had* downed three espressos in a row. Hadn't wanted to yawn midinterview.

Then again, was he even capable of yawning with a woman like Dani beside him? Probably not. His dick had been hard before he'd even crossed her threshold. He'd never seen her wear anything other than black, never seen her barefoot and braless without a scrap of makeup, so the way she looked tonight had hit him like a fist to the gut. Who else saw her like this? Not many people, he'd bet. It was a tiny and ridiculous and meaningless thing, but to Zaf, it whispered *intimacy*, and the fact that it was all in his head didn't stop him from biting his fist. Hard.

The pain didn't help; it just reminded him of that tattoo. He'd bite her all right, if she wanted it. He'd kneel at her feet, put his hands on her hips—soft, she'd be so soft—and turn her around. Slowly. Drag down those shorts to expose the full, fat curve of her arse, and sink his teeth so fucking gently into all that ripe flesh, until every inch of her was marked by him.

Then, obviously, he'd stand up, push her against the wall, free his greedy cock and spread her pussy open. Cram her full of him and rut until he couldn't see, burying his face against her neck, all that lovely skin so bare and vulnerable for him and, holy fuck, his dick was thick and leaking in his jeans and he really needed to stop this or they'd never get to the fucking radio station.

Slow and deliberate, he breathed in through his nose, then out through his mouth, a twisted smile curving his lips. He was officially using his old anxiety tactics to deal with an erection. His brother's laughter rang in his head, so real he almost turned around to see if Zain Bhai was there. But he didn't turn, in the end. Because Zain was never there.

"Nope," he muttered under his breath. "What we're *not* going to do is swing straight from horny to depressed." He rubbed a hand over his freshly trimmed beard—what? Every guy wanted to go out looking his best—and turned away from the window, since Dani wasn't around to spot the fucking baseball bat stuffed down his jeans. "Distraction. That's all I need, a distraction." He had a feeling he was going to spend this entire fake relationship looking for distractions, because Danika got impossibly prettier and sweeter and smarter and sexier every time he saw her, like a very sophisticated torture device.

But he wasn't going to think about that, not when he couldn't do anything about it just yet. He was going to think about . . . about all the things in this huge studio apartment he'd never seen before. Like the books and statues and the pink sticky notes on the wall. Like the countless plants packed onto windowsills and counters, standing tall in ceramic pots, hanging from the ceiling, even. He ran his fingers over the fine prickles of a nearby cactus, and when that didn't help, he wandered across the room to the bookshelf. It was made of some glossy wood, taller than Zaf and twice as wide, taking up the whole sunshine-yellow wall by the front door. He squinted at the titles, failed to find any he'd heard of, and gave up when he saw something called *Summa Theologica*, which didn't sound like English, Punjabi, or Arabic, and was therefore none of his business. Some of the shelves held glass jars, too, like fishbowls—but instead of water, they were filled with cut leaves and dried flowers and random crystals. He recognized lavender in one of the jars. Another held a teardrop stone that gleamed like the moon.

When Zaf and Zain were kids, their dad used to tell them stories about the moon, just before bed. Zaf should've flinched away from the memory, but he didn't. And nothing bad happened. Instead, for a moment, he thought about sharing it with Danika, and how she'd probably say something weird and wonderful like "Moons are eminently important. Your father sounds a very sensible man."

Or maybe that was wishful thinking. Maybe she'd be like everyone else, and say, "Your father and brother died at the same time, and then your mental health plummeted and your life spun out of control? Sounds awful. Tell me all about it, every gory detail."

That didn't seem likely. But it hadn't seemed likely with anyone else, either.

Zaf left the strange little bowls and moved on to the coffee table in the center of the room. It was small and sturdy and polished, with a golden statue of a woman planted dead center. The woman had a head full of curls, bees on her wrists and collarbones like tame pets, and a mirror in one hand. There was a marble cup of water in front of her, along with a little dish of orange slices. There were candles all around her, solemn white things with wax dripping at their edges and burnt-black wicks. It took him a moment to realize this was probably an altar, and he was gawking at it like it was a circus sideshow. Oops.

He turned away, moving on to the last oddity in the room: a wall of pink sticky notes beside Danika's desk. He studied them for a few moments, taking in the scrawled words and phrases, most of which he'd only ever heard from her mouth. Then he realized what he was looking at. This wall of sticky notes was Danika's brain.

Well, part of it. Probably a tiny part, considering how smart she was. Once, a few months back, she'd come into Echo looking kind of annoyed, and when he'd asked her what was up, she'd launched into a speech about thesis statements, specificity, and cissexist understandings of gender and family in an essay about something called Creolization. He was awed, not because he didn't understand most of the words—although, no, he didn't— but because he understood just enough to realize how quickly she was jumping from point to point. How many logical steps she didn't even feel the need to say out loud because, apparently, they were obvious to her. Kind of like how, if he were going to do a spin pass, he wouldn't consciously think about his sight or his hands or his wrists, because he wouldn't have to. He'd just *know* how to do it, and that would make him faster and sharper than someone who didn't.

Danika Brown was faster and sharper than a whole lot of people. And by the time he'd read all of her haphazard, sticky, pink thoughts, Zaf was grinning.

"Good Lord. I've never seen you so cheerful." Dani's voice came from the doorway she'd disappeared through. He looked up and found her standing there, transformed in a way he could only call impressive. The pajamas had been replaced by painted-on black jeans and some kind of tight, sleeveless top that did gravity-defying things to her chest—which he really could've done without. Especially since she was still wearing her usual black leather necklaces, and they disappeared between her epic cleavage like arrows to paradise. Her makeup was the glossy, shiny, heavy kind that made a woman's entire bone structure look different, the kind his niece had attempted last Eid before Kiran had seen her, frowned, and said, "Really, Fatima? Go up-stairs and wash your face."

Dani was much better at it than Fluff.

"Wow," he said. "You look . . ."

"Aggressively sexy and mildly terrifying?"

He paused. "Yeah, actually."

"Thank you." Her smile was privately pleased. Apparently, that was exactly what she'd been going for. He didn't know why, since they were going to be on the *radio*, but—

The *click* of her high heels cut through his thoughts as she stepped closer. "You like my Wall of Doom?"

"Your . . . ? Oh, the sticky notes?" He turned back to the sea of pink and felt another smile tug at his lips. He had no idea why the sight of her chaotic, almost-impossible-to-read handwriting and her brilliant, almost-impossible-to-follow thought processes fizzed through his mind like sherbet on his tongue, but they did. "Yeah, I like it. What's with the doom?"

"This is my preparation for the Daughters of Decadence symposium in a few weeks. I agreed to sit on a panel discussion about intersectionality in feminist literature, and, since my lifelong idol will be there, too, it's possible I'm overpreparing." Her shoes kept *click*ing, and Zaf looked down to study them. Silver high heels covered in little diamonds, her black-painted toes peeking out, tiny skulls lining the ankle straps. His smile widened.

Then her words sank past the adoring fog blanketing his brain. "A few weeks?"

"Mm-hmm. Eighteen days, to be precise." Dani was standing beside him now, tall enough to kiss, thanks to the heels. He would take advantage, only kissing was a slippery slope that might lead to his dick inside her when they should both be inside a taxi, and also—

"You never mentioned a . . . a symposium. Or the fact that you've been doing all this work to get ready."

"Of course I didn't. I bore you with my work often enough by accident. I certainly won't subject you to a mind-numbing speech about my quest to cover every topic that might come up on a panel you don't care about."

He stared. "Dani . . . you don't bore me when you talk about work."

She gave him a look that reminded him of a GIF his niece liked to use. The one that dripped pure skepticism, with the caption *Sure, Jan.*

"You don't," he insisted. "I mean, I wouldn't read the books you read, and I don't always understand the words you use, but I like your voice, and it's cool when you get excited about nerd stuff."

She blinked a few times, as if she'd just walked into a cloud of dust, then looked away. "Oh. Uh. Hmm. I . . . see. Right. Hmm."

If Zaf didn't know any better, he might think she was blushing. But Dani should already know how adorable she was. She should've been told a thousand times by a thousand different people, and the suspicion that she *hadn't* been was making Zaf feel personally offended.

"Anyway," he went on, brushing that spark of annoyance away. "If I'd known you were this busy"—he nodded at the chaos of the wall—"I wouldn't have asked you to come with me to-night." Because he knew her well enough to realize she'd rather be holed up in here like Gollum, stroking books and murmuring, "My precious."

But she looked at him as if he'd said something ridiculous and replied, "You didn't ask. I insisted, because you're my friend. You do know that, don't you, Zaf? That we're friends?"

Well—when she put it like that, yeah, he supposed he did. He'd always known. But lately he was starting to realize what friendship with Dani really meant, just how strong and deep and powerful it ran, how much she'd do to support the people around her. And he couldn't help but wonder how a woman who was so secretly, subtly lovely had gotten to a point where discussing romantic relationships put shadows in her eyes.

"Thank you," he said softly.

"I've told you about thanking me," she grumbled, but now he saw the discomfort and the sarcasm for what they really were. She was the sweetest person on earth, only she wasn't used to getting any of that sweetness back.

Which was a fucking crime.

"Are you nervous?" he asked. "About the panel, I mean?"

Her smile was more like a wince. "I'm never nervous."

"Sure. Who's your lifelong idol?"

Dani shifted on her heels like a little kid, her lashes fluttering as she looked down, her mouth curving into a just-can't-stop-it grin. "Inez Holly. She's one of fewer than thirty black woman professors in the UK, and her essay on the politics of desire changed my life, so I sort of need to impress her or I might die."

Something blossomed in Zaf's chest, as fresh and delicate as a flower, and it smelled like honey and candlewax. It smelled like Danika. "That is the cutest thing you've ever said."

When Dani was surprised, she looked especially catlike. She gave him that look now, lips pursed and brows arched, as if she was annoyed by her own astonishment. "Oh, piss off," she muttered, but he could tell she was blushing again. Precious, she was so fucking precious. The look in her eyes, a tentative, self-conscious pleasure, made him want to grab her and kiss her and never let go.

But if he tried it, they'd be late, so Zaf satisfied himself with sliding an arm around her shoulders and squeezing. "Is this panel thing open to the public?"

"Yes, indeed," she murmured.

"Want me to come?"

"No," she said instantly. But then, just as quickly, she looked up at him and blurted, "Would you? Why would you? You wouldn't. Would you?"

Well. That was interesting. "It's like cheering someone on at a match, right? I've got to come."

"Because I'm your fake girlfriend."

"Because you're my real friend," Zaf said, and meant it.

She flashed a bemused smile, as if she didn't understand him but wasn't willing to argue. "It'll be terribly boring."

"If you're talking," he said, way too honestly, "I won't be bored at all."

Her smile widened, so bright and beautiful, he felt like he was stepping into sunlight after months in the dark. And Zaf could say that with certainty, because he knew exactly what it felt like. Something deep inside him shifted and *thunk*ed and . . .

And if he didn't change the subject soon, he might do something foolish. He scrubbed a hand over his beard and checked his watch. "Oh. Crap."

She caught his wrist and angled her head to read the time. "We're going to be late."

"Not if we get a taxi."

"*Genius*, darling."

Even though he wasn't either of those things, the words curled around him like affectionate cats. They kept him warm as he and Dani ordered a cab and ran downstairs, as they drove through the city to the building Radio Trent shared. It was only when Zaf stood in front of the place, the evening breeze nipping at his skin and the light from the building spilling through its glass doors, that his warmth disappeared like smoke and memories bombarded him.

Shouted questions as he left practice, strangers stabbing at an open wound. Headlines, the smooth voices of sympathetic commentators, sober newsreaders mentioning his family's devastation in calm, measured tones during the sports update. Pictures of him and Dad and Zain, grinning side by side, posted in "tribute" by people who didn't even fucking know them, who couldn't feel it, who'd *never* feel it, but who wanted, for some twisted, suffocating reason, to be involved. And now here he was, voluntarily walking into a place full of people just like that, with nothing but a fake girlfriend and a polite request "not to discuss certain topics" as his shield. The fact that noth-

ing about this situation was safe or easily controlled slammed
into him like a big, panic-stricken fist. He felt his chest tighten,
felt the tide trying to pull him away, and why the fuck was this
happening when it had been so long and he'd been doing so
well and—

It doesn't matter. It doesn't matter. It's okay. Zaf caught his
self-recriminations by the throat, threw them aside, and focused
on making himself feel better, not worse. He knew what to do.
He'd done it countless times before. So he thought, as clearly as
he could, *Zaf. You're having a panic attack. But that's okay.*

Then he sank down onto the ground and breathed.

CHAPTER TEN

A lot of people considered Dani oblivious, but that wasn't true: she simply chose to ignore the things that didn't interest her in favor of the things that did. People, as a group, were therefore pushed to the back of her mind in favor of more relevant topics, such as snacks and poetry and panel research. But Zaf had a strange tendency to squeeze through the bars of her mental cage (which made no sense, since he was bloody huge) and stroll into her zone of focus like he belonged there.

Which is why Dani noticed the instant his breathing changed. It wasn't that she could hear it—not with her ears, anyway. They were on the pavement outside the boxy, modern building that housed Radio Trent's headquarters, the traffic behind them busy enough to drown out the sound of one man's inhalations. And yet, when that slow, steady rhythm faltered, Dani *felt* it, somewhere deep inside her own chest. Zaf sucked down his next breath as if dragging in the oxygen against its will, and she turned as if pulled. Then he bent down into a crouch, right there on the street, and she did the same without a second thought. It felt as if some shining tie was braided between them and if one of them couldn't stay upright, neither of them could.

"Sorry," he told her, his voice strained and rough as sandpaper. "Sorry."

"Don't you dare," she said softly.

"I'm just—I just need to—"

"You can tell me later. Right now, do what you need to do." Dani sat on her bum—some people didn't have the quad muscles required to crouch, thank you very much—and added, "If I can help, let me know. Otherwise, feel free to ignore me. I'll still be here."

He swallowed hard. "I'm fine, though. This is fine."

"Zaf."

"You're right," he said with a tight little laugh. "Not fine. Not fine at all."

"No," Dani agreed. "But no one can be fine all the time. So we'll stay here while you're busy being not-fine, and we won't move until you're done, and that's okay." It was ridiculous, it was babble, it was the best she could offer. But she saw the tremor in his hands and the worryingly pale gold of his skin, and for the first time in a long time, she wished like hell that she could offer more.

Zaf, meanwhile, went quiet.

At least she knew what *not* to do. When Zaf had mentioned his anxiety disorder, natural curiosity had led Dani to spend a few hours researching the topic. So she wouldn't grab him, or ask silly questions, or do anything else that might make him feel worse, and that was something, wasn't it?

Well, it was all she had, so she supposed it would have to be.

After a while, his breathing slowed, and his broad shoulders relaxed inch by inch. With every infinitesimal sign of release, the thick rope of concern wrapped around Dani's throat started to ease. Then Zaf opened his eyes and gave her one of his hard, impenetrable stares, the one that meant *I'm going to be a bit of an arse now,* and she knew he was back to his usual self and annoyed as always. She waited for him to say something brisk and grumpy and vaguely annoying. He opened his mouth, as if preparing to do just that. But after a long moment, he scrubbed a hand over his beard and sighed.

She bit her lip. "Are you okay?"

He grunted.

"Should I . . . cancel the interview? Because we can do that. If you want."

He stared at her, his expression unreadable. "Ten minutes before we're due to go on?"

"I don't care if it's ten seconds. Tell me," she said firmly, "and I'll go in there and tell *them.*"

After a long moment, his lips twitched. "Are you being nice to me right now? Because that's twice in one day. Would you also take me somewhere with coffee and cake and try your best not to bitch about the evils of caffeine? None of the cheap shit, mind. I know you've got money."

The spluttering noise she made was half amusement, half a sigh of relief. "If you can be irritating, I assume you're much improved."

"Yeah, actually. I guess, with some associations, you just have to . . . get through them. And if that's what's going to happen tonight, I'll do my best to handle it." His words were cryptic, his expression pensive, and she almost wanted to ask more questions. To learn what was going on inside his head, every tiny detail.

Luckily, before she could embarrass herself like that, he spoke again. "But you should know for future reference that I could be irritating with one foot in the grave."

Dani couldn't help it: she laughed. It was a quick, guilty bubble of sound—but then he smiled in response, slow and sweet like spilled honey, so she laughed some more, and suddenly he was laughing, too. They sat in the middle of the pavement, giddy and giggling and breathless like a pair of schoolchildren, and Zaf put an arm around her shoulders and sort of . . . leaned on her. Even though he didn't give her half his actual weight, it felt good. So good Dani forgot she was supposed to be laughing.

And then they were simply very close, and Zaf's eyes were very dark, and his face was very soft and very dear.

"You know what, Danika Brown?" he said.

She snuggled deeper under his arm, but only because she was cold. "What?"

"You're all right."

"Just all right? What a disgraceful understatement." But *all right* from Zaf felt a thousand times better than self-conscious compliments from someone else. *All right* from Zaf made her twinkle inside as if he'd made a night sky of her. Except people weren't allowed to make things of Dani, so she snorted and shoved him, and everything was easy again. "I hope our online stalkers aren't lurking somewhere, filming all this."

"Fuck 'em," Zaf said cheerfully, but she didn't miss the faint remains of wariness in his eyes. He caught her hand and hauled them both to their feet.

It was ridiculous to feel a little flip in her stomach every time he manhandled her, but apparently, Dani was a ridiculous human being.

"All right," he said. "We'd better go in." Except he didn't move. "Am I sweating?"

She pressed a hand to his forehead. "No."

"Feels like I'm sweating."

"Is that usually how it feels?"

He shocked her by answering with honesty rather than a roadblock of a grunt. "Yeah. You know when you exercise in the freezing cold, and your sweat is hot but your skin is like ice, and you can almost feel the salt?"

She nodded, pressing her lips together. There was a sorry little hollow in the space between her stomach and her ribs, and in that hollow lived a very sad gnome who was greatly displeased that Zaf struggled this way, but glad he hadn't been alone this time.

She hoped he wasn't ever alone.

"Feels like that," he said. "And then there's the whole lungs-clogged-with-water sensation."

"Oh. Delightful."

"And my stomach dropping out of my body like it's made of lead."

"Sounds ideal."

Zaf nodded solemnly. "Fan-fucking-tastic. Dan?"

"Yes?"

"Is this your version of being supportive?"

"Yes," she said. "You can probably tell it doesn't come naturally. I apologize."

"Don't," he murmured, so quiet she barely heard him over the passing traffic. "I like it."

Three words, and the familiar ache of not quite being enough vanished in a B-movie flash. "Oh. Really?"

Her heart pounded in time with the rhythm of his reply. "Yeah. Really."

Zaf might've been embarrassed about dealing with a full-blown panic attack in front of a woman he wanted to sleep with—*if* he hadn't spent the last couple of years developing a curriculum designed to teach boys that mental health struggles didn't make them less masculine, and that there was nothing wrong with being less masculine, anyway. So, once he pulled himself together, he felt nothing but familiar exhaustion, and the glitter of laughing with Dani, and a slight annoyance that he hadn't brought his antianxiety meds.

He'd handled things, though. He'd handled things *well*. So he'd focus on that. Or maybe on Dani, who was so pretty, he could stare at her all day.

Until she ruined things by asking hard questions like "Should we talk about the fact that you're nervous?"

Zaf sighed and made himself concentrate on words instead of the fine little creases at the corners of her eyes. "I'm not *nervous*. It's just, if I disgrace myself on the radio, my mother will beat me with a slipper every day for at least the next year. And I bruise like a peach."

She swept a laughing gaze over him. "You do look rather delicate."

"You have no idea." Questions and concern successfully dodged, as always. Now they'd leave the conversation there, go inside, and never, ever discuss exactly what had triggered him, because Dani wasn't his family or his forever, which meant she didn't need to know.

But she looked at him—just looked at him, with this quiet, conscious acceptance, as if to say *Maybe you're hiding the whole story, but if you need to, I'll let you.* And something about that look leaned on every last one of Zaf's pressure points—not in a painful way, not exactly. More like a massage that hurt really fucking good.

Maybe she wasn't family or forever, but she was a really good friend. Beneath his memories of moments like this going pear-shaped, one undeniable fact shone like a star: Dani didn't hurt people and she didn't make things worse. She always—*always*—tried to make them better. That must be why, for the first time in a long time, he wanted to keep talking more than he wanted to shut someone down.

He could trust her. He did trust her. He would trust her.

"The thing is," he said, "I'm nervous because, back when I

used to play, something bad happened. One day my dad and brother were in a car crash, and they, uh, died." He always stumbled over that part. Not because it hurt—although it really fucking did—but because it seemed so . . . small. So simple and flat and anticlimactic a phrase for something as monumental as death. You told people "they died," and hell was folded up inside those two short words. Some people got it. Some people didn't.

He knew the minute he met Dani's eyes that she did.

"Oh," she breathed, and caught both his hands in her own, as if she knew instinctively that once upon a time, he'd fallen apart—but if she just held him tightly enough now, the memory of it might be a little easier.

And it *was* easier with her hands on him and her eyes so soft and warm. Suddenly, he had no idea why he'd worried she might react the wrong way to any part of this story. Well, yes, he did: anxiety. That was why. But still. Dani was never going to treat him like a sideshow, because she was a good person. And if she had, she *wouldn't* have been a good person, so what she thought wouldn't have mattered anyway.

He'd never . . . he'd never quite looked at it like that.

"I was at practice," he said, steeling his spine because if he didn't, he might wobble, just a little bit. "My phone was off. But it was a big crash, locally, and there were a couple of sports outlets that paid extra attention to me—I don't know if you know, but there aren't many Muslim rugby players. It was a, er, point of interest." He rolled his eyes as he said the words. "Most of them were just waiting for me to fuck up. But anyway. I got more press than I technically should've, and when I left practice, there was a reporter waiting for me."

Dani's eyes widened. "Zaf . . ."

"He told me. He said, 'Zafir, how do you feel about the tragic death of your father and brother?'"

She pressed a shaking hand to her lips. "Oh my God. Oh my God."

"I broke his nose." Zaf paused. "That's what I heard, anyway. I don't really remember." He flashed her a smile, because telling this story shouldn't be sad; it was already too much to bear inside his head. "I was always surprised he didn't press charges, but—"

"But you would've been well within your rights to murder him, and he probably knew it," Dani snapped, rage flickering around her like flames, so intense he could feel the heat. He wasn't angry anymore, had worked hard not to be, but for some reason he liked seeing that anger in her. Maybe because it was for him. She was feeling for him, and it made him hungry for more.

Get a grip. He cleared his throat and continued. "Life went downhill from there. Everything fell apart, or maybe I ripped it apart with my bare hands. I don't know. I was kind of going through some shit." She laughed softly then, just like he'd wanted her to, and even more pressure slipped away. "I made some bad choices, wanted to fight the world. And for about a week, a few of those right-wing rags decided following me around was their new favorite thing. It didn't last long—I wasn't famous enough. But it felt like forever to me. So now, I guess, I'm a bit . . . private." That wasn't the full story, just a fraction of it. Because the press had left Zaf alone eventually, but grief hadn't. Not for a long, long time. He wasn't going to tell her about the heights his anxiety had reached, or how it turned out depression could fuel rage like nothing else, or how bleak it felt when the fire ran out and the demons were all you had left. Not right now, anyway.

But the unexpected lightness in his chest made him think that he could. Some other time, he could.

Which was . . . novel, to say the least.

"I see," Danika murmured, and he felt oddly certain that she did, at least a little bit. Her gaze was steady on his, and beneath the sadness, nothing had changed. There was no pity, no judgment ready and waiting to crush him. He was still himself, but the biggest relief was the fact that she was still Danika.

She would always be Danika. She would always be just fucking right.

Then she continued. "And I see what you meant, now, about your past, and not wanting to bring it into the present."

He shrugged, clearing his throat. "Yeah. Well, what you and me are doing, it's, er, changing associations, according to Fatima. Which helps."

"Changing associations," she repeated gently. "Interesting."

He arched an eyebrow, because he could practically hear her mind whirring. "Tell me what you're thinking."

"Just . . . I understand wanting to shift the narrative. But changing it completely—is that possible, in this case? I mean, your loss, and your anxiety, they're at the root of why you started Tackle It. Aren't they?"

He stared at her, unnerved by the ruthless way she drilled down into something he wasn't always comfortable thinking about. "Well—I don't know. Maybe. But it's not—I'm not going to parade my family's death like it's part of the organizational ethos." He realized he was sounding a little defensive, mostly because right now she reminded him of Jamal. And Kiran. And his own doubtful midnight thoughts, wondering if he was making the right decision by keeping things separate, or just the easiest one.

"Of course not," she replied firmly, but her eyes burned into him as if she saw things he'd rather hide. She put a hand over his chest for a moment, just the lightest touch, as if she'd needed to reach out and check his heart was still okay in there. "I was just thinking, Zaf, that . . . you're brave. Most people, when something scars us, we hide it. When you started Tackle It, you framed a scar in gold. Don't you think?" She waited, as if she actually thought he'd be able to respond to that.

Sorry, no. He was too busy trying to figure out why those words unraveled the knots in his chest so easily.

After a moment of silence, Dani shook her head and gave an embarrassed little laugh. "Sorry, that was . . . weird. Very weird."

"No. No, that was—" *Truer than I know what to do with, and I think I need a moment.*

"Inappropriate," she supplied wryly, "and dangerously close to maudlin." He could hear the discomfort in her voice, knew she hadn't meant to get emotional with him. Danika didn't get emotional with anyone, and usually, he'd lecture her about that—but right now, it didn't seem right.

Because Zaf was beginning to wonder if he had some shit of his own to sort through. When he'd started therapy, he'd been determined—*really* determined—to heal. To move on from a grief so huge that it might crush him if he couldn't find a way to fold it up and make it safe. He would never be over Dad's and Zain's deaths, but fighting the darkness in his head had been like . . . like his battle cry.

Was it possible to move on too hard? So hard you became afraid of even glancing back? He didn't know, and standing outside a radio station while his fake girlfriend tried to pretend she was the friendly neighborhood robot didn't seem like a good time to figure it out.

"Anyway," Dani was saying, "if anyone brings up your family during this interview, don't worry. I'll eat them."

That startled a smile out of him. "Good to know. Jamal pretended to be my publicist and outlined what they could and couldn't ask. So it should be fine, but . . ."

"But some people struggle with basic listening skills," she finished, facing his fears head on. "Well, I can promise you this: I'll be right beside you to misdirect whenever necessary. All right?"

She was too fierce and too smart to doubt. The only thing he could say was "All right." The only thing he could feel was relief.

"And," she went on, "I have something that might help your nerves. I mean, it always helps *me* when I'm nervous, so . . ." Dani's voice trailed off as she began fiddling with the mess of leather cords she always wore around her neck. Zaf had spent way more hours than was healthy wondering what hung off those cords. His current favorite theory was that she kept every engagement ring she'd ever been given, kind of like how Russian princesses used to sew jewels into their clothes before they fled the country. He'd read about that in an older romance novel he'd found at the local library.

A woman like Dani must deal with proposals at least once a month, and since she was mind-numbingly posh, all the rings were probably platinum-and-diamond situations from white guys whose great-great-great-great-grandmas once fucked Henry VIII. So when she pulled off the necklaces and Zaf caught sight of loose, colorful stones hanging from each one, he knew straightaway that his favorite theory was 100 percent wrong.

Which was fine, since he was about to learn the truth.

"Here," she said, disentangling a small, bloodred stone from the rest. "Just for the interview."

Zaf held out a hand for the swinging pendant. "Thanks . . ." he said slowly. "What is it?"

"It's a garnet. I wear it for my grandma Gigi—her name is Garnet—but it also brings balance, strength, courage. Good for career things." She dropped the cord into his palm where it curled like licorice. The stone was warm against his skin— warm from *her* skin. This was what she wore every day, tucked safely under her clothes like a secret? He looked up and found her watching him, her teeth sinking into her lower lip.

"You believe in this?" he asked.

She lifted her chin, her gaze sharpening. "Yes."

"I'm not trying to say shit," he told her.

The tension left her shoulders, but she shrugged as if she didn't care either way. He didn't believe it. Zaf was beginning to notice that Danika cared about more things than she let on, including him. The evidence was warm against his chest right now: she believed in this gem stuff, and she'd given him one, like sharing a slice of faith. That mattered. It mattered so much his bones ached. He put on the necklace, tucking the little red gem safely under his clothes. "Thanks," he said again, and this time the word came from somewhere deeper.

"You're welcome," she said softly, and for a moment he thought he saw the same hazy tenderness that filled him reflected in her eyes. But then she shook her head, standing a little straighter and flashing a little brighter, like Hollywood lights. "All right," she told him briskly, hooking her arm through his. "Let's do this. Don't forget: we are young and in love and boundlessly affectionate." As if she were an actor coaching herself before she went onstage.

But nothing—*nothing*—about the last twenty minutes had been acting. None of it had been performance, none of it had been fake. And suddenly, Zaf was gripped by the urge to pull her back, look her in the eye, and make her admit it.

The only thing stopping him was the knowledge that pushing too hard made things snap.

Ten rushed minutes later, Dani found herself seated on a surprisingly uncomfortable but chic-looking bench in a surprisingly well done but tiny room. Apparently, she was way behind on the norms of modern radio, because there was a camera blinking at them from the right, and the footage it recorded would, they'd been informed, eventually find its way to YouTube. Seemed like everyone had to diversify their income these days.

Luckily, Dani had dressed to impress one Zafir Ansari, so she looked generally presentable. And Zaf himself was always disgustingly hot, so no problems there. For a moment, when the teenage assistant had explained the filming element to them, Dani had worried it might trigger more anxiety for Zaf. But he'd touched the slight bump created by the garnet beneath his shirt and nodded.

A burst of something tender and possessive had hit Dani then, leaving her breathless. It was just as strong as the sorrow that had carved itself into her bones when he'd told her about his family. She'd wanted to kiss him. She'd wanted to cry. She'd wanted to tell the world how incredible he was, because he'd dealt with all that but look at him—*look* at him—he was still fucking going.

Only, she couldn't do any of those things, because they all seemed excessively passionate, and the only passions Dani typically permitted herself were sexual and professional. Anything else had to make it past the committee, and the board had not approved Feeling Intensely for Zafir. The board had approved Shagging Zafir, which, more to the point, was the only proposal Dani had actually submitted.

At that moment, Zaf's hand nudged hers on the cool, plastic surface of the bench, cutting off her thoughts. She looked up, met the dark honey of his gaze, and saw a secret smile, just for her. Pleasure zipped over her stomach, skating between her breasts, warming her from the inside out. Then he hooked his little finger over hers, a tiny connection hidden between their bodies, one the camera wouldn't catch—one even the radio presenter wouldn't see across the equipment-laden table—and Dani was forced to remind herself that Zaf was just getting into character. Method acting, or something. They were performing their relationship, and he was putting his all into this scene. Nothing more.

The music filling the room faded away as the presenter, a beanpolelike white man who was all messy hair and huge, horsey teeth, fiddled with a slide-y type thing on the table. Apparently, his name was Edison. Dani had never heard of him, as she preferred Radio Four.

"Allll right, then," he began, before nattering away about the song he'd just played in a smooth, dark-chocolate voice that didn't remotely match his appearance. With his oversized, raggedy jumper and enormous eyes, he looked like the ghost of a Victorian child shoved into skinny jeans.

Dani was in danger of zoning out completely to explore the parallels between Radio Trent's evening presenter and nineteenth-century children when she heard their pre-discussed cue. Which was, for the sake of simplicity, Zaf's name.

". . . Zafir Ansari, former rugby union flanker for our very own Titans, and his girlfriend, Danika Brown. These two have kicked up a storm recently as the social media sensation #DrRugbae. Welcome to the show, guys."

"Cheers, mate," Zaf nodded.

Having decided that feigning demureness was the best route

(until Zaf needed her to leap in and attack, anyway) Dani dimpled prettily and murmured, "Hello."

"So, how do you guys feel about the whole Dr. Rugbae situation? That first viral video—what was that like?"

"It was . . . unexpected," Zaf said ruefully. Dani had wondered if he'd clam up, but now that he'd gotten past his initial nerves, he was cool and collected and charming in a way he usually hid. If she were a stranger watching this, she'd think he was absolutely fine—confident, even.

But she wasn't a stranger. She felt the rigidity of his hand against hers, and knew he was concentrating so it wouldn't shake. She heard the rough edge to his voice, and knew he was uncomfortable speaking to so many listeners. She saw him rub a hand over his short, thick beard, and knew he'd probably planned this carefully, so carefully, but was still worried about the unpredictability of the format.

So Dani leaned into his side and pressed a useless, impulsive kiss to his shoulder. Then she wondered what the fuck she was doing and if she'd been briefly possessed by the spirit of a 1970s local politician's wife.

Zaf looked down at her, flashing the ghost of a grateful smile that melted her middle like gooey chocolate. And suddenly, kissing his shoulder—*faking casual affection*, rather—felt like the smartest, most accomplished thing she'd ever done.

Which, considering her general excellence, was really saying something.

"And what about you, Dani?" Edison asked. "How are you

coping with social media stardom?" He said the words with a wry irony she appreciated.

"It's . . . quite sweet," Dani said, which was an absolute lie. In reality, being a social media sensation for a week had started to feel slightly creepy. "I must admit," she added with a laugh, "I could do without the comments from women who want Zaf for themselves. He's otherwise engaged." That was Fake Girlfriend Dani talking, obviously, not Actual Dani. Actual Dani didn't care about that sort of thing because Actual Dani had no claim on Zaf whatsoever.

Something in her stomach lurched.

Zaf frowned down at her. "You shouldn't read those."

"And you should know very well by now, darling, that you can't tell me what to read." Although he was right, and after the third comment she'd come across describing how gross and bald she was, and how she and Zaf were disgracing and/or diluting their respective races, Dani had decided to return to her life-long avoidance of social media. She was lucky Gigi had coached all the Brown girls on the nature of fame long ago, just in case any of them ever followed in her show-biz footsteps—or, alter-natively, took part in *The Great British Bake Off* and got caught screwing Paul Hollywood in a field. That had been the example provided, anyway. Gigi was a firm believer in Paul's raw, animal magnetism.

"Just so everyone knows," Zaf grumbled, leaning closer to the microphone like an old man with a poor grasp on high-tech sound equipment, "I go through that hashtag every night and report anyone who says sh—*stuff*," he corrected himself, his scowl deepening, "about Danika. Or about us being together. And if I see any of you—"

Dani squeezed Zaf's hand and laughed loudly before he could threaten anyone with bodily harm on public record. He was clearly invested in the protective boyfriend role, because she could almost feel the heat rising off him. "Relax. What really bothers me is the hashtag itself. I'm not actually a doctor," Dani said. "I'm a Ph.D. student. So Dr. Rugbae isn't entirely accurate."

Edison burst out laughing, though she had an inkling his amusement was more frantic gratitude that she'd changed the subject. "There's a note for all our listeners—she's not a doctor, she's a *doctor in waiting*. Academic types are strict about this."

Her cheeks heated. Wasn't *everyone* strict about factual accuracy? They should be, anyway.

Edison chuckled some more, then moved on with impressive efficiency. "You two were filmed at work, during that famous fire-drill rescue. You're in security now, right, Zaf?"

"That's right." Zaf still seemed vaguely annoyed that he'd been prevented from issuing threats, but he was clearly trying his best to sound pleasant and interested.

"That's not all you're up to these days, though, is it?"

Oh, lovely. Edison was steering things quite nicely, and once you got past the haunted eyes of a starved Victorian infant, he seemed a friendly and capable man. Dani smiled beatifically and kept her mouth shut as Zaf launched into an explanation of Tackle It, while Edison, bless his soul—he was growing on her by the second—asked all the right questions and delivered all the right prompts.

While Dani had planned to cast her mind elsewhere during this segment—there was only so much interest she could feign for anything rugby related—she found herself strangely fascinated by the discussion. Perhaps because Tackle It was less about rugby itself, and more about equipping young men with the tools to understand their emotions and express them beyond the boundaries of toxic masculinity. Or perhaps it was because Zaf lit up with passion as he spoke, and the gentle glow she'd always been drawn to now burned from his gaze like the sun.

He was . . . wonderful. Brilliant and bold, especially when he said things like "I love sports, of course I do—but the culture can easily become toxic. It's not enough to say, *That's not me*. Like, all right, nice one, but what are you doing to fight it?" She'd always known his grouchy grump routine hid an unexpected softness—but she was starting to notice something else in him, too, a steady core that radiated strength and peace and other cool, immovable things. She heard it echoing in his voice when he said, "You'd never tell an athlete to just get over a sprain; you'd give them time to recover, physical therapy, whatever they needed. Why are mental health conditions any different?"

At one point, Dani realized with a blush that she was nodding along beside him like some sort of hypnotized acolyte. She stopped, of course. But as she leaned closer to him, like the tide drawn in by the moon, it occurred to her that she could think of no one she'd rather fake date. Whoever ended up with Zaf would have a partner to be dizzyingly proud of, wouldn't they?

Well, maybe. Or maybe the romance he prized so highly would go to his head and his desire for the ideal partnership would devolve into a toxic need for perfection that led him to ultimately and brutally betray his lover. Based on personal experience, empirical evidence, most literary canon, and plain old probability, that seemed far more likely than a boring, uneventful life of contentment and faithfulness.

Even if, for some reason, she couldn't quite envision Zaf in the role of Textbook Arsehole.

Most likely, then, he'd be the one who ended up hurt, all his sweet illusions shattering like glass. That possibility caused a discordant *clang* inside Dani that she found quite disturbing.

Eventually, the discussion of Tackle It was expertly wound down by Edison, and Dani waited for more music to be played so she and Zaf could be ushered away. Instead, the deejay rubbed his hands together menacingly—if the poor, juvenile victim of a centuries-old workhouse could be considered menacing—and said with obvious glee, "All right! Before we say good-bye to #DrRugbae, the team and I have cooked up a fun little game to find out if you guys are couple goals"—he pressed a button that created some sort of cheering effect—"or a total fail." Another button, this time with a boo.

Dani shifted in her seat, frowning over at Zaf. What on earth was this? No boos. She was too accomplished to be booed. And Zaf spent his free time teaching little boys how to feel, so he *certainly* shouldn't be booed. In fact, if anyone dared to boo him, she'd stick her stiletto firmly up their arse. Dry.

While Dani's temper continued to quietly unravel, presumably due to the stress of the unknown, Edison reached beneath his desk and produced two small whiteboards with dry-erase pens Blu-tacked at the top.

"So how this works is, I'll ask you questions about each other." He handed them each a board. "You write down your answers, then we see if they match. It's a bit like they do on *Love Island*—you watch *Love Island*?"

Zaf looked bewildered. "Er . . ."

Apparently, he'd completely missed that particular phenomenon. Fascinating.

"Never mind, never mind," Edison said. "Let's jump right in, shall we?"

Dani narrowly resisted the urge to say, *No. We shall not.*

At her side, Zaf veered with impressive speed from confusion to horror to unmistakable panic. Their eyes met, and Dani could almost read his mind. She'd bet money on him thinking, at this very moment, *How the fuck are we supposed to answer these questions when we're not really together? I haven't even shagged you yet.*

She tried to send back something along the lines of *All in good time. And at least you know about my arse tattoo.*

Perhaps the telepathy attempt didn't work, because he failed to laugh.

"Question number one," Edison said, blissfully unaware of his guests' simultaneous internal meltdowns. "We'll start easy. Zaf, how does Dani take her tea?"

Zaf stared. "So now I . . . ?"

"Now you write down your answer, Dani writes hers, and we see if they match."

Zaf looked dubious. "All right."

"Also, you have ten seconds." Edison flashed them a toothy grin, tapped a button, and a rather high-pressure clock noise filled the room.

"Oh, Christ," Dani muttered, staring at her whiteboard. She suddenly had no idea how she took her own tea—and, more important, neither did Zaf. If they were really together, he'd be able to answer this, wouldn't he? Oh *dear*. If a ridiculous game on a local radio station exposed their lies, Dani might just burn this place to the ground.

After a tense few seconds, she scribbled down her answer without much thought—since they were utterly doomed and absolutely nothing mattered—and waited with dread for the timer to end and Zaf to get this question hideously wrong. Really, it wouldn't be the end of the world, she told her racing heart. No one would hear them fail some radio game and come to the ludicrous conclusion that their entire relationship was a sham. But they might decide that Zaf was a shitty boyfriend, or that their relationship in general was shitty—how had Edison put it? *A fail?*—and for some reason, that idea bothered Dani severely.

"All right, time to share." Edison grinned. "Zaf, what's your answer?"

Zaf flipped his board, looking distinctly uncomfortable. "Green. She, er . . . well, she doesn't drink regular tea. But she drinks a lot of green tea. So. Green."

Dani stared.

Edison was clearly horrified that she drank anything other than breakfast tea, but he hid it well. "Dani, what's your answer?"

She flipped her board.

And now Zaf was the one staring.

"Green tea!" Edison said cheerfully, when it became clear Dani wasn't going to.

She was feeling rather dazed, actually. A rush of relief and a flash of surprise combined to intoxicate her, until she returned to her senses and pulled herself firmly together. *Of course* Zaf knew she drank green tea. When she brought him coffee, he teased her about the contents of her own cup. And really, what was tea, anyway? Minor, that's what. Practically public information. There were people Dani *despised* who knew her tea preferences.

Of course, those were usually people she'd worked with in close quarters, people who'd been forced to actually make her said tea as a matter of courtesy when it was their turn to be on kettle duty. But still.

Still.

"Next question!" Edison appeared to be enjoying himself. Either he had the intellect of a puppy, or he was unusually invested in #DrRugbae. Dani suspected, with no little discomfort, that it was the latter. "Dani, what's Zaf's favorite flavor of crisps?"

Well, she knew *that*; she'd seen him eating them often enough. Dani scrawled *salt and vinegar* onto her board and flipped it over before the ten seconds were up. What sort of relationship quiz was this if two work friends could win so easily? Although, some might say she and Zaf were a little more than work friends these days. Coconspiracy tended to intensify a relationship. Perhaps they'd leveled up to general friends, or some other platonic relationship status that explained the magnetic pull she felt sitting beside him, as if every second she spent not looking at him or smiling for him or laughing with him was a second wasted.

Perhaps they were *best* friends. How cute.

More questions flew by, all of which were answered correctly. But Dani refused to be impressed that Zaf knew her favorite season—autumn—and she wasn't remotely happy with herself for remembering that he preferred dogs to cats. He had once told her, over the security desk, that cats were sneaky creatures who hid their toilet business, and an animal that hid its toileting could easily make a habit of pissing behind your sofa, and you wouldn't even know until you died of ammonia inhalation. Really, when he'd displayed such an unexpected passion on the subject, how could she forget?

"All right," Edison said finally. "Last question. Zaf, what is Dani's area of academic interest?"

Those words popped Dani's buoyant mood like barbed wire—which made very little sense, because they were doing well enough to excuse a single mistake. Zaf answering this question incorrectly shouldn't throw any real doubt on their relationship. Ph.D.s were slippery and frequently boring things.

"Zaf, show us your board!"

In fact, this time last year, Dani might have struggled with such a question herself. It was a tricky—

"Race and gender in the West after slavery," Zaf said.

At which point, Dani released a garbled sound of astonishment, one that sounded like a cross between a cough, a burp, and a squawked "*What?*," into the ears of the entire city.

Zaf shot her a look of concern, as if he suspected she'd accidentally swallowed a passing pigeon. Which would be quite a feat, considering the room's lack of windows.

"Dani," Edison said patiently, "what's your answer?"

Slowly, she turned her board over. "Evolution of misogynoir post–chattel slavery,"

"That's close, right?" Zafir looked inordinately pleased with himself. He actually smiled, a big, beaming grin that made him achingly handsome, all white teeth and dark beard and lovely, lovely mouth. But she mustn't get distracted by the mouth. In fact, for once, she *couldn't* be—she was too busy staring at his whiteboard in astonishment. There it was, in black and white: a valid understanding of her general thesis topic.

"How did you know that?" Dani demanded in a whisper.

Zaf arched an eyebrow. "You think I don't listen when you talk?"

"When I'm rambling about work? I was absolutely certain you weren't listening, correct."

"Yeah, well." He tapped his lovely nose and looked smug.

"Zaf, that's almost the title of my most recently published article." In line with her twenty-year plan toward professorship, Dani had, of course, secured bylines in minor academic journals over the past few years.

"And now you think you're the only one who knows how to use a library."

Her voice reached dolphin pitch. "You've been *reading* my *articles* at the *library*?"

He shrugged, and she got the impression common sense had broken through his competitiveness, because he now looked slightly hunted. "Er . . . yeah. I mean, they're interesting."

Interesting?

It wasn't that Dani didn't find her own work interesting—of course she bloody did. She had to, or she might have stabbed herself in the throat with a ballpoint pen by now. And she knew very well that lots of other people found her work interesting, too. It was just . . . well. She'd never *been with* one of those people.

Not that she was *with* Zaf. But still. Even Dani's *sisters* didn't read her papers. The only friend who did so was Sorcha, and that was because Sorcha had studied a similar field at undergrad. No one outside Dani's profession had ever withstood her disjointed ramblings about literary theory and come away with a burning desire to learn more about it all. She simply wasn't as fascinating as the written work itself, as evidenced by the number of dates who had gently informed her that she was more boring than thrilling in long-term conversation.

Back when she still did silly things like date, that is.

So Dani couldn't think of a single damned reason why Zaf would carry himself to the library to read her essays. Then he slid one big, warm hand over the nape of her neck, squeezed, and said, "Don't look so surprised. You know I love your brain." At which point, Dani stopped thinking of anything at all. Her throat dried up like the desert, and tiny darts of sheer, sun-lit happiness zipped through her blood, and her eyes prickled oddly hot at the corners because—actually, she didn't know why. All she knew was no one had ever said a thing like that before.

And Zaf, she realized abruptly, wasn't saying it, either. He was lying. He was performing. He was faking it.

"Well, *that* was adorable," Edison cooed, dragging Dani rudely back to earth. She tucked her stormy confusion away and hoped her expression on camera hadn't been too shocked, or alarmed, or bewildered.

Meanwhile, the deejay continued. "And there we have it, folks! Zaf and Danika, aka #DrRugbae, are most definitely couple goals."

Edison was getting on her nerves, all of a sudden. Back to the workhouse with him.

CHAPTER ELEVEN

Zaf wasn't the only person in the world who'd noticed Danika was kind of a genius. He couldn't be. For one thing, she had a B.A. and an M.A. and they were letting her get a Ph.D., and that didn't really happen by accident. For another, journals published her articles, which meant they got it, too. So it must be the people in her personal life who were oblivious dipshits. Clearly, none of them appreciated her enough—not if Zaf admitting he'd read her work was enough to make her wide-eyed and stutter-y.

He only understood about 60 percent of the things Danika wrote, but even that 60 percent made him feel smarter. More interesting. Educated, and all that good shit. She was talented, damn it. Why was no one reading her stuff?

"You're brooding," she told him.

Zaf looked up. They were standing in her kitchen, steam rising between them from the boiling kettle. As soon as they'd gotten home, Danika had changed into pajama shorts and that nearly translucent white T-shirt that reduced his concentration to tatters. Barefaced and barefoot, arranging mugs and teaspoons, she looked . . .

She looked like a fantasy he had no business entertaining. Not when she'd made it clear the only relationship she'd bother with was a fake one.

She arched an eyebrow at him as she poured the hot water, and Zaf remembered they were talking. Or Dani was talking, and he was staring at her mouth like some kind of sex-starved animal. Which made sense, since he felt like one.

"Brooding's kind of my thing," he told her, and she laughed.

"Is that what the heroes do in those books of yours?"

"For someone who isn't interested in romance, you ask a lot of questions about it."

She rolled her eyes—*which isn't an answer, Danika*—handed him a mug, and wandered off toward the living room. He followed, and they sat down on her vast, purple velvet sofa, side by side. Close, but not close enough. She could never be close enough. His hands always ached to touch her, and tonight was no different—fuck, tonight was *worse*. But he wasn't about to mention it. Changing into pajamas and making tea didn't really scream *Plough me, Zafir*, so he wasn't sure if their whole gentleman's-agreement thing was still a go. If he wasn't twice her size and strong enough to throw her around, he might be pushier about it.

But he was both those things, so he kept his hands to himself and looked down at his mug, eying the murky liquid skeptically. "Dan. There're plants in my tea."

"Tea is a plant, Zaf." Her tone was severe, but when he looked up he saw her lips twitch.

"Are you trying to poison me?"

"It'll help you sleep."

"Don't start complaining about my sleeping patterns," he snorted, "or I'll stop answering your texts at two A.M."

"I'd know you didn't sleep even if we'd never texted."

"Oh, yeah? Why's that?"

Instead of pointing out the bags under his eyes, she said, "You have the energy of a newborn baby."

He spluttered.

"Which suggests that you are, amongst other things, pure of heart and always hungry."

"I don't know about that first part."

"And tired," she continued. "You're always tired."

She wasn't wrong. But she *was* soft—her voice, her eyes, her words—and that softness wrapped itself around his heart like a blanket.

Don't think like that. I promise nothing good will come of it.

"While we're on the subject," he said, "you don't sleep great, either."

"I'm a machine," she said airily.

"No, you're not." The words were fiercer than he'd intended. "You're a human being, and staying up all hours of the night isn't good for you, any more than it's good for me. If you can sleep, you bloody well should."

The eyeroll she gave was dismissive, but he knew the way the air crackled when Dani was thinking. And she was thinking, right now, about everything he'd just said. But all she did was mutter, "Drink your tea."

Like an obedient puppy, he bent his head and inhaled. Caught lavender and spices, heat and comfort. "Can I ask you something?"

"When people start with a question like that, it usually means they're about to be rude."

His lips quirked. "I'm not trying to be."

"Well, in that case," she drawled.

Zaf tried his tea, enjoyed it more than expected, and sipped again. Then he nodded at the little table in front of them—the one with the golden goddess and the orange slices. "This statue, the tea, the garnet you gave me." He'd given it back, but he still felt the phantom pressure against his chest. "What's all that about?"

"I'm a witch."

"Oh," he croaked after a moment. "Witch. Okay." *Crap.* Knowing Zaf's luck, she'd received the mystical equivalent of a push notification every time he thought about her tits. "So how does that, er, work?"

Dani sipped her own tea, clearly hiding a smile. "It depends, really. It can be very personal. For me, my Nana—my maternal grandmother, Rose—she was an obeah woman. It's a spirituality that started with enslaved Africans in the Caribbean, so it has a lot of influences and variations, but . . ." She trailed off, her eyes distant in a way that told him thoughts were arcing through her mind faster than lightning.

"Is that what you do?" he asked, nudging her gently. His knee brushed her legs, which were curled up beneath her like a cat's.

She blinked back to him. "Oh—hardly. It's passed down through generations, but I was never interested in learning, not until Nana died and left me her statue of Oshun. And then, of course, it was too late." Dani flashed a smile Zaf recognized: the kind that hid grief and longing and regret and a secret wish for five more fucking seconds. Five more seconds with the person you'd lost. "I sort of cobbled things together on my own, after that, so I could feel closer to her. I'm a hodgepodge of modern witchiness, I think. Whatever feels right. Whatever feels real."

You. You feel so fucking real to me. Zaf held out his hand, and Danika took it. The braid of their intertwined fingers, the pressure of her palm against his, lit up the shadows inside him. If this touch could take away a fraction of her sadness, too, then his right hand had never been so useful.

Which, considering how often it had wanked him off recently, was saying something.

"Oshun and I get along well," she continued, nodding at the statue. "She's the goddess of beauty, purity, abundance, and"— she flicked a glance in his direction, and suddenly the curve of her mouth and the sweep of her lashes became a slow, hot tease—"lust," she finished, her tongue flicking against her upper lip. "Which is why I asked her to send me you."

Funny thing about the human body: it went haywire so fast. Dani's words shot through Zaf's veins like liquid pleasure, his heart pounding like a war drum against his rib cage. In the space of a second, his cock became the center of the universe, and it fucking ached. *Lust.* He'd thought she'd changed her mind, which would be an absolute travesty, but the look in her eyes said she hadn't. She hadn't. Thank fuck.

Zaf needed to sleep with her so he could stop wanting her so bad. Needed to take the edge off, to know the unknown, because unfulfilled desire had her on his mind 24/7.

Kiss me. Cure me. Please.

Danika gave his obvious hard-on a satisfied glance and murmured, "Well, that's encouraging. I thought you might be too tired."

He stared at her in disbelief. "Too tired for you? Aren't you supposed to be the smart one?"

She laughed, and just when he stood a chance of gathering actual human thoughts for a moment, maybe holding a coherent conversation to follow that *I asked for you* thread, she ruined everything by rising up on her knees and straddling his lap. Just like that, he couldn't move. He might've forgotten how. She sank down like soft, fluid sin, her incredible arse smothering his dick, her fingers digging into his shoulders, and the tips of her breasts brushing his chest, and Zaf shouldn't be able to feel her nipples through both their clothes, not really, but, holy fuck, he could.

And judging by the flutter of her pulse at her throat, the spilled ink of her blown pupils, she felt something, too.

Just as his options narrowed to either kissing her or exploding, Dani arched an eyebrow and looked pointedly over her shoulder. "Are you enjoying that?"

Only then did Zaf realize he'd grabbed a healthy handful of her arse. Apparently, he *did* remember how to make his limbs move, but only for important things. Fair enough.

"Yeah," he said honestly, and squeezed some more, his hips jerking up into her soft, warm weight. He could feel the little ripples and dimples of her skin, could feel her tattoo, the lines of ink slightly raised, and maybe it was the fact he now knew what Danika Brown's arse felt like, or maybe it was the sound of her breathing heavy and the way she pushed against his hand, but Zaf's dick felt like it might break in two. He was leaking precome so slow and steady, he wouldn't be surprised if he soaked through his jeans.

"Well," she said graciously, "if it helps you concentrate."

"It does," he lied. "So. You . . . asked for me?" He had to clarify, because it was possible Dani's magic tea was slightly hallucinogenic and he'd only heard what he secretly wanted to.

"I asked for the perfect fuck buddy," she said, "and various signs pointed me in your direction."

Zaf stared. "You prayed for a fuck buddy."

"That is correct," she said calmly.

"You do realize," Zaf told her, "that you're . . . you."

"Me?" A smile played at the corner of her lips.

"Yes, you. Danika fucking Brown. A woman who does not

need divine assistance finding someone to shag on a regular basis." People should be lining up for her attention. He'd always imagined she lived like a fertility goddess: appear to a village of cowering mortals, choose the hottest one, crook a finger. Like that.

But for some reason, Zaf acknowledging her perfection— even slightly—made Dani uncomfortable for the first time all evening. She looked away, that teasing smile fading to something more serious, her fingers fiddling with the seam of his shirt. "Well," she murmured, "that's rather flattering. And I do know I'm wonderfully attractive."

Now he wanted to laugh, or kiss her, or both. Of course she knew. And of course he loved that she knew.

"But I'm not the easiest person to get along with," she continued. "And—"

"Aren't you?"

She faltered. "Pardon?"

"Aren't you? Easy to get along with?" Because he'd never had any trouble.

"No, Zaf, I'm not. And I don't want to be. So relationships aren't my thing, but sex definitely *is* my thing—"

Thank fuck for that, because if he had to let go of her arse anytime soon, he might actually cry.

"—and I think you can give it to me. No strings attached."

No strings attached? *Ha.* Zaf had never had casual sex in his fucking life. His relationships so far had been *made* of strings, and they'd only ended due to incompatibility, not because he hadn't wanted them to last. But Dani was in his blood, and this was the only way he could have her—the only way he should want her. And the only way she wanted him.

That thought shouldn't hurt, so he didn't let it.

"Zaf?" she whispered, her eyes searching his face. Waiting.

"Yeah," he said softly. "No strings. I can do that." *I hope.*

Her smile was pure sunshine. "Good. I do have some conditions, just to make sure we're on the same page."

"Okay, but I can feel my actual pulse through my dick right now, so I don't think I'm legally compos mentis."

She grinned, leaned closer. Now her tits were pressed hard against his chest, and her mouth was brushing his ear, and he might be having a heart attack. "I'll be clear, then. One: make me come. Two: don't catch feelings. And three: don't spend the night."

Well, that was a fucking cold shower. Not that it made his dick relax or anything—at this point, a horse tranquilizer probably couldn't do that—but it did punch a hole through the lies he'd told himself, laying the truth of his feelings bare. No matter how hard he rationalized this, Zaf was barreling headfirst into meaningless sex with a woman he'd accidentally started to adore. Which most people would consider, at best, *bad.*

And he still wasn't sure that sex *could* be meaningless. Not for him, anyway. Did that make him a liar, or just a trier? Shit.

A question spilled out before he could think better of it. "Why are you so against relationships?"

He felt her cool and stiffen into iron. "They don't agree with me."

"I'm not trying to say you're wrong," he added quickly, squeezing her hip. "You know what you're doing, Dan. And I respect your choices. I'm just . . . wondering." *I want to know the parts of you that aren't on display.* But only because he'd shown her a little of himself, earlier, sharing the details of his past. He wanted this friendship to be balanced. That was all.

Zain's voice rang through his head, full of stifled laughter. *Lying is haram, little brother.*

Yeah, well.

Zaf's words seemed to relax Dani, because she stopped giving him a death glare and shrugged, her lips pursed. "I've attempted romantic relationships before, and it never ends well. I don't have the necessary qualities to make a 'good girlfriend.'" She made air quotes around the words, rolling her eyes as if that would hide the vulnerable edge to her voice. "I'm too work-focused. I don't say the right things, or remember romantic little anniversaries. I find excessive affection obnoxious and I don't enjoy putting other people's priorities before my career and my family. These facts tend to disappoint prospective partners, and I'm too busy to deal with someone else's disappointment or the punishment that comes along with it. So I avoid the dynamic altogether."

Zaf frowned. "But that's . . ."

She arched an eyebrow.

"That's not how relationships should be," he finished, thrown a little off-balance. She'd said those words with such flat, empty hopelessness, as if this was a lesson she'd learned the hard way. As if it was a simple fact that love would ask too much of her, and so she wouldn't or couldn't try. He wasn't sure if the look in her eyes was weariness or an echo of something sharper, harsher. Either way, he didn't like it.

"I know," she told him slowly, as if explaining something to a child. "I don't do things right, and I don't think I want to. It all seems awfully dull and inconvenient. That's why I've chosen to abstain."

"No. I meant—priorities that don't match, punishments for being yourself, that's not how a relationship should be."

She opened her mouth, then closed it. Apparently, he'd surprised her.

"People harp on about compatibility for a reason. If you value family and work, you just need someone who feels the same way, someone who admires that about you. If you can't do the sappy shit, you just have to find someone who's okay with that. Someone who understands how awkward you are—"

"I beg your pardon?"

He ignored her. "—and loves it. I know you have a busy life, but you make room for the stuff that matters. If it was worth it, and you wanted to, you could make room for a relationship, too. What you get out of being loved, it's supposed to be worth the compromise. When it's good, it makes you *want* to compromise."

She eyed him steadily for a moment, her expression unreadable. But something about the line of her mouth, the slow rhythm of her breaths, told him she was thinking. Hard.

In the end, though, it came to nothing. "I have no idea how you aren't married yet," she murmured, studying him like he was some kind of exotic insect. Then she sighed and shook her head, as if brushing away fairy tales. "Maybe you're right. Maybe there's some lucky individual out there who's just dying to spend forever with a bookish workaholic who wants to vomit at the prospect of romance, but I don't care enough to bother searching for them. I'm not interested in the, er, transformative power of love, or what have you. I don't need it. I know what I want from life, and I know how to get it."

Each word landed with a thump in Zaf's chest, like a series of death knells, though he couldn't say exactly what was dying.

I know what I want from life, and I know how to get it. "So do I," he said softly.

Dani nodded. "We're not that different, you know, even if we're facing opposite directions. I don't want to waste my time looking for a diamond in a pile of shit. And you don't want another unhappy ending."

Another. The way she looked at him, as if she saw his every fear and secret hope, was almost enough to make Zaf sweat. He still wanted to chase away the ghosts in her eyes, but if that meant she got to chase his, too . . . no fucking thank you.

Besides, he hadn't been lying when he'd said he respected her choices. Didn't mean he had to like them. But he respected them, because he respected her.

"I accept your conditions," he said finally. "But I have a couple of my own." Needed them, he realized, if he was going to come out of this unscathed.

"Hit me," she murmured. Then she wiggled on his lap, and he narrowly avoided biting off his own tongue. "Quick."

"First: we can't do this forever."

She arched an eyebrow. "Forever isn't really my thing."

"I know." His cheeks heated. "I meant . . . maybe, since we

put a deadline on the fake relationship, we can put a deadline on this, too." That would save him from stumbling over boundaries or breaking rules he'd never learned. Dani was so committed to this no-strings shit, she'd actually *prayed* about it—and Zaf knew from experience that when you started praying, it meant you were deadly serious or about to die or both. The last thing he wanted to do was embarrass himself by holding on too long.

She eyed him carefully, and if he caught a flash of disappointment in her gaze, it was either wishful thinking or a protest from her sex drive. "All right. Once our charade dies down, you'll probably get back to looking for your one true love, anyway. I wouldn't want to get in the way," she said wryly.

The idea that Dani could get in the way of *anything* felt wrong—wrong enough to wrench at something vital in his chest. But she'd made a good point, one that tied up their loose ends neatly. "We should end this when we end the fake relationship. We'll have to stage some kind of breakup around then, anyway." Which Zaf had managed to avoid thinking about until this moment. "It'll be good timing. Which gives us . . . three weeks."

"Three weeks," she echoed. "I can work with that."

"Good," he said, but it didn't feel good at all. He pushed away nameless, shapeless misgivings and pulled her closer, where she belonged. "I have one last condition." Because there were a thousand things he wouldn't push her on, but this? This was different. "I get that you want casual. But as long as we do this, Danika," he murmured, "no one touches you but me."

She swallowed hard, but to his relief, she didn't argue. When she nodded, something vicious inside him sang to life. "Only you," she whispered.

It was terrible, how perfect those words sounded on her lips. Dangerous, how much he wanted to hear them again, in a thousand different ways.

This might be the best bad idea he'd ever had.

CHAPTER TWELVE

Dani bit her lip and tried to look sexily expectant as opposed to painfully, desperately horny. It wasn't easy, not when Zaf was watching her with a focus that shivered its way across her skin. Not when she could feel him, thick and hard, between her thighs. Not when every inch of her shook with a lust so obvious, she was considering throwing her whole, treacherous body out with the recycling tomorrow.

She was unraveling for him, as if she *needed* him, and the intensity of it made her feel alive and horribly exposed all at once. It was dangerous, to be like this, to crave like this. It had to be. But then she realized that Zaf was unraveling, too, and suddenly things weren't so bad. Through the fog of her own hunger, she noticed the heavy rise and fall of his chest, the way he wet his lips as if he'd been thirsty for centuries and she was an oasis. He reflected her own frantic need right back at her, and Dani's worry faded until only anticipation was left, dancing through her stomach like starlight. *Only you*, she'd said, and the words had seemed to vibrate with something like power.

Which was probably a spiritual pat on the shoulder from Oshun. You know: *Well done for taking the hint, darling! Now take an orgasm or two, as well, so you can stop whining all the time.*

Dani was mentally promising to do just that when Zaf's free hand rose to cup her nape, and her thoughts scattered.

Then he kissed her.

This wasn't like their first kiss: that had been a test, a surprise, and technically, a fake. It hadn't *felt* fake, not when he'd taken her apart piece by piece with each cautious stroke of his tongue, but still. It hadn't been for them, not really—it had been for show. The same went for their second, short kiss at the security desk, even if that had felt . . . different, at the time.

But this? This was so real and so raw, Dani might have flinched away if it wasn't so fucking *good*.

Zaf's mouth was lush and firm against hers, sending electric shivers racing up her spine. His free hand cradled her cheek, and his thumb pushed at the edge of her lips, coaxing her to open wider, to take his tongue deeper. He was always so gentle with her, so unassuming, that she'd never expected his lust to fill the air like rich humidity—but it did. He surrounded her, his taste in her mouth and his hard cock between her thighs, and she wanted to succumb.

When his other hand kneaded her arse with shameless hunger, heat flooded her pussy in response. She rubbed her swollen nipples against the solid breadth of his chest, rocked her desperate clit against the crude ridge of his erection, and helpless need rose in her like the tide. His tongue slid across the tender seam of her upper lip, and she felt that trembling pleasure in her cunt. He pulled her hard against him, and she felt the damp fabric of her underwear draw tight over her folds. Fuck. *Fuck.* Thirty seconds of making out on the sofa like teenagers, and she was already fighting the urge to shove him onto his back and sit on his face.

Oshun, I'm sorry I ever doubted you.

Even sorrier that she had him for just a few weeks. But she wouldn't think about that right now—wouldn't remember the odd pang that had hit her when he'd laid out his first condition. Like she'd said, Dani didn't do forever.

A strange melancholy nipped at the heels of her lust, but then Zaf bit her lower lip and squeezed her jaw—just enough to say, *Me. You're with me. So come back.* And she did, delicious tension squeezing her core, desire pooling thick and sweet as honey.

Faintly, she murmured against his mouth, "Are you a sex wizard?"

His laughter was strained, as if he didn't have enough air in his lungs to do it properly. "No. But I've been thinking about this for a long fucking time."

Her breath hitched in her throat, and she pulled back slightly. "How long?"

"Long enough," he said, low and rough, "that I've thought of a thousand ways to kiss you. So let me."

Let me. She slid her fingers into the raw silk of his hair and pulled him closer. He slipped his hands under her shirt, high enough to cradle her ribcage. And then he stopped.

"Touch me." Her voice was tight with need.

"I want to take this off," he rasped, tugging at her T-shirt.

"So take it off. And take yours off, while you're at it." She dragged at his shirt, and then they broke apart enough to fumble with their clothes until they were both bare-chested and panting. Zaf was as gorgeous as she'd known he would be, big and strong and golden, with a wealth of chest hair that arrowed down to the bulge in his jeans. His eyes seemed almost black as he watched her, his lips slick and parted. He looked like sin and sex and hers.

"Fuck, Danika," he breathed, his fingertips skating over the stretch marks on her hips. "You're so . . ."

"What?"

"Beautiful," he said softly, so softly she almost didn't hear. Wanted to pretend she *hadn't* heard, because the word shook with a reverence that shouldn't be there, that shouldn't fill her up inside. She'd never been so conscious of her own breath before, of the rise and fall of her tits and the shift of her lungs and the movement of her belly. But everywhere Zaf looked at her felt realer than before—almost too real, teetering on the line between intensity and discomfort.

Dani liked walking that line, if the wet fabric clinging to her pussy was any indication.

Zaf's palms slid up over her rounded belly, and then his thumbs caressed the sensitive undersides of her breasts.

"Christ," she groaned, pleasure igniting over her skin.

"Like that?" Their gazes held as he stroked his thumbs over her tight, needy nipples. Then he pinched gently, and sweet relief sparked through her, quickly followed by even more tension than before. She leaned forward, pressing her brow against his, trapping them both in a world of heat and skin and soft, slow moans.

"Tell me," he murmured, rolling her nipples between finger and thumb. "Tell me you like it."

Each quick circle tightened the coil inside her so violently that she could barely speak. "Yes," she gasped as he kissed her jaw. "Yes, I like it." Pleasure pulsed through her clit until she had to slide a hand beneath the waistband of her shorts.

She felt his lashes flutter against her skin as he looked down.

"Are you touching yourself?" he asked, an edge to his voice that sounded like urgency.

She spread her legs wider and eased her middle finger through hot, slippery folds. "*Yes.*"

"Want some help?" His voice was slow, velvet sin.

She rubbed her clit frantically, her breaths labored. "Fuck, yes. Please."

"Stand up, then." He leaned back, watching her like an animal waiting to strike. She stood and shoved off her shorts and her underwear in one fast, thoughtless, unsexy move, and his jaw clenched so tight she worried it might break. His hips lifted, just a bit, as if he'd started to thrust against thin air and had barely managed to stop himself. "Turn around," he said, his voice like iron.

She turned, and saw her altar, and the statue of Oshun, and thought, *Thank you, universe, for sending me—*

Meaningless sex, she ought to have thought.

—Zafir, her mind supplied.

If she'd had another second, her lust-soaked brain might've sobered in surprise, and she might've realized that it wasn't normal for her entire body to be on fire for one person, wasn't normal for his voice to thrill her as much as his touch did, wasn't normal for his hands to squeeze her heart as much as, you know, her tits.

But Dani's mind never got the chance to hurtle down Danger Avenue, because Zaf was still talking in that strained, hungry, *God, I want you* voice. "Bend over," he ordered, and she leaned forward at the waist until she heard his low, tortured groan. Closing her eyes, she imagined what he could see: the curve of her arse, the hint of her swollen, glistening pussy.

Then she felt his big hands on her, his fingers digging into her hips. "What's with the tattoo?" he asked.

She flushed at the reminder of the words inked onto her arse. "Undergrad. Sorcha."

"Ah." Since Zaf had met Sorcha a few times, that was probably explanation enough. She felt his teeth graze her skin, biting gently, as per the tattoo's instructions. Something in her stomach clenched like a fist. Then cool air hit her sensitive folds, and the vision in her head changed: now he was holding her open, exposing her ruthlessly, and he'd see more than just a hint. He'd see her cunt, soft and wet for him, and—

One of his hands slid between her thighs, his finger nudging her clit. Dani's whole body jerked, so hard and so sudden that he wrapped an arm around her hips to keep her still.

"*Fuck.*" The word shuddered out of her, as unsteady as her legs. She put her hands flat on the altar and bit her lip.

Zaf tapped her clit again and murmured, "Good?"

"So good," she gasped, rocking back. "Fuck, Zafir."

His finger, wet with her want, circled her clit with brutal slowness, and whatever scraps of cool she'd been clinging to disappeared.

"Oh my God, Zaf, just lick me or fuck me or something, I need to come so badly—"

"Can you do something for me, love?"

"Anything, I promise, I'll—just—"

"If you like it," he said softly, "scream." And then he put his mouth on her.

At which point, Dani realized it was entirely possible, maybe even *likely*, that Zaf had sold his soul to some dark god in exchange for incredible oral sex skills. If so, Dani thoroughly supported—indeed, approved of—his decision.

The man didn't just lick her; he practically fell inside her vagina face-first. Which was a lot sexier than it sounded. His tongue slid through her folds like warm, wet silk, his beard rasped against the tender curve where her thighs met her arse, and his finger worked her stiff little clit so firm and fast that if he stopped, she might kill him. She'd at least try. She'd smack him over the head with her statue of Oshun, probably, because the feel of him burying his face in her pussy was fucking intoxicating, and his tongue made her knees weak, and the arm he wrapped around her upper thighs was the only thing keeping her upright.

"Please," she panted, words rushing out like a fall of shattered glass. "Zaf, please." He rubbed his tongue over her cunt with deliberate, ruinous decadence. The twist of need inside her grew tighter and tighter, until the pressure was just too much. She did exactly as he'd asked: she screamed.

The sound was short and sharp and shaking, her orgasm hard and unescapable. It ripped through her on a wave of sheer ecstasy, then stuck around, sinking into her bones even as her muscles turned to liquid. Zaf's tongue stroked her softly through each aftershock. And then, when her knees finally gave out, he caught her in his arms and stood.

Dani screwed her eyes shut as her stomach flipped. "For heaven's sake," she mumbled, each word shivering and breathless. "I am in too delicate a condition to be thrown around right now."

"Delicate, hmm?" Zaf sounded amused and . . . smug. The bastard. "I better put you to bed," he said mildly, at which point Dani discovered heretofore unmined reserves of energy.

"Yes." She grinned, opening her eyes. "You'd better."

"On it."

With his eyes gleaming hungrily and his mouth swollen and slick, Zaf looked like exactly what he was: an unholy tool of sexual devastation, also known as Dani's greatest fantasy. He shouldered his way into her room, dropped her onto the bed, and then stripped off the rest of his clothes with little fanfare.

"This is very efficient," she said as his trousers disappeared.

"I have a one-track mind."

"I approve."

He laughed and took off his underwear. Now he was gloriously naked under the glow of her bedside lamp, prowling toward her like an advancing god. He had a broad, heavy body, with amber skin dusted by pitch-black hair, but Dani found 100 percent of her attention sucked up by his cock. Which was appropriate, since she'd like to suck his cock. It was thick and dark and curved slightly to the left, the head shining with pre-come, a fine vein pulsing along the underside that practically begged for her tongue.

"Gosh," she blurted, blinking hard. "That's . . . your . . . penis."

"Yep." He looked down at himself, frowning a little. "Er . . . this isn't your first one, is it?"

"No," Dani squeaked. She was simply experiencing a moment of mild alarm because . . . well. She didn't think she'd ever wanted anyone quite this much.

Of course you have. You must have. These were just sex chemicals, dopamine and other traitorous substances making her feel oddly attached in the heat of the moment. God only knew what would happen when he put his dick in her. Maybe she'd lose her mind.

And maybe none of that mattered, because Zaf lay over her then, and the skin-to-skin contact felt like sinking into a warm bath after a long day, and Dani quite lost her train of thought.

He traced the line of her jaw and whispered, "You still with me, sweetheart?"

"Al—" She broke off just in time, her voice caught in her throat.

Always. That's what she'd been about to say. *Always.* The word sat in front of her, too bright and awful to look at, like a ray of sunshine through the blinds at 6 A.M. What in God's name was that? Had she fallen asleep in front of a Hallmark film recently and absorbed its bullshit into her subconscious? Dani swallowed hard, bit her lip, and remembered she was sex-drunk. Yes. Chemicals, et cetera. Zaf's tongue was basically a drug. She'd been over this.

He watched her with a furrow between his thick eyebrows that she suddenly wanted to kiss. "Dan?"

Don't panic. Everything is fine. But she needed to change the subject, both internally and externally. Which, in this case, meant licking her palm and reaching between their bodies to grasp his cock.

He choked out a moan and his hips jerked. He was so smooth, so hot, so hard. Addictive. She swept her thumb over the fat, swollen head and watched his eyes snap shut. "Danika," he said, the word ragged. "Fuck. That's good."

That's good. She liked that, coming from his mouth. Liked putting that agonized look on his face, liked the way his control dissolved. This was what she wanted from him. This was *all* she wanted.

"Tell me what else is good," she murmured, and stroked him, slow and deliberate, drinking down the way his muscles tightened.

"Yeah," he grunted when she twisted her wrist. "*Yeah.* Harder."

She squeezed, he growled. Before she knew it, he was kissing her, hot and aggressive, his teeth tugging at her lower lip. She kept stroking him, and the faster she jerked his dick, the more he fell apart. Soon he was making hoarse, breathless sounds, catching her wrist with one strong hand, begging her, "No more. Don't make me come before I get inside you."

She pouted and ran her thumb lightly along that fine, raised vein.

"*Ungh*. Fucking hell, Danika."

"What? I stopped." She tapped his arse, about to tell him to get up so she could search for condoms. Then she realized his arse was *incredible* and, firmly distracted, grabbed a good handful. "Mmm. I like this."

"I like yours. Get up and show me."

"You're so bossy."

"Only works because you like it."

She gasped in mock outrage and pushed him off her. But she also arched her back for him as she bent over the bedside table. Zaf, both wonderful and predictable, palmed her arse immediately. He cupped one heavy cheek, squeezed, then slid his hand sideways until his thumb glided through her wet folds. She finally found a condom just as he pushed inside her, forcing a breathy little moan from her lungs. "*Zafir*."

"Yeah?" His thumb massaged a spot that sent raw pleasure surging through her blood. She must have made some unholy sound—though she couldn't be sure, since she lost a little awareness for a moment—because he laughed softly and said, "Ah. There."

"God, you sound so smug."

"You have no idea." He eased out of her pussy—which was tragic in the short term, but good in the long term since the current goal was to get his cock in there—and caught her hip, tugging her back onto the bed. "Condom?"

"Here."

But Zaf didn't accept the little square of foil; instead, he cradled her jaw in his hand, his thumb tracing Dani's own wetness over her lips. She slid out her tongue to taste, and the next thing she knew she was sucking the digit deep.

Zaf moaned. "You look fucking good with your mouth full, Danika."

She released him with a pop. "If you think that's good, you should see how I look on your dick."

He laughed, the sound low and strained. "I'd like to."

And yet, she had the oddest feeling he was stretching this out—touching her here or there, playing her like an instrument while trying not to come, as if he didn't want any excuse for this to end.

Or maybe she was projecting. Because, although her pulse pounded *more, more, more* and her pussy grew softer and wetter, just for him, she didn't exactly want this to end, either.

Calm down. You have almost a month to shag him senseless. That's more than enough.

It is. It is. It's more than enough.

She pushed him onto his back and straddled his thighs, ripping open the condom and rolling it on as he hissed out a breath. Tension rippled through his body at her touch, muscles flexing before her eyes, skin flushing with heat, and it was all so . . . so intensely Zaf, and so perfect because of it.

"Now," he told her. "Dan, please." He cupped her breast, ran his palm down the length of her body until it curled around her hip. "I need you here."

She bit her lip and crawled over him, needing it just as much. Moaned when he parted her sensitive folds with his thumbs. Obeyed, breathless and eager, when he ordered, "Put me inside you."

Then she sank onto his hardness inch by inch, until she was achingly full of him.

But she still wanted more.

In the moment before they joined, a warning siren screamed at the back of Zaf's mind. Just the usual sensible bullshit, reminding him that he actually wasn't that great at keeping sex physical, and that catching feelings was kind of his MO. Zaf listened to the sirens for a second, then decided he wouldn't mind being eaten alive by unrequited adoration if it happened *after* he felt Danika come on his dick. Apparently, this was how he made terrible sex-based decisions: with total enthusiasm.

Then she took him inside, her pussy tight and wet around his aching cock. Her moan was a whimper, his breaths were the gasps of a drowning man. Their eyes met—and when searing tenderness burned him just as hot as lust, Zaf knew he'd made a mistake. Because after months of wanting Dani, he had her, and the hunger wasn't fading. It was already stronger. So strong it threatened to crush him, or worse, to crush the dam he'd set up against all his forbidden feelings.

Ah, shit.

She planted her hands on his chest, rolled her hips, and the ecstasy on her face . . . he would kill to see her look like this, to *make* her look like this, and she was just giving it to him. How was he supposed to live the rest of his life like a normal human being when he knew the texture of her skin, knew the tiny, pale stretch mark that arrowed through her left nipple like a lightning bolt through a dark berry? This was what the word *intoxicating* really meant: Danika trusting him to touch her, wanting him to touch her, and choosing to touch him.

But only for now.

She rose up, and the slick squeeze of her cunt chased that single, hopeless thought away. Then she sank down again, her tits bouncing as she used him, her brows drawn together like she needed this as desperately as he did. She was spellbinding, she was fucking him so good he couldn't think straight, and when she gasped, "God, Zaf," that warm, velvet voice stroked him like a touch. He'd heard her say his name a thousand times, but not like this. Never like this. He drank in the sight of her spread open by his cock, saw her plump clit peeking out and rubbed it gently with his thumb. Then he sucked in a breath as her cunt spasmed around him, gripping him so tight he almost lost it.

"Fuck," he managed, once he could speak again. "Perfect. You're so perfect."

Her breath caught, and she looked down at him with wide eyes. "I—"

"Sweetheart. Don't argue with me right now."

Her surprise softened into laughter. Then he stroked her again and her giggle cracked right down the middle, her eyes glazing over with lust. "Don't come," she gasped, as if she could feel the tension building at the base of his spine. "Oh my God, not yet, don't come, don't stop."

He gritted his teeth and took a deep breath and tried to obey. Then she leaned forward and kissed him, her breasts rubbing his chest, her weight anchoring him, and all he could think was *Mine*. Something deep inside him cracked beneath a tidal wave of lust, something that had once been called *control*. Zaf wrapped his arms around her and found he couldn't let go. He felt almost feral, trapping her against him, trapping himself inside her, and when she moaned into his mouth, a shaking, shuddering sound, the hunger, the possession, the desperation got worse. His hips twisted as he fucked deeper inside her, and she rocked against him, her hands tugging at his hair.

"Baby," she panted, and this time it wasn't fake. Nothing right now was fake. The vulnerability in her voice, the shameless need, was so real it almost hurt—and it was all for him. "Baby, please, I need more."

Anything. He'd give her anything. Especially when it was this damn good.

He repeated his hard upward thrusts and held her in place so she could do nothing but take it. Again, again, again, and then she screamed and tightened so impossibly around him, he didn't have a hope in hell of holding back. His orgasm tore down his spine and through his aching balls, his come releasing in hot, almost-painful spurts.

All he saw was Dani, all he tasted was her kiss, and all he felt was her body shaking for him as his world spun off its axis.

CHAPTER THIRTEEN

Zaf's dick had Jedi-mind-tricked him.

That was the only explanation. Because now that he'd actually slept with Danika Brown, it seemed painfully fucking obvious that sex was not the magic pill to cure him of his attachment to her. As a matter of fact, without the months-old fog of lust clouding his brain, he saw quite clearly that his feelings for her were honestly out of control.

And those feelings couldn't be described as friendship. Friendship was there, sure, but so was something else, something dangerous, a bloodred poppy of affection trying to bloom in his chest. He absolutely adored this woman—and he'd just agreed to be her no-strings friend with benefits for the next three weeks. Clearly, he had the intelligence of a rock—a small pebble, a little chip of fucking *gravel*—because on what planet did intimacy ever cure anyone of affection?

Especially affection like this. Bright and beautiful and wild and terrifying, just like a forest fire.

Beside him, she murmured dryly, "Orgasms are meant to relax you, Zafir."

He turned his head on the pillow, met her soft, tired eyes. Felt a punch of dizzying warmth, a soul-deep possessiveness, a tender pleasure that made him want to smile. And he'd thought this was a crush. He'd thought *this* was *a crush*.

Seriously. Intelligence of a fucking rock.

"Seems like I do things backward," he told her.

She smiled, all plump cheeks and white teeth, and he felt it in his chest. Beautiful, so beautiful, he couldn't fucking breathe. "Backward," she said. "Sounds like you."

Yeah, it did. Backward, like developing feelings for a friend and only noticing *after* you swore to keep things platonic. Barbed wire wrapped its way around his heart.

What the hell had he done?

"Hey," Dani murmured. "Are you okay?" She raised a hand, hesitated, then touched his cheek. Just a brush of her fingertips, but the sensation smacked into him like a fist. He caught her wrist, swallowing down a thousand pointless words, and wondered why she was doing this, anyway. They'd finished ten minutes ago. She'd been to the bathroom, he'd fetched her water from the kitchen. She should be throwing him out, not lying beside him, all soft and naked and warm, touching him as if she gave a shit. This should be pissing him off.

It wasn't.

"I'm fine," he told her, because if he said, *I'm realizing my feelings for you are way too intense and I never want to leave,* she might panic and smother him with a pillow.

She arched an eyebrow and tugged her wrist free of his grip. "Sure. That's why you've been scowling at the ceiling like it shit in your slippers."

Despite the churn of emotions in his chest, he couldn't help but smile. "Where do you come up with this stuff?"

"My sterling jokes? Why, I find them on the back of chocolate bar wrappers like everyone else."

Reckless tenderness took over his brain, and the next thing Zaf knew, he was kissing her. It was sweet and soft, lazy and gentle, her taste ambrosia in his mouth. She raked her fingers through his hair as if she owned him, and fuck, he wished she would. If this was any other woman, he'd say, *Let me convince you to be mine.* He'd say, *Let me learn you.* He'd say, *Do you feel that? We could have something.*

But Dani didn't feel it, and he couldn't make her, and sticking his tongue in her mouth seemed like the opposite of accepting those facts. He needed to get away from her addictive warmth, needed to think, even if all he wanted to do was stay here and stay mindless.

When Zaf pulled back, she was smiling. Then he blurted, "I should probably go," and that smile cooled and hardened into something sharp and silver.

"Oh," she said. "Yes. Yes, you should." The words were calm—but her voice held a slight, embarrassed edge, and her gaze slid away from his. Like maybe she'd forgotten her own rules there for a second, and he'd just reminded her.

Ah, shit.

"Unless," he said quickly, "you don't want me to."

She sat up, turning away from him. A second passed before she looked over her shoulder and met his eyes again—and in that second, all the uncertainty had vanished from her gaze. Maybe he'd imagined it in the first place. Maybe he was made of wishful thinking.

"I'm far too tired for another round, so yes, I want you to go." She stretched lazily as she stood. "No offense. I hope you haven't forgotten the rules already, darling."

Yeah, right. Those rules were the only lighthouse he had in the storm of his own feelings, and right now, he should follow that glow all the way out of Dani's flat. *Should* being the operative word.

"I haven't forgotten," he said quietly, grabbing his clothes off the floor as she threw on a robe. He felt like throwing a farewell ceremony when she covered that magnificent body, but now didn't seem like the time. "I was wondering if maybe *you* forgot. For a moment."

She shot him a sarcastic look as she sauntered out of the room. "Oh dear."

"What?" He zipped up his jeans, threw on his shirt, and followed.

"Already searching for excuses to stick around?" She reached the front door and leaned against it, a teasing smile playing at the corners of her lips. "Why do I get the feeling you're falling tragically in love with me as we speak?"

"No idea," Zaf lied, planting his hands against the door, one on either side of her shoulders. "Why do I get the feeling you'd be terrified if I was?"

Her chin lifted. "I hope you're not psychoanalyzing me, Zafir. The last person who tried that ended up defenestrated."

"Which means what, exactly?"

She arched an eyebrow, slow and sexy as fuck. "Keep looking at me like that and you'll find out."

"Looking at you like . . . this?" he asked, holding her gaze. "Do I make you uncomfortable, sweetheart?"

Dani stepped closer, moving away from the door and into his chest. She was a head shorter than him, but there was steel in her eyes and confidence in her smirk, and he felt like they were players squaring up before a match. "I'm never uncomfortable, Zafir," she whispered. "I lack the necessary social awareness, and anyway, in case you hadn't noticed, I'm kind of a badass."

"You're impossible, is what you are."

She cocked her head, shooting him an incandescent smile. "You say the sweetest things."

"Why do I want to kiss you so badly right now?" The question was more for himself than for her. In fact, he hadn't meant to say it aloud—it just rushed free on a breath of frustration. He should be horrified, or panicking, or *concerned*, at the very least, by his affection for a woman who didn't want it. He should be leaving fast enough to make tracks on her shiny floor.

Instead, he was seriously considering fucking her all over again. On the aforementioned shiny floor.

No, Zaf. Stop that. He couldn't process his emotions and shit while he was balls-deep in the source of his conflict. That much seemed obvious.

"You want to kiss me," Dani said, "because I'm incredibly good at it."

"Your middle name is modesty, right?"

"Close." She grinned. "My middle name is honesty." But then she sobered. "This is how people work, Zaf. We want what we want, and we get it however we can, and when morals or ideals or promises get in the way, we say *fuck it* and push right past."

He didn't want to agree with that kind of cynicism—not even now, when he was ignoring the warning sirens in his head in favor of the ache in his cock. So he slid his hands beneath her short robe to cup her arse and pulled her close until they were pressed together, their heavy breathing in synch. "There's nothing immoral about the way I want you, and what I promised was three weeks of making you come. So say the word, and I'll take you to bed again."

Danika tilted her head back, rising up on her toes until her lips brushed his. "And fall asleep right after," she murmured, "and snore all night like a big bear, and develop delusions of romance in the morning because you read too many novels."

A reluctant smile curved his lips. "I'm not that easily carried away, you know. I won't forget what this is."

"Good," she said. "Now bugger off."

He laughed, and kissed her cheek, and let her go. She practically shoved him out the door, and as soon as he was alone in the hallway—as soon as he was without her—the confusion he'd been looking for crushed him like a brick wall.

I won't forget what this is.

Fuck, he was such a liar.

The thing about mental health was, you couldn't take a course of antibiotics and be magically healed. Some people's brains just thought too much or felt too much or hurt too much, and you had to stay on top of that. Zaf, for example, would always be an anxious motherfucker—which was fine. He'd learned to handle it. And, like he taught the kids at Tackle It, taking the time to work through your feelings was never a bad thing.

Unless working through your feelings involved walking home from a friend's house after she'd screwed you senseless, coming to terms with the fact that something about her made you wonderfully, dangerously silly.

Zaf shoved his hands into his pockets and watched the cracks in the pavement as he moved. Fact was, he had . . . *feelings* for Danika Brown. Soft, mushy, *I need you* feelings that made him want to hold her hand, or introduce her to his mother, even when she was threatening him with words he didn't understand. The problem: Dani didn't *want* his feelings. In fact, she didn't want any of the things Zaf wanted, which made him wonder how he'd managed to develop this attachment in the first place. Weren't you supposed to prefer people who shared your core values, or whatever the fuck? Yeah, that seemed right. And yet, here he was, pining after a woman who'd never be interested. Typical. Bloody *typical.*

It wasn't like he could convince Dani to change everything she believed and be with him for real. She was a person, not a doll or a character in a book, and expecting something she hadn't offered would feel like . . . It would feel like trying to change her, like saying what she had to give wasn't enough. But it was. Their friendship, it meant something. It meant *everything*, because it was from her.

Which was why he couldn't do the sensible thing and cut her off completely. Avoiding her would probably stop these feelings getting any worse, but for fuck's sake, he didn't *want* to avoid her. They worked together, and they were in the middle of a fake relationship, here, and he'd promised her three weeks of sex, and—and who the hell was he kidding? None of that shit mattered. None of it. He just didn't want to go without her smile.

Zaf stopped in the middle of the street, rubbed a frustrated hand over his beard, and glared at a passing car, just because. Then he decided it was officially time to call Jamal.

Fuck, he'd never hear the bloody end of this.

But when he dialed Jamal's number, no one picked up—which meant he'd either gone to bed earlier than usual or was dead in a ditch somewhere. Zaf racked his brain for their last conversation, remembered calling his best friend a pretty-boy twat with his nose in everyone else's business, and decided to mentally rewrite that as something more poignant and loving. Then he reminded himself sternly that not everyone in his life was doomed to die (well, they were, but hopefully not yet) and called Kiran's number instead.

After a few rings, *Jamal* answered the phone with a gruff, irritable, "What?"

Well. That was unexpected.

Actually, no it wasn't.

"Who's this?" Jamal grumbled, and Zaf realized he hadn't said anything yet.

His surprise wore off, and he felt himself smile. "Why are you answering Kiran's phone?"

Jamal's sleepy tone vanished. "Zaf?"

"Yeah. Bet you wouldn't have picked up if you'd noticed it was me, you shit."

In the background he heard Kiran's voice, faint and yawning. "Jamal, who's that?"

"I only came over for dinner," Jamal said quickly. "Your mum was there. But we went upstairs to talk, and then we fell asleep—me and Kiran, I mean. Not me and your mum."

"I should bloody well hope not. Are you ignoring her?" Zaf asked, sounding vaguely threatening and trying not to laugh.

"Am I ignoring your mum?"

"No, dipshit, Kiran. I just heard her ask you a question. Are you ignoring her right now? Because I really don't appreciate that."

There was a pause before Jamal sighed. "You're fucking with me, aren't you?"

"Who, me? Never. Now piss off and let me speak to my sister."

"God, you're a dick." There was some fumbling as the phone was passed around. Then Kiran's voice floated down the line.

"Stop tormenting my suitors," she said dryly, "or I'll beat you."

"It's not torment. It's just my personality."

"Shut up." There was a pause, and her next words were hesitant.

"Jamal and I have technically been misleading you about just how often we speak. I asked him to—"

"Lie out his arse, yeah, all right."

"I just didn't want to put any pressure on . . ."

"I know," Zaf said softly. "It's fine."

"Really?"

"Obviously. Your business. Actually, you can't see me, but I'm jumping for joy."

"That sounded extra sarcastic, so it must be true."

Zaf's lips twitched into a smile. Of course, the smile might have been wider if the night's events weren't still weighing on him.

Sleeping. Jamal and Kiran had been sleeping, and judging by the acidic bite beneath his happiness, Zaf envied them. He tried to imagine ever falling asleep beside Danika and drew a big fucking blank. His steps echoed down the empty street, his shadow stretching ahead, dark and alone.

But then he remembered the feel of her fingertips brushing his cheek, that moment of perfection, trapped in amber, when it almost seemed as if she cared for him. Not the way she had a month ago, or even a week ago, with that sweet but strictly friendly concern. He'd seen something different in her eyes . . . And she'd almost let him stay. He could swear she'd almost let him stay.

"Zafir? Are you okay?"

"I'm fine," he murmured. *Or falling apart. One of those.*

"You're quiet," Kiran said.

"Thinking. But I really am fine. Better than fine. I'm glad." Because Kiran had been through the absolute worst—the fucking *worst*. But here she was, trying again. It reminded Zaf why he loved this romantic shit so much: because it was all about hope, about finding sparks of light in a world that could be so fucking dark. And there'd been a time in his life when the promise of hope and light were the only things keeping him anchored.

"Kiran," he said, "are you in love?"

He could practically hear her blushing. "Well—I—"

"I'll take that as a yes."

"Oh, shut up," she muttered.

"Were you scared?"

There was a pause before she answered, her voice soft. "Of course I was, Zaf. I'm still scared now. A little bit of me is always scared. But I was also terrified that this might never happen. That I'd never . . . move past the loss. The thing is," she told him, "feeling is always worth it."

Feeling is always worth it. The words were too true to ignore. After Dad and Zain had died, the family had spent so long numb with grief. Now the idea of stifling his emotions on purpose felt like a sin. He couldn't do it. He didn't want to. And maybe that was okay, because things couldn't grow without water or light, and there was no way in hell Dani would ever water him. So he'd keep his desperate, aching feelings to himself, and then three weeks would pass, and their deal would end, and Zaf would get over all this.

He didn't have to kill the scarlet poppy in his chest: it would die naturally. Because pining after someone who only wanted him for sex had to be the definition of an unhospitable environment.

There was no need to overthink, or panic, or fix things: he was just going to let shit happen. Go with the flow. No more uptight

Zafir. His old therapist would be shitting herself with pride. He was making a good decision, here. He definitely was.

"You know what, K?" he murmured. "Thanks."

He could hear his sister's bemusement through the phone. "For what?"

CHAPTER FOURTEEN

Dani had a problem, and it had started last night.

She'd known exactly what she and Zaf were doing—right up until the moment he'd called her perfect. It shouldn't have mattered. It *didn't* matter. She was willing to bet that a large percentage of the nation would call her perfect when she was in the middle of providing them with an excellent orgasm, and really, who would blame them?

The trouble was that, for a moment—high on sex chemicals and dopamine and whatnot—she'd *believed* Zaf. And she'd liked it.

After coming to her senses and throwing him out, she'd lit a candle for Oshun and spent a short while meditating. Dani had meant to focus on setting positive intentions—you know, as in: *I intend to enjoy my new friend with benefits until his tongue falls off.* But Zaf's voice kept sneaking its way into her head, shattering her concentration with sweet, nonsensical rubbish.

There's nothing immoral about the way I want you.

Why do I want to kiss you so badly right now?

She went to bed in a foul mood.

By lunchtime the next day, her temper had fermented into violent urges. When they met for their usual fake lunch date, and Zaf greeted her with a smile that turned her muscles to jelly, Dani fantasized briefly but passionately about throwing a chair at him. When he bought her a Coke and made her laugh, she seriously considered pushing him into a fast-moving river. The knowledge that these feelings were unreasonable did little to make them stop.

"Fluff says our hashtag engagement is declining steadily," Zaf whispered between mouthfuls of his baked potato. The food court was quiet today, so they were risking strategic updates.

Dani looked up sharply, jolted from a daydream about biting his arse. "Really? Declining?"

"Steadily," he repeated. "But I think that's normal, after a week." Then he frowned. "Actually, I don't know what the hell I'm talking about, so I could be wrong. Do you think it's normal?"

"I—I don't know," she stammered. Social media moved quickly, that was just the way of things. So why did she feel a flare of panic, a sudden determination to stretch this "viral moment" out a little longer?

Probably because they'd agreed to stop having sex when they ended their fake relationship—so if they ended things *early*, Dani would be unfairly deprived of dick. Yes, that must be it. Zaf was so good in bed, she'd feel cheated if she missed out on her allotted three weeks.

But he clearly didn't feel the same, because lunch was almost over, and he had yet to suggest a repeat of last night. Usually,

Dani would bring it up herself—she had needs, after all, which was the whole point of this bloody arrangement. But various sex chemicals had made her slow to boot him out yesterday, and he'd latched on to that fact with disturbing enthusiasm. If she came on too strong now, he might get the wrong idea again, and then she'd have to horribly disappoint him.

"We're still benefiting from the popularity," he was saying, oblivious to her inner (sexual, purely sexual) turmoil. "Donations are increasing daily."

"That's great," Dani murmured, and meant it. She smiled when he told her about the connections he was making with local schools. She nodded when he described the funding budgets he'd applied for from bigger trusts. She absolutely did not fantasize about shoving their food off the table, climbing across it, and kissing him senseless, because that would be ridiculous. Public kisses could not lead to orgasms, and she was in this thing for the orgasms.

Unfortunately, lunch ended without Zaf offering another one.

By the time Dani returned home on Wednesday evening, she'd decided Zaf's lack of interest in sexual shenanigans was actually a good thing. Her schedule was far too busy to accommodate daily boinking, anyway. The symposium was less than three weeks away. She had seventeen days left to prepare for a panel discussion with the one and only Inez Holly, so a calm, quiet, Zaf-less night sounded absolutely ideal. Definitely conducive to research.

Unfortunately, for some reason, Dani found she couldn't get much done.

While she sat at her desk and stared blankly at the Wall of Doom, the sunlight through her window grew richer and sank lower, throwing long shadows across the room. At some point, she got up, rummaged through the freezer, and threw some vegetarian nuggets in the oven. Ate them. Sat down again and continued to be useless. Briefly considered dunking herself in a saltwater bath to exorcise whatever demon of mediocrity had occupied her body.

And then, just as the sun's last rays died, Zaf called.

"Hey." His voice was low and rich and comforting, whiskey and maple syrup.

"Hi," she said, pushing her necklaces aside and rubbing her chest. There was an odd sensation beneath her breastbone that might be heartburn. "Is everything all right?" He didn't usually call her. She called *him*, during her five-minute rest breaks, because he knew better than to possibly interrupt her work.

"Yeah," he said. "Everything's fine. Except for the fact that you were kind of weird today."

Dani swallowed and twitched one of the pencils on her desk. "No, I wasn't."

"Yes, you were. Is it because you had a great time last night and you want to lock me up in a sex dungeon forever, but you're scared I might get the wrong idea?"

She stared at the phone for a second before putting it back to her ear. "Did you . . . did you just read my mind?"

When Zaf spoke, she heard the hint of surprise he was trying to hide, knew her response had been unexpected. "Nah. That's just the reaction I'm used to after sex."

She snorted. "Sure. And when was the last time you had sex, Mr. Happily Ever After?"

"Last night," he said.

"Smooth."

"Shut up. Danika . . ." His words became slower, more serious. "Just so you know, I've been thinking that maybe—maybe I should let you take the lead, when it comes to our friends-with-benefits situation. You know," he added, "since you're the one with the rules. And since you're already doing a lot for me, with the fake dating, and everything. Seemed like I shouldn't ask for too much. So. That's why I didn't mention it today."

Yet again, it was as if he'd read her mind. Actually, it was as if he'd kicked down her mental front door and riffled through her metaphorical knicker drawer, which was, among other things, extremely rude and profoundly uncomfortable.

"And you're telling me this why?" she demanded.

"No reason," he said mildly.

"I should hope not. I'm very busy, you know. It's not like I spent all day wondering about—about what you were thinking, or some such rubbish. And I certainly don't sit around fantasizing about your dick all the time."

"Sure you don't, trouble. Just like you *definitely* didn't spend lunch staring at my mouth and drooling into your baked potato."

"Zaf Ansari, you are the cockiest little shit I've ever—"

"Ah, don't feel bad, Dan. I spent the whole day fantasizing about you, too."

Dani wheezed a little, then pulled herself together through sheer force of will. Her heart pounded like a drum, fairies fluttered their way through her stomach, but her voice remained steady. "Of course you did. I'm very memorable."

"And very pretty when you come. Can't get it off my mind." But his voice was so low and rough and raw, she almost heard something different.

Can't get you off my mind.

God, did he have to be so fucking—*open* about it? Did he have to want her so *obviously*? Did he have to make her feel so safe and so golden and so out of control?

"Well," Dani said faintly. "Well. If that's the case, you're probably struggling to concentrate."

"I am," he sighed. "I really fucking am."

"Maybe . . . maybe you'd better get over here, then." *Please get over here. Now. Before I expire.*

"Yeah," he said. "Maybe I should."

Their phone calls dwindled after that, because Dani developed a new routine: she'd finish her research at 9 P.M., and then Zaf would come over. She'd fuck him into exhaustion, catch her breath, maybe kiss him a little while she made herself come again—which wasn't the same as cuddling. Cuddling didn't count if you masturbated while you did it, not even if the person in your arms whispered things like "Go on, sweetheart. I've got you. Fuck, I love how you love to come."

Once all that was . . . dealt with, she'd send Zaf home, and he'd call her when he got back safely. It was a cursory phone call, of course, a security measure—but sometimes they started chatting, and she occasionally fell asleep listening to the deep, familiar rhythm of his voice.

On nights like those, she'd wake up the next morning to the sound of his alarm through the phone. Would hear him mumble sleepily, "Shit," before cutting off an hours-long call neither of them had been conscious for. The only reason Dani allowed this particular habit to continue was—well. If she heard him waking up, at least she knew he'd managed to fall asleep.

All of this meant skipping her late-night study sessions, but within a few days, she was waking up earlier and more energetic in the mornings, so she supposed it all balanced out. Perhaps that was why her research for the panel had started going swimmingly, and why her nerves had faded, just a touch. Excellent sex had always worked wonders for Dani's stress levels.

Sorcha said as much on Tuesday afternoon, when she found Dani in the library and announced, "As your best friend, I think it's high time I was introduced to your *wonderful* boyfriend."

Dani marked the page of her book and stared. "I beg your pardon?"

"I'm tired of tracking your adorable dates through the Dr. Rugbae hashtag, so I thought I'd join you for lunch today."

Dani added some startled blinking to her staring, just to emphasize the sheer what-the-fuck-ness of all this. "First of all, Sorcha, I can't introduce you to Zafir. You already know him."

"Barely."

"And second of all"—Dani lowered her voice to a whisper—
"you do realize he and I are not actually . . ."

"What I realize," Sorcha said with a smirk, "is that you're
rather relaxed and glow-y, lately. Yesterday morning, you spent
an hour discussing possible *Game of Thrones* endings with me
instead of compulsively working, even though your panel is
less than two weeks away—not to mention all the thesis work
you're keeping up with and the classes you have to teach. You're
seriously unclenching these days, which means—drum roll,
please . . ."

"You're an evil cow and I hate you."

"Danika Brown is getting laid *good*," Sorcha finished gleefully. "Amongst other things. Other mushy, happy things."

Dani had learned long ago that there was no reasoning with
this woman, so she responded with silence.

"Now, since you're obviously super happy with Zaf—"

"Sorcha, you know I am ethically and philosophically opposed
to the idea of being happy with a person."

"—he is officially important to my best friend. And the rules
are the rules. Meet him, I shall."

Dani pinched the bridge of her nose. "Zaf is not important
to . . ." She'd been going to say, *Zaf is not important to me*, but
that felt so horribly false she couldn't force the words out of her
mouth. "He's no more important to me than—than—" She considered and discarded several options. *My vibrator? My favorite mug? My laptop? My thesis manuscript?* No, she must have
taken a wrong turn somewhere and gone too far. Either way, Zaf

couldn't be any of the things Sorcha was patently insinuating, because the universe itself had pointed him out to Dani *as a fuck buddy*. Nothing more. What that man wanted, she simply did not have.

"Zaf and I," Dani tried again, wrenching her mind back on track, "are just—"

Sorcha growled. *"Meet him, I shall."*

"Oh, for God's sake. Fine."

When Dani showed up at the food court with a tiny, brown gremlin in tow, all Zaf did was arch an eyebrow and grunt, "Sorcha."

"Rugbae," Sorcha purred with a shit-eating grin.

They chose a food truck with surprisingly little fanfare, Sorcha prattling on as they waited for their subs, Zaf distracting Dani completely by going all . . . quiet. He was obviously listening as Sorcha spoke, his eyes focused and his nods coming at the right moment, but the sarcastic responses Dani had grown used to were replaced by a gruff, steady calm. He answered direct questions. He offered tiny, one-sided smiles. And that was it.

Dani watched him all the way back to their table, wondering if perhaps he was horribly ill, or had dropped his attitude down a well and needed help to rescue it.

Then Sorcha disappeared to find barbecue sauce (something about dunking over spreading; Dani preferred not to ask). As soon as they were alone, Zaf's posture relaxed. That forbidding furrow between his eyebrows disappeared, and he flashed a smile that made his eyes crinkle at the corners and Dani's brain melt at the edges. "So. Sorcha's fun."

Oh. Something clicked into place. "I forgot," Dani blurted, then wanted to kick herself.

He raised his eyebrows. "What?"

"I . . ." Well, she'd committed now; might as well reveal her creepy fluency in Zafir Ansari. Painfully glad that he couldn't see her blush, she cleared her throat and said primly, "I forgot how you are around people you don't know."

His eyebrows, if possible, rose higher. "Meaning?"

She, if possible, blushed harder. "Meaning nothing. I just—I suppose I'm used to you being yourself around me. I'm glad—" *No. Nope. Stop. Danika Alfreda Brown, stop fucking talking.*

But it was too late. Zaf's eyebrows displayed previously undiscovered Olympic potential and rose even higher. His grin was unselfconscious and familiar, and in the midst of her embarrassment, Dani felt a rogue flare of pleasure that he was showing it to her. This man didn't share himself with everyone, which was just fine, but he shared himself with her, which was—exhilarating. Fucking fantastic.

Ah, the wonders of friendship.

"You're glad that *what*, Dani?" he nudged.

"Shut up." She sank vicious teeth into her sandwich.

"Glad you flossed this morning?"

She rolled her eyes.

"Glad . . . you wore your favorite shoes?"

How did Zaf know these were her favorite—? Oh. Because the other night, during one of their exhausted, babbling phone calls, she'd waxed lyrical about the blessed style-and-comfort combo of her suede block-heel ankle boots. The man absorbed information like a sponge. But she couldn't allow herself to be impressed, not while he was currently ruining her life.

"Glad . . ." He trailed off as if thinking, then leaned in closer, his arm sliding around her shoulders and his lips brushing her earlobe. She fought a shiver of pleasure and lost. "Are you glad, Dani," he asked, his voice smoky, "that you know me?"

She put down her sandwich. "Do you enjoy making me say hideous, unnecessary, and mortifying things?"

His answer was instant, delivered with a smile. "Oh, yeah."

Dani was saved from crawling under the table and hiding there forever by the reappearance of Sorcha, who popped up out of nowhere and took a picture of them on her phone. With flash.

"A close-up of the lovely couple," she trilled. "I see a platinum tweet in my future."

Dani studied her lunchtime companions and wondered which of the two she should murder first.

Perhaps they both sensed the silent threat, because Zaf slipped easily into fake boyfriend mode—which involved lots of secret smiles and very little emotional torment—while Sorcha zipped her lips and put her phone away. This newfound peace lasted for thirty blessed minutes. But the moment Zaf kissed Dani's cheek and headed back to Echo, Sorcha's bullshit began.

"Hmm," she said.

Dani pointedly ignored her. "Do you think Zaf knows he left his muffin? Maybe I should go after him."

"Hmmmmm," Sorcha repeated.

Dani picked off one of the muffin's chocolate chips and popped it in her mouth. "Or not."

"*Hmmmmmmmm.*"

"Sorcha, darling, do you have something in your throat?"

"Who, me?" Sorcha batted her lashes. "Not at all. I'm simply overwhelmed by Dr. Rugbae's cuteness. All those meaningful looks, and the tender way he wiped milkshake off your nose . . . Adorable."

"Good," Dani said, keeping her voice low. "It's supposed to be."

"And why's that?"

Dani shot her a look. "You know why."

Sorcha snorted. "I know *something.*"

"I beg your pardon?"

Sorcha smiled and shrugged one narrow, black-clad shoulder.

"You're very irritating when you're being enigmatic, did you know that? And"—Dani squinted—"are you wearing my Benetton jumper?"

Sorcha waved a hand as if she could brush the question away. "You might as well eat that muffin. He left it for you."

Dani looked down at the little cake. "What? No, he didn't. I told him I didn't have time for dessert."

"Because you're very strict about your schedule when you're stressed. But you're also easily tempted out of said strictness when faced with the temptation of sweets, which Zaf clearly knows." Sorcha leaned forward, an odd, almost excitable expression on her face. "So he bought it. And left it. For you. How does that make you feel, Danika?"

Dani doused the flicker of warmth in her chest, pinching her own thigh beneath the table to ward off nonsensical emotions. "How does that make me feel? Is this some sort of therapy role-play?"

"Are you pleased?" Sorcha prodded. "Are you happy that he bought you a muffin?"

"I don't think he did buy me a muffin," Dani insisted, because if she allowed herself to think that he *had*—well. She didn't know what would happen, but the giddiness blossoming in her stomach and the completely unauthorized smile tugging at her lips suggested it would be bad. Terrible. Mortifying.

Foolish. If she let herself follow Sorcha's thread, she would make a fool of herself.

"It doesn't matter," Dani said firmly, and took a bite of the dessert because finders were keepers anyway. Through a mouthful of fluffy chocolate goodness, she mumbled, "For Christ's sake, it's only a muffin."

Sorcha huffed out a sigh and leaned back in her chair. "Oh sweet Lord, you have *got* to be kidding me."

"What is going on with you today?" Dani demanded.

Sorcha rolled her eyes. "Absolutely nothing at all."

For some reason, the muffin was still on Dani's mind later that night.

It was ridiculous, of course. Zaf had serious dadlike tendencies; she'd always known that. His habit of feeding her didn't mean anything, and anyway, she didn't *want* it to mean anything. He was her universe-mandated fuck buddy, and fuck buddies didn't run around making gentle romantic gestures. Fuck buddies didn't know or care that explicit expressions of affection gave Dani hives; nor did they find subtler, easier, low-pressure ways to make her feel special. Fuck buddies just . . . fucked.

Zaf might be a hopeless romantic, but he wasn't romantic about *her*. She was hardly his ideal. She was hardly his forever.

Still, Sorcha's waggling eyebrows nagged at Dani for hours.

Perhaps she felt guilty for stealing the muffin, or maybe she couldn't forget its particular yumminess. Whatever the reason, when she and Zaf lay panting in bed that evening, some sort of dessert demon took over Dani's body. She turned to him and murmured, "I think I ate your muffin today."

He laughed, still slightly breathless. Then he nudged her in the ribs, a familiar tease that soothed the awkward tension in her belly. "Good. That was for you, you dork."

Shit. "Why?"

He raised an eyebrow. "Why did I get you a muffin?"

She nodded tightly.

"Because I knew you wanted one." When Dani remained silent, her feelings an uncertain tangle, he cupped her face. His thumb brushed her lower lip, and her cheeks warmed, even though he'd touched far more intimate places minutes ago. "Do I need a reason to make my friend smile?"

Well, when he put it like that. "I suppose not," she said on an exhale. *Friends.* That's the way things were between them, and there was no danger in friendship, no pressure, no expectation. She'd been silly to worry.

Because she *had* been worried. Most definitely. This hollow hunger in the pit of her stomach was . . . erm . . . relief.

"Good." Zaf ran his hand down her throat, over her collarbone. Cupped her breast, bent his head, kissed her there. "You're so reasonable when we're naked."

She smacked his shoulder. "Don't get cocky."

"If I made a pun right now, would you throw me out of bed?"

"Best not to find out," she said dryly, and pushed his head back to her breast.

Their phone call that night was slow and easy, almost as if Zaf had called just to talk instead of to prove he'd gotten home safe. Dani tried to mind, and failed. The pillow he'd lain on smelled just like him, and if she fell asleep with her arms wrapped tight around it . . .

At least there was no one there to see.

Hi Zaf,

I'm happy to inform you that our head teacher was as impressed by your work as I am. We'd love to have you teach a workshop to one Year Nine class and one Year Eleven class over the summer term. Please find a proposed schedule attached.

Kind regards,

Emma Cheung

By the third week of their arrangement, and the second week of their, er, sexual arrangement, the scarlet flower of affection in

Zaf's chest—the one that was *supposed* to die—had multiplied. He was housing a brightly colored meadow, beautiful and dangerous.

Every morning, he woke up and told himself, *This is minor. This will pass. At least you're not in love with her.* And every night, he ran his hands over Danika's skin, kissed the moans from her mouth, lost himself inside her, and pretended the squeeze of his heart was some kind of deadly arrhythmia, or a hallucination, or something he'd eaten. Anything but that reckless thing he was absolutely not allowed to feel. Anything but that.

Weekends were the best and the worst. Best, because he couldn't see Dani at work, didn't have to spend his lunch worrying about how many of his reactions to her were just for show and how many were an overflow of affection. Worst, because trying not to pine over Dani might be uncomfortable, but waiting all day to see her was starting to feel like torture.

Which couldn't be a good sign.

It was Saturday morning, a week before Dani's symposium—and ten days until their fake relationship and their fuck-buddy status were both due to end. *Just ten more days,* he told himself, *and you can start getting back to normal.* Then he pulled out his phone and texted her, not because he needed to, but because his day would be a thousand times better once she replied.

ZAF: Hey. Are you free tonight?

She was always free, but he always asked. He kept it simple, though, kept it light. Wouldn't want to come on too strong, or she might notice that he, you know, adored her beyond reason.

Then again, he was starting to think Danika wouldn't notice adoration if it smacked her in the face with a feather pillow, so he was probably safe. Kindness from someone other than her sisters or Sorcha left her baffled. Every time he asked how her day had gone, or fed her snacks while she prepared for her symposium instead of telling her to stop, she looked at him like he might be some lizard overlord wearing human skin. Then she shrugged and went on with her day, because, presumably, Dani didn't have a problem with lizard overlords as long as they left her books alone.

She must be buried in those very books right now, because the text he hoped for never came. In the end, Zaf spent his Saturday the way he usually did: taking the kids to a local league game with Jamal in the morning, bringing his mother vegetable pakoras at the shop, and listening to Fatima talk about a show called *Fleabag* for way too long. Then he went home, clicked through some promising emails, and thought about the one from Mac Stevens that he still hadn't answered.

It was past time he did something about this.

Despite his subconscious fears, Zaf knew, logically, that there was no connection between his grief and the time he'd spent playing for the Titans. Blurring lines between past and present wouldn't unravel all his progress or take him back to the dark place he'd been in when his family had shattered. Only one thing about pro rugby had made his experience worse: the part where his minor claim to fame led the press to swarm him like mosquitoes.

But faking it with Dani had overwritten those memories with

newer, lighter ones. This time around, he had control. He had the power. And something about that caused his fears to fade until they were blurry at the edges.

Still, when he opened Mac's email, he heard the thump of his pulse in his ears and felt himself hesitate. Zaf sat with his anxiety for long, long moments, until his breathing slowed and he was calm enough to push past it. Fast. With gritted teeth.

Yes, he told Mac, of course I remember you, and the family's okay, what about yours? I . . . I can definitely offer the emotional workshop stuff without the coaching, if that's what you need. We can work something out.

Then Zaf hit Send, ran a hand over his beard, and realized he was grinning. Adrenaline flooded his veins like he'd just roared in a tiger's face and come out unscathed. "All right," he told himself, shutting the laptop. "Take five." This called for a celebratory cup of tea or twelve.

He was in the bathroom ten minutes later, humming under his breath and getting undressed for the shower, when Dani's name lit up his phone.

DANIKA: Not tonight. Currently drowning in my own blood.
ZAF: ???

She didn't reply.

Buttnaked, Zaf sat on the edge of his bathtub—shit, that was cold—and stared at the screen, waiting for her reply. Obviously, Dani wasn't actually drowning in her own blood right now. Usually, when people were in the middle of something like that, they didn't text about it. On the other hand, Dani wasn't particularly usual, and she *wasn't* texting him anymore, and he could definitely imagine her, say, trying to open a bag of Skittles with a kitchen knife, accidentally stabbing herself in the hand, and texting him about it shortly before passing out from blood loss.

Fuck it. He hit Call.

She picked up after a few seconds, sounding fairly healthy, if a little tired. "Hello?"

Zaf sighed, closing his eyes and raking a hand through his hair. His heart pounded against his chest—and yes, he knew that was unreasonable, but he was always going to be himself. "Fuck's sake, woman. I thought you were dying or something."

Her pause seemed to crackle with amusement. "And you thought this *because*..."

"Because you—" He broke off. "Oh. Ohhhh. I see. Never mind. Got it."

He supposed he couldn't blame her for laughing.

"Zaf," she gasped between giggles, "just to be clear—"

"Yeah, I got it."

"I'm on my period."

He cleared his throat, his cheeks burning. "Mm-hmm. Sorry. I always forget people have those."

"Must be nice," she snorted.

"I mean, ye—"

"Before you finish that sentence, you should know I've taken enough codeine to plea diminished responsibility after I murder you."

"Duly noted."

"But I'm sorry for, er . . . causing concern. In the depths of my misery," she drawled, "I momentarily forgot about your protective instincts."

That was a very sweet way to phrase *I forgot your Worry setting is permanently turned up to a thousand.* "It's fine," he said. "I take it you're not feeling great?"

"Oh, goody, you're interested in my menstruation. Did anyone ever tell you about rectal cramps?"

"No, no they did not. Can I come over?"

There was a moment of silence. "I said *rectal cramps.*"

"I know."

"As in, your arsehole—"

"Yeah, I know what a rectum is. Stop trying to freak me out. Are you hungry or not?"

"Hungry?" Dani repeated. Her voice was a mixture of suspicion and intrigue.

"That's what I said."

"Hmm. Well. I ate all my emergency Skittles this morning, and I'm out of cereal, so . . ." A pause. "I want egg fried rice, salt and pepper potatoes, and crispy seaweed." She put the phone down.

Zaf decided there must be something deeply wrong with him, because somehow, he'd managed to enjoy that conversation.

Less than an hour after his unexpected phone call, Dani opened her door to find Tall, Dark, and Shouldn't Be Here on the doorstep. Along with a bag of Chinese food, since he clearly knew

what was good for him. Obviously, the food was the only reason why Dani let him in—well, that and the fact that the sight
of him soothed her never-ending PMS tummy ache by a solid
10 percent.

Zaf soothed rather a lot of things, even when she didn't want
him to, and apparently without trying. The fucker.

"Hey," he said softly, putting the bag down and catching her
by the shoulders. He was big and handsome and he smelled like
oranges, and she wanted to swim around in his eyes as if they
were pools of rich, dark honey. Also, it was entirely possible Dani
had taken too much codeine. Oops.

"You okay, sweetheart?" He squeezed her upper arms, which
felt quite lovely, so she grabbed his arms and squeezed back.
The corners of his mouth tugged up into a smile. "What are
you doing, Dan?"

Good question. She stopped squeezing. "Nothing."

"Are you tired?"

"Yes."

"Are you high?"

"It's a possibility," she admitted.

"Is your rectum doing unholy things?"

"The good kind or the bad kind?"

He laughed and dragged her into a hug, which was fabulous, because Zaf was the most huggable person on earth. He
was very sweet and very soft and very firm. He held on to you,
not enough that you felt suffocated, but more than enough to
make it clear you should stay right there. With him. Because
he wanted you to.

The circumstances of this particular hug made Dani wonder what else he wanted. There was no one to fake it for here, and despite his earlier moment of obliviousness, he must realize now that she wasn't in the mood. So why, exactly, had he come over?

Friend. He came over because he's my friend. And she shouldn't ask herself questions like that, because what was the point of them? If he looked at her as if she mattered, if he asked about her day, if he bought her fucking muffins, it didn't mean a bloody thing. She didn't *want* it to mean a thing. In fact, she was already sick of him and his hugs and his kind, steady calm, and she should probably tell him to leave because there was no good reason for him to—

Then Zaf kissed her forehead, her cheekbone, the corner of her mouth. Instead of pulling away, Dani turned her head. Their lips met.

Her heart ached with shy excitement, as if they'd never touched before. The kiss was a chaste brush of lips, barely there, yet powerful enough to dislodge an uncomfortable truth inside her. She wanted Zaf here, and just the act of wanting in itself made her exhilarated and afraid—as if she were falling slowly enough to enjoy the sensation, but fast enough that landing would hurt.

He raised his head, studying her face as if he sensed some infinitesimal change in her. "Dani," he said, his voice strange— quiet but urgent, gentle but burning. "You do know—you do realize that soon—" He broke off.

Her mind filled in his gaps: *Soon enough, all this will be over. We'll be over.* She'd checked the calendar that morning. They had eleven days until their arrangement ended, until everything between them disappeared.

No—not everything. They'd been friends before all this had started, before the video and the fake dates and the deal they'd made. They'd be friends after it. And that was what really mattered, insisted a panicked voice inside her mind: the friendship.

She couldn't lose him. She refused. He was so dear, he was so—

Dani choked down the words that threatened to escape, swallowing her feelings like a blade. "Of course I know," she said calmly. "Soon, the symposium will be upon us and I will either tragically fail or reign triumphant."

"Yeah," he said after a moment. "Yeah, that's right. My money's on triumph, by the way." He let her go and bent to pick up the Chinese food. "Still shitting yourself over Inez Holly?"

"Absolutely."

He laughed as he headed to the kitchen. "Well, after we eat, you can tell me about all the prep you've done. It'll be like practice or something."

Dani stopped walking. "You . . . want to talk about the panel?"

"Yeah. Why not?" He bent to search the cupboards for plates.

"Because . . ."

"Because what?" He found the plates, put them down on the counter, and walked over to her. "Because you don't think I'm interested?" Their gazes caught, and he shook his head. "But that can't be right. You know I've read your articles. And back when we only hung out at work, you told me about that stuff all the time. You didn't give a shit if I was bored or not—which I wasn't, by the way. So that can't be it." He cocked his head, almost theatrically. Something precious unfurled in Dani's chest at the familiar, teasing sparkle in his eyes. "Maybe it's because you're not used to the people you sleep with giving a shit about you. Except that can't be right, either, because you told me once that you've slept with friends before. And honestly, I don't see how anyone could know you and not give a shit about you, Danika. The way you act sometimes," he said softly, "I know it must have happened. But I just don't understand it."

She swallowed. Hard. "Zaf . . ."

"So maybe that's it. Maybe you don't think someone who looks at you the way I do should care about every part of you. Maybe, before, you stumbled across people who only wanted bits and pieces of you. Never the whole package. Never enough."

Each word tugged her apart at the seams until all she could do was stammer out a nervous laugh. "You're . . . direct today."

He looked at her. "Yeah, I am. Know what I was doing before you texted me?"

"No." Some strange and starving beast inside her wanted to know what he was doing every second of the day, but that was clearly bonkers and possibly the result of a period-induced mental break, so she pushed it aside.

"I was emailing an old coach. Because I decided you were right before, that I should use my contacts to help Tackle It. I think the only reason I hesitated was—sometimes I get these barriers in my head. And I get anxious about what might happen if I cross them. If I don't stick to what's safe. But I've started blurring lines and crossing boundaries." His eyes drilled into her, as if urging her to see—to see *something*. "It was easier than I thought it would be, because it was worth it. What do you think about that, Danika?"

"I think I admire you," she whispered, cautious pride warring with the nerves thrumming under her skin.

"Then maybe you should try crossing some boundaries, too. If you want."

She didn't want to understand him. Didn't want to know what he meant. Because if she understood, they'd have to talk about it, and everything would be—

Different. Ruined. Over. She'd fuck it up, whatever *it* was. She was already fucking it up, standing here in silence while his chest rose and fell, and hope died in his eyes. She didn't know how to do this. She hadn't prepared or researched or practiced, had nothing even vaguely coherent to offer him beyond a familiar rasp of fear.

But Zaf wrestled with fear every day, and even when he lost, he came away bruised and bleeding because he'd *tried*. She couldn't show her pathetic, nameless panic to a man like that. It would be fucking insulting.

The silence between them stretched before Zaf looked away. "Okay, sweetheart," he sighed. "Okay."

Dani knew what sighs meant: disappointment, dark and heavy, to match the sudden shadows in his eyes. Protecting him from that felt almost as important as protecting herself from drowning. "Zaf, I—I just have a lot going on right now. And interpersonal issues are not my strong suit."

She watched his lips tip into a cautious smile and wanted to celebrate. "Interpersonal issues," he repeated. "Is that what we're having?"

"I—" *I'm a coward. I'm lost. I'm addicted to being around you and I don't know what I'll do when it stops.*

Maybe it shouldn't stop.

"I don't know what we're having," she said finally, "because I'm not best placed to analyze the situation at present."

"Bad timing, huh?" His gaze caught hers and held. "You want me to wait, Dan? Ask me. Just ask, and I will."

The words spilled from her lips without rational thought, pushed out by some needy, ravenous thing she couldn't control. "Wait. Please."

"All right," he murmured. "I'm waiting."

Something shimmered between them, something strange and dizzying. She was building up the nerve to examine it when Zaf turned away, heading back to the kitchen.

He opened her steaming egg fried rice and his own chow mein, grabbing cutlery as if nothing had happened and switching back to their previous topic. "We don't have to talk about work if you don't want to. We can watch TV instead."

Dani hesitated. Felt a little ashamed of her weakness, and a lot like kissing him in gratitude. Finally, she asked, "Do you like zombie films?"

He looked up, and, God, he was so fucking beautiful. "Hell yeah, I do."

CHAPTER FIFTEEN

The next week flew by so quickly, Zaf barely had enough time to be anxious. He still managed, obviously. But it was a tight squeeze.

Dani went into overdrive, preparing for the symposium, and Zaf . . . well, Zaf did what he could. There'd been a moment, on the night he'd brought her dinner, when he'd thought he'd ruined everything. That he'd been too honest, hinted too hard, reached for something bright and been doomed to burn.

Then she'd surprised him. Danika always surprised him.

Wait. Please.

They still didn't talk about their feelings or sleep in the same bed. But that meadow of affection he'd been trying to starve, the one that bloomed inside his chest for her? All of a sudden, she wouldn't let it die. When they had lunch together, her feet nudged his under the table where no one could see. When they rode the library elevator alone, she played with his hair. One night, after sex, she put her arm around him with such painful awkwardness, it took Zaf a while to realize what she was doing.

"Is this cuddling?" he asked, incredulous. "Just straight cuddling, no sex? Is that a thing we do?"

"Quiet, Ansari." She smothered him with a pillow until he tickled her into submission.

Before long, he started coming over early to cook dinner. She'd eat saag paneer with one hand, the other clutching a book. "Sorry," she'd say every so often. "I'm—sorry. I'm busy. You don't have to do this."

"I know," he'd say. "I want to."

She'd smile, and eat, and read. He'd crack out his laptop and catch up on work. But when the clock struck nine, without fail, she'd pull the computer gently from his grip and drag him off to the bedroom.

Not that he was complaining.

On one of those near-perfect nights, it happened. Zaf, his nerve endings still tingling from his orgasm, was pressing Dani against the living room wall as he kissed her good-bye. They did that, now: they kissed good-bye, like a couple who couldn't wait to see each other again.

"All right," he panted against her lips. "All right. I'm going." He stepped back, already missing her.

Instead of opening the door to kick him out, she hesitated. "Wait. I, erm, mumfupdumpin," she mumbled, padding over to the kitchen.

He squinted after her. "You what?"

Silence as she riffled through a drawer, then returned, clutching a little black pouch in her hands. She cleared her throat. "I made you something." And then, while his brain was still processing those words, she shoved the pouch at him like a toddler presenting a finger painting.

Except this definitely wasn't a finger painting. He took it, a smile spreading over his face and a whole herd of feelings rampaging through his chest. Butterflies, birds of fucking paradise, all that shit.

"You made this," he repeated. "For me?" Through the black gauze, he felt dried-out plants and little stones.

She nodded, looking like she might die of embarrassment. "Um. Yes."

He still had no fucking clue what it was, but— "It smells like you." Like peace and candlelight.

A hint of pleasure warmed her features, erasing her self-consciousness. "It's a charm. It'll help you sleep. I know you don't like taking your meds when you have to get up in the morning, so I thought maybe—"

"You thought you'd make me this," he said, emotion spilling from his voice without permission. His feelings for Dani were like sunlight: they'd always find a crack to slip through, a way to light things up. "Careful, Danika. Keep being so sweet and I might think you give a damn."

She pursed her lips. "Well. You're no use to me if you're too tired to get it up."

"Bullshit."

"Be quiet." She grabbed a handful of his shirt, dragged him closer, and kissed him again.

Changing. Everything was changing.

But time slipped through Zaf's fingers like sand, and the end of their deal loomed like an axe over his head. When their fake relationship became unnecessary, would she take the leap with him and start something real? Another man might assume the answer was yes, but he knew Danika well enough to realize that soft touches and significant looks meant nothing. When she made a decision, she *spoke*.

She hadn't spoken yet.

The Friday before the symposium was full moon night, which meant Zaf found himself banned from Dani's flat and discouraged from calling. Something about a standing date with Sorcha, witchy business, and "the baffling quality of heterosexual energy." He decided not to follow that particular thread.

But the next day, Saturday, dawned bright and brilliant. He got up with a smile on his face and a determination to put his pining on the back burner, because today was about one thing and one thing only: Dani sitting on a panel beside her idol. So he combed his hair into something like an actual style, dressed carefully, and used the beard oil Kiran always badgered him about. Then he made his way over to Dani's flat, knocked three times, and waited.

And waited. And waited.

Just when he was wondering if he'd missed a pretty vital text, the door burst open and there she stood, wild-eyed and . . . brown-haired?

"I'm sorry," she said, "sorry, sorry, sorry. I heard you, but I didn't hear you."

"That's o—" She was already gone, whirling so fast, her black dress fluttered around her shins.

Zaf shut the door and watched her pace across the room, muttering to herself under her breath, her hands rubbing that newly dyed hair. There was a pile of books and paper in the middle of the floor and a small mountain of shoes by the desk that looked like they might have been thrown. The candles on her little goddess table were burning, surrounded by half-empty mugs of different-colored tea.

"So," he said, "you seem perky."

Dani ignored him.

"And obviously in a very healthy place right now."

She ignored him harder. A passing bystander might claim she hadn't done anything at all, but they would be wrong.

He sat on the arm of the sofa and said, "Want to talk about it?"

She turned to glare at him, which was progress. "You are profoundly annoying and extremely troublesome."

"Good thing I have a big dick."

There was a flicker of surprise, a hint of a smile. "Shut up."

"Come here." He caught her hand, pulled her closer. "Yesterday at lunch, you were fine. Now your hair is brown and your laptop is balanced upside down like a tent on your kitchen counter, all of which suggests you're losing your shit. Want to tell me why?"

She raised a defensive hand to her curls. "It's not brown! It's very dark blue."

"Danika. I've seen your hair blue. That's brown."

She folded her arms over her chest and made a strangled, jerky sound, kind of like a frustrated kitten. "Well, maybe it is! Maybe I need to look as ordinary as possible to make up for the fact that I don't know what the *hell* I'm doing."

"There has not ever," Zaf said mildly, "been a time when you didn't know what you were doing. Including your actual birth. I'm pretty sure about that."

"I just—after you left, I may or may not have had a rather unpleasant nightmare, in which I made a complete fool of myself in front of Inez Holly"—it was always *Inez Holly*, Zaf had learned, and never *Professor Holly* or *Inez*—"and she gave me a look of chilling disdain midpanel in front of everyone—"

"Danika," Zaf began.

"And then she got me thrown off my Ph.D. for being so utterly useless—"

"Sweetheart, come on. She doesn't even work at our—"

"And then she called someone who knew someone, and they somehow stripped me of my master's, which—"

He caught Dani's face in his hands, held her gaze with his. "Which is not ever going to happen. Do you know who you sound like right now?"

She scowled at him, but she didn't pull away. "No," she muttered. "Who?"

"Me," he said softly. "You sound anxious, you sound under pressure, you sound like me. Happens to the best of us. So we're going to try something, okay?"

He saw her throat bob as she swallowed. He waited for a sarcastic comment, for a deflection, but one didn't come. Instead, she said quietly, "Okay. What?"

"We're going to breathe together."

She arched an eyebrow. "And by that you mean . . ."

He laughed. "Just trust me, okay?"

"I do," she said, and those two little words all but knocked him out.

Slowly, he drew her into a hug. Zaf knew, logically, that Danika wasn't a small woman—actually, that was one of the things he liked about her. But sometimes, she really *felt* small. Like right now, when the tension leaked out of her, drop by drop, and she relaxed slowly into his arms. Zaf kissed the top of her head, then pressed his nose into her hair and breathed deeply. Once, twice, as many times as it took, until her breathing slowed, too, and they were in calm, steady synch.

It was good, doing this for someone—with someone—instead of just himself. Perfect, doing it for Danika. Time seemed to slow, or dissolve, or disappear, and his heart rate sank so low he was either totally at peace or a little bit dead.

Eventually, she tipped her head back to look at him. "Thanks," she murmured.

"Anytime." *Seriously, anytime. All the time. Forever. Just say the word. Holy shit, please say the word before I die.*

Instead of reading his mind, she took a breath and raised a

hand to her own chest. He knew she was touching the gemstones beneath her dress, reminding herself what each one meant to her. Finally she murmured, "I can't keep doing this."

He arched an eyebrow. "Breathing?"

Danika's glare, as always, was a thing of beauty and impressive venom. "This," she repeated. "Fixating on my goals, pouring all my energy into my work until there's nothing left." She faltered, swallowed hard, and Zaf's heart squeezed. He tried to remember if he'd ever heard Dani address the obsessive way she worked, and came up blank. There'd be a self-conscious joke here, a wry comment there—but the way she was looking at him now, solemn and serious, was different. This was different.

He held her closer, kissed her temple, and waited.

"I don't let anyone else do the things you do for me," she said. The words rushed out, all jumbled together, her awkwardness as obvious as it was adorable. "I don't let anyone feed me or force me to take breaks or drag me outside to see the sun. And lately I've been thinking—what did I do before you? Did I just . . . not eat? Not sleep? Not breathe? I don't even remember, like it was so unimportant my brain didn't retain the information. But that's not okay. Taking care of myself matters just as much as my work."

"More than," he said mildly.

"Don't push it." She pinched his side, then bit her lip, that mind of hers whirring so fast he almost felt the heat. "I love my job because it never demands more than I can give. But lately I think I've been offering too much. Like maybe I've forgotten . . . balance. So last night, that's what Sorcha and I asked for. Balance."

"That's good, Dan," he said softly. "That's really good."

She snorted. "It's really good that, at twenty-seven years old, I've finally committed to eight hours a night and regular trips outside?"

"It's good that you realize you're more valuable as a person than an idea-machine."

"Oh, gag." She smiled—just the tiniest tilt of her lips, but it left him feeling as if he'd been knocked over the head with perfection. "I can tell this is your job. You're very good at supportive pep talks."

"You're not my job, Danika. Not even close."

Her eyes caught his for a second before easing away. "I know."

If Zaf judged correctly, she'd just hit her weekly threshold for emotionally vulnerable conversation in the space of ten minutes. Still, he couldn't let the moment fade, couldn't take the truths she'd offered without sharing some of his own. "I've never really thought of Tackle It as my job, anyway."

"Oh?" she murmured, and he caught a flash of gratitude for the slight subject change.

He shrugged. "Security is my job. Tackle It is . . . my dream, maybe. Or my duty. Or both. Something I can't leave alone. Which is why I, er, changed the 'About' section on our website the other day and started altering the mission statement I put in our funding requests. Just to reflect my reasons for doing this. To mention that I went through loss, that I struggled with my own mental health. You were right, before," he said, cupping her cheek. "I was worried about the mechanics of moving on, but that's not who I am. Putting gold frames around my scars. That's who I am."

"I know," she said again, this time with an incandescent smile. "I'm glad you know, too. I'm proud of you, Zafir." Then she rose up on her toes and kissed his nose, and he thought he might never recover.

It turned out that a symposium was some big, academic event involving panels, presentations, research displays—all of that. Zaf stayed by Danika's side for the first hour or so, and, even though he doubted #DrRugbae watchers would be in high supply here, she held his hand. If she weren't stressed out as fuck, he'd have teased her for that—but she was. Stressed out as fuck, that is. So, as the minutes ticked by, he concentrated on keeping her calm. And when it was time for her to go, he caught her by the hips and kissed her with just a shadow of the devotion in his blood. When she pulled back, she was dreamy-eyed and smiling, as if she felt it, too.

Tell me you feel it, too.

"There we go," he murmured, and tapped her chin.

"Fuck off," she said crisply, and kissed his cheek.

When he took a seat in the audience, the place where she'd kissed him still fizzed, warm and alive. He breathed in, rubbed his hands over his face, wondered if the way he felt about her shone out from him like starlight. It was so bright and so fucking obvious, everyone in a five-mile radius must be able to see it. When someone tapped him on the shoulder, he turned, certain they'd say something like *Wow. You're a goner, huh?*

But they didn't. Instead, he found himself face-to-face with an excited-looking older man, a tall, lean guy with carefully combed wisps of gray hair and flushed pink cheeks. "You're Zaf Ansari," he whispered, "aren't you?"

Zaf grunted and turned his attention back to Danika. There were three other women sitting at the table with her. Only one of them was black, so she was probably Inez Holly. Then he saw the nervous way Dani shifted in her seat, the awestruck glance she sent in the older woman's direction, and decided that was *definitely* Inez Holly.

"I'm a big fan," the balding, pink-faced man whispered in Zaf's ear. "Supported the Titans all my life. I was really gutted when you left. I—"

"Shut up," Zaf said. Professor Holly was short and compact, with graying, natural hair in a cloudy halo around her lined, nut-brown face. Like Danika, she wore all black, and when she spoke, her voice was low and slow and considered, her accent broad and northern. Something about the way she held herself, from the steady set of her shoulders to the no-nonsense line of her mouth, seemed to say, *Respect is mandatory and I comfortably await your payment.*

She kind of reminded him of Danika.

"Excuse me," the pink-faced man hissed after a blessed few moments of silence. "What did you say?"

Zaf huffed out an impatient sigh and turned to face him. "I said my girlfriend has been worried about this panel for fucking centuries, and now it's happening, and if anyone talks over her or gets in the way of me hearing how incredibly smart she is, I will put that someone through a wall. So it's really in both our interests for you to *shut up*." He paused. "Cheers, though. Appreciate it."

"Right," the man said faintly.

Zaf turned back to the panel—and realized with a little start that, when he'd called Danika his girlfriend, it hadn't been for show. He'd meant it. Because she felt like his.

He needed to keep an eye on that. The problem was, he didn't want to.

Up on the platform, the speakers were invited to introduce themselves, and then the real discussion began. A moderator asked questions and made sure everyone had a turn to comment on concepts that went straight over Zaf's head. The talk still managed to be compelling, though—or maybe that was just Dani's voice, a shining golden thread gleaming out at him, husky and electric with enthusiasm. It took her a little while to really get going—not that anyone who didn't know her would notice. But after a few questions, she forgot to worry and lost herself in the topic, holding her own just like he knew she would.

At one point, she said something about examples of historic erasure being available "in real time, right before our eyes, if we need a blueprint to justify our interpretation of past texts," and Inez Holly nodded her head approvingly and murmured, "Mmm. Mm."

For a moment, he was worried Dani might actually dissolve from sheer pleasure and float away. Or that she might jump up out of her seat and scream, *Did you see that? Did you see that, everyone? Inez Holly just nodded at me.* But she limited her reaction to a beaming smile. Her gaze wandered across the crowd and found his, as if she'd been searching for him, as if she wanted him to be a part of this moment.

And Zaf knew. He knew, once and for all, that he loved her. So hard and so hopelessly that he couldn't deny it, couldn't fight it, couldn't hide from it for another fucking second. He loved her intelligence and her ambition, her crystals and her sticky notes, her charming smiles and her dreamy ones. He loved the way she thought in straight lines and facts but believed in magic to honor someone she'd lost. He loved her chameleon curls and her passionate speeches and her awkward unfamiliarity with her own emotions. He just—he loved her.

Zaf remembered the man he'd been three weeks ago, the man who'd decided never to fall in love with Danika Brown, and realized he'd discovered the meaning of hubris.

Oh fucking well.

Worth it.

It took Dani a good thirty minutes on the panel to realize that, even though she could *feel* her voice shaking with nerves, no one appeared able to hear it. She didn't know how that was possible; she just knew that the audience watched her speak as if nothing strange was afoot, and her fellow panelists responded to her points with thoughtful respect, and *Inez fucking Holly* appeared to agree with her more than once, which must mean . . . it must mean . . .

It must mean everything was fine, and Dani was doing well.

It must mean that when Eve and Sorcha and Zaf had sworn she could do this, they hadn't been lying or soothing or biased. They had been right. Which she'd already known, logically, but now, as her heart slowed and her clammy palms dried and her confidence grew, she *felt* it. And it felt good.

When the panel finally ended and Dani headed over to Zaf, she was so exhilarated that she practically ran. He caught her, thank goodness. Wrapped his arms around her and pressed her safe against his chest, kissed the top of her head and lifted her clean off her feet for a moment. It was enormously undignified and completely unnecessary. It wasn't as if anyone here cared about #DrRugbae's public displays of affection, or even *wanted* those displays.

But Zaf loved touching her. And Dani—Dani was quite fond of Zaf.

She was still grinning like a loon a couple of hours later, when she abandoned him by the table of watered-down juice in the postsymposium reception room to nip to the loo. But when she entered the bathroom, it wasn't empty. Inez Holly stood in front of the sinks, slicking on a nude lipstick and throwing Dani into a spiral of excited, starstruck panic simply by existing. Any urge Dani had to pee vanished like smoke. Inez Holly could not be subjected to the sound of her bodily functions. In fact, Dani was in the midst of a passionate mental debate about the pros and cons of backing slowly out of the room when Inez Holly's eyes met hers in the mirror.

"Danika," Inez Holly said, "isn't it?"

It took Dani a disgracefully long time to splutter, "Er, yes. Me. My name, rather. That is indeed my name. Correct. Thank you." *Oh dear goddess, did I just say 'thank you'?*

Inez Holly gave a quirk of the lips that might, on a less stately lady, have been referred to as a smirk. "Did you need the toilet?"

"Pardon? Oh, no." Then, realizing that sounded quite odd, Dani added, "I just wanted to come in and . . . check my hair." Wonderful. Now, rather than odd, she sounded both vain and ridiculous, since hair less than two inches long was not exactly in need of regular checking.

But Inez Holly refrained from passing judgment, for she was great and merciful. "Well, by all means, claim a mirror."

Would it be awkward to take the mirror next to Inez Holly? Would it be insulting *not* to take the mirror next to Inez Holly? Dani considered this for a few feverish seconds before realizing it was a moot point, since there were only three mirrors and Inez Holly was in the middle.

Pull yourself together! She pressed a hand to her chest, feeling the reassuring lump of her garnet beneath. *Self-confidence.* She never lacked it, usually, not in this arena. And she was on something of a roll today; she'd properly acknowledged her ever-so-minor workaholic tendencies and aced the panel she'd spent so long preparing for. She could certainly handle this.

Inez Holly gave her an amused sideways glance as Dani squared her shoulders and chose a mirror. "Has anyone ever told you that you think very loudly?"

"Yes." Dani fished out Charlotte Tilbury's Legendary Queen from her handbag. "I do hope it wasn't distracting, out there."

"Not at all. I enjoyed sitting on the panel with you, you know. It's always nice to meet other sensible people in one's field."

Dani very nearly drew a line of wine-red lipstick across her own face. "Oh." She cleared her throat. "Right. I—thank you." *Inez Holly called me sensible!* Just wait until Zaf heard about this. Then it occurred to her that she should probably take advantage of this miraculous moment. "Professor Holly, would it be all right if I asked you a question?"

Inez Holly turned to face her. "The teacher in me wants to point out that you just did. By the way, great lipstick, but you should probably . . ."

"Oh, yes." *Apply lipstick to bottom lip as well as top lip,* then *ask meaningful question.* That done, Dani forged on. "I was wondering—well, you're quite inspirational to me. I hope to be where you are in some years' time. I'm working toward it, but it's not always easy, and I was wondering if you might have any advice." Which was the sort of open-ended question Dani usually abhorred, but she thought it best to leave Inez Holly with options. She might prefer to share advice like "Always wear matching underwear in case you get hit by a truck" over the personal, in-depth secrets of her career so far.

At least, Dani had assumed she might. But that assumption, like so many she'd made lately, proved wrong. "My advice?" Inez Holly arched an eyebrow. "I'd say . . . anything you want to do, you can. Hurdles were made to be jumped, glass ceilings were made to be smashed." She leaned in closer. "But all that can be exhausting, so make sure you take care of yourself, too. There's great value in the things that bring you joy."

Dani blinked, taken aback. "Things that bring me joy?"

"Outside of work," Inez Holly added pointedly. "Don't forget that part. I know your type. I *was* your type."

Dani suspected she should feel chastened right now, rather than pleased by any comparison to Inez Holly.

Regardless, the word *joy* circled her mind, refusing to be ignored. She could hardly write off the very advice she'd asked for, even if it was somewhat unexpected, so she let the word settle and noticed the memories it produced. Apparently, joy was dinner with her ridiculous sisters, bingeing Netflix shows with her nonsensical best friend, arguing with her ludicrous grandmother. Repotting her plants, dyeing her hair for no discernable reason, being with Zafir—

She cut that last thought off for now. Whacked a fence around it and resolved to deal with it later. Then she asked, "Is it a bad sign if all the things that bring me joy seem to be vaguely absurd?"

"Certainly not," Inez Holly said serenely, and waggled a mauve gel manicure in Dani's direction. "Once every two weeks, I drive an hour to my favorite salon to get my nails done. I don't give a damn what else is on my to-do list; this is nonnegotiable. Major or minor, if something keeps you human when pressure makes you feel like a volcano, hold on to that thing by whatever means necessary."

"I see," Dani said quietly, letting those words sink in. "I— thank you." It was a shame she couldn't be more eloquent, but she was still grappling with the mental fence she'd created, the one that wouldn't stay put. Because every time she thought *joy*, Zaf zipped to the front of Dani's mind and refused to vacate.

Teasing him at lunch in front of sneaky camera phones, shagging like rabbits as if sex were vital to their continued existence, watching him make dinner from the corner of her eye as she tried to concentrate on research. It was mortifying and inconvenient and sure to bite her in the backside, but clearly . . . clearly, joy was *Zaf*.

The realization left her dazed, even if it wasn't entirely out of the blue. The giddy, tender swirl of her feelings shouldn't matter: you weren't supposed to put your happiness in someone else's hands. It never worked. It was foolish. It was dangerous. Only, Dani had been struggling for a while to see any part of Zaf as dangerous, not when he looked at her as if she were the world. Now here was Inez Holly herself, like an unwitting sign from the universe, telling Dani to stop stalling, stop making him wait, and choose joy.

This *was* a sign, wasn't it? Clear as vodka, and just as intoxicating. Especially when mixed into the cocktail of today's success.

Dani thanked Inez Holly again, possibly a little too profusely. Then Inez Holly wrote down the shade of Dani's lipstick, which was rather thrilling, and took Dani's email address, because "It's always good to stay in touch," which was *excessively* thrilling, and by the time Dani left those toilets she felt as if she could rule the world.

She strode back into the reception hall and saw Zaf instantly. He was leaning against a faux-marble column, wearing his usual resting bitch face, and for once, she let herself smile soppily at the sight of him. After all, Inez Holly had practically told her it was safe. And Dani was hardly one to avoid such an obvious cosmic hint.

"Hey." He grinned as she rushed into his arms. "Whoa. You're cheerful."

"Yes. I'm going to start jogging."

"Er . . ."

"I used to run long distance at school," she said. "I liked it."

"Oh. Cool."

"I think I want to try breeding orchids."

Zaf burst out laughing. "What the hell did you find in the bathroom? Cocaine?"

"Inez Holly," she told him breathlessly.

"What?" Pure excitement spread over his face. Then he said, "Did you talk to her?" And Dani realized that excitement was for *her.*

Zaf felt things for her. She knew because she felt things for him, too, bright and terrifying, like a brand-new sun over a world that had been dark for ages. She should be afraid—and part of her was.

But in that moment, she felt so powerful, and he felt so precious, and the thought of letting him go was impossible. *Impossible.* She couldn't let it happen.

So instead of answering his question, she pulled back and told him quietly, "You . . . you're supposed to be my perfect fuck buddy."

His eyebrows flew up, and his mouth tightened. "Yeah. I know."

"Which means, amongst other things, not getting attached."

His expression turned wary. Or maybe guilty.

"The trouble is," she went on, "I think I've gotten quite attached to . . . to the way you make me feel. And to making *you* feel—oh, I don't know. I don't know how I make you feel, but I like trying to make you—smile." Her voice was choked and strange, and her words tasted like little white lies. If she were an honest woman, she would say, *I love to make you smile.*

Because the mortifying truth was this: Dani had grappled with ravenous affection for Zafir Ansari far longer than she liked to admit. She'd tried to turn away from it, but suddenly she couldn't remember why. Zaf wasn't like anyone else she'd been with, and their relationship didn't have to fit some romantic ideal she would never measure up to. All they had to do was keep things exactly as they were. If they stayed like this—just like this—everything would be fine.

Everything would be perfect.

She saw the moment he began to understand, his eyes widening. "Danika . . ." he said slowly, "is this you—?"

"I'm not very good at saying things," she told him firmly. "Okay? I don't like it. So this is me *not saying things*. I'm just saying, that's all."

He arched an eyebrow. "You're just saying that you're not saying?" But there was a slow smile spreading across his face, one that made her cheeks heat.

"We spend a lot of time together," she told him, "and it's not awful. So maybe we could . . ." God, she really hadn't thought this through, and it turned out sheer, shining adoration was incredibly difficult to express out loud.

But apparently, that was okay with Zaf, because he swept in and rescued her. "Maybe we could keep being not-awful?"

"Exactly," she managed.

"Together," he pushed. "Without faking it. And without limits."

"Right," she said faintly.

"You know what that is," he murmured, "don't you, Danika?"

Maybe she did—all right, yes, she absolutely did—but her nerves were already frayed enough. "Baby steps," she told him firmly. "Okay?"

"Baby steps to . . ."

"To being with you," she blurted out.

"Glad to hear it," Zaf said gravely. Then he kissed her with a barely restrained passion that verged on scandalous.

CHAPTER SIXTEEN

Despite Dani's newfound boldness, she was not—and would never be—the sort to make a vomit-inducing speech about Zaf's many virtues and her many feelings. Not unless they were both trapped on a train hanging off the edge of a cliff, and therefore moments from gruesome death, or something along those lines. So when they left the reception, instead of turning to him with some romantic declaration, she dragged him into an outdoor alcove where students kept their bikes, and kissed his gorgeous face off. Again.

Judging by the heat in his eyes before their mouths met, he didn't mind.

Kissing Zaf was like drinking ice water in a heat wave: slow sips might work, but hungry, gasping gulps felt better. When Dani's lips brushed his, every pleasure center in her body flashed firework-bright. She slid her hands into his hair, pressed herself closer against him because she just couldn't stop, and explored that solemn mouth without restraint. He tasted of sweet, dark honey, of peace and quiet comfort, of fresh white sheets and dawn. He tasted of things no man should, as if he were something greater. Something more. Something she'd been searching for.

Dani pulled back. "Let's go home."

"Definitely on board with that."

"To your place. Didn't you tell me you're closer to campus than I am?"

He grinned. "And I'm so irresistible, you just can't wait?"

"Don't be smug." But she liked him smug.

Fifteen minutes later they slammed into his flat, and Dani was pushing him around once more—against the door, this time. Since she knew from experience that she couldn't *actually* move Zaf, that meant he was letting her. The thought sparked another burst of tenderness even as lust set her alight. He looked down at her with lips parted and kiss-swollen, his hair a mess from her hands, and he was simultaneously sexier and more divine than anything she'd ever seen.

She sank to her knees without conscious thought. Only need drove her now.

Mine, mine, mine.

"Danika," he breathed, and cupped her face as she undid his belt. "Fuck. You're going to ruin me." But he made the prospect sound like heaven, like a gift.

She undid his zipper, shoved aside every barrier in her way until he was naked from the waist down, his cock hard and thick and dripping. Then he dragged his shirt off over his head, and the sight of him completely bare while she stayed fully clothed made her dizzy with want.

She wrapped a hand around his shaft, hot and velvety with that fine, thrumming vein along the underside. Then, since they'd somehow never done this before, she said, "Not to ruin the mood—"

"Literally impossible," he choked out.

"—but don't forget about my overenthusiastic gag reflex."

His laughter was faint and cracked. "Never going to forget you coughing up noodles on my lap."

"Oh, be quiet," she muttered, her cheeks warm. Then she brought up a second fist to join the first, until just a few inches of his cock remained uncovered. She eased the fat, gleaming head into her mouth, squeezing with her hands as her tongue flicked out to taste him, and the noise Zaf made sounded inhuman.

That low, ragged growl zipped straight to her clit like a tiny electric shock. The taste of him, that salty musk, teased her tongue.

She sucked.

He hissed out a breath. "Holy shit, yeah. Sweetheart—" The word broke. She looked up to find him staring down at her, something endless and unnamable in his eyes. She could see his restraint in the pulse thrumming at the base of his throat, the rigid line of his hips as he tried not to thrust deeper—and God, God, she fucking loved it.

Dani released his cock with a pop, grabbed his arse with both hands, and felt more of that delicious control. Bent her head to lick and suck the weight of his balls, heard him turn the air blue, and felt pure, filthy power. The sparkling, sensitive *something* between her thighs grew more and more intense with every curse he spat out. When his shaft was slick and his voice was rough and frenzied, she palmed his cock again and stroked him hard, kissed and sucked his tip, and watched him lose it.

"Shit," he gasped. "Shit, you're so fucking—keep—" He reached down, grabbed the neckline of her dress, and pulled hard. She heard, or felt, a slight rip, and then the fabric loosened and her bra was exposed. "Sorry, sorry," he panted, even as he pushed down her bra cup. Her breast spilled free and he squeezed the aching flesh, an unapologetic grope that felt dirty and presumptuous and absolutely delicious. Then his thumb swept over her stiff nipple and she moaned, her blood heating and her patience melting away.

She released his dick, tried to stand, and realized her knees were weak. Zaf picked her up a second later, and she wrapped her legs around his waist. "Perfect," he told her. "You're perfect." It wasn't the first time he'd said it. But this time, she was almost sure he meant it.

Then he kissed her hungrily, his teeth tugging at her bottom lip, and she felt him put her down on something cold and hard. A table, she realized, as he pulled away to find his wallet. He'd taken her into what must be the closest room—the kitchen—and put her on the table. Dani quite agreed with, and indeed approved of, his sense of urgency. Then he was back, rolling on a condom and pushing up her skirt, dragging off her thong and tugging her close.

He eased a finger into her wetness and she took him easily, found herself begging mindlessly for more. So he gave her another, and another, until she was finally full of him. Zafir, invading her body, stroking all the soft, shivering flesh inside her as he murmured against her mouth, "Want you so bad, Dan. Want you, just *want* you—"

"I know," she panted. "I know."

He groaned, and then his fingers left her, and she was lost for a second before he replaced them with his cock, splitting her open slow and steady. She rocked her hips, leaning back on her hands, spreading her thighs wider as the pressure turned her liquid from the inside out. "Yes. Oh my God, yes."

"You're mine," he told her.

"I'm yours," she said, and nothing had ever felt so good.

Zaf was losing control and he didn't care, because Danika was right there with him. She sobbed his name as she took him deep, sinking her nails into his shoulders, vulnerable to him in a way she'd never been before, not once. When he looked her in the eyes, she didn't flinch away. She met his gaze steadily, and dragged him closer, as if she wanted every fucking part of him and couldn't even pretend otherwise.

Something inside him snapped, shifted, transformed, and all he could do was fuck her, fuck her, fuck her.

Zaf pounded into her with mindless hunger, her every breathless moan urging him on. He couldn't stop touching her, couldn't stop his hands from sliding over her thighs, stroking her spread sex, running up over her torso to her tits, her throat, her face. Her fucking *face*, mouth open, brow furrowed, those impossible eyes pinned to him.

"Say my name," he grunted, like some kind of animal, and she said—

"*Zafir*," like petals floating over water, and then she pressed her palm flat against his chest and he swore his heart felt the touch. "Mine," she told him softly. "You're mine, too, you know."

He kissed her, cool mint and desperation.

When he couldn't get close enough, deep enough, he pushed Dani onto her back and climbed halfway across the table himself. Ignored the way it groaned, and shoved into her hot, wet cunt until he couldn't see straight. So good, so fucking good. When he thrust against that tender place inside her and she screamed and squeezed around his cock—oh, fuck, he wanted more of that. So he reached between their bodies and rubbed her swollen clit, tight little circles the way she liked, and kept the angle of his hips just right.

"Come on, love," he panted.

"You can't—tell me to—"

"Come."

Her sob of pleasure ripped him open. He felt her pussy spasm around his cock as she climaxed, and then—

And then he came harder than he ever fucking had, which wasn't exactly surprising, and the table collapsed beneath them, which was.

CHAPTER SEVENTEEN

Dani had been distantly aware of an ominous creaking sound, but in the midst of various emotional revelations— *God, I'm in love with Zaf's voice,* and *Wow, the way he kisses me slowly while fucking me senseless is life-ruiningly perfect,* for example—she hadn't really paid any attention. She certainly noticed, however, when the sturdy-looking table groaned dramatically and one of its legs gave out.

Luckily for her, she happened to be sleeping with a former athlete who had unholy reflexes. Zaf wrapped an arm around her and dragged them both backward—away from the collapsed table leg and sliding tabletop. They ended up on the floor, him clearly winded, Dani safe and fairly comfortable on his massive chest. His quick movements were especially impressive given he'd only just finished coming, but she was too dazed and confused to offer appropriate praise.

After a long moment of silence, during which Zaf caught his breath and Dani wondered if anything this awkward had ever happened in the history of the world, he finally spoke. His first words were, predictably, "Fuck's sake."

Dani had always thought sex became boring and unbearably solemn once you, er, *felt things* for someone, but that clearly wasn't true when it came to her feelings for Zaf, because she took one look at his familiar, grumpy scowl and burst out laughing.

"Hey," he said, but he was grinning. "I blame you for this."

"Me? You're the one who put me on the bloody table!"

"And you're the one who's so sexy I forgot about, you know, physics and shit." He ran a hand over her hair, down her spine, all the way to the swell of her arse. Which he then grabbed. "You okay?"

"Is this you checking for damage?"

He winked.

She sighed and pretended she wasn't utterly thrilled by everything about this. But she was. She always was. Whenever they were together, whenever he touched her, all she could feel was happy.

Ick.

She looked over her shoulder at the drunken, three-legged table leaning against the floor. "Sorry about that. Should we—?"

"The only thing we should do right now," he said firmly, "is go to bed."

Dani hesitated, because—*We. Bed.* Hmm. For more sex, or for something . . . else? Clearly old habits died hard, because despite her best intentions, the idea of spending the night with someone she cared about for the first time in forever made her gut clench with nerves.

But that was silly. She was fearless. She was chasing joy. She shoved her apprehension into a box and tried not to notice that the lid wouldn't quite lock.

Zaf must have caught her uncertainty, because he helped her to her feet with a solemn expression. "It's very late, Danika. You can't go home on your own."

Laughter chased away the shadows in her chest. "Zaf, it's barely seven o'clock."

"You're talking too much." He scooped her up in his arms and carried her off to the bedroom.

And she let him.

It was dawn when Dani woke. For a moment, staring blearily across an expanse of deep blue pillow, she wasn't quite sure where she was. Then, slowly, sensations trickled in: the weight of a heavy thigh slung over her waist. The slow dance of fingertips across the bare skin of her back.

"Zaf," she whispered into the churchlike silence.

His voice was low and sleep-roughened. "Good morning, Danika."

The way he said her name, lazy and tender, made her smile into the pillow—but beneath that pleasure, a hint of panic flared. Deciding to be brave and getting swept up in the moment was one thing—but she hadn't woken up beside another person in years, and she'd *never* wanted another person in quite the same way she wanted Zaf. Maybe she was overthinking things slightly, but . . . but she wasn't entirely sure what was supposed to happen next, and fuck, she didn't want to get anything horribly wrong.

Really, darling? You're twisting yourself in knots over how to say good morning? The voice in her head sounded oddly like Gigi, and as always, Gigi was right. Dani's worries were ridiculous. This was why she hated relationship bullshit: it turned her into an uncertain, alien mess.

"Did you sleep okay?" Zaf asked, as if all this was normal—and the sweet familiarity of his voice almost made it so. Almost.

"Yes," she said, because it was true. "Did you?" The answer seemed to matter more than it should, but then, everything mattered more than it should with Zaf.

"Yeah. I sleep pretty well ever since you gave me that charm. And I think you wore me out last night."

The way that made her smile was sickening. Sickening! But she couldn't quite stop.

Then Zaf asked softly, "Will you look at me?" His soothing, barely there touch on her back faded away.

"Of course I will!" Dani rolled over so fast that she got tangled in the sheets like a blushing duvet sausage. But it didn't matter, because she thought she'd heard something like trepidation in his voice, and she didn't want that. She didn't want anything bad or sad for him, not even if it meant maintaining her own comfort. Which seemed a disturbing and potentially dangerous outlook, but she'd worry about that some other time.

Fortunately, Zaf didn't look upset by the time she faced him. In fact, he was clearly trying not to laugh. "Did you know you hog the sheets?"

"Shut up," she muttered. God, he was even handsome first thing in the morning, which was both pleasing and extremely irritating. The shy dawn light suited him, making his brown skin glow. His bedhead was incredibly sexy, and the sleepy slowness of his eyes made her blood heat.

He ran a fingertip over the curve of her ear, his smile tiny and teasing. "So. We broke a couple rules."

Don't spend the night. Don't catch feelings.

"Yes," she murmured. "We did. But, in my defense, Inez Holly told me to."

His fingertip's journey stuttered to a stop, and he blinked. "What?"

"Er . . ." Hmm. That might have been a weird thing to say, mightn't it? But then, she *was* weird, and she'd always been weird with Zaf, and he didn't seem to mind, so she cleared her throat and continued. "Yesterday in the bathroom Inez Holly told me a key part of success is remembering to chase joy, so. Here we are."

For a moment, Zaf looked so taken aback, she was worried she'd monumentally fucked up. Possibly by coming on way too strong. She'd been a little high on happiness yesterday, when she'd had her *Zaf is joy* moment, and now in the unforgiving morning light, it all seemed quite . . . embarrassing.

But then he gave her a slight, crooked smile, and the tension in her chest eased. "That's—sweet," he said. Then a teasing light entered his eyes, and he murmured, "Joy, huh?"

Dani blushed. "Whatever." Definitely time to change the subject. Avoiding his gaze, she searched the room for another, safer topic and found one almost immediately.

"Oh my God," she said, leaning over him to reach for the bed-side table. "The infamous romance novels."

Zaf snorted as she snatched up the book balanced next to his alarm clock. "I take it you didn't notice the entire bookcase in my living room last night."

"I didn't make it to your living room last night," she reminded him. "You fucked me on the table, you fucked me in the bed, you produced cheese on toast from somewhere—"

"The wonders of having a kitchen stocked with food instead of tea and plants," he said dryly.

"And then we fell asleep." She sat up and studied the glossy little book in her hands. A pair of scandalously attractive black people in old-timey clothes graced the cover, each looking slightly pained by the intensity of their undying love. "*Tempest*," she murmured, running her fingers over the title font. "Are you reading this right now?"

"Almost done."

"What's it about?"

He lay back and gave her a lazy smile. "If you want to know, I'll buy you a copy. No spoilers."

"Except for the happy ending."

He laughed. "That's not a spoiler. That's a safety net."

Dani paused, the words catching at something in her mind. "A safety net. You know, you never did tell me—why do you read these books, Zaf? How did you start?"

His smile softened into something older, sadder. "Because after Dad and Zain died, I was clinically depressed for three years, and then my sister-in-law told me I was scaring her and threw a Harlequin Romance at my head. After she left, I wanted to find her and say sorry, but I couldn't. I just couldn't. So I picked up the book and started reading it. And . . ."

He trailed off, and Dani's heart stuttered, threatened to shatter. "Zaf," she whispered. There was an ache to his words, old, but no less powerful for it. She set the book aside and lay back, rolling over to hold him whether he'd asked for it or not. Because she knew this man, and the look in his eyes told her that he had more to share, but couldn't do it without a little help. When she rested her head on his chest, he relaxed as if he'd been waiting for her.

"Sorry," he said, his voice rough.

"You apologize unnecessarily," she told him, and turned to meet his eyes. "I know you put a lot of stock in the fact that you're 'better' now. That you handle things. That you cope. But coping takes a lot out of a person, too. And handling things doesn't mean never struggling or slipping up. Life isn't that black-and-white, not even close. So I want you to do or say or feel whatever the fuck you like, about everything, but especially about this. And I never want you to tell me you're sorry for feeling things. Not ever again."

With every word she spoke—or rather, every word that some higher power tugged unwillingly from her mouth—Zaf's gaze softened, and the tension she felt thrumming through his body trickled away. He looked at her with something tender in his eyes, and Dani knew she should regret the emotional honesty she'd just spewed all over him—but she didn't. Not if it made him smile like that. Not if it made him breathe a little easier. She didn't.

Which was mildly terrifying.

"Thank you," he murmured, his hand moving to stroke her hair. For once, she couldn't bring herself to push that quiet, meaningful *thanks* back in his face, so she closed her eyes and waited.

Before long, he continued his story. "After the accident, I went a little bit off the rails. I think I already mentioned that. I've had anxiety ever since I can remember, but being without my dad and Zain—especially Zain . . ." Dani felt herself move with the rise and fall of Zaf's chest as he took a deep breath. "There were seven years between us. My parents thought they couldn't have another kid, but then I showed up. So he was kind of like a junior dad, you know what I mean? He was always there, and then he was gone, and I just couldn't fucking breathe. People think anxiety makes you nervous all the time, and it can. But no one ever talks about how it makes you angry. Eventually the anger faded, though, and after that, I was . . . nothing. For a long, long time, I was nothing."

Dani felt the pain in his voice like a punch to the chest. "No, you weren't. You're always something, Zaf. Even when you don't feel like it. Even when you don't feel *anything*, you're still kind, and smart, and thoughtful, and one grumpy mother-fucker. You're still you."

His smile was faint but real, and she was greedy for it. "Yeah. Yeah, that's true." He pulled her closer, kissed her cheek. "At the time, it was romance novels that reminded me. Since you've never read one, that probably sounds weird. But it's all about emotion, Dan—the whole thing, the whole story, the whole *point*. Just book after book about people facing their issues head on, and handling it, and never, ever failing—at least, not for good. I felt like my world had already ended unhappily, but every book I read about someone who'd been through the worst and found happiness anyway seemed to say the opposite. Like my story didn't need to be over if I didn't want it to. Like, if I could just be strong enough to reclaim my emotions, and to work through them, maybe I'd be okay again. That's kind of what inspired me to, er, keep going. To make good choices, even when feeling better seemed impossible."

There was a flood of something soft and all-consuming in Dani's chest, and it was entirely for him. She didn't know how to express something this big—couldn't even give it a name. But she wanted him to feel it. So she pressed little kisses into his skin, every part of him that she could reach, and when he slowly started to relax beneath her, she knew he understood.

She also knew now, *really* knew, why romance meant so much to him—not just the books, but that search for his own happily ever after. She'd thought he was just sweet, loving, maybe a little old-fashioned, but now she realized he was . . . inspired. That he was one of those people, one of *many*, whose lives had been forever changed by someone else's words. And that wasn't something Dani treated lightly. She made her living out of words. She knew very well that they could be everything.

Which made this new information intimidating, to say the least.

This fresh glimpse inside Zaf's head made her lungs constrict, made her bones creak with the threat of extra weight, extra pressure. But she steeled her spine and tried to breathe through it, because now wasn't the time to worry about all the ways she could disappoint him. And anyway, it wasn't as if they were in *love* or something. They were just together, and trying. That was all. Baby steps.

But a nervous little voice in the back of her mind whispered, *You know where he wants those baby steps to take you.*

She pushed the voice away and focused on what mattered—on Zaf.

"Will you tell me about your family?"

"Yeah." He heaved a breath, and smiled. "You've met my niece. I know she acts like a normal human being in public, but don't trust it; she's feral."

"You must be very proud."

"Obviously. As for the rest of them . . . you'd like my sister—my sister-in-law, Kiran. She's always in control. Thinks big. Focused. She runs a dress shop with my mum, and thousands of people follow her on Instagram to, er, look at her outfits."

"Really? Good Lord, she must dress well."

"Yeah."

"That explains why you have such firm opinions on clothing."

"No, it doesn't. I only have firm opinions on *your* clothing. The opinions are that you look great in it and even better out of it." He said these things with a matter-of-factness that had her grinning like a loon. "My mum," he went on, "is bonkers, good at hiding it, and spends most of her life silently laughing at the rest of us while pretending to be calm and dignified."

"Oh, she sounds wonderful."

"She is," Zaf said, with feeling. "And then, of course, there's my dad and my brother. Dad was big into computers and had no idea why I hated school or why I liked running around on a pitch getting beat up, but he supported me anyway. He came to my games and cheered whenever I touched the ball, even when everyone else was silent." He laughed at the memory, and the sound made Dani's heart lift. "And Zain Bhai . . . Zain was my hero. He loved books and he loved rugby, almost as much as I did. He actually got up for dawn prayer every day, but he didn't judge me if I overslept. When I started struggling with anxiety as a kid, he's the one who noticed and figured out what was going on. He explained to my parents that it was serious and it was real, and he took me to the doctor. He was just . . ." Zaf's voice cracked slightly before he recovered. "He was just special. And I miss him."

Dani bit her lip, because if she didn't, a tsunami of emotion might spill out and drown them both. "Thank you," she managed eventually, "for telling me."

"Thanks," he said softly, "for being someone I can tell. I wish . . ."

"What do you wish?"

"That they could meet you." He shrugged. "But at least Mum can."

The solemnity of the moment was cracked by the strained, wheezing noise Dani made as she choked on her tongue. "You . . . want me to meet your mother?" she squeaked.

"Er . . ." He gave a cough that sounded suspiciously like a laugh. "You sound like you want to jump out of a window right now."

"No! No, nooo, no. It's just . . ." She could count on one hand the number of family meetings she'd been involved in, post-Mateo. Actually, she could count on one finger, and that had been an unfortunate accident involving bad sex (there had been whipped cream, much to the dismay of both Dani and her vaginal pH), mind-blowingly poor timing, and a spare key under the doormat.

"Relax," Zaf snorted. "I'm not trying to wheel you out already. I'm just assuming it'll happen eventually, unless you develop some seriously impressive avoidance skills."

Dani gave a nervous laugh and wondered just how serious those avoidance skills might have to be. Not that she'd ever avoid Zaf's last remaining parent, whom he spoke about with such love in his voice, and with whom he was clearly quite close, and who might easily hate Dani's guts or generally disapprove of her hair and her boobs and her witchcraft, not that Dani would *care*, but Zaf might care, and—

"All right," he said firmly, a slight smile curving his lips. "New subject, before your head explodes."

"My head's not going to explode."

"No, it's not, because we're changing the subject."

She laughed. How could he always make her laugh? And why did he seem so much calmer about all this, as if things between them hadn't transformed out of nowhere? Not that she was complaining, exactly. One of them needed to stay calm through all this new territory, and it made sense that Zaf would be that one. Even now, the way he touched her, the easy rhythm of his breaths and the warmth in his eyes, made her heart rate slow a little more.

His thumb stroked her cheekbone, a soothing motion that went on for long moments before he spoke again. "I once asked you why you didn't believe in relationships."

"I remember."

"You gave me an answer. But I've been wondering lately," he said, his tone careful, "if you told me everything."

Dani swallowed. "No. I didn't."

Beneath the sheets, his hands found her waist and held on tight. "Do you want to tell me now?"

Not really. That was her gut instinct, anyway, but for once, she didn't quite agree with it.

She thought about all the things he'd told her, all the troubles he'd shared with her simply because she'd asked him to. The pain he'd endured, and fought, and beaten, and how honored she felt every time he gave her a glimpse of it. If he could tell her all that, surely she could tell him an embarrassing story or two, couldn't she?

Yes. Yes, she could.

So Dani began. "I did fall in love once. During undergrad, I met a boy called Mateo. I'd never been in a relationship before him—I suppose I was a late bloomer. And a giant nerd."

Zaf squeezed her hip. "You're still a giant nerd."

"This is true, but I was worse back then. Finding time to balance my giant nerdery with actual human interaction has never come naturally to me."

His lips twitched. "Really?"

"Oh, shut up."

"I'm just saying, I hadn't noticed."

She flicked him in the chest.

He burst out laughing, and she bathed in the warmth of the sound. "Go on," he managed eventually. "Tell me the rest."

"Ah. Yes. Well. I realized I wasn't as naturally emotive as other people. I knew I could be hyperfocused on my work, that I could be blunt and unsentimental. But I wanted to be a good girlfriend," she said, wrinkling her nose at the memory. She'd been so young and so ridiculous, thinking she could fake certain qualities to make someone else happy. Thinking that she *should*. She'd never make that mistake again.

Won't you?

She cleared her throat. "In the end, it didn't matter. We were together for four years before I caught him fucking someone else. I mean, he was literally fucking someone else when I walked into the room. He didn't know I was coming home. I was trying to surprise him. Because, you know. Romance."

Zaf growled. As in, that noise predatory animals make right before they eat someone. His expression was just as ferocious, too. "What an *arsehole*."

"Mmm," Dani nodded. "That's what I said. But then he told me that he'd been forced to begin an affair because I was so dull and inattentive and *ice cold*—that's a direct quote, I suppose he was feeling poetic. Apparently, being with me left him lonely."

The hand on her hip tightened for a moment before relaxing

finger by finger, as if by force. Zaf's jaw was hard as he gritted out, *"What?"*

"Mm-hmm." Dani attempted a smile. It wasn't her best. "The thing is, I'd been trying so hard—and I'd been so blissfully oblivious, certain I was getting it right—and the whole time, I was failing."

"Failing?" Zaf didn't just scowl. He looked angrier than she'd ever seen him, practically bristling with it. Since he was bare-chested and dangerously handsome, Dani rather enjoyed it, but she tried not to look too thrilled, because he was clearly serious.

Seriously pissed, that is.

"You didn't fail, Danika," he snapped. "You loved someone, and you tried to make them happy. The fact you were incompatible isn't a failure on anyone's part. Failure is lying and cheating and blaming it on anything but your own sleazy, spineless bullshit. You know that, right?"

"I—" She faltered, taken aback by the fire in his eyes. She'd been angry, too, of course she had. But maybe not quite *this* angry. Because, at the time, no—she hadn't known that at all.

"I know it now," she said finally.

"Good." He held her tighter, pulled her closer, and looked even more murderous. "What a piece of shit. What did you say his last name was, again?"

She arched an eyebrow. "I didn't."

Zaf grunted.

"Anyway." She swallowed. "After that, I refused to change myself for a relationship ever again. I wasn't about to make a fool of myself by putting romance before my work, or bending over backward to make time for inane chats about how someone's *day* was, or forcing myself to make grand gestures, or pretending to give a shit about anniversaries—"

Zaf raised his head to squint at her. "You don't give a shit about anniversaries?"

She waved a hand. "Valentine's Day exists for a reason. Marking the passage of time within your relationship as if it's a prison sentence seems unnecessarily depressing." She paused. "My point is, after I stopped compromising, every relationship I attempted went straight down the toilet. In the end, it seemed like a waste of everyone's time and energy to keep trying. So I stopped." And now she'd hopped back into the saddle by developing an attachment to the sweetest man on earth, who deserved the best relationship in the world and was smart enough to know it. *Nice training wheels, Danika.* Suddenly, her throat felt tight, her heart pounding against her ribs.

"Hey," Zaf said, squeezing her arm. "Listen. Not only was that guy a piece of shit, he had maggots for brains if he couldn't see that you're perfect. But *I* see it. And you do know how to make someone happy, Dan. Remember when I told you relationships shouldn't feel like a drain? That, when it was worth it, and it was right, you'd *want* to compromise?"

"I—yes?"

"Well, maybe that's where we're at. Because all those things you think you can't do, Danika, you already do them for me." He paused. "Except for the anniversary thing. We'll talk about that later."

She wanted to laugh—she was supposed to laugh. Or to

smile and say, *Oh, gosh, you're right!* and realize perfection had crept up on her. Except it hadn't. It couldn't. That wasn't how life worked. Instead, discomfort crept up her throat, warm and prickling, as if she was up to her neck in hot water.

"No," she said slowly. "These things don't change overnight. I—I'm still bad at relationships." Of course she was. She had to be. She'd only just decided yesterday that they were going to do this thing, and talking about Mateo reminded her that she was 100 percent fuzzy on the details of *how.*

How the hell was she going to give the man she cared about so deeply the kind of relationship he wanted? Her lungs felt five sizes too small. She sat upright, just to get a little more air.

"Danika," Zaf said softly, sitting up beside her. His hand on her shoulder felt heavier than usual. "You're not bad at relation-ships. You're lovely. You're smart, and sweet, and generous, and you make me smile, and you listen when I need you—when *any-one* needs you. So don't—"

"Stop," she said tightly. "Just stop, okay? I know I have positive qualities, Zafir, of course I do. Just like I know that I'm antiso-cial and abrasive and occasionally boring, and utterly inflexible, and—and not perfect. Not even close. I'm trying, here, but don't get your hopes up. I'm not going to turn into someone else." She hunched her shoulders, focused on the sheets in front of her—but she couldn't stop sneaking desperate glances at Zaf from the corner of her eye. Watching his face fall at her words, even though it hurt her. Like picking a scab.

Some distant part of her brain pointed out the sudden changes in him, a clinical list: *He's stiff. He's worried. He's not smiling anymore*. He'd been smiling all fucking morning, even when they talked about the hardest thing he'd ever gone through—but she'd just wiped the happiness clean off his face. She was fucking up already, acting like this, but she couldn't make herself relax.

"I don't want you to be someone else," he said firmly, but she caught the barest edge of panic in his voice, too. "That's what I'm saying, Danika. I—" He hesitated, then forged on. "I love you as you are. Exactly as you are."

Her thoughts slammed to a stop. "What?" she said weakly. Or maybe her voice just sounded weak over the roar of her pulse in her ears.

He eyed her steadily. "I think you heard me, sweetheart."

Her mind stuttered over various explanations and couldn't find a single one that seemed reasonable. She opened her mouth with no idea what would come out, choking on a tide of anxious fear before croaking, "How?"

"I—what?" Beside her, Zaf looked painfully uncertain.

"How could you love me?" Because now she'd managed the question, she realized it was the right one to ask. The only one to ask. "When would you even get the chance to start? I mean, I know I'm a good time, don't get me wrong." Her attempt at a laugh came out disturbingly bitter. "But I've spent the last month pushing you away, using you for sex, and boring you to death with various work-based neuroses, so when, exactly—?"

"Stop it." She could see he was trying to stay calm—but she also knew him well enough to see the tension in his jaw, hear the slight edge to his voice. "You've spent the last month making me happy, making me come more than I thought was humanly possible, and carrying out a ridiculous scheme just to help me and my business. And you really don't see why I might love you? Sweetheart, loving you is the easiest thing I've ever done."

Loving you is the easiest thing I've ever done. If only she was ridiculous enough to believe that, despite all evidence to the contrary. If only it sounded remotely like a fact instead of a fairy tale. But she wasn't, and it didn't, and her heart—her heart didn't just fall. It collapsed.

"Oh God," she breathed. Realization was finally dawning, slow and terrible, like a bloodred sun in some postapocalyptic nightmare. She scrambled to her feet, dragging the sheets with her.

"Danika, whatever you're thinking right now, I can tell by your face that it's absolutely wrong."

Except she wasn't wrong, because it all made sense. *This* was the only logical explanation. "I know what you're doing, Zafir."

He stared, apparently at a loss. Because of course he wasn't doing this on purpose. He'd never do a thing like this on purpose. "What—?"

"We've been faking it, and sleeping together, and blurring all kinds of lines. So we both—we both got confused, and did *this.*" She gesticulated wildly, as wild as the panicked rush of her pulse. "And now you're romanticizing everything, trying to turn us into some epic love story, trying to make me something I've never been—"

"Are you serious?" he demanded.

"Don't act like I'm not making sense," she snapped, searching the floor for her clothes. "Just—just ask yourself for a second if what you're feeling is really about me or if it's part of the . . . the story you want to weave for yourself." *And then tell me. Tell me the truth, and make it good, and make me believe it, and then I can calm down and get back into bed and stop—stop feeling like I'm dying—*

Zaf stood with a curse, stabbing his legs into a pair of sweatpants. "Danika, the first night we slept together I left your place in fucking knots because I knew I had feelings for you and I couldn't see how it would *ever* work out. I thought the best I could hope for was just getting over you. You think that's the kind of thing I romanticize? It's not like you're the easiest option!"

She stopped in her tracks and turned to stare at him. "You're right," she whispered, because if she spoke any louder she might . . . she might cry. "I'm not the easiest option at all."

He looked stricken. "I didn't mean it was a bad thing! It's the exact fucking opposite. I am not just stumbling into this." He walked toward her slowly, the way you might approach a wounded animal. They'd woken up together, and he'd told her she was perfect, and that he loved her, and instead of it being the sweet, romantic moment he deserved, she'd turned it into this.

Jesus fucking Christ, couldn't she have just said thank you and made him some coffee?

"I love you," he repeated softly. "And it's not in spite of this or that. It's not because I don't see you as you are. It's not because I want you to be someone else. I just . . . love you."

He didn't, of course. He couldn't. He was deluded. And she wanted to be deluded with him, she wanted that so fucking badly, but—but it wouldn't last. It never did.

Would Zaf still think he loved her when she fucked up, when

she started to buckle under the pressure of his expectations? When she made everything hard all the fucking time just to see if he'd bend or break, if this or that time would be the last straw? In that moment, she could visualize a thousand ways her rough edges might wear away his shine, and she just—

In every relationship she'd ever had, someone was ruined and someone did the ruining. Danika didn't want to play either role. Not with him.

"I'm sorry," she said.

He knew what she meant. He always knew what she meant. "Don't. Danika, *don't.*"

"This was a mistake."

He stepped back as if she'd slapped him. His expression crumpled like paper, and her heart did, too. "No," he said. "We're—we're trying. Try with me, Dan. Give me something."

"We *tried*," she corrected, because she had to get the hell out of here before the first tears came and snapped her in two. "But trying didn't work."

CHAPTER EIGHTEEN

Four hours later, Zaf was standing on the rugby pitch, waving good-bye to the last of the lads, mentally patting himself on the back for pretending to be a real, live human during the length of a Tackle It session.

In reality, he wasn't human at all. He was a thousand shattered pieces, and for the first time in a long time, he honestly couldn't see a way to glue himself back together.

Trying didn't work.

He couldn't forget the look on her face, the horror and fear and disbelief when he'd told her he loved her. Why the *fuck* had he told her—when he *knew* how scared she was, when she'd just admitted how badly her twisted ex had fucked with her head—that he loved her?

Because he'd wanted her to be okay again, to stop worrying. He'd seen her panicking, and instead of remembering that she was Danika and she needed time and space, he'd treated her like she was someone else—someone who'd be pleased with a big *I love you* moment. Zaf realized that when he cared about something, he had a tendency to be . . . rigid. To draw harsh lines and stick to them, to follow the path he knew. But she'd asked for baby steps, and he'd fucking *sprinted*. Since when did following the perfect script matter more than the woman he actually wanted to be with?

Trying didn't work.

He was still struggling to swallow that fact, its thorns drawing blood in his throat, when he looked across the field and spotted a familiar reed-thin figure haunting the edge of the pitch. Mint-green hijab, cream blouse and trousers, with matching mint-green shoes peeking out. Hollywood sunglasses and a tiny, glossy handbag. Hands on her hips and a posture that said, *Ugh, grass.*

Kiran.

Something in Zaf crumbled, just a little bit. He strode over and snatched her into a hug, lifting her off her feet.

"Watch it," she groused, whacking him with the handbag. "You're crushing my silk."

He hugged harder. And she, despite her supposed annoyance, hugged back, grounding him like an anchor.

Kiran's blood siblings, all sisters, were scattered across the globe: an engineer in Toronto, a scientist in Nairobi, an artist in Lahore. But Kiran was the type who found family everywhere, one of the shining silver links that held the shitty world together. She'd loved the Ansaris, loudly, from the start. And Zaf loved her, too.

After a while, she whispered in his ear, "Sweetie, are you crying?"

"No," he said. "I'm leaking masculine pain from my eyeballs."

Kiran laughed. Zaf tried to, since that had been the point of saying it, but he couldn't quite make himself. Because he hurt. He was hurting. Just thinking the words chipped away at some cold, concrete dam inside him, and the full force of his technicolor feelings spilled out like the world's most violent waterfall. *Fuck*, he thought. *Nope, no thanks, don't want that.* But it came anyway.

"Ouch," he muttered, and put Kiran down so he could rub his chest.

She peered up at him, concern creasing her brow. "Zaf. What the hell happened?"

"Nothing."

"*Nothing?*" She shot the word back at him with a spade of skepticism.

Jamal strolled over, which was a surprise, because Zaf had been so out of it he'd kind of forgotten his friend was even on the pitch. "I called Kiran because you looked like you were dying and you wouldn't talk to me."

"You're a snitch," Zaf muttered.

"And when I was leaving," Kiran interjected, "Fluffy told me that if you're upset it's probably because you're in love with your fake girlfriend."

"Your daughter," Zaf said, "is also a snitch."

"Or you're just really obvious," Jamal supplied.

Kiran pointed a finger at him. "You're not helpful. Go and finish clearing up." She hooked her arm through Zaf's, which might have been awkward if they didn't have years of experience navigating the height difference, and tugged him off down the field. "Let's walk."

"All right," he sighed, leaving Jamal huffing indignantly behind them.

After a few strides and long moments of silence, she nudged Zaf in the ribs. "And talk. Let's walk and talk."

"About?" he asked dully, as if he didn't know.

"Stop being annoying before I hit you with my bag again."

Really, what were sisters even *for*?

Making you feel human when you're teetering on the brink of abandoning your mortal name and moving into a box in the woods.

Well, yeah. There was that.

"This morning I told Dani I loved her. And she didn't believe me."

Kiran stared at him. "Oh. Oh, dear. How long have you two been dating for real?"

"Er . . . At that point, about twelve hours. Depending on your perspective."

Kiran stared at him some more. Then she whacked him with her bag.

"*Ow.* What? I talked!"

"Let me guess. You sprang all the emotional stuff on her before she was ready, she reacted badly, and now you're moping around like someone peed in your cereal." Kiran threw up a hand, which contained the Bag of Terror, and Zaf tried not to flinch in response. "*Men.*"

"I know I messed up," he said. Holy fuck, did he know. There were stones in his rib cage, burning coals in his belly, cement blocks set around his feet. He felt as if a part of him had been hacked raggedly away. The only thing keeping him upright was the knowledge that he'd weathered worse storms, and that he'd survive. That he'd always survive.

But that didn't stop him fucking hurting.

"I don't think she's ever going to want the things I want," he admitted, the words almost choking him. "She told me from the start, and I acted like I got it, but . . . Part of me hoped that if I showed her things could be good, she'd change her mind. And that's just fucked up. Dani was the only one who could change her mind about us, and maybe she was going to, but I couldn't give her the time she needed to do it." He paused. "Or maybe she wasn't changing her mind at all, and she only spent the night with me because Inez Holly told her to. One of those."

Kiran's eyebrows flew up. "I'm not entirely sure what that last part means, so I'm going to ignore it, if you don't mind."

"Wish I could ignore it," he muttered. *Trying didn't work.* The words haunted his mind again, and this time he noticed they were taking on the familiar, taunting cadence of an anxious fixation. He took a breath, and another. Kept talking, because sometimes that was the only way to untangle his own knots. "Bottom line is, I think I hurt her, going too far, too fast. And I definitely hurt myself. I don't know if we can do this, and she's positive we can't, so . . . maybe that's that."

"Oh," Kiran murmured after a while. "I see. I'm sorry, Zaf. I'm really sorry."

"I know," he said softly.

"Are you going to . . . talk to her?"

"I don't know." He wanted to. More than anything, he wanted to go after her and make everything right—because that's what he was supposed to do. That's how you got to a happily ever after. Except Zaf's desire for a happily ever after, and his idea of how love was *supposed to* look, had pushed him into this mess. He thought for a moment longer, then shook his head. "I've chased her too hard for too long, and all that did was make her panic." Zaf knew panic. He knew the squeeze of fear, knew the way it left you shaken and unsure of who you were, and he didn't ever want to cause that feeling in someone he loved again. Just the idea made him physically sick. "I don't know what else to do except leave her the fuck alone."

"If you've overwhelmed her," Kiran said slowly, "that might be a good idea. I know sometimes you worry about things being . . . right or wrong, ruined or perfect. But there are shades of gray, too, Zafir."

"Yeah," he agreed. "Yeah." He wanted to learn those shades—or rather, to get better at remembering them. He knew he could do it.

But one thing would never change: Zaf loved Danika in bold black-and-white, stark and completely unsubtle, no shades of gray to be found. He loved her absolutely and he loved her uncompromisingly. And if that was all wrong for her, he'd just have to deal with the loss.

Ah, he was so fucking screwed. But at least he wasn't alone.

Zaf came to a stop, turning to face his sister. "Kiran . . . have I ever said thank you?"

She blinked, raised her eyebrows. "For what?"

"For staying with me. Back then. When Dad and Zain—when they died. I tried to make you leave me alone. Or hate me. But you wouldn't."

"Well," she said with a smile, "you're impossible to hate." Then her expression softened. "You stayed with me, too, you know. And Fatima, she couldn't ask for a better uncle." Kiran reached up to put a hand on his cheek. "You're my little brother, Zaf. I love you. I don't leave you. Your mother and I, Jamal and Fatima, we're all a family."

A family. A broken one, true, but broken didn't mean ruined. He and Danika had broken clean in half this morning, but nothing about her was ruined, either. Because the world wasn't split into unhappy endings and happily ever afters. There were blessings everywhere and a thousand shades of joy all around him.

Every shade should be savored.

Danika wasn't entirely sure what death felt like, but she was certain her current state must be close. True, nothing had actually harmed her. And yet, the minute she'd slammed Zaf's front door behind her, she'd felt as if several vital organs had been wrenched from her body all at once. As if they were trapped on the other side of that door, slamming against the wood to reach her, and she could feel every last bruising smack.

Now, for what felt like the thousandth time today, a sob racked her shoulders, and the hollow of her empty insides ached.

Beside her, on Chloe's vast, marshmallow-y sofa, Eve grimaced.

"Oh dear." She speared Sorcha with a grave look and murmured, "You did the right thing to bring her here."

"No, she didn't." Dani sobbed (yes, sobbed, *again*—her tear ducts appeared to be malfunctioning) from beneath a wad of Kleenex.

"And to call me," Eve continued.

"No, she *didn't*." Dani glared across the living room at her best friend. "When have I ever ratted you out to *your* sisters, you traitorous . . . *lizard*!"

Sorcha arched her magnificent eyebrows. The effect was quite severe. "If I ever call you in a flood of tears and request an emergency rescue from the back of some random chip shop because I'm crying too hard to walk home, I give you formal permission to contact whichever of my sisters you wish." She paused. "Except Aileen. Don't you dare call Aileen."

Dani's attempt at an acerbic response was cut off by her older sister. "Redford," Chloe said imperiously, phone pressed to her ear, "if you have any dodgy friends who might be persuaded to dump someone in the River Trent, gather them now and tell them I pay very well."

Dani tried to laugh, but it came out as a choked squeak, accompanied by a bubble of snot.

"Oh, darling." Eve shuddered, passing her another lavender-scented tissue. "What an atrophied state of affairs."

"It's fine," Dani insisted, after blowing her nose. "I'm fine. Everything's fine." She'd tried, and she'd failed, but that was to be expected, so why should it hurt? It shouldn't. And neither should the knowledge that Zaf had deluded himself into loving

her, because it wasn't as if *she* loved *him*. She'd simply been high
on Inez Holly's approval and had made some shoddy decisions
last night. This morning's events had been a warning shot from
the universe, a reminder of who Dani was and the lessons she'd
learned about attempting romance. That was all. That was *all*.

She opened her mouth to explain as much in a clear and calm
manner, but all that came out was another ear-splitting wail.

Oops.

"When I picked her up," Sorcha said grimly, "she was essen-
tially unintelligible, but I did hear *Zaf*."

"That's why I'm calling instead of texting," Chloe was saying
patiently into her mobile. "No paper trail. I see no reason for
your line to be bugged, so this is a fine method of arranging a
man's imminent death."

"Chloe, honestly," Dani managed, "Zaf hasn't done—"

"Little sisters should be seen and not heard," Chloe said
grimly, before her concentration went back to the phone. "I'm
not implying anything, darling, I'm just saying that you're a very
resourceful man who might possibly know other resourceful
men, especially since artists are known to have an excess of feeling. Yes. Yes. Well, of course I don't want you to go to prison; I
wasn't suggesting you get *caught*. No. I'll ask her. Danika, would
you like orange chocolate or dark?"

"Both," Danika said glumly.

"Same for me," Eve piped up.

"And me." That was Sorcha.

"We'll all have both. Oh, stop moaning, our teeth have survived this long. Good-bye. I love you, too."

Dani's stomach lurched, a stab of pain flaring behind her ribs. *I love you,* Zafir had said. *I love you as you are.* It had sounded so wonderful, coming from that beautiful mouth in that slow, familiar voice, and she'd wanted it so badly she'd felt dizzy. But she couldn't—she just couldn't—

Why would he *say* that? Why would he say that to her, and make everything so much more impossible? She was only just coming to grips with the fact that they could be together properly, that she might not fuck *that* up, and he expected her to believe he'd somehow fallen head over heels within five minutes?

Yes. He expected you to believe him, because he never lies. And because being a romantic doesn't make him a fool.

But he must've been mistaken. He *must* have been, because Dani hadn't even *tried* to be lovable. Except . . .

Except he'd sort of told her that she didn't need to try. Which, now she could breathe again, and think without the weight of his entire life's hopes and dreams crushing her, did sound quite reasonable and very Zafir-like.

Oh dear. Oh dear, oh dear, oh dear.

The tears started again.

"Good Lord," Chloe said, putting the phone down. "You really must tell us what's happened, Danika, or I might be moved to call Gigi."

"I think—I think Zaf *loves* me," Dani wailed.

There was a moment of silence before Sorcha piped up cautiously, "Oh . . . no?"

"But I didn't—he *shouldn't*," Dani sobbed. "Or he couldn't! Except he does really seem to like me, and he's inhumanly wonderful, so perhaps he *could*, and if he did, I've just ruined everything."

"Sorry, don't let me throw you," Eve said, "I'd just like to check before we go any further. Are you telling me that your fake boyfriend, who you have, obviously, been sleeping with—"

"Bravo, by the way," Chloe interjected.

"—told you he *loved* you, and you decided, for some reason, that he'd . . . made it up?"

"Yes," Dani managed in a very small voice.

"And what," Eve asked delicately, "did you say to him in return?"

"I said . . . I said we'd made a mistake."

"Oh sweet fucking Christ," Sorcha muttered. "Baby Jesus in a manger, give me *strength*. Danika Brown, if I strangle you—"

"Don't be angry with *me*," Dani snapped. "It wasn't—I wasn't ready for this! All I asked for was a nice, goddess-mandated fuck buddy, and the signs led me to believe that I'd gotten one."

"Oh, for shite's sake, Dani!" Sorcha cried. "You *know* that's not how signs and invocations work. You're not supposed to use random happenings as an excuse to avoid dealing with what you really want. You're supposed to pay attention to what resonates. You're supposed to take a fucking hint!"

"Is that *honestly* your best solution?" Dani demanded. "Focusing on what I want? Because that would involve letting myself be lost and confused and in love with him, which is a lot to fucking deal with, Sorcha!" She hadn't had a chance to work through the pros and cons, or check it for safety from every angle. For heaven's sake, she hadn't even written it down, and nothing even *counted* until you wrote it down, which meant that Dani was currently engaged in the highly dangerous practice of loving Zaf without a permit, so no wonder she'd fucked it up, and—

"Oh my God," she gasped. Her thoughts, her breaths, her *heart*, all lurched to a stop.

Loving him. Shit.

Shit, shit, shit.

She loved him.

Dani turned the idea left and right, examined it cautiously as if a vicious alien might burst out from its middle, and finally judged it to be irrefutably true, if not totally safe. She loved Zaf. Which would explain why she'd felt as if she were being crushed by a wheel of terror when he'd had the audacity to love her, too.

Sorcha clapped her hands. "Oh, there we go. *There* it is. Give the girl a prize."

Dani burst into tears again.

"Sorcha," said Eve, who appeared to be—for once—concentrating fully on the matter at hand. She'd even taken her AirPods out. "I'm not entirely following this conversation, and Dani is alarming me. Tell us what you know, or we'll sic the cat on you."

Sorcha looked around. "What cat?"

Chloe removed her glasses and polished them on the edge of her cherry-printed swing skirt, a gesture she no doubt hoped was threatening. "He prefers to avoid company unless absolutely necessary," she said, "but make no mistake, he is a fearsome creature, indeed."

"What on earth are you—?"

Dani decided now might be a good moment to pull herself together and explain things to her sisters. "When Zaf and I started sleeping together," she said, her voice shaking slightly, "we had rules. I always have rules. It makes things . . . safer."

"Safer than what?" Chloe frowned.

Dani took several deep breaths and dabbed at her face with more tissues before answering. She laid out the facts for herself as much as for anyone else, building a map to her own emotions—emotions she'd clearly kept locked away for far too long, if she barely recognized them when she stumbled into their path.

"Safer than feeling things," she said. "Because feelings hurt. Rules don't. But everything with Zaf was so easy that I forgot the risks—until things went too far, and suddenly, he loved me. It just . . . it didn't seem plausible. Or safe. I didn't want to fail or fuck it up. I didn't want to hurt him, and I didn't want to admit he could hurt me."

Chloe eyed her carefully. "I see. Completely understandable. But, darling . . . you seem hurt right now, and I'm willing to bet he is, too. So whatever path you chose to avoid that issue—"

"Was the wrong one," Dani whispered, cradling her head in her hands. "I know. I know. You don't need to tell me that." Not anymore, anyway. Because she was using real logic now, not fear-driven desperation, and it was achingly clear that trying her best for Zafir and failing would've been far less painful than . . .

Than giving up. He'd told her he loved her, and she'd just given up.

Her first instinct was that he might be better off without her. But then she remembered that she was Danika fucking Brown, that she had Inez Holly's email address, that she achieved her goals no matter what, and if she made loving Zaf—properly, the way he deserved—one of those goals, she *could* do it.

Assuming he wanted her to, which, after this morning's fiasco, was doubtful.

"I'm going to fix things," Dani said, because speaking the words aloud would make them realer. "I'm going to do my best, anyway."

"I'm glad," Chloe said gently. "But, darling, I have to ask: this unfortunate incident aside, are you all right? With your . . . feelings, and such?"

Dani hesitated. Then she whispered honestly, "I'm not sure."

Chloe pinned her with an all-seeing, older sister stare and made a soft, encouraging sound that meant, *Do tell, before I drag it out of you on pain of death.*

Apparently, by engaging in a very snotty relationship-related breakdown, Dani had tipped her hand. Her strange-and-possibly-unhealthy-attitude-toward-relationships hand. For the sake of her remaining shreds of dignity, she tried her best to resist spilling her guts. Unfortunately, her iron will was more aluminum today, so after a few seconds, the whole story came tumbling out.

Mateo and the things he'd said, Dani's abject humiliation and gut-wrenching pain. The failures and rejections that came after, and the decision she'd made to avoid romance for good. All the things Dani had learned about love—or rather, about protecting herself from it—flooded the room, and her sisters descended into solemn silence. As she spoke, her shoulders lifted and her stormy emotions calmed, all the fears she'd never admitted to finally flowing free. By the time she was done, a weight that had lived in her gut for years had disappeared. Without it, she stood taller and saw things from an angle she hadn't been able to reach in a while.

Hmm. Fascinating. Perhaps discussing emotional nonsense did have some uses after all. It certainly made her feel better, and wasn't that her latest goal? Taking care of herself as if she deserved it?

You do deserve it. Maybe if she'd really understood that fact, she wouldn't have hyperventilated at the unreserved tenderness in Zaf's eyes that morning.

As Dani's halting speech ended, everyone—even Chloe— left their various seats to join her on the carpet, slipping an arm around her shoulders or squeezing her hand. She was surrounded by her sisters and her best friend, and it felt like being wrapped up in a blanket as soft as clouds and strong as armor. This was love, and part of her had always known that if she shared her darkest thoughts with these women, she'd receive such love instantly. Maybe she'd held off because deep down, she hadn't thought she deserved it.

Dani was starting to realize she'd treated the opinion of everyone who'd ever left her as an irrefutable truth: *Danika Brown is not worthy of love.* The trouble was, building a conclusion based on irrelevant or unreliable sources never worked. And when it came to Dani's worthiness, the only source she should really value was herself.

"Well," Sorcha said after a moment. "I had no idea about all *that.*"

"Nor," Chloe murmured broodingly, "had I." She paused. "Possibly because you never really tell us anything, darling."

Dani sniffed and scowled under the weight of three patient stares. "Yes, I do," she lied.

"No, you don't," Eve said. "I used to just read your diary, but then I got too old to avoid feeling guilty about it."

Dani stared. "Remind me to smack you for that at a later date."

"Why would I possibly remind you to smack—"

"Girls," Chloe interrupted. "Let's focus on the issue at hand, shall we?"

The issue, Dani assumed, being her sudden verbosity in the case of emotional sharing. She supposed her siblings' and even Sorcha's stares of astonishment were warranted; she certainly couldn't remember ever word-vomiting all her pointless problems at anyone before. Except these days, they didn't seem so pointless, and she had a feeling that Zaf—Zaf, who always listened; Zaf, who always cared; Zaf, who wanted everyone to know themselves—was partially responsible for that.

She'd hate him for it, only she was quite tragically in love with him, so hate was proving difficult.

"I remember that little shit Mateo," Chloe went on. "Never liked him. I don't trust southerners."

Oh. Apparently, the issue at hand wasn't Dani's attitude change; it was everything she'd just admitted. She dried her eyes and murmured, "Mateo was Welsh."

Chloe sniffed. "Wherever he was from, I don't trust them."

Sorcha laughed. Eve snorted. And Dani felt incredibly light, despite the lump of sadness blocking her throat and making it hard to breathe.

"You know," Eve said thoughtfully, "you really ought to share with the class more often, Dan. Because now we know all of this, we can tell you helpful things, like: Mateo was a total scumbag. And: you should marry the Superman security guard. And: we love you."

Dani managed a wobbly smile and forced out a mortifyingly honest response. "I love you, too."

"Awwww!" Eve slapped a hand over her heart and pretended to faint. "You know what else I love? That this witch stuff actually works. You might have to teach me."

Sorcha rolled her eyes. "It's not about whether or not it works, Eve."

But Dani was suddenly sure that it absolutely had.

Before she could examine that thought further, the front door opened with a creak and the jangle of keys. "All right," Redford called from the hallway. "If the guy I'm supposed to kill is that big fucker from the video, we'll need an airtight plan."

CHAPTER NINETEEN

Texting Zaf after what had happened really didn't seem like an option. The idea of talking to him over the phone, without being able to see his face—or, worse, calling and him not picking up—felt even more ill-advised. And turning up at his house after storming out just that morning wasn't acceptable, either, not in Dani's mind. She wanted to get this right. Not someone else's idea of perfect, but *right*, for both of them.

To put it simply, they needed to talk. *Shudder.* After she'd apologized. *Double shudder.* So Dani spent Sunday evening trimming her hair and dyeing it red for confidence while on the phone with her grandmother, searching for sage advice.

"Men are difficult creatures," Gigi said as Dani slapped scarlet gloop onto her head. "And it does sound as if you hurt his feelings, my dense little darling. Not that I blame you. You're far too delicate to be expected to weather the drama of sudden romantic confessions."

Dani did not consider herself remotely delicate, but she decided now wasn't the time to argue the point. "I was hoping you'd have some sort of magic tip to help me win him over." Because if the tables had been turned—if she'd been brave enough to admit she loved Zaf, and he'd thrown it back in her face—Dani knew very well she wouldn't be particularly understanding. Not even if she knew all about his reasons.

Hurting a loved one was like running over someone's foot; you rarely meant to do it, but the bones still broke.

"Tips?" Gigi mused. "Hmm. I rarely bother winning people back, darling, so I'm afraid I won't be much use. Unless you want to hear about oral techniques—"

"*Nooo*, thank you. Nope. No. Definitely not."

"I didn't think so. In that case, my beautiful buttercup—you know him best. You know how to explain and how to earn his forgiveness. I don't think anyone can help you with that."

The advice rang in Dani's ears as she rushed to Echo bright and early Monday morning, Zaf's cup of bitter black coffee warming her hand. She'd been too jittery to order a green tea for herself, gripped with the urgent need to see him, even if she had no idea how to explain herself, or make it up to him, or anything else. She just had to see him, and tell him she loved him, and then she'd figure it out from there.

Except Zaf wasn't at his desk.

"Morning, duck." George beamed as she strode into the foyer. "Nice hair."

"Oh," Dani murmured, her steps faltering. "It's . . . you." She couldn't help it if *you* came out sounding a bit like *dog shit*. She didn't want George's pink-cheeked smile. She wanted a grim-faced scowl.

George appeared unperturbed by her less-than-warm welcome. "That for me?" he asked hopefully, reaching for the coffee.

"No." Dani jerked back, which was ridiculous. Zaf wasn't here, and *she* certainly wasn't going to drink his awful brew. But he must be around somewhere. He had to be. She needed to give him this, and tell him she was sorry, and see if he'd still brought her morning protein bar or if he'd absolutely washed his hands of Dani and her poor nutrition, which she wouldn't blame him for. Not because of the nutrition itself, but because she'd been a shit. "Where is Zafir?"

George gave her an odd look. "Called in sick. Thought you'd know."

Sick? "Right," Dani said calmly, as if she weren't absolutely stricken. "Of course." But there was no *of course* about it. Zaf never called in sick. Never. She'd noticed that the same way she'd noticed everything about him, for months and months now: easily, without ever once realizing how closely she watched him or how fascinating she found even his mundanities.

He was wonderful, he was everything, and she'd hurt him, and now he'd called in sick. Shame curdled like sour milk in her belly. "See you," she muttered to George, and scurried up the stairs.

The next day, she brought another coffee, but Zaf still wasn't there. Dani swallowed hard in the face of George's slightly pitying smile, walked past the lift with a wistful, teary glance, and dragged herself up the stairs, which suddenly seemed to go on for miles. She didn't know exactly what it meant when the person you loved stopped coming into work so they wouldn't have to see you, but it certainly didn't seem good. She took a sip of Zaf's coffee, then squeaked in horror and dribbled it back into the cup. Good Lord, that was disgusting. Were the man's taste buds made of concrete?

And now she'd dribbled coffee on her chin, so she should probably go to the bathroom before continuing the day's tragic move-fest.

She turned the corner that led to the nearest bathroom just in time to see a familiar brown bob disappear behind the closing door. *Jo.* Or maybe it wasn't, but it might be, and just that possibility stopped Dani in her tracks—because suddenly, in the midst of all her own pain, it seemed really, really urgent that she speak to Jo.

Jo, her friend. Jo, who'd committed the grievous crime of developing feelings, which human beings often did, and had been punished for it because Dani wasn't in touch with her own. Well, she was certainly in touch with her feelings now, every last stomach-churning one of them, and when it came to Jo, guilt was at the forefront. Along with regret and honest-to-God sorrow, that Dani had hurt someone she cared about just because they'd wanted something she hadn't.

So, like any reasonable ex–fuck buddy with stalkerish tendencies, she leaned against the wall and waited to hear a flush.

Five minutes later, the bathroom door opened, and Jo emerged, her brown bob razor-sharp as ever. Beneath her lab coat, she was wearing black trousers and a midnight-blue shirt, one Dani used to love on her. Of course, there were lots of things Dani had loved on Jo, or about Jo. She'd just never dared to consider the idea of loving Jo herself.

Which now struck her as a damned shame.

"Christ," Jo yelped as she caught sight of Dani. "Oh my God. What are you doing here? I mean—sorry, you probably just want the toilet—"

"No, actually," Dani said. "I followed you."

Jo sighed. "God, Dan, you're not supposed to admit that sort of thing. People will think you're weird."

"I am weird, but that's beside the point. I wanted to talk."

Jo's lips tightened for a moment, but then she released a breath and shrugged. "I suppose you can't still be angry with me, since you've moved on with Mr. Big and Brooding. So what, exactly, do you want?"

Dani ignored the twinge she felt at that mention of Zaf. "I want," she said quietly, "to apologize."

Jo blinked. "Apologize? Really."

"Yes."

"I wasn't certain you knew the meaning of the word."

"Don't be irritating, Josephine. I am attempting to prostrate myself before you."

Jo looked theatrically at the ground. "I don't see it."

I missed you, Dani realized, and wanted to kick herself. *I didn't deserve you.* Not in any context. But it was better to attempt to do right by someone than to give in and refuse to try.

Jo sighed. "God, you look so serious. And tired. You never look tired. Are you sick or something?"

"No. I'm not sick. Simply repenting for my many mistakes."

Jo gave her a considering look and leaned against the wall. "Go on, then. What's this apology for?"

"The entirety of our relationship."

Both women eyed each other for a moment, then smirked almost simultaneously.

"I was a bad friend," Dani went on. "You can't control feelings, but I blamed you when you felt things for me. You were hurt and I didn't give you space to feel that. I didn't respect that it was real. You were my friend and if you'd come crying about some other woman, I would've supported you. So I should've supported you when that woman was me"

Jo took a deep breath and looked away. After a long moment, she shrugged. "I was barking up the wrong tree with you. You made that clear from the start; I just didn't want to hear it. Or maybe I thought I could change you. But I couldn't, and that's okay, because people shouldn't be changed."

Dani agreed with that, to a certain extent. People shouldn't be changed—but perhaps they should grow. Which would explain the constant, hollow ache that had filled her chest whenever she tried not to care about Zaf and failed.

Growing pains.

"Thank you for apologizing," Jo said. "I appreciate it."

"Yes, well. Record the incident in your diary tonight, because I doubt it'll ever happen again."

"I'm sure you're right," Jo snorted. "And I'm sorry, too. Honestly, I just . . . I kind of want us to be okay again."

"Oh thank God. Yes. Let's be okay again."

Jo grinned. Then, after a slight hesitation, she held open her arms.

It was a wonderfully awkward hug, and Dani felt better for it—just as she felt better for being open and honest, for engaging with emotion even if the vulnerability made her uncomfortable. For trusting Jo enough to accept that she cared, and daring to care in return.

They went their separate ways with uncertain smiles, and Dani felt as if she'd been reunited with the best parts of herself. Not the parts so obsessed with staying safe that they electrocuted anyone who got too close. But the strong parts, the determined parts, the ones that made her the woman she was. And she remembered Gigi's words: *You know him best. You know how to explain and how to earn his forgiveness.*

Click.

She knew what to do.

Dani hurried off to her seminar, ideas sparking, mentally cataloguing every romance novel she'd ever seen Zaf read or heard him talk about. While her students got to grips with the horror of close reading on a Tuesday morning, she opened her laptop and ordered digital copies of every love story she could recall.

Dani might not be good at everything, but she'd always been damn good at learning.

When the seminar ended, she looked up at the girl with Zafir's—no, with *Zain's* eyes—and murmured, "Fatima. Could I have a word, please?"

The girl nodded, clearly nonplussed.

When the rest of the students had filed out, Dani stood. "I'm sorry if this makes you uncomfortable, and please feel free to say no." She knew she was being wildly inappropriate. All things considered, Dani had expected Fatima to be yanked from her class long ago. But apparently, none of the Powers That Be realized Dani was teaching her fake—ex . . . oh, whatever—boyfriend's niece. Clearing her throat, she continued, "I was hoping to . . . arrange something for your uncle. And I wondered if you might have any idea how I could contact his friend Jamal."

Fatima, thankfully, didn't seem alarmed by the request. "Sure," she said with a shrug. "I have his number, if you want it."

"Oh, thank you! Although—would he mind you giving it to me?"

Fatima huffed out a laugh. "*Everyone* has Jamal's number. He might as well stick it on lampposts at this point. He likes to know people will call him if they're in trouble, you know?"

Now, that certainly boded well. Surely such a lovely man wouldn't give Dani too hard a time for brutally rejecting his best friend's heart, would he? No. Definitely not.

And he didn't—but when she rang him later that day, he was certainly cautious.

"This is Danika Brown," she said, and there was a heavy pause.

"Hi, Danika," Jamal replied, his voice gentle but steady, moss over immovable earth. "May I ask why you're calling?"

"It's, erm, about Zafir. You see, I know him from work, and—"

"I know who you are."

Well, yes, she supposed that made sense, what with their fake relationship and Jamal being Zaf's best friend and so on and so forth. Dani cleared her throat and pulled herself together. "I suppose I'd better get to the point, then. I need to apologize to Zaf. I want to do it in a very particular way, and I could really use your help."

There was an unnerving moment of silence. Then came Jamal's voice, several degrees warmer. "All right, Danika Brown. Let's talk."

Spending time without Danika did wonders for Zaf's clarity.

For example, he was now even clearer on the fact that he loved her, and that said love was most likely doomed. Which was a shame, because the feeling seemed to have worked its way into his DNA, and he didn't know how to stop. Hence calling in sick to work all week: he did have *some* pride. Enough that he'd rather Dani didn't see his face until he got better at hiding the slapped-arse, brokenhearted expression he'd been wearing since she'd stormed out of his flat.

Falling out of love with her might take a fucking lifetime, but he'd at least *seem* calm and collected while he did it.

"Here, my boy," Mum said, cutting through his thoughts. She plonked a bowl of sweet phirni in front of him and kissed his head. "Eat up. You are wasting away."

"Er . . ." Zaf looked dubiously down at his belly. He didn't know who'd snitched to his mum about this Dani situation, but whoever it was, he'd hunt them down and deliver payback very soon. After he'd had enough of all these home-cooked meals, obviously.

Across the table, Fatima groused, "When are you going to come back to uni? It's weird not seeing you around."

Zaf dredged up a smile, because he always had one for his Fluffball. "It's only been four days. You miss me? Hmm?"

She rolled her eyes.

"You *do*." His smile widened. "You know, when you were a baby, I used to sneak you spoonfuls of my phirni and you'd smile at me so big. Except you didn't have any teeth, so it was kind of scary."

"Ya Allah, not the baby stories."

"Fatima," Kiran sighed. "Watch your mouth."

"Don't mind your uncle," Jamal piped up through a mouth of rice pudding. "He's just feeling emotional."

Mum poked her head out of the kitchen to pout in Zaf's direction. "Oh, my poor, sweet boy. Look at you. Depressed, overeating—"

"Hang on," he said with a scowl, "what happened to 'wasting away'?"

"—and soon to be unemployed. I knew that teacher was trouble from the moment I saw her. Didn't I say, Kiran? Didn't I say, *She looks like trouble*?"

"No." Kiran frowned. "You said she was beautiful and that her haircut was very French."

Mum huffed and disappeared into the kitchen again. "I don't remember that at all."

"Lay off Danika," Zaf called after her. "I . . ." He stopped, suddenly aware that the rest of the table was staring at him.

"You *what*?" Fatima nudged with a grin.

I love her. I miss her. I know that if she can't love me back, I need to let her go. But I can't stop remembering that Danika always surprises me.

He shook his head and told Fatima firmly, "This is an adult conversation."

"I'm eighteen!" But she didn't sound as outraged as usual. And then he caught her exchanging an oddly significant look with Jamal, which never boded well.

"What are you two up to?" Zaf demanded, narrowing his eyes.

"Nothing. You're paranoid," Jamal said sweetly, which might as well have been a sign flashing BULLSHIT. "And don't worry, Auntie Maya," he called toward the kitchen, "Zaf's not going to be unemployed. He's too stubborn for that."

"I don't think that's how employment works," Zaf said with a snort. "But actually . . . Mum, could you come back in here? I have something to tell everyone."

Mum reappeared with a bowl of her own and sat down at the head of the table. "What? What is happening?"

"Nothing," Zaf said. "It's just, well—things have been going really well for Tackle It since . . . since we got so much publicity." He paused for a moment to work through the catch in his throat, the pang in his chest. The woman in his mind's eye.

Danika. If there was one thing he'd learned from their month together, it was that risks were always worth it. Even if you fell instead of flying.

He cleared his throat and started again. "Things have been going well. Really well. You all know I got the chance to offer my program to four local schools in the summer. I got positive responses to some of my funding bids for the first time—maybe because I was more open about what we went through, and how that led me to start Tackle It. Which is cool. But then . . . this week, I got the opportunity to sign a deal with the Titans." Everyone sat up a little straighter at the mention of his old team. "You know they're doing a lot better than they were, back in the day. And now they have this whole nonprofit, grassroots campaign to find more kids for their training academy. So they want to—to join forces with Tackle It, I guess. The idea is, they fund me, I carry out my workshops for them and elsewhere, and I funnel talented kids into the academy, too. Plus, the owner gets to look extra charitable or whatever." Deep breath. "So I've decided it's time to give up security and really go all in."

The stunned silence went on long enough for Zaf's nerves to balloon a little bit. Then, one by one, his family's faces split into slow, proud grins, and the balloon popped, leaving nothing but relief.

"Chacha," Fatima whispered, wide-eyed, "are you serious?"

He nodded. He knew this was huge, logically. He'd just been having trouble getting excited about it when his mind and his heart ached with other things. But now his mother whooped and clapped her hands, and Kiran was clutching her chest and beaming like a lightbulb, and Jamal was punching him in the shoulder and laughing, saying, "I see you, I see you," and some-how all their enthusiasm broke down his own cautious, hurting wall and shoved excitement directly into his veins.

And just like that, Zaf was smiling, too.

An hour and another bowl of dessert later, the whole family still buzzing with congratulations, Jamal dragged Zaf into the hall.

"Come on, man. We need to go somewhere."

Zaf followed along with a frown. "What? Since when?" Then Jamal pushed Zaf's jacket into his hands and kicked his shoes toward him. "Where are we—?"

"Just taking Zafir for a walk, auntie," Jamal called over his shoulder. "Be back in a minute. Come on, get your shoes on."

"Why?" Zaf demanded, but he did it anyway. Jamal just winked. Then he opened the door and they broke out into the cool, spring evening, the sky above them a calm dove-gray. March was officially over, just like Zaf and Dani—but then, that had always been the plan. Yesterday had marked the end of their four weeks of faking it.

So much had happened between them, he barely even thought about that Dr. Rugbae shit anymore. Except when he was scroll-ing through the practically dead hashtag to find old, creepy pic-tures of them holding hands all over campus. Which was not healthy behavior, he realized that, but whatever. He was working on it.

Jamal flicked him in the back of the head. "You're moping."

"No, I'm not."

"Look at your face—you're moping." Jamal steered him around a corner and down the street.

"Maybe I'm pissed because you just dragged me outside for no reason. What's going on?"

"*Nothing.* Nothing you need to panic about, anyway. I promise."

A promise from Jamal was good enough to ease the threat of flickering anxiety, but Zaf still couldn't stop himself from guessing. "Is this about one of the kids?"

"Nah. All good."

Zaf thought some more. "Are you going to propose to Kiran?"

Jamal rolled his eyes. "Inshallah, *obviously* I'm gonna propose to Kiran."

"And you're taking me to discuss this on the . . . rugby field?" Because that's where they'd wound up, he realized, as they stepped onto the familiar grass. "Right now? Is it that urgent?" A thought occurred, and Zaf thumped his friend in the shoulder. "Are you doing it *today*?"

"No. I haven't even got a ring." Jamal looked genuinely nervous for once in his laid-back life. "What kind of ring do you get a woman like that? Plus, it has to match the first one."

The ring Zain Bhai gave her, the one she'd never taken off. Zaf's heart squeezed, but it wasn't discomfort so much as awed, gentle envy.

Love could hurt so bad, but fuck was it *good*.

Zaf was going back to work tomorrow. He had to. Maybe Danika would sail right past him as if they'd been nothing, maybe he'd have to chain himself to his desk so he wouldn't chase after her like some lovestruck hero, but he needed to see her. Or he'd never get the chance to tell her he was sorry. Or to tell her that, if she didn't want his love, fine—but if she did, it would always be there.

Always.

"So," Zaf croaked, "you want ring advice?"

"From you? For what? Like you're some fashion icon. I'll ask Fluffy, thanks very much."

Zaf laughed—and then, freed from the distraction of his sister's possible proposal, he finally noticed the goalposts at the far end of the field. The ones they were walking toward right now. The ones that usually stood plain and unadorned, the white paint chipped and the metal rusting in places, against the backdrop of the field and the cluster of silver beeches just behind it.

Today those posts had countless bunches of huge, bright flowers wrapped around them. Every inch of metal, up to the crossbar, was hidden by white and red carnations, each bigger than Zaf's fist, a sea of petals scattered on the mud beneath the goal. Behind that spectacle, in the long evening shadows cast by the beeches, was a group of teenage boys perched on BMXs, who all started waving. They shouted over each other like excitable puppies given human form.

"Here he is!

"Here, Zaf, we kept an eye on all this because—"

"Fucking Ollie Carpenter was sniffing up here, but—"

"Quiet, quiet, we're supposed to fuck off now."

"Cheers, lads," Jamal called, and they all dispersed.

Zaf stared. "What—?" Then someone else walked out of the shadows. The last person he'd ever expected to see, a living fantasy—but he felt the evening breeze on his cheeks and the familiar give of the earth beneath his feet and knew this was real. "Danika," he breathed.

"Right," Jamal said, nodding happily. "You don't look pissed, so this is my cue. In a bit."

"What? Wait—"

Jamal was already jogging off, back in the direction they'd come. Which left Zaf alone, confused, cautiously hopeful, and absolutely dizzy with longing.

He looked at Dani. Dani looked at him. There were only a hundred meters between them now, but he couldn't make his feet move. He also couldn't stop his eyes from devouring her. Her hair was red, just like the day they'd met—when she'd looked up from her phone and her smile had hit him like a sledgehammer. He might have been doomed from that moment on.

Or maybe *doomed* wasn't the right word anymore.

Today, she wore a black sundress covered with tiny, silver moons and black sandals with a blocky sort of heel that couldn't be comfortable on mud and grass like this. She looked perfect, of course. She always looked perfect, even wringing her hands like she was right now.

"Zaf," she called across the distance. "Are you—are you going to come over here?"

He swallowed. Examined his own buzzing mind and frozen feet. Replied honestly, if a little hoarsely, "Can't."

She hesitated. "Okay."

Another pause as they studied each other. Maybe he was a fool, to look at her now and feel so much hope. But he'd read enough romance novels to suspect things might be looking up.

Did he dare suspect they might be looking up?

"I'm sorry," she said finally, her voice clear and steady. "For hurting you. And for resisting love so hard that I almost didn't notice everything I felt for you."

His breath caught, but he forced down a lungful of air and took a step forward.

"I love you," she said, her voice lifting at the end, like it was a cautious offering. Like she thought he might reject it.

Zaf didn't think he was physically capable. The words seemed to stroke over him, sink into him, surrounding him with a shimmering, starlight happiness he'd never known before.

She loved him, she loved him, she loved him, and he felt like he could fly.

"I know I didn't act like it," she went on. "I was scared, and I used that as an excuse to hurt you. I thought I had everything figured out, but I really don't. I do know for a fact that I trust you—I believe you, when you say you love me. And I love you, too. I'm kind of terrified by it, but clearly not terrified enough, because I can't stop." She was nervous; he could tell by her slight, self-deprecating laugh, by the lopsided smile on her face. She continued to wring her hands, and shifted her weight on her heels, and suddenly all Zaf could think was—

Why the fuck am I not touching her yet?

So he took a step forward, and another, and then he was running.

"Erm," Dani said, her eyes widening. "I hope you're not going to tackle me or something." But her smile had grown bigger and her words fluttered like doves, like cautious hope, and she didn't move. She stood right there until he reached her, and picked her up, and spun her around like she was the greatest gift he'd ever gotten. He heard the breath rush out of her in a long, laughing gasp, and he felt her, soft and lovely, in his arms, and he smelled her candles-and-warm-skin scent and wanted to drown in it. In her.

"I'm sorry," she kept saying, the words muffled against his shoulder, her fingers twisting at his shirt. "I'm sorry, Zaf, I'm sorry."

He put her down and cradled her face in his hands, studied those gorgeous eyes and the crease in her lower lip and the little scar on her nose. "Say it again."

"I'm sorry. I was—"

"Danika." He lowered his head and brushed his lips against hers, electric perfection flashing through every nerve in his body. His stomach swooped like he was on a roller coaster, and a giddy smile spread across his face. Her hands wrapped tightly around his wrists, as if to stop him from letting her go. Like he'd ever let her go. He felt the curve of her answering smile against his mouth.

"That you love me," he corrected softly. "Say you love me."

"I love you," she breathed, and he inhaled the words and exhaled bliss as she continued. "I love you a ridiculous amount, and I can't promise I'll never freak out or mess up—"

"Sweetheart, I don't need promises like that. I just need to know you'll try anyway."

"I will, Zaf, I will—"

"And *I'm* the one who's sorry."

"You're sorry?" She looked at him like he'd dropped his brain on the floor, then laughed. "Of course you are, because you're lovely."

"You asked me for baby steps," he said, every regret tumbling out. "I knew you weren't ready for everything I wanted, but I got carried away. I'm not surprised you panicked."

"It's okay," she told him softly. "It's okay. Now shut up, I'm de-claring myself, and you're making me lose my nerve." Then she kissed him, just the slightest touch, just like he'd kissed her. But he felt it down to his bones.

"Oh," he breathed. "Cool. Yeah. Declare yourself." *Quickly, before I die of happiness.*

She grinned, but her expression sobered as she cupped his face. "I've spent a long time trying not to get hurt, Zaf, but until you, I never stopped to think about why. I'm a confident person. I really am. Which is probably why it's taken me so long to real-ize that I'm also insecure. When it comes to my own value in this—in this context, and the things I'm capable of. Socially." She cleared her throat. "Romantically." Her voice was stiff, and he knew she was probably embarrassed just saying this.

So he held on to her, and hoped she'd understand what it meant. He was speaking her language, the silent one he'd always worried might be in his head, the one made up of touches and looks. *It's okay. It's always okay, when it's you and me.*

She smiled a little, slow and trembling, like she heard him loud and clear. "Now that I've realized all this, I'm planning to . . . you know, work on it. Take a page out of your book, and know myself a little better. Because I deserve it, but also because of you, Zaf. I don't ever want to hurt you to protect myself. I want to be brave."

"You are," he told her. "You are."

"And you're worth it." She kissed him again, slower, deeper, and he let everything he felt for her overflow, because all of a sudden, he didn't have the words to express it. So sipping at her lower lip became *I missed you*, and easing her mouth open meant *I adore you*, and the touch of his tongue against hers meant *You're mine*.

Then he pulled back and said it, just said it. "I missed you. I adore you. You're mine." Wait. He hesitated. "But I don't know what you want, what you're really asking for. And I promised myself I'd always be clear on that. Dan—"

"I want you. In every way I can have you. And I trust you to have me, too," she said softly.

He felt dizzy. "Even though I hit you with the love thing like it was a brick?"

"Yes, despite that." She laughed, and he felt the puff of her amusement against his lips because he still hadn't moved away. Couldn't. Although, he was getting a crick in his neck, bending down for her like this, so he let go long enough to pick her up.

Just like he had the first time: princess style. Since she was his princess and all.

"Zaf," she spluttered. "We've talked about this."

"You should really expect it at all times. Kiss me again."

She didn't hesitate.

When she'd orchestrated this scene, Dani had entertained modest hopes. In her wildest dreams, she'd imagined Zaf deigning to hear her out, then returning to his desk and letting her ply him with coffee and chocolate until his feelings toward her slowly thawed.

Instead, he was kissing her with unreserved joy into a breathless, horny heap, and all she'd done was make a verbal declaration. Dani made a mental note: *Zafir likes verbal declarations.*

She had decided, these last few days, to study everything Zaf liked and do her very best to give it to him.

After one last, lingering kiss, he pulled away slightly and asked, "What's with the flowers?"

Dani's heart was in danger of flying out of her chest, which made concentrating on explanations quite difficult, but she managed anyway. "White and red carnations—it means love. I was being romantic. You know, like in the books."

He grinned wide. "The books?"

"I . . . may or may not have read a few romance novels in order to research how I might win you back."

"You did *what?*" he choked out. Then his shock dissolved into laughter. "Ah, but of course you did. Danika fucking Brown."

He made her name sound like a blessing.

Then, suddenly, he sobered, studying her face with a frown.

"What?" she asked, trying not to panic. If she'd gotten something wrong, he wouldn't throw it back in her face—she knew that now. He never had, and that wouldn't change just because she'd decided to call this connection romantic instead of convenient. So she willed her pounding heart to slow . . . and it did.

"I just—it's not that I don't appreciate the grand gesture," he said, "because, trust me, Dan, I really fucking do."

She exhaled a sigh of relief. "Well, thank goddess for that."

"But I know you don't enjoy things like this. And I hope you didn't feel like you had to do something that wasn't . . . that wasn't you. Because I meant what I said the other day, even if I said it at the wrong time. I don't want you to change, Danika. I just want you to be mine."

Dani was really starting to see the benefits of this romance shit, because at those words, her conservative little heart kicked off its shoes and started to dance. "Well," she said, fighting a grin, "that's quite wonderful to hear. In fact, feel free to repeat it whenever."

He brushed his nose over hers. "As many times as you want," he said softly, and the promise washed over her like warm water.

"But no," she went on, "the flowers haven't triggered some sort of existential crisis in me, if that's what you're worried about. Actually, I've decided this sort of thing might suit me. Perhaps I find it a little difficult to describe how I feel about you—but if I can do something like this to *show* you . . . well. I don't mind that." Actually, she loved it. Loved the smile she'd put on his face, loved the happiness radiating from him even now. He was like the sun, but twice as vital to her existence. She was certain of that.

"All right," he said softly. "All right." Then he sank onto the puddle of petals at their feet, and she curled up in his lap and held him tight, as if he might disappear.

Lord, how she prayed he'd never disappear.

A slight breeze rustled her skirt, and his calloused thumb swept over her bare forearm in that slow, lazy arc she'd missed so fucking much. "I know this isn't going to be easy," she whispered. "But I want to try. I want to try with you, and not give up this time."

"Good," Zaf said. His eyes burned into hers as if he could stamp his words into her mind, into her heart. "I would rather be trying and stumbling with you than doing anything—seriously, absolutely *anything*—with anyone else."

Dani swallowed back a lump of adoration and tried to sound lighthearted as opposed to disgracefully emotional. "Even if I don't change my mildly controversial stance on anniversaries?"

"Fuck anniversaries," he said promptly. "As a very smart woman once told me, that's what Valentine's Day is for."

Dani's laughter became tears after approximately two seconds. She threw her arms around him with such force that anyone else would've fallen—but Zaf didn't. He took the hit and held her tight against his chest where she could feel his pounding heart, or maybe it was hers, or maybe they shared hearts now—she wasn't quite sure how this romance arrangement worked. But she was sure she wanted it, no matter the risks.

"This love business is absolutely nonsensical," she told him unsteadily.

"I know," he replied. "Isn't it great?"

EPILOGUE

One Year Later

Zaf shut the front door and hung up his coat, sweaty from an evening's practice with his local amateur rugby league, and vibrating with a certainty that Danika was up to something.

They had a routine, on nights like this: as soon as he got home, she'd jump his bones and ask about his day. Apparently, she liked sweat. She also liked grilling him about meetings and workshops while playing with his dick, because it made her laugh when he got his words mixed up.

But today? Zaf clocked her shoes in the hallway, but Dani herself was nowhere to be found.

"Hey, trouble," he called as he put his Tesco bags down in the kitchen. "Where are you?"

There was a pause before she shouted from the bedroom, "Nowhere."

The last time Dani had *nowhere*'d him, it was because she'd accidentally bought a fern on Facebook Marketplace that was almost as big as Zaf—*despite* being banned from buying any more plants because they could no longer see their TV.

She was taking her newfound work–life balance, and the accompanying hobbies, very seriously.

Zaf shook his head and followed her voice with a sigh. He had visions of his bedside table being replaced by a giant pot of bamboo. "Dan. Sweetheart. You know we don't have space for any more—"

"Don't come in!" Her voice was muffled through the closed door. "I'm in the bedroom. But don't come in! And don't worry, I didn't buy another plant."

"I don't believe you."

"I *didn't*! Well, not unless you count that teeny, tiny cactus from Urban Outfitters—"

"Danika!"

"He's only a baby, Zaf, darling, have a heart. And stay out of the bedroom." She was laughing, but there was a squeaky edge to her voice that sounded almost like . . . nerves?

Hmm.

In the year since they'd decided to be together—*really* together—Dani had treated keeping in touch with her emotions the same way she treated everything else: as a goal to be hit so hard and so accurately, she split the target in two. But when it came to feelings, and learned behavior, and past hurts, you couldn't just read a few books and try really, really hard and be better. No one could. So, a little while back, they'd made a deal. It was a simple one.

When Zaf was worried about Dani, he pushed. And if it felt like too much, she told him.

"Are you okay?" he asked now.

"Peachy. Golden. Flying without wings."

"Right," he said dryly. "Listen. I'm going to take a shower, and then I'm going to make dinner, and we're going to eat and talk about whatever's bothering you."

"Yes, sir, emotional drill sergeant, sir."

He snorted and flipped her off through the door.

"Are you giving a slab of wood the finger right now, Zafir?"

"You know me so well," he said fondly, and left her to it.

An hour later, Zaf was clean, the kitchen was filled with the scent of homemade Chinese food (which looked pretty damn good, if he did say so himself), and his girlfriend was still locked in their bedroom.

He knocked on the door.

"Yes?" she called innocently.

"Food's almost done."

"Crap."

"What?"

"I said, *great*."

He sighed. "You know, I'm starting to wonder if there's a dead body in there."

"Don't be silly, darling. This is my favorite room in the house, not to be defiled with murder and gore. I'd keep a dead body in the bathtub. Much easier to clean."

"Good to know. I'm coming in now."

Dani released a sigh so mighty he actually heard it through the door. Then she said, "Oh, for heaven's sake. I suppose this will have to do."

Er . . . *what* would have to do? Zaf opened the door to find Danika sitting on the floor with pieces of paper in her hand and a pile of books next to her. Which wasn't exactly an unusual sight—except for the expression on her face.

"Sweetheart," he said, hurrying over to sink down beside her. "What's wrong?"

"Nothing," she said with a scowl. But the trepidation in her pretty brown eyes and the way she pressed her teeth into her plump lower lip all said otherwise.

Zaf dragged her into his lap. "Bullshit."

Dani laughed, slid her hands into his hair, and pulled him close. Her kiss was quick and soft and almost shy, as if they barely knew each other again. She tasted like tea and honey and comfort, and by the time she pulled away, he was light-headed, as always, grinning and drunk on her. Seemed like he'd never build up a tolerance.

Then she asked him out of nowhere, "What did you make for dinner?"

"Nothing special," he said. "Just, you know . . . egg fried rice. And stuff."

She smiled, slow and sweet. "Ah. Good choice."

"Well, it's—"

"For our anniversary, correct?"

Zaf froze. "That . . . is not what I was going to say."

"But it's true, though." She didn't look upset. Actually, she looked *pleased*.

That pleasure spilled over to him, her sunlight too bright to contain. "My girlfriend doesn't believe in anniversaries," he said, fighting a smile, "and I don't like to pressure her. Not when she does Valentine's Day so well."

Dani flicked imaginary hair over her shoulder and looked adorably self-satisfied.

"Plus," he continued, "we only moved in together six months ago. I'm still trying to make sure she won't run off into the night."

"You know I'm not going to do that, Zafir." She rolled her eyes, but there was nothing mocking about what she said next. "I can't. I love you. And you're mine."

"I know," Zaf said softy. And he really, really did. He'd never known anything the way he knew that, because she showed him in a thousand perfectly *Danika* ways every day.

"Anyway," she continued, "you sleep half on top of me and you're too heavy to push off, so I couldn't sneak away if I tried."

He burst out laughing.

She crawled out of his lap and back to her stack of books—which, he now realized, were romance novels. Ones he recognized. Zaf frowned at the familiar spines as she said primly, "Since you raised the topic of anniversaries—"

"Oh, yeah. Since *I* raised it."

"Shut up. Here." She picked up the first book in the pile and shoved it at him.

Zaf blinked down at the cover and wondered if Dani had

forgotten he already owned this. It was one of his favorites, although, in fairness, he hadn't seen it for a while. Thought he'd lost it or something.

Then he eyed an old scuff on the corner and realized this was *literally* his book.

"Er . . . thanks, sweetheart," he said. He meant it, too. It was sweet that she'd decided to go against her weird theories about *temporal markers in relationships as an unnecessary source of external validation*, or whatever, even if she'd done it by . . . gifting him his own book.

"I was trying to write you a letter," she said, waving her paper around. "I've been working on it for hours. I thought I could finish it before you got home, but then you returned *disgracefully early*—"

"Pretty sure I didn't."

"Don't split hairs, darling. The point is, it's not my finest work, but it'll do." She handed the paper over with a grimace. He looked down at the few lines she'd written and wondered if it was possible to pass out from adorableness overload. Then he actually read the words and decided that, if it *was* possible, he was in serious danger.

Dear Zaf,

I suppose you were right about this anniversary rubbish. On the one hand, it seems twisted to celebrate the growth of your embryonic connection to another, ultimately fallible human being, but on

the other, I enjoy finding excuses to make you happy.
And I suppose it is quite nice that I've had you for a
whole year. I love you. Also I have been systematically
stealing, defacing, and hiding some of your favorite
paperbacks for almost the entire length of our
relationship. Hope that's all right.

Danika

He read that last part with a frown and looked up. "I love you, too. Seriously. A lot. But I'm not sure I understand what you mean about the books."

Dani pursed her lips and rubbed her hands over her thighs. Nervous. She was still nervous, even after she'd given him the letter. "I considered buying brand-new copies to be signed, but that seemed silly. Then you'd have multiple copies of the same book, and we barely have enough shelf space as it is, and—"

"Signed?" Zaf cut in, and picked up the book again, flipping it open. There it was, right on the title page:

For Zaf.

And then a signature. From one of his favorite authors.

He stared at it for a moment in disbelief. Then he took another book, and another, and opened each one, and saw . . .

"When did you *do* this?" he murmured, flicking through them all. "*How* did you do this?"

"I began eight months ago, with some copious research," Dani said, "and identified the authors amongst your favorites who were likely to assist in a romantic gesture—which was, unsurprisingly, almost all of them. I went with Eve to a few conventions—"

"You told me she was forcing you to do that!"

"Ha. I'm sure she would rather have gone with one of her book-club friends, but I had a task to complete. Other than the authors I met in person, I have been in correspondence with a few for some time, and used Gigi's many creative connections to persuade the rest." She paused her matter-of-fact recitation and flicked him an uncertain look, one that wrapped around his heart like a fist and squeezed. "*I* don't want presents, you understand." He believed her. She looked mildly horrified by the idea. "I'm very pleased with dinner and I'm very pleased with you. And maybe anal, since we're celebrating," she added thoughtfully.

"Noted," Zaf murmured, still feeling dazed.

"But what I really wanted was, erm . . . I suppose, to do something that would make you . . ." She trailed off with a slow smile, then pointed at his face. "Yes. That. I wanted to do something that would make you look absolutely thrilled. So, mission accomplished." She clapped her hands and beamed, clearly impressed with herself.

"Dan," he said slowly. "You didn't . . . you didn't have to do this."

"I know." She came to kneel in front of him, her hands on his shoulders. When their eyes met, he saw a fierce, burning love in hers that reflected everything inside of him, and when she spoke, he heard it in her voice. "I know I didn't have to do this, Zaf. I never *have* to do anything with you. But you make me want to. You make me feel like myself, and you make me feel like I'm enough, and you even make me feel like I would be just fine without you. The thing is, I don't *want* to be without you, and so I don't ever plan on it. We are going to have many more anniversaries, and you will continue to make me dinner, and I will continue to make you smile, and I believe that is what they call—"

He arched an eyebrow. "Living happily ever after?"

She nodded. "Sounds about right."

Don't miss the next steamy, fun romantic
comedy from Talia Hibbert . . . The last
Brown sister finds love in Spring 2021!

Read on for a sneak peek at Eve's book . . .

CHAPTER ONE

Eve Brown didn't keep a diary. She kept a journal. There was a difference.

Diaries were horribly organized and awfully prescriptive. They involved dates and future plans and regular entries and the suffocating weight of commitment. Journals, on the other hand, were wild and lawless things. One might abandon a journal for weeks, then crack it open one Saturday evening under the influence of wine and marshmallows without an ounce of guilt. A woman might journal about last night's dream, or her growing anxieties around the lack of direction in her life, or her resentment toward the author of the thrilling Ao3 fanfic "Tasting Captain America," who hadn't uploaded a new chapter since the great titty-fucking cliffhanger of December 2015. For example. In short, journaling was, by its very nature, impossible to fail at.

Eve had many journals. She rather liked them.

So, what better way to spend a lovely, lazy Sunday morning in August than journaling about the stunning rise and decisive fall of her latest career?

She got up with a stretch, clambered off of her queen-sized bed, and drew back the velvet curtains covering her floor-to-ceiling windows. With bright, summer light flooding the room, she tossed off her silk headscarf, kicked off the overnight tea tree and shea foot mask socks she'd slept in, and grabbed her journal from her bedside table, leafing through the gold-edged pages. Settling back into bed, she began.

Good morning, darling,

—The journal, of course, was darling.

It's been eight days since Cecelia's wedding. I'm sorry I didn't write sooner, but you are an inanimate object, so it doesn't really matter.

I regret to report that things didn't go 100% to plan. There was a bit of a fuss about Cecelia's corset being eggshell instead of ivory, but I resolved that issue by encouraging her to take a Xanax from Gigi. Then there was a slight palaver with the doves—obviously, they were supposed to be released over Cecelia and Gareth for the photographs, but I discovered just before the ceremony that the dove's handler hadn't fed them for two days so they wouldn't shit all over the guests. I may have lost my temper and released them all. Unfortunately, the handler demanded I pay for them, which I suppose was fair enough. It turns out doves are very expensive, so

I have had to request an advance on my monthly payment from the trust fund.

Finally, Cecelia and I have sadly fallen out. It seems she was very attached to the idea of the aforementioned doves, and perhaps her tongue had been loosened by the Xanax, but she called me a selfish jealous cow, so I called her an ungrateful waste of space and ripped the train off her Vera Wang. By accident, obviously.

Knowing the lovely Cecelia as I do, I'm sure she'll spend her Fiji honeymoon badmouthing my services on various bridezilla forums in order to destroy my dream career. Obviously, the joke is on her, because I have no dream career and I have already erased Eve Antonia Weddings from the face of the earth. And Chloe says I lack efficiency!

Hah.

Eve finished her entry and closed the journal with a satisfied smile—or else, a smile that should be satisfied, but instead felt a little bit sad. Hm. Apparently, she was in a mood. Perhaps she should go for a walk, or read a romance novel, or—

No. Breakfast. She must begin with breakfast.

Decision made, Eve chose her song for the day—"Rain on My Parade," to cheer her up—hit Repeat, and popped in one of her AirPods. Soundtrack established, she got up, got dressed, and headed down to the family home's vast marble-and-chrome kitchen, where she found both her parents in grim residence.

"Oh dear," she murmured, and stopped short in the doorway.

Mum was pacing broodily by the toaster. Her pale blue suit made her amber skin glow and really highlighted the fiery rage in her hazel eyes. Dad stood stoic and grave by the Swiss coffee machine, sunlight beaming through the French windows to bathe his bald, brown head.

"Good morning, Evie-bean," he said. Then his solemn expression wavered for a moment, a hint of his usual smile coming through. "That's a nice T-shirt."

Eve looked down at her T-shirt, which was a lovely orange color, with the words SORRY, BORED NOW written across her chest in turquoise. "Thanks, Dad."

"I swear, I've no idea where you find—"

Mum rolled her eyes, threw up her hands, and snapped, "For God's sake, Martin!"

"Oh, ah, yes." Dad cleared his throat and tried again. "Eve," he said sternly, "your mother and I would like a word."

Wonderful; they were in a mood, too. Since Eve was trying her best to be cheerful this morning, this was not particularly ideal. She sighed and entered the kitchen, her steps falling in time with the beat of Barbra's bold staccato. Gigi and Shivani were at the marble breakfast bar across the room, Shivani eating what appeared to be a spinach omelet, while Gigi stole the occasional bite in between dainty sips of her usual Bloody Mary smoothie.

Unwilling to be contaminated by her parents' grumpiness, Eve trilled, "Hello, Grandmother, Grand-Shivani," and snagged a bottle of Perrier from the fridge. Then, finally, she turned to face Mum and Dad. "I thought you'd be at your couples' spin class this morning."

"Oh, *no*, my lovely little lemon," Gigi cut in. "How could they possibly *spin* when they have adult children to *ambush* in the kitchen?"

"I know that's how I approach disagreements with my twenty-six-year-old offspring," Shivani murmured. When Mum glared in her direction, Shivani offered a serene smile and flicked her long, greying ponytail.

Gigi smirked her approval.

So, it was official; Eve was indeed being ambushed. Biting her lip, she asked, "Have I done something wrong? Oh dear—did I forget the taps again?" It *had* been eight years since she'd accidentally flooded her en suite bathroom badly enough to cause a minor floor/ceiling collapse, but she remained slightly nervous about a potential repeat.

Mum released a bitter laugh. "The *taps*!" she repeated with frankly excessive drama. "Oh, Eve, I wish this issue were as simple as *taps*."

"Do calm down, Joy," Gigi huffed. "Your vibrations are giving me a migraine."

"Mother," Dad said warningly.

"Yes, darling?" Gigi said innocently.

"For God's sake," Mum said . . . rage-ing-ly, "Eve, we'll continue this in the study."

The study was Mum's office, a neat and tidy room on the ground floor of the family home. It had an atmosphere of focus and success, both of which Eve found singularly oppressive, and the only comfortable chair in the room was the vast leather one behind Mum's desk. Of course, Mum sat in that particular chair,

Dad standing behind her like a loyal henchman, which left Eve to perch on the edge of the stiff-backed guest seat opposite. It wasn't the most comfortable of positions, physically or metaphorically.

"Where," Mum asked, straight to the point as always, "is your website?"

Eve blinked. She had, in her time, owned many websites. Her oldest sister, Chloe, was a web designer, and Eve had always been a loyal client. "Erm . . ." Before she could formulate a response—a nice, precise one that covered all relevant information in exactly the way she wanted—Mum spoke again. That was the trouble with Mum. With most of Eve's relatives, in fact. They were all so *quick*, and so uniformly relentless, their intellect blowing Eve about like dandelion fluff in a hurricane.

"I directed my good friend Harriet Hains," Mum said now, "to your business, because her daughter is recently engaged, and because I was so proud of the success you made of Cecelia's wedding last week."

For a moment, Eve basked in the glow of that single word: *proud*. Mum had been proud. Eve had, for a day, achieved something her brilliant and accomplished mother valued enough to deem it a *success*. Giddy warmth spread out from her chest in cautious tendrils—until Eve got a grip and clamped firmly down on those rogue emotions. Any external source of validation that affected her so intensely was not to be trusted.

She had planned Cecelia's wedding, and now she was done with it. Simple as that.

"Harriet told me," Mum forged on, "that your website URL led her to nothing but an error message. I investigated for myself

and can find no trace of your wedding planning business online."
Mum paused for a moment, her frown turning puzzled. "Except a
largely incoherent forum post claiming you stole an entire bevy of
white doves, but that is an obviously unhinged accusation."

"Obviously," Eve agreed. "I paid for those doves, that lying cow."

Mum gave a glacial stare. "I beg your pardon, Eve Antonia
Brown."

"Let's focus on the issue at hand, shall we, love?" Dad interjected. "Eve. What's happened to your business?"

Ah. Yes. Well. There was the rub. "The thing is, Dad,
Mum . . . I have decided that wedding planning isn't for me
after all. So, I dissolved the business, deleted the website and
disconnected the URL, and closed down all associated social
media accounts." It was best, Eve had found, to simply rip off
the bandage.

There was a pause. Then Mum said tightly, "So you gave up.
Again."

Eve swallowed, suddenly uncomfortable. The cadence of that
single word, the world of disappointment in Mum's voice, made
her feel small and cold and trapped. "Well, no, not exactly. It was
just an experience I stumbled into—Cecelia's original wedding
planner was rubbish, so—"

"She was an ordinary woman who couldn't deal with a spoiled
brat like Cecelia Bradley-Coutts," Dad cut in, frowning deeply.
"But you could. You did. And you seemed to enjoy yourself, Eve.
We thought you'd—found your calling."

A cold bead of sweat began to drip, slow and steady, down
Eve's spine. Her calling? Eve wasn't the sort of woman who had

callings. She was free and loose, thank you very much. It suited her disposition far better than—than—

Than shoving everything she was and everything she had into a single dream, and failing, and hurting herself as punishment. There was a little demon in her head that lived for punishment. But that was okay; she knew how to outwit that demon now.

What she didn't know was how to explain all this to her parents. "It's for my own good, really," she began, light and airy. "Everything went suspiciously well—you know I probably couldn't recreate such success again. Wouldn't want to disappoint myself."

Dad stared, crestfallen. "But Eve. You're disappointing *us*."

She flinched.

"You can't avoid trying at anything in case you fail," he told her gently. "Failure is a necessary part of growth."

She wanted to say, *That's what you think*. But she couldn't. She couldn't, because she wasn't about to slice open years-old scars for them now. Mum and Dad didn't need to know about all of Eve's little imbalances. She handled things just fine.

But clearly, her parents didn't agree, because Mum was shaking her head and saying, "Enough is enough, Eve. You're twenty-six years old, perfectly intelligent and absolutely capable, yet you waste time and opportunities like—like a spoiled brat. Like Cecelia."

Eve sucked in an outraged breath. "I am *not* spoiled!" She thought for a moment. "Well, perhaps I am mildly spoiled. But I think I'm rather charming with it, don't you?"

No one laughed. Not even Dad. In fact, he looked rather angry as he demanded, "How many careers do you plan to flit through while living at home and surviving on nothing but the money *we* give you? Your sisters have moved out, and they work—damned hard—even though they don't need to. But you went from performing arts, to law school, to teaching. From graphic design to cupcakes to those tiny violins you used to make—"

"I don't want to talk about the violins," Eve scowled. She'd quite liked them, but she'd developed a large social media following by filming her musical carpentry. Then various magazines had started writing about her skills, or some such rubbish. When that Russian prodigy had shown up on her doorstep, she'd known things were going too far.

"You don't want to talk about *anything*!" Dad exploded. "You dip in and out of professions, then you cut and run. Your mother and I didn't set up the trust so you girls could become wastes of space," he said. "We set it up because when I was a boy, I had nothing. And because there are so many situations in life that you've no hope of escaping from without a safety net. But what you're doing, Eve, is abusing your privilege. And I'm disappointed."

Those words burned, charring her edges with hurt and shame. Her heart began to pound, her pulse rushing loud enough in her ears to drown out Barbra's comforting beat. She tried to process, to find the right words to explain herself—but the conversation was already racing off without her, a runaway train she'd never been fast enough to catch.

"We have decided," Mum said, "to cancel your trust fund payments. Whatever savings you have will have to do until you can find a job."

Savings? Who the bloody hell had *savings*?

Dad took over. "You can stay here for three months. That should be more than enough time to find a place of your own."

"Wait—what? You're throwing me out?"

Mum went on as if Eve hadn't spoken. "We've discussed things, and your father and I would like you to hold down a job for at least a year before we restart your trust fund payments. We know finding decent work might be difficult with such a . . . unique CV, so we've lined up positions for you in our own companies."

Eve jerked back in her seat, her head whirling as she tried to keep up. "But—I already quit law." And for good reason. Eve had enjoyed law school a disturbing amount, had recognized the warning signs, and had quit before she could sublimate her entire sense of self-worth into her ability to nitpick linguistics around Tort law. She considered that a lucky escape.

Mum's mouth tightened. "Well, there's always your father's accountancy firm."

Now Eve was truly appalled. "Accountancy? I can barely count!"

Mum narrowed her eyes. "Don't be flip, Eve."

"You're right. I don't *want* to count. And I don't want my parents to hand me a job because I'm too useless to get one on my own. I'm *not*."

"No," Mum agreed, "just too feckless to stick with one. To do the hard work, after the excitement and glamour has faded. Too immature to be an *adult*. When are you going to grow up, Eve? I swear, it's embarrassing—"

And there it was. Eve sucked in a breath and blinked back the hot tears prickling at the corners of her eyes. They were more shock than pain, like the tears that came with a banged elbow—but she shouldn't be shocked at all, now, should she? Of course her parents saw her this way. Of course her parents thought she was an immature little brat. She'd never given anyone a reason to think she was anything else.

"I—I need to go," she said, standing up quickly, her voice thick with tears. Embarrassing. She was so fucking embarrassing, crying like a baby because her mother had told her the truth, running away from everything because she wasn't strong enough to cope with the pressure.

"Eve, darling," Mum began, already sounding softer, full of regret. Next, she'd say, *I'm sorry, I didn't mean that,* and everyone would decide that was enough for today, and the poor, delicate baby of the family would be let off the hook for a while because everyone knew Eve couldn't handle difficult conversations.

No one in this family had any idea of the shit Eve could handle. *No one.* And while that wasn't their fault, she suddenly resented them all for it. Every last one.

"Don't worry," she said sharply. "I've listened to everything you've said, and I'm taking it very seriously. I don't need you to baby me anymore. I will deal with this on my own, and I will try not to disappoint or—or *embarrass* you in the process." *But now I need to go before I completely undermine myself by bursting into tears.* She turned her back on her stricken parents and bolted.

CHAPTER TWO

It had taken Eve seven attempts to pass her driving test.

She was used to passing tests immediately and without much effort, but driving had proved unexpectedly difficult. Apparently, she had serious spatial awareness problems that had taken four years of weekly lessons to overcome. But driving was one of the few things Eve hadn't ever given up on, because a license promised the sort of freedom that wouldn't turn sour.

For example: the freedom to drive fast and aimless down abandoned country roads while blasting music at full volume. Her mood had taken a sharp turn, and Barbra would no longer do.

As she sped past turn after turn that would take her back to the main road—to the city, to her sisters—Eve debated the pros and cons of running to Chloe or Dani for help. What, exactly, would she say? *Help, Mum and Dad have cruelly demanded I hold down a job and take on some adult responsibilities?* Ha. Chloe, who was hideously blunt and who had overcome more difficulties in her thirty-something years than many people did in a lifetime, would tell Eve outright that she was being a pathetic brat. Dani, who was similarly blunt and absolutely addicted to hard work, had never and would never understand why Eve avoided committing to a profession. Or to anything.

Eve had told her parents she'd handle things herself, and she would. After she finished undoing the instinctive panic caused by this morning's conversation.

She turned up the music and drove, until the sun faded behind gray clouds and pre-rain mist soaked into her skin through the open windows. It was so safe, in that music-pounding, rain-shielded, ever-moving bubble, that Eve drove for over two hours without even noticing.

Just when she was beginning to feel the first pangs of hunger, she caught sight of a sign that said SKYBRIAR: FIFTEEN MILES.

"Skybriar," she murmured over the thrum of cleopatrick's "hometown." It sounded like a fairytale. Fairytales meant happily ever after. She took the turn.

Skybriar looked like a fairytale, too. Its main road unraveled down an impressive hill, with woods standing tall on either side of the pavement. It was the kind of deep and vivid greenery that looked like it must, by rights, contain pixies and toadstools and all the rest. The air through Eve's open window tasted fresh and earthy and clean as she drove deeper into the town, past adorable, old-fashioned, stone-built houses and people in wellies walking well-behaved little dogs.

Another turn, taken at random, and she struck gold. Up ahead, guarded by a grand oak tree and fenced in by an old, low wall of moss-covered stone, was an impressive redbrick

Victorian with a wine-red sign outside that read CASTELL COTTAGE. EXCELLENT ACCOMMODATION, DELICIOUS CUISINE.

She was feeling better already.

Actually, that was a categorical lie. But she would feel better, once she ate, and took a moment to think, and generally stopped her drama queen behavior.

Eve threw the car into the nearest sort-of parking space—well, it was an empty spot by the pavement, so it would do—and cut off her music. Then she slipped in an AirPod, chose a new song—"Shut Up and Groove," Masego—to match her new determinedly positive mood, and pressed Play. Flipping down the car's mirror, she dabbed at her red eyes and grimaced at her bare mouth. Her waist-length braids, lavender and brown, were still tied back in a bedtime knot. She set them free to spill over her shoulders, then rifled through her glove box and found a glittery, orange Chanel lip gloss.

"There." She smiled at her reflection. "Much better." When in doubt, throw some color at it. Satisfied, she got out of the car and approached the cute little countryside restaurant thingy through softly falling drizzle. Only when she reached the grand front door, which had yet another sign pinned over it, did she notice what she'd missed the first time.

CASTELL COTTAGE.

BED AND BREAKFAST.

Eve checked her watch and discovered that it was now far from breakfast time.

"Gabriel's burning bollocks, you have *got* to be kidding me." She glared at her warped reflection in the front door's little stained-glass window. "Has the trauma of the morning's events killed off your last remaining brain cells, Eve? Is that it?"

Her reflection did not reply.

She let out a hangry little growl and started to turn—when a laminated notice pinned up beside the door caught her eye.

CHEF INTERVIEWS: FIRST DOOR ON THE RIGHT.

Well, now. *That* was rather interesting. So interesting, in fact, that Eve's witchy sister Dani would likely call this literal sign . . . a *sign*.

Of course, Eve wasn't Dani, so she simply called it a coincidence.

"Or an opportunity," she murmured slowly.

Eve, after all, could cook. She was forced to do so every day in order to survive, and she was also quite good at it, having entertained brief fantasies of opening a Michelin-starred restaurant before watching an episode of *Hell's Kitchen* and developing a Gordon Ramsay phobia. Of course, despite her private efforts, she had never actually cooked professionally before—unless one considered her ill-advised foray into 3D genital cakes *cooking*.

Still, the more she thought about it, the more this seemed like the perfect job for her. Wedding planning had been too satisfying, too exhilarating, the kind of career she could easily fall in love with—which meant that when she inevitably failed at it, she'd be left broken. But cooking at some small-town bed and breakfast? She certainly couldn't fall in love with that.

"*Your father and I would like you to hold down a job for at least a year before we restart your trust fund payments.*"

Her parents didn't think she could get a job on her own and clearly doubted her ability to keep one. They thought she needed supervision for every little thing, and if she was honest with herself, Eve understood why. But that didn't stop their doubt from biting like too-small leather boots. So, securing her own job the day she left home? And also, quite conveniently, *not* having to return home with her tail between her legs after this morning's tantrum-like disappearance? That all sounded ideal, actually.

One year to prove herself. She could do that. In fact, Eve knew better than anyone that she could do anything.

She opened the door.

Contrary to popular belief, Jacob Wayne did not create awkward situations on purpose. Take right now, for example: he didn't *mean* to subject his latest interviewee to a long, glacial pause that left the other man pale and jittery. But Simon Fairweather was a certified prick and his answers to Jacob's carefully considered interview questions were nothing less than a shit show. With each meaningless response, Jacob felt himself growing even colder and more distant than usual. Perfect conditions for the birth of an accidental awkward pause.

Simon stared at Jacob. Jacob stared at Simon. Simon began to fidget. Jacob reflected on how bloody irritating he found this man and did nothing to control the derisive curl of his lip. Simon started, disturbingly, to sweat. Jacob was horrified, both by the rogue DNA rolling down Simon's temples and by his obvious lack of spine.

Then Jacob's best friend (all right, *only* friend) Montlake heaved out a sigh and leapt into the breach. "Cheers, Simon," he said. "That'll be all, mate. We'll get back to you."

"That's true," Jacob allowed calmly, because it was. He watched in silence as Simon scrambled up from his chair and exited the room, nodding and stuttering all the while.

"Pitiful," Jacob muttered. As the dining room door swung shut, he wrote two careful words on his notepad: FUCK. EVERYTHING.

Not his most adult choice, granted, but it seemed more mature than flipping the goddamn table.

Beside him, Montlake cleared his throat. "All right. Don't know why I'm bothering to ask, but . . . Thoughts on Simon?"

Jacob sighed. "Are you sure you want to know?"

"Probably not." Montlake rolled his eyes and tapped his pen against his own notepad. He, Jacob noticed, had written a load of intelligent, sensible shit about today's applicants, complete with bullet points. Once upon a time, Jacob had been capable of intelligence and bullet points, too. Just last week, in fact. But then he'd been forced to sit through the seven-day-straight parade of incompetence these interviews had become, and his brain had melted out of his fucking ears.

"Well," Mont went on, "here's what I put: Simon's got a lot of experience, but he doesn't seem the sharpest tool. Bit cocky, but that means he'll eventually be confident enough to handle that thing you do."

Jacob narrowed his eyes and turned, very slowly, to glare at his friend. "And what *thing* is that, Montlake?"

"That thing, Bitchy McBitcherson," Mont said cheerfully. "You're a nightmare when you're panicking."

"I'm a nightmare all the time. This is my ordinary nightmare behavior. *Panic*," Jacob scowled, "is for the underprepared, the out-of-control, and the fatally inconsistent."

"Yeah, so I've heard. From you. Every time you're panicking."

Jacob wondered if today would be the day he murdered his best friend and decided, after a moment, that it was entirely possible. The hospitality industry had been known to drive men to far worse. Like plastic shower curtains and brown carpets.

To lessen the risk of imminent homicide, Jacob pushed the fine frames of his glasses up his nose, rose to his feet, and began to pace the B&B's spacious dining room, circling the antique table that took up its center. "Whatever. And you're wrong about Simon—he isn't right for Castell Cottage."

"You don't think anyone's right for Castell Cottage," Mont said dryly. "That's kind of why I'm here. Voice of reason, and all that."

"Actually, you're here because you're a respected local business owner, and proper interviews need more than one perspective, and—"

"What's wrong with Simon?" Montlake interrupted.

"He's a creep."

Mont, who had a habit of leaning everywhere—probably something to do with his ridiculous height and the natural effects of gravity—sat up straight for once. "Who told you that? The twins?"

A reasonable assumption, since Mont's sisters were the only women in town who actually spoke to Jacob—aside from Aunt Lucy, of course. "No one told me. Just watch the guy some time. Women bend over backward to avoid being alone with him."

"Christ," Mont muttered, and ripped a page out of his notepad. "All right. I know you hated the first two, and you've written off all the *previous* candidates." He paused significantly. If he was waiting for Jacob to feel bad or something, he'd be waiting a long fucking time. "So that leaves us with Claire Penny."

"Nope," Jacob said flatly. "Don't want her." He stopped midpace, noticing that one of the paintings on the aubergine wall—a landscape commissioned from a local artist—was slightly crooked. Scowling, he stalked over and adjusted it. Bloody doors banging all day, knocking things out of whack, that was the reason. "Can't have a chef who slams my doors," he muttered darkly. "Doesn't create a restful atmosphere. Bastards."

"Is that the issue with Claire?"

"What? Oh." Jacob shook his head and went back to his pacing. "Claire knows how to shut a door properly, so far as I can tell. But she smiles too much. No one smiles that much. Pretty sure she's on drugs."

Mont gave Jacob the dirty look to end all dirty looks, which was a natural skill of his. "You can't be serious."

"I'm always serious."

"She's sixty-four years old."

Jacob rolled his eyes. "You think people stop making bad decisions when they hit sixty? Nope. Anyway, you remember before I left for the city, she used to work at Jimmy's? I ordered a slice of her apple pie once, and there was a hair in it."

"*That's* why you don't want to invite her back?"

Jacob frowned at his friend. "Why are you using your *Jacob's being unreasonable* voice? I don't want hairy pie, Montlake. Do you want hairy pie? Because if you're that hot for hairy pie, I will make you a hairy pie."

"You couldn't pay me to eat your cooking, which is kind of why we're here." Mont scrubbed a hand over his face and screwed his eyes shut for a second. "Come on, man. You left five years ago. You think she hasn't learned how to wear a hairnet in five years? Call her back, let her cook for us, give her a chance."

"No." Jacob knew he sounded like a dick. He knew even Mont, who got him better than everyone, probably thought he was being a dick. But sometimes it was easier to keep his thought processes to himself because other people either had trouble following them, or thought they were unnecessarily blunt.

Bluntness was never unnecessary.

ABOUT THE AUTHOR

TALIA HIBBERT is a Black British author who lives in a bedroom full of books. Supposedly, there is a world beyond that room, but she has yet to drum up enough interest to investigate. She writes sexy, diverse romance because she believes that people of marginalized identities need honest and positive representation. Her interests include beauty, junk food, and unnecessary sarcasm.

FROM TALIA HIBBERT

GET A LIFE, CHLOE BROWN

Chloe Brown is a chronically ill computer geek with a goal, a plan, and a list. After almost—but not quite—dying, she's come up with seven directives to help her "Get a Life", and she's already completed the first: finally moving out of her glamorous family's mansion. The next items?

- Enjoy a drunken night out.
- Ride a motorcycle.
- Go camping.
- Have meaningless but thoroughly enjoyable sex.
- Travel the world with nothing but hand luggage.
- And... do something bad.

But it's not easy being bad, even when you've written step-by-step guidelines on how to do it correctly. What Chloe needs is a teacher, and she knows just the man for the job.

Redford 'Red' Morgan is a handyman with tattoos, a motorcycle, and more sex appeal than ten-thousand Hollywood heartthrobs.

But when she enlists Red in her mission to rebel, she learns things about him that no spy session could teach her. And what really lies beneath his rough exterior…

TAKE A HINT, DANI BROWN

"Talia Hibbert is a rockstar! Her writing is smart, funny, and sexy…"

—Meg Cabot, #1 *New York Times* bestselling author of the Little Bridge Island and Princess Diaries series

One of *Oprah Magazine*'s 21 Romance Novels That Are Set to Be the Best of 2020

USA Today bestselling author Talia Hibbert returns with another charming romantic comedy about a young woman who agrees to fake date her friend after a video of him "rescuing" her from their office building goes viral…

Danika Brown knows what she wants: professional success, academic renown, and an occasional roll in the hay to relieve all that career-driven tension. But romance? Been there, done that, burned the T-shirt. Romantic partners, whatever their gender, are a distraction at best and a drain at worst. So Dani asks the universe for the perfect friend-with-benefits—someone who knows the score and knows their way around the bedroom.